YOU MADE ME

JAMIE MILLEN

TITLES BY JAMIE MILLEN

CLAIRE WOLFE THILLERS

YOU DID THIS
YOU MADE ME
YOU ARE NEXT

JAMIE MILLEN

YOU MADE ME

Copyright © 2022 by Jamie Millen

jamiemillen.com

ISBN-13: 978-1-950139-09-5 (ebook)

ISBN-13: 978-1-950139-10-1 (paperback)

ISBN-13: 978-1-950139-19-4 (large print)

ISBN-13: 978-1-950139-11-8 (hardcover)

ISBN-13: 978-1-950139-12-5 (audiobook)

FIC031080 FICTION/Thrillers/Psychological

FIC022020 FICTION/Mystery & Detective/Police Procedural

FIC022040 FICTION/Mystery & Detective/Women Sleuths

FIC031010 FICTION/Thrillers/Crime

FIC030000 FICTION/Thrillers/Suspense

FIC027110 FICTION/Romance/Suspense

Cover design by 100 Covers

First edition

CHAPTER 1

Carmine Hannover loved cheap hotels. They made her feel dirty and sensual. She perched on the narrow double bed and ran her fingers over the stiff white sheets. The scent of dust and mothballs wafted in the air. In the pokey bathroom, a leaky faucet dripped. Her parents would cringe with disgust at The Barnett Inn. That's why Carmine had selected the hotel for her romantic rendezvous. Her parents' disapproval also motivated her choice of lovers. With each passionate encounter, Carmine gave her parents the finger. *Take that, you stuck-up bastards. You don't control me. Not anymore.*

She dropped her tote bag on the bedside table. The Kate Spade cost ten times what she'd paid for the room but only half the nightly rate at her parents' hotels. Carmine always paid in cash, and the hotel manager never asked questions. He understood the needs of his clientele. Nobody checked into The Barnett Inn to be recognized.

Carmine flopped on the bed. She pressed her back to the hard mattress and ran her palms along the curve of her thighs. The light fixture on the ceiling had collected dust and dead flies. A damp stain snaked around the light. The shape resembled a giant python that had swallowed a small deer. But the foreboding image didn't dampen her spirits. Tonight was going to be magical. This lover was special. Their relationship wedded pleasure with business. Together, they'd change the world—and her parents wouldn't know what hit them.

A knock on the door launched Carmine to her feet. Her lover had arrived early for a change. She touched her hair, a final act of preening before their reunion. But when she opened the door, her excitement faded. The man with the ill-fitting uniform and folded white towels was not her lover. Carmine had never encountered the cleaning staff of the hotel, and she'd assumed The Barnett Inn didn't employ bellhops.

"Your towels, ma'am."

The black strap of a duffel bag dug into his shoulder. The incongruous detail ignited a warning light in a primal corner of her mind, but her annoyance at the intrusion extinguished the internal danger signal.

"I didn't order towels."

He smiled earnestly, and her skin crawled.

"I have to put these in the bathroom."

Her senses heightened, and her heart rate accelerated. Something about the bellhop had activated her fight-or-flight response. He seemed harmless enough. The bellhop was average in every way—hair, height, and build—the invisible sort of man she'd never give a second glance or remember meeting. Thanks to years of martial arts classes, Carmine never feared for her safety. She could floor this guy without breaking a sweat. Why was she overreacting? Letting him in might be the quickest way to get rid of him.

Carmine stepped aside. "Make it snappy."

The man entered, swung the door shut behind him, and dropped the towels.

"Scream and you're dead. Do as I say, and nobody gets hurt."

Carmine blinked at the handgun he aimed at her chest. She knew better than to resist. A brown belt in karate offered no protection against bullets. He issued a series of terse commands, and she obeyed. Within seconds, she lay on her back, her wrists and ankles bound to the bedposts with zip ties.

Her heart thumped, but still, she didn't fear for her life. The petty criminal must have spotted her expensive bag and followed her to the room. *Let him take what he wants and go.* He didn't seem interested in rape or kidnapping. He didn't know who she was—and thank God for that. She'd be more discreet in the future.

He stood over her, a silver roll of duct tape in his hand. "Hold still. I need you to keep quiet so I can get away."

Carmine nodded and let him tape her mouth shut. The ordeal was almost over. Her lover would arrive soon and release her. They wouldn't report the crime to the police. The incident would expose their relationship and compromise their shared goals. *No matter.* Carmine was a confident and independent young woman. Soon, she'd look back on this holdup and laugh.

But the man didn't escape with his loot. He stared at her and smirked.

"I admire your work, Carmine."

Panic flared within her. *He knows my name.* He'd mentioned her artwork. This was no opportunistic robbery. Carmine pulled at her restraints but only bruised the soft flesh of her wrists.

He chuckled. "Oh, yes. I know exactly who you are, Ms. Hannover. I've been watching you. I've been watching you for a long time."

Chills snaked down her spine. The creep had been stalking her, and she'd had no idea. Had her parents sent him? Had they hired the thug to spy on her and scare her into "mending her ways?" Worse yet, had they discovered her plans and decided to silence her?

The stranger sat on the edge of the bed. "You've lived a charmed life, Carmine. But inside, we're all the same. I'll show you."

He shot to his feet. Steel tools clinked as he rummaged in his duffel bag on the floor and out of sight.

Carmine's breath came in quick, shallow gulps. *I'll show you.* What did that mean? Was he going to rape her? Hurt her? *No!* Carmine was a Hannover. Her parents were too proud to have their daughter abused like a street hooker. But what if her parents hadn't sent this stalker?

She glanced at the closed door. Any moment now, her lover would come knocking and send the attacker fleeing. *Where are you?*

Movement drew Carmine's attention to the foot of the bed. In a gloved hand, her captor wielded a large carving knife.

Carmine strained and shifted on the bed, but her sealed mouth turned her screams into muffled groans. Nobody passing by in the corridor would hear her or know of the danger she faced. Her lover was her only hope. But would her savior arrive in time?

Still brandishing the knife, the stranger leaned over her legs. Carmine shut her eyes and braced for the pain. But he didn't stab her. He slid the blade inside her pant leg and tore through the length of her slacks. Carmine froze, too terrified to flex a muscle. He sliced her slacks from her body and tossed them aside. Her blouse followed, then her panties and bra. She squirmed, completely naked and utterly vulnerable. Fear flooding her, she hazarded a glance.

The stranger feasted his eyes on her exposed body. His trousers bulged at the crotch, but he made no move to undress.

He didn't plan to rape her. He just wanted to see her naked. She clung to that conviction for all she was worth.

"You've taken good care of your body, Carmine. Good for you."

Rage washed away her fear, and the old Carmine returned. *How dare he talk to me that way!* He'd pay for this. Her parents' lawyers would make sure the pervert spent the rest of his days behind bars.

The stranger studied his knife blade with interest. "We have something in common, Carmine. I'm an artist, too. From one artist to another, I want to apologize for lying to you. I said I wouldn't hurt you. But this will hurt. This'll hurt a lot."

Her rage evaporated. "Please don't hurt me. My parents have money—lots of money. They'll give you whatever you want. Just, please, don't hurt me."

But the tape over her mouth turned her pleas into a pathetic, inhuman wail.

"Save your strength. Nobody can hear you. And frankly, I don't care. But I want you to know one thing. Your art inspired me. We're going to recreate your iconic design, right here and now."

At that moment, Carmine understood exactly what he'd to do to her. Her life was over. *No. No!* This couldn't happen to her. She stared at the door, willing her lover to rescue her.

The stranger laughed. "Nobody's coming to save you, Carmine."

She studied him in terror. *How could he know that?*

"Nobody knows you're here. Not even your secret lover."

He knew about her lover. *I've been watching you.* He knew everything. A horrific thought gripped her. Had her lover sent him? No, that made no sense. Why was this happening to her?

The killer sat beside her on the bed. He ran gloved fingers

over her flat, naked belly, and goose bumps broke out on her skin.

"You like to make artistic statements, Carmine. Together, we'll send a powerful message."

He placed the blade to the delicate skin at the base of her full breasts.

Please don't. I beg you. She searched his eyes for a hint of human compassion and found none.

"We'll create a masterpiece. Only this time, you're the canvas."

CHAPTER 2

S ome days, Claire Wolfe could murder her mother. Monday morning was one of those days.

"Would you hurry up already? I'll be late for the ceremony."

Claire stood in the open doorway of her mom's house, Claire's childhood home, her car keys jingling in her hand. An icy breeze tickled her face. March had arrived, but Newburgh's weather still chilled her bones.

The swearing-in ceremony for Charles Emmerso, Claire's former captain and Newburgh PD's new chief, was only one reason to leave home on time. Claire didn't want to arrive late on her first day back at the Investigations Bureau. Long months had passed since she'd worn her plain brown detective suit or sensed the reassuring weight of her service weapon on her waist. The gunshot wound to her shoulder had healed, and Internal Affairs had cleared her of wrongdoing in last year's shootings. Claire had said goodbye to her physiotherapist and was ready to rejoin the Bureau. And if she had to stay home with her mom one day longer, she'd go insane.

"Mo-om!" Claire called in a singsong voice. Around her

mother, she became a frustrated, eye-rolling teenager. "We talked about this. I can't be late today."

The timing of Emmerso's ceremony was perfect. Claire could return to work without being the center of attention. She checked her wristwatch again. Was her mother dragging her feet on purpose?

Her glance drifted to the framed photograph on the kitchen counter. Tina, blonde-haired and blue-eyed, smiled at her from the portrait, forever fourteen years old. Claire's late sister was not the only ghostly presence in their lives. After the tragedy and trauma of the Middle School Murders last year, Claire had banished the likeness of William "Bill" Wolfe from their home. But the purge didn't exorcise her father's ominous presence from her mind.

Diane Wolfe descended the stairs, her gym bag in hand and her trademark scowl on her face. "Since when are you such a hard worker?"

The biting comment fooled nobody. In school, Claire had been a star student and qualified for the track team. She'd graduated from the police academy at the top of her class, and she'd applied the same determination and hard work to her mother's rehabilitation.

In the six months since Claire had moved back home, her mother had shed twenty pounds. She looked twenty years younger, too. Claire had hoped her mother's irrational fury would subside along with her alcohol intake. But the years of hatred and suspicion hadn't evaporated. Which reminded her —Claire had another bombshell to drop today. She'd save that explosive news item for the car ride.

"I told you a hundred times, Mom. Chief Emmerso's cere- mony—does that ring a bell?"

Emmerso deserved the promotion. Claire would miss reporting to him directly. He'd treated her well. In a way, she'd returned the favor. By exposing the crimes of the former chief, Harry Wallace, she'd set up Emmerso for his new position. Claire's other actions during that investigation haunted her dreams. She pushed those memories from her mind.

Mom trudged through the living room. "Well, don't let me slow you down. Go ahead without me."

"Nice try, but you're not skipping the gym today."

Her mother shuffled past Claire and onto the street. Claire locked the door, got into her battered white Ford Focus hatchback, and they hit the road.

Mom sighed. "No booze. No cigarettes. Gym every other day. You're trying to kill me, aren't you?"

There was no humor in her words, only contempt. And her casual talk of murder was no accident. Diane needled her daughter with a morbid relish. She lived to make Claire feel guilty. For caring. For breathing. Was blaming Claire for crimes she hadn't committed simply a habit she couldn't shake?

"It's important to keep to your routine."

"I had a routine," her mother snapped, "before you moved in."

Claire scoffed. "TV and beer don't qualify."

"Whatever."

Mom stared out the window at the panning scenery of suburban Newburgh. Election fever was in the air. Posters on every street corner promised to make Newburgh safe again. Last year's multiple murders were still fresh in the voters' memory, and every politician and his mother had decided the time was ripe to unseat Thomas Thornton, the city's long-sitting mayor.

A billboard with a young female candidate snagged Claire's eye. Sarah Malik had olive skin and a black pixie bob haircut. Dressed in a no-nonsense business suit, she promised to "drain the swamp." Not to be outdone, a pudgy and graying Mayor

Thornton labeled himself the "responsible choice." The advert didn't mention that Thornton had appointed the former chief of police, Harry Wallace, who was serving time for the dual felonies of Misconduct in Public Office and Obstruction of Justice.

An uncomfortable silence stretched between Claire and her mother. Claire hated the silences. The only thing she dreaded more was the decision she needed to share. *Bombs away.*

"I signed you up for AA."

"AA?" Mom spat the word. "I am not an alcoholic."

"Said like a true alcoholic. We tried cutting back, Mom. It didn't work. Your first meeting is tonight."

Her mom fumed for three long seconds. "I'm down to one six-pack a day."

Claire snorted. "Not counting the bottle of red. I take out the trash. Did you think I wouldn't notice?"

Diane's next long silence was a seething admission of guilt.

"You need to get back on your feet, Mom. Nobody's going to hire a drunk. Dad didn't exactly leave you a fortune."

Claire had stopped by the local Bank of America with Mom to size up her finances. The only thing keeping her mother off the street was Claire's detective salary, which barely covered the household expenses.

"So you keep telling me." Mom spoke as though her financial plight was Claire's fault, too. "You should have thought about that before you killed him."

Claire clenched her jaw. She hadn't killed her father. But the accusation still hurt. Although Claire hadn't pulled the trigger, his death still weighed heavily on her conscience.

Mom wasn't done. "I'm surprised they want you back at work. Everybody around you dies—Tina, your partner, and now Bill."

Claire could hold back no longer.

"Would you rather I had died instead?"

Her mother smirked. Her arrows had found their mark. Mission accomplished.

Claire lost her appetite for conversation. That's the trouble with family—they know your pressure points and can inflict the most pain. When Claire stopped the car outside Planet Fitness, Mom got out and slammed the door without turning back.

Claire swallowed her heartache and pulled off. She'd looked forward to this day for months, but her mother had ruined her mood. Claire should never have moved back home. Mom had spent twelve long years wallowing in grief and self-pity. She'd never loved Claire before Tina's death. Why should she start now?

News vans hogged the sidewalk outside Newburgh PD. Claire had expected reporters to cover the ceremony, but she hadn't predicted a media frenzy. The Middle School Strangler had put Newburgh on the news map. Claire fought the urge to turn her car around and flee the cameras. She'd promised Bella Winters of *The Newburgh Herald* an exclusive interview about the case, but Claire had screened the newshound's calls and ignored her emails. Would Bella hold a grudge? Avoiding the reporter gave Claire another reason to bolt. But she had promised Chief Emmerso she'd attend the ceremony, and she'd keep her word. "Today is not about you," she reminded herself.

Claire parked her car in the department lot, dodged the newshounds, and slipped into the building. A pretty, blonde-haired woman in a brown business suit stood in the hall. Her eyes lit up as Claire walked in.

She held out her hand. "Detective Wolfe, welcome back!"

They shook hands. Blue-eyed and young. No press card. They had met before, but the details eluded Claire's memory.

"I'm sorry, remind me..."

The young officer's enthusiasm didn't flag in the slightest. "Jessica Long."

Claire remembered. The patrol officer had assisted with the murder investigation last year. "Sorry. I didn't recognize you out of uniform." In Newburgh, Claire had spent more time on medical leave than on the job, and the effects of her extended absence showed.

"Chief Emmerso is expecting you in his office."

"Oh. Thanks."

"Have a great day."

"You, too."

Claire left the cheerful off-duty officer behind and headed for the chief's office. She knocked before entering. The office was double the size of his previous room. Emmerso knotted his tie in the reflection of a certificate mounted on the wall.

He treated her to a broad smile, and his kind eyes twinkled. "Detective Wolfe, I was beginning to worry you wouldn't show."

"I wouldn't miss this for the world, Chief."

Emmerso grimaced. "*Chief*. I still haven't gotten used to the title. Soon I'll be buried in politics and red tape."

"You'll do fine, sir. I know it."

During their short time working together, Emmerso had struck her as both an honest man and a smooth political negotiator, a rare combination of talents.

"Thank you."

"You wanted to speak before the ceremony?"

"I want to let you know of some recent changes. Captain Morris Washington is the new Investigations head."

The news caught Claire by surprise. "I thought Nakamura was tapped for the job." She knew Detective Haruto Nakamura and liked him. The new captain was a wildcard.

"That was a temporary arrangement while I was acting chief. Nakamura doesn't seem to want to abandon Mahoney.

Don't tell their wives. He stepped down when Washington and Gomez got back from the DEA task force."

"Oh."

Washington *and* Gomez. Two wildcards. The Investigations Bureau wasn't the same group of officers she had left.

Emmerso seemed to register her doubts. "Washington's a stand-up guy. I think you'll like him. There are a few more changes, so brace yourself."

He gave her a mysterious grin. Was he hinting at a promotion for Claire? She'd spelled out her desire to remain a homicide detective. Investigations were what she did best, and she didn't want to derive any personal gain from the death of those poor girls and her former partner, no matter how indirect.

Emmerso adjusted his tie and ran a hand over his thinning hair. "I'll fill you in later. They're waiting for us."

"Us?"

He gave her an apologetic grin. "The mayor wants you onstage."

The floor seemed to fall away beneath Claire's feet. She was going to appear on camera. Last year, Claire had become an unwilling media sensation, and the mayor was using her notoriety to boost his reelection campaign. Emmerso hadn't told her in advance. Either he hadn't known or he'd feared, correctly, that Claire would skip the ceremony. Emmerso had outmaneuvered her.

He guided her toward the door. "It sucks, I know. But that's the price of fame."

CHAPTER 3

Claire's insides squirmed. A dozen camera lenses eyeballed her in the Newburgh Police Department conference room as she stood at attention on the stage. Newspeople whispered in each other's ears from the rows of chairs. Claire ordered her hands not to fidget. Thankfully, she was not alone on the stage. Mayor Thornton took the podium, Chief Emmerso at his side. Claire stood in a short line of officers behind them. She was not the focus of attention. Her intense discomfort was unjustified. The crowd had assembled to honor Charles Emmerso and celebrate his well-deserved promotion. Claire was merely the token female officer in the backdrop. Today's ceremony was not about her.

Mayor Thomas Thornton gripped the podium with his pudgy hands as though to prevent anyone from stealing the limelight. The mayor leaned into the bouquet of microphones, and his oily voice boomed on the conference room speakers.

"Members of the Newburgh City Council. Our friends in the local and national media. And of course, Newburgh's finest, our brave and tireless officers of the Newburgh Police Department. I feel honored and privileged to stand before you today."

Claire scanned the crowd beyond the flashing cameras for familiar faces. Her fellow homicide detectives, Haruto Nakamura and Brendan Mahoney, sat in the fourth row among a sea of patrol officers in blue uniforms. Nakamura gave her a subtle nod, and Claire responded in kind.

"Today, we have gathered to congratulate one of our own, Charles Emmerso, on his first day as Newburgh's new chief of police."

The officers in the audience put their hands together, and Mahoney whooped. Even Captain Ronaldo Rodriguez of Patrol, a rival contender for the top job, applauded.

Mayor Thornton gave Chief Emmerso a friendly smile. "In the five years since Officer Emmerso joined our department, he has proved to be a very capable and valued asset to our community. He presided over the Investigations Bureau during a troublesome period and handled complex and high-profile cases with integrity and devotion."

Chief Emmerso shifted on his feet, uncomfortable under the barrage of compliments. Claire agreed with every word. During the Middle School Strangler case, Emmerso hadn't rushed to arrest suspects, despite pressure from the media and within the department to show progress in the homicide investigation. Claire also suspected Emmerso had played a moderating role when the investigation had turned against her. She probably owed her former captain her life.

"I have every confidence," the mayor continued, "that with Chief Emmerso at the helm of local law enforcement, we will all sleep better at night, secure in the knowledge that he and his officers are working around the clock to keep our city safe."

Mayor Thornton had hit every note. He'd recognized the child homicides that had terrorized Newburgh last year but recalled none of the unsettling details. By appointing Emmerso as chief, he assured the community that such periods were a thing of the past. Thornton was not Newburgh's longest-sitting mayor by accident.

He called on Captain Ronaldo Rodriguez of Patrol to pin the badge on the new chief. Then, the mayor presented Emmerso with his certificate in a leather portfolio and invited him to say a few words.

Emmerso welcomed the attendees. "I thank you, Mayor Thornton, for entrusting me with this great responsibility. Many challenges lie ahead of us, and we will do everything humanly possible to assure the safety and security of our fellow citizens. Some changes will be necessary. I'd like to thank Mayor Thornton for approving our plan to deploy Police Observation Devices, or PODs, in the city's high-crime areas. This network of mobile cameras and sensors is a proven strategy for both preventing crime and bringing criminals to justice."

The audience clapped again. The police department was taking concrete steps to reduce crime. Claire doffed her imaginary cap to Emmerso. He'd traded compliments with the mayor and emphasized his role in advancing the city's safety, earning the mayor points in the upcoming mayoral elections. Emmerso could swim with the sharks like the best of them.

"But none of this would be possible," he continued, "without our teams of dedicated officers. Mayor Thornton called them Newburgh's finest, and I couldn't agree more. I'm fortunate to be among you and look forward to working together to serve and protect."

The crowd loved him, offering applause and bursts of camera flashes.

Mayor Thornton took the podium again. "Speaking of our fine officers, I'd like to take this opportunity to recognize one member of our police force in particular."

Claire's gut clenched. Adrenaline burst into her bloodstream. She sensed an ambush. *He wouldn't dare, would he?*

"A few months ago," Mayor Thornton continued, "this officer went above and beyond the call of duty to bring a killer to justice."

A hot fever gripped Claire as every eyeball and camera lens turned to her.

"She risked her life and took a bullet, and the injury put her out of action for months. Today, we are proud to welcome her back to the department. Ladies and gentlemen, please give a warm round of applause for our very own Detective Claire Wolfe!"

Claire forced her twitching lips into a grateful smile while the world shifted around her. If by "above and beyond the call of duty" the mayor meant escaping attempts by her fellow officers to end her life, then he was on the money.

So that's why Emmerso had sent Officer Long to greet Claire at the station. The mayor had roped Chief Emmerso into his reelection campaign and now he was doing the same to Claire.

At the podium, Mayor Thornton lifted an engraved rectangular plaque from beneath his notes, and he beamed at Claire. If he thought he'd get her to play his game, he was in for an unpleasant surprise. When Claire refused to budge, Chief Emmerso jerked his head for her to join them at the podium. "I don't like this either," his defeated smile hinted. "Take one for the team."

She gave in. Her legs carried her to the podium between the mayor and the chief of police.

The mayor spoke into the microphones. "Detective Wolfe, on behalf of the city of Newburgh, we thank you for your service. We're glad to have you back. Please accept this Award

for Valor, signed by me and Chief Emmerso, as a small token of
our appreciation. Congratulations!"

The crowd went wild. Flashing lights blinded her. Claire bit
her tongue and accepted the award with as much grace as she
could muster. She hadn't wanted to remember last year's
events, never mind receive an award for the role she'd played.
The homicide investigation had ended with Claire shooting her
partner dead. And although Claire had acted in self-defense,
the death would haunt her for the rest of her life.

Claire smiled for the photo op with the mayor and chief of
police, then slipped away, returning to her post, irritation and
shame mixing in her thumping heart. She gripped the plaque
and stared at her feet.

"We'll take a few questions," the mayor said. "Yes, over
there. Please hand her a microphone."

A woman spoke, and Claire looked up. She recognized the
voice at once. There was no mistaking the painted face and
mane of auburn hair of Bella Winters. *Perfect.* In her coverage
of the Middle School Strangler case for *The Newburgh Herald*,
Bella had been highly critical of the local police department.
Then again, she'd also aided the investigation, bringing crucial
information to the department before publishing her findings.
She had atoned for her earlier sins, but Claire still owed her
that exclusive interview.

Bella Winters gazed at Claire and spoke into the microphone. "This question is for Detective Wolfe."

Claire swallowed hard. The mayor shot a glance at Claire.
For the first time during the press conference, he seemed
worried. But he'd opened the floor to questions and couldn't
retract the offer.

"Of course."

He motioned for Claire to return to the podium. Claire

sucked in a deep breath and stepped forward. Once again, she felt the press of every eyeball in the room.

"Detective Wolfe," Bella said. "How does it feel to return to the department that considered you a suspect in the Middle School Murders?"

Blood pounded in Claire's ears. The reporter did hold a grudge, after all. With a single question, she had jammed her fingers into Claire's open wounds. Pitting the recently decorated detective against her department might create a juicy news story, but the conflict wouldn't ease Claire's return to work or restore the public's confidence in law enforcement. And although Claire itched to stick it to the mayor for trotting her out in front of the cameras, she sidestepped that deadly snare.

Claire cleared her throat. "Investigators follow the evidence wherever it leads, and those cases have been closed. But to answer your question, I'm looking forward to getting back to work."

She had dodged the trap, but Bella didn't give up on a tantalizing scoop so easily.

"Your investigation exposed corruption at the top levels of Newburgh PD. Has the swamp been drained?"

Whispers circulated the room, but whether they expressed shock at the reporter's audacity or concerns about the department's corruptibility, Claire couldn't tell. Either way, she didn't get to answer the question.

Mayor Thornton leaned into the microphones. "Thank you, everybody. That's all we have time for today."

CHAPTER 4

Claire lingered on the threshold of the squad room. Inside, the Investigations Bureau buzzed with ringing telephones and the plastic chatter of computer keyboards. Was she ready for this?

After the press conference, she'd found refuge in the women's restroom. She'd drawn deep breaths while she waited for her fingers to stop shaking. Claire was a good detective. No, she was an *excellent* detective. But she'd made mistakes. Lethal mistakes. Her last investigation had ended in bloodshed, and she'd wrestled with guilt throughout the winter. Now the reporter's question rang in her ears. Was Claire a part of the swamp that needed draining?

You can do this. Claire held her breath and crossed the threshold. Her computer and monitor remained on her desk as she'd left them. Someone had occupied the workstation opposite hers, the desk of her former partner, Detective Jed Wallace, who'd never return. Claire placed her Award for Valor on her desk, facedown.

Brendan Mahoney rose from his desk. "The leading lady has arrived."

His partner, Haruto Nakamura, followed his example. "Good to have you back."

"Thanks. It's good to be back." Claire's voice sounded unconvincing to her own ears.

"Captain Washington is waiting for you." If he resented being passed over for the promotion, Nakamura hid his disappointment well.

Claire said, "I was...hoping they'd give you the job."

"Nah, they couldn't promote me. Who'd keep this loser out of trouble?" He swatted Mahoney on the back of the neck.

Mahoney pretended to take offense. "Don't blame me." He winked at Claire. "Not my fault he's underqualified."

Nakamura placed his hands on his hips. "Underqualified? How so?"

Mahoney spoke as though his partner wasn't there. "A captain needs to read and write, and our Asian friend is still illiterate. Very embarrassing."

Nakamura scoffed. "All right then, Mahoney. *You* write up today's report. Ha!"

Mahoney smirked. "Fine by me." The joke had landed him with a chore, but he paid the price gladly.

Nakamura turned to Claire. "Wait a minute. You've never met Washington, have you?"

"Your detective skills are as sharp as ever." Claire had slipped back into the Bureau's familiar banter and already felt more at ease.

"He's all right. Done his time. Mahoney and I will make sure the promotion doesn't go to his head."

"Hey, I heard that!" A stocky Latino with a shadow of a mustache swaggered over and offered Claire his hand. "You must be Detective Wolfe. Lucas Gomez." His grip was tight, challenging.

Mahoney snorted. "These days he goes by Your Highness."

Nakamura explained. "Ever since *Prince* Gomez and Captain Washington helped the DEA take down that drug ring upstate, they think they're too good for the rest of us."

"Your words, not mine." Gomez eyed Claire and hooked a thumb toward Nakamura. "Inferiority complex. So sad."

Claire found an excuse to avoid further questioning. "Time to meet the new boss."

She knocked twice on the door of Captain Morris Washington's office and stepped inside. Claire recognized the bulky black man behind the desk. He'd stood on the other side of Chief Emmerso in the conference room that morning. Captain Washington gave her a broad smile and stood.

"Detective Wolfe, welcome back." He shook her hand. "I've heard so much about you."

"Don't believe any of it, sir."

"Please, sit."

He settled back in his seat and studied her closely, his eyes unblinking in his wide, clean-shaven face. Like Gomez, deep suspicion lurked behind his friendly facade. Suspicion or fear? Claire didn't blame them. Most police officers never discharged their service weapons during their careers. Claire had fired hers twice within two days. The second time, she had killed a fellow officer. What else was she capable of doing?

"Quite the dog-and-pony show this morning, don't you think?"

"Yes, sir."

"You handled that pretty well."

"Thank you, sir."

Washington leaned forward, placing his elbows on the desk. "I'll be upfront with you. As you probably guessed from his speech, the mayor has increased the department's funding. We're hiring new officers, which means our more experienced officers will take on more responsibilities. Congratulations, you've made sergeant. You'll complete your training on the job. I've emailed you the application forms and study materials."

Claire's lips parted with surprise. Captain Emmerso had hinted at a promotion, and Claire had made her wishes clear. Were they trying to keep her off the streets?

"Sir, as I told Chief Emmerso, I prefer to work cases."

"You'll still work cases. The promotion just means a bump in salary and the opportunity to impact more cases and guide new detectives."

"Sir, with all due respect, there are officers here with more experience. Both Detective Nakamura and Detective Mahoney know the lay of the land better than—"

Captain Washington raised his hand for silence. "I understand, Detective. I had the same reservations when I was in your shoes. If it's any consolation, this isn't just about you. Climbing the ladder is as much luck and timing as talent. Lucky breaks don't come knocking every day. But that's beside the point. We have no choice in the matter. This comes straight from the top."

He gave her a commiserating frown, and Claire understood. The mayor wanted a female sergeant, and Claire Wolfe was a household name in Newburgh. Had Washington also received his promotion thanks to the diversity agenda of the mayor's reelection campaign?

Claire considered his words in silence. If she refused, she'd piss off Mayor Thornton and give Chief Emmerso a bureaucratic headache. After everything Emmerso had done for her, refusing the promotion reeked of ingratitude. Maybe they were right and the streets would be safer with Claire behind a desk?

"Thank you, sir."

"We'll delay the official ceremony until you've completed your training. And if you're worried about spending all your time behind your desk, don't. We're drowning in cases and short on detectives. Which reminds me..." He picked up his desk phone. "I want to introduce you to your field trainee."

Field trainee? The floor fell out of Claire's stomach. Emmerso had said nothing about her serving as a field training officer.

Washington spoke into the phone. "Yeah." He hung up.

Claire tried to stay calm. "Sir, I prefer to work alone. I spoke with Chief Emmerso—"

"I know, but the Bureau needs you. As an FTO, you'll get another bump in salary. I think you and your trainee will get along well."

Claire doubted that. The FTOs she'd known at Boston PD had always griped to their colleagues about the "hand-holding" and "diaper-changing." The door behind Claire opened, and on cue, her new partner entered, bright-eyed and eager.

"Sergeant Wolfe," Washington said, "this is Detective Jessica Long."

The pretty young detective beamed at Claire. "We've already met. Sergeant Wolfe, it's an honor to work with you."

CHAPTER 5

Special Agent Robert Cline climbed out of the Bureau car that morning and glanced at a familiar rustic landscape. The ranch house loomed in the shadow of the woods. Strands of torn police tape dangled from the front porch. The scent of decaying pine needles carried in the chilly air. The abandoned homestead whispered of evil deeds and deadly secrets. After a frustrating month away from Newburgh, Rob had returned to the crime scene for one last shot at cracking the case.

Special Agent Tom Brown slammed the driver's door shut, the noise spooking birds in the trees and sending them flying. "We could've stopped by the motel first to unpack, you know."

Rob ignored his old partner, but he had a point. Their suitcases were still in the trunk, along with their thermal underwear. Spring had arrived, but Massachusetts hadn't received the memo. A burning question spurred Rob on despite the inclement weather.

The shootout in the ranch house basement last year had left two people dead and exposed a treasure trove of evidence. Photographs and personal effects hinted at additional victims of the murderous pack that had used the isolated house as its base of operations. The agents of the FBI's Behavioral Analysis Unit had extended their visit to the small city to study the items, and Newburgh PD had provided them with office space. For long months, they had analyzed the new evidence for connections to unsolved crimes. The number of potential victims had sent shivers down Rob's spine.

But despite the team's best efforts, the victims remained nameless. The agents had dug up the stony yard outside the ranch house but failed to discover the victims' bodies. Without corpses, their investigation into the multiple homicides was one big conspiracy theory.

Rob tried to sound upbeat. "Sixth time lucky?"

This was their sixth trip to Newburgh in six months and probably their last. Tom had lost his enthusiasm for the search long ago. Their boss at the BAU, Unit Chief Madelaine Alda, had given Rob one last week to make progress on the case before she froze their investigation indefinitely to stop "wasting Bureau resources."

Rob had an ulterior motive for returning to Newburgh. But he also believed the key to the murders lay here, right under their noses. This was his last chance to find that elusive piece of evidence that would blow the case wide open.

"Whatever," Tom grumbled. His breath frosted in the air. "Let's get this over with."

Gravel crunched underfoot as they approached the darkened house. The agents unlocked the front door and walked through the hallways. The rooms stood empty. Forensic teams had bagged and labeled every item that wasn't nailed down and combed every square inch for trace evidence. The fingerprints had matched the perpetrators of the Middle School Murders, both of whom were dead. But the house hadn't yielded a single hair or smudge of blood belonging to the nameless victims who appeared among the serial killers' mementos.

Floorboards creaked while the agents toured the four bedrooms and living room. The house belonged to Anabelle Mervis. She'd paid her utility bills on time until a year ago when she'd evaporated into thin air, leaving no next of kin. The secluded location was a perfect murder den. William Wolfe's pack had committed their gruesome crimes here without fear of discovery. Rob was not optimistic about Anabelle's chances of survival.

The agents knocked on walls and floorboards, testing for hidden compartments and crawl spaces. They found none. Only one area remained—the basement.

Rob drew a deep breath and opened the door. Stairs led downward into inky darkness. A light bulb dangled from the ceiling, a replacement for the one that had shattered during a shootout. Rob felt the wall for the light switch, which clicked dutifully but provided no light.

Tom rubbed his arms. "I guess the electricity company finally ended the party."

Rob turned on his phone's flashlight and made a sweep of the interior. The basement was an empty shell. The forensic teams had cleared out the cabinets and drawers along with the moving boxes and their mementos. This was where Lisa Evans, the killer's protégé, had died, along with Detective Jed Wallace. Detective Claire Wolfe had almost become corpse number three.

Rob descended the steps. Bloodstains marked the floor, and bullet holes peppered the walls. The agents split up to inspect the space, their flashlights casting ghostly shadows.

Rob placed his hands on his hips. "Any ideas?"

Maybe Chief Alda was right about wasting Bureau resources? What had he expected—a flash of inspiration? A secret trap door their earlier searches had missed?

"Yes." Tom had Rob's undivided attention. "There's one possibility we haven't considered."

"Let me guess. We'll never find the bodies?"

"No, but that's a close second. The killers led Jed Wallace to this place. They wanted the authorities to find the mementos."

"True. They planned to frame Wallace for these killings along with the murdered girls."

"What if there are no other victims?"

Rob considered the suggestion. "The mementos are a hoax?"

"A diversion. We'd chase our tails for a few months while they set up shop somewhere else."

Rob laughed ironically. "Well, we fell for it, all right."

Tom placed the flashlight under his chin, and the shadows played devilish games on his sunken cheeks.

"I'm sorry to tell you this. But we've been chasing ghosts."

"You're creepy, you know that?"

"Rob, you have no idea. Come over to our home next Halloween. That'll freak you out."

"I'll try to remember that."

They headed back upstairs. Maybe Tom was right? Hitting a brick wall didn't mean the cosmos wanted you to try harder. It hinted that you should stop. While he was wasting Bureau dollars on this dead end, other killers roamed the nation. It was time for this investigation to cut its losses.

As Rob stepped onto the front porch, a hand closed on his arm. Tom pointed toward the edge of the woods, where an oversized gray dog tilted its head into the wind.

"Is that a wolf?"

"Coyote."

"How can you tell?"

"Wolves are larger and hunt in packs. Isn't she a beauty?"

Rob agreed. He was about to ask how his partner knew the

coyote was a she when the animal turned and stared right at them. Something protruded from the side of her mouth.

"Is that a rabbit?"

Tom swore under his breath and ran for the animal. The coyote dropped its prey and darted back into the woods. Rob followed. Why had his partner charged at the creature?

When he caught up, he understood. On the ground where the coyote had stood lay a pale, furless object. Not a rabbit. A severed human forearm.

CHAPTER 6

"Diane?"

The black woman had called her name twice. Diane Wolfe sank lower on the plastic chair, her gaze on the floor and her arms folded over her chest. Maybe if she ignored the woman, she'd leave her alone?

The past twenty minutes had seemed like twenty hours. In the event hall of the Second Presbyterian Church, the men and women in the discussion circle had shared their sob stories. Diane had watched the clock on the wall, praying for the meeting to end before her turn arrived. As with everything good in her life, that hope died a miserable death.

Judy, the annoyingly polite counselor, glanced at her clipboard to make sure she'd gotten Diane's name right. She had.

"Diane, this group depends on participation. We need to hear your story."

Diane scoffed. "I don't belong here. I'm not an alcoholic."

Knowing laughs circled the room. Their mocking eyes and patronizing smiles bored into her, and Diane felt hot in the face. *Are you happy now, Claire? This is what you wanted.*

"Diane, the first step to sobriety is to admit you have a problem."

"I don't have a problem. I don't see why I—"

"Let's try something different. When did you start drinking?"

Diane sighed. She had no energy to fight. Her memory of the past decade was wonky, but she remembered when she'd begun drinking. She'd never forget that day.

"The day my little girl, Tina, didn't come home from school. It was her fourteenth birthday. The police found her body that night. She'd been murdered."

Her words wiped the smiles from their faces. Served them right for poking their noses where they didn't belong. Maybe now they'd back off.

"How long ago was that?"

"Twelve and a half years."

"That must have been devastating."

Diane nodded, blinking back her tears. "That's when I started drinking. My husband added the painkillers and antidepressants."

"Diane, it's important to take responsibility for our addiction. It's easy to blame others."

"He did that on purpose. Slowly but surely, he was trying to kill me."

"I know it feels that way sometimes. Our loved ones might have the best intentions but—"

"You don't understand. My husband killed our daughter."

The woman beside her gasped, and a man swore.

"He killed her to hurt me. Then, he medicated me for years, so I'd think I was crazy. I only learned the truth last year."

She let her words sink in. "So you see, I don't belong here. Can I go now?"

But Judy was a stubborn woman. "Alcohol isn't the solution."

"It's all I've got left."

"And yet, here you are, Diane. I guess a part of you wants to be sober."

"I'm only here because my daughter forced me."

"Nobody can force you to attend our meetings, Diane."

"*She* can. She pays the bills. I've got to exercise and eat healthy food. I think she's trying to kill me, too. *That is not funny!*" The fresh wave of chuckles subsided. "She got my husband killed. Gunned down in our basement while I lay unconscious upstairs."

They were whispering among themselves now. Every man, woman, and child in Newburgh had heard about the Middle School Strangler from the news. Now they knew who she was. The pity in their eyes was more than she could bear.

A phone buzzed in her bag. The AA meetings outlawed cellular phones, and Diane jumped on the excuse to leave. She fished the offending device from her bag. The screen read "private number." Only Claire had her number. The caller must be a telemarketer.

"I have to take this." She hurried out of the room and into the foyer of the Second Presbyterian Church.

A man said, "Mrs. Diane Wolfe?"

"Who is this?"

"Mark Manson of Riddle and Ember Investments."

"Investments? You've got the wrong number. I don't have any money."

The man on the phone laughed. "Mrs. Wolfe, that is about to change."

CHAPTER 7

When Claire drove home that evening, a black SUV with tinted windows idled across the street from her mother's house. Was the media hounding her?

All day long, Claire had sensed invisible eyes following her. Her first case had involved a string of date rapes. She and Detective Jessica Long had visited a local bar to investigate, and the hairs on the back of Claire's neck had bristled. Someone was watching her. But when Claire had spun around, she'd found no ominous stalkers, only the framed portrait of a pirate on the wall. She had chalked up the paranoia to her unpleasant encounter with the press that morning. Now, the vehicle outside her home vindicated her premonitions.

Claire slammed the door of her white hatchback. She marched toward the Chevy Suburban and realized her mistake. Bella Winters couldn't afford the luxury SUV. Her mystery visitor was no newshound.

As Claire neared the vehicle, a Latino with a well-trimmed goatee got out of the driver's side. His lime-colored suit and shiny dress shoes looked expensive. His musky aftershave assaulted her nose at ten feet. This was no reporter, unless he wrote for a male fashion magazine.

He spread his hands in an appeasing gesture. "Sergeant Wolfe, we're sorry to disturb you at home."

Sergeant Wolfe. News travels fast. His apologetic manner neutralized Claire's rage. Who was this man, and what did he want?

"That makes two of us."

"Ms. Malik wanted to speak with you without attracting any...unwanted attention."

"Ms. Malik?" Where had Claire heard that name before?

The lack of recognition seemed to dishearten him. "Sarah Malik. She's running for mayor."

"Oh."

Claire remembered the campaign poster and the young Middle Eastern woman who promised to "drain the swamp." Claire's heart hardened. Was the politician in league with Bella Winters?

Interpreting her hesitation as permission to engage, the man grinned and extended his hand. "Alexandro Menendez, Ms. Malik's personal assistant. You can call me 'Al.'" He chuckled, then swept his arm toward the back door of the SUV. "Would you mind? Ms. Malik asks only a moment of your time."

At the end of a long, frustrating day, Claire yearned for privacy and a hot bath. But the visitor had aroused her curiosity. *Fine.* Her day couldn't get any weirder.

Alexandro "Al" Menendez opened the back door for her. The spacious interior of facing seats and lacquered wooden finishes reminded her of a limousine, although Claire had never set foot in a limo. *There's a first time for everything.*

The slender young woman inside crossed her legs over the luxurious leather upholstery. Claire recognized the black pixie bob hair and olive skin from the campaign poster, but Malik had selected a different business suit today.

Sarah Malik placed her brand-new iPhone on the wooden island beside her. She smiled at her guest and waved Claire to the seat opposite her. Her PA closed the door.

Malik's voice was pleasant and deep. "I apologize for the cloak-and-dagger approach, Sergeant Wolfe. In my line of work, privacy is hard-won."

"I'm OK with cloaks. But I draw the line at daggers."

Malik laughed, playful and appreciative.

"Spoken like a true homicide detective."

Her eyes drank Claire in, savoring her every detail. "Congratulations on your award."

Claire inclined her head. "Thank you."

"I've been following your career for some time. It's not easy to succeed in a profession dominated by men. I admire that."

The politician had selected her words to create empathy and forge a bond of sisterhood. This girl was good. But her smooth talk triggered Claire's defenses. In politics, there was no such thing as a free compliment. What did she want from Claire in return?

"Pity Thornton turned the ceremony into a campaign ad. That was tacky, even by his standards. The press conference was supposed to honor Chief Emmerso."

Claire agreed with her new friend and surrendered to her magnetic charm. No wonder Thornton was panicking. Claire might be chatting with the future mayor of Newburgh.

"And congratulations on your promotion, Sergeant." A knowing grin curled her lips. "You deserve it. But the timing is...suspicious. Thornton needs the female vote to win this election, and women are poorly represented in local law enforcement. Your award and promotion improve his image. I'd do the same thing in his situation."

The confession disarmed Claire. Chief Emmerso swam with the sharks, but Sarah Malik ran circles around them. Why was she contending for Mayor of Newburgh? This woman should run for President of the United States.

"What I don't understand, Claire," Malik added, leaning forward, "is why you're still working in law enforcement."

"Excuse me?" The question undermined her compliments. Didn't Malik believe Claire was a capable detective?

"As I said, I've been following your career. I saw how you handled that reporter this morning. You're far too intelligent to be chasing thugs and writing police reports."

Malik had hit a raw nerve. A top student at both Hannover High and the police academy, Claire had only joined the Force to uncover the truth of her sister's murder. Sure, she was an excellent homicide detective. But why waste her talents on solving crime when she could treat cancer or earn millions at technology startups?

Claire gave the politician an ironic smile. "You mean, why work for Thornton if I can work for you?"

Claire had called her out. Malik had criticized Thornton for using Claire to further his political agenda, and a moment later, she had tried the same tactic. Malik leaned back on her seat and shrugged off her hypocrisy.

"With me, you won't be a foot soldier. You'll be on the team that decides public policy. Imagine the impact you'd have, and not just as a woman. Your years in law enforcement add a lot of value. Why catch criminals one by one if you can change the rules of the game and neutralize hundreds. Newburgh needs you. I need you. And it doesn't hurt to know you'll be well compensated for your work. You won't have to worry about providing for yourself and your mother."

Malik had done her homework. But the invasion into Claire's personal life annoyed her.

"And you'll have Newburgh PD's new hero at your side during the campaign."

Malik's smile cooled. "I wouldn't offer this position to anyone, Claire. Like it or not, you're a celebrity. Embrace it. Let your reputation work for you."

The spell had broken. Malik had dressed her appeal to Claire's ego, ambition, and greed in saintly robes. But if Malik's election bid failed, Claire would find herself out of work and options. Still, she couldn't fault the politician for trying.

"Thank you for the offer. I'm flattered, but politics isn't my game."

"You're already playing, Claire. Make sure you're on the right side."

Claire grinned. "I'm happy where I am."

Malik inclined her head, accepting her defeat gracefully. She handed Claire a business card.

"Call me when you change your mind."

Claire exited the vehicle, and Malik's fancy SUV drove off. Claire's expectations for her new chapter at Newburgh PD hadn't included overtures from hopeful politicians. Life was full of surprises.

She crossed the street and glanced over her shoulder. Again, her skin crawled with that unsettling self-conscious sensation. Claire scanned the deserted street for suspicious observers. Finding none, she went indoors.

CHAPTER 8

From down the street, the killer watched the house in Pine Hills. He loved the hunt. Even more than the kill. The women went about their daily business completely unaware of his presence. They had no idea he held their lives in his hand. They were powerless to stop him. He was like an earthquake or a tornado. He was the hand of God.

A white Ford hatchback pulled up outside the Wolfe home, and Claire got out. Claire was beautiful. Perfect. She looked even better in person.

He'd first seen her on TV. Then, he'd collected newspaper clippings. He'd surveilled her from a distance. Each day, he circled closer, a Great White in the murky depths, drawn to the splash of a swimmer's legs.

But this was no ordinary hunt. Claire was unlike the other women. Claire was his soul mate. They shared a deep bond. And soon, he'd steal her heart.

Claire crossed the street toward the souped-up SUV. He wasn't the only one following Claire Wolfe. He observed the interchange with the man in the lime suit and glimpsed Sarah Malik before the door closed. *Well, well, well.* The politician had taken an interest in Claire, too. That was intriguing. Did the development threaten his plan? Perhaps not. In fact, the two dovetailed nicely.

He remembered the girl at the hotel. She'd lasted longer than expected. The rich bitch wasn't his type. Carmine was merely a pawn in his game. Claire was the queen. He and Claire would make a perfect, royal couple.

Claire got out of the SUV, and the Chevy Suburban drove away. Claire crossed the street and scanned her surroundings. Her gaze passed over him, and a thrill tickled his core. *Claire sensed him.* Yes, she was different. She longed for him, too.

Claire turned back to the house and let herself inside. Seconds later, a light went on upstairs. Was that her beacon? Was she inviting him to join her right now? The anticipation was almost painful.

"Soon, Claire," he promised her. "We'll be together soon."

CHAPTER 9

The knocking on the front door came while Claire was drying her hair. She'd had a long, hot bath and wasn't expecting visitors. Even shameless journalists knew better than to bother her at home after ten o'clock. Had Sarah Malik returned to change Claire's mind?

She padded downstairs, barefoot and in her pajamas. Diane snored softly from her bedroom. An earthquake couldn't wake her mother. Claire might as well be alone in the house. At the foot of the staircase, she paused. She'd left her gun upstairs. The crime statistics didn't lie. Even a female police officer would be a fool to open the door to late-night strangers. *Never mind.* She'd dispatch the would-be mayor quickly. This would only take a moment.

Claire put her eye to the peephole. She'd been mistaken. A young man in a cheap brown suit stood on her doorstep. This was no politician. But he was cute. She opened the door.

The man's face was an expressionless mask. "Detective Claire Wolfe?"

"Yes?"

He flashed an identity card. "Special Agent Cline, FBI. You're under arrest."

Claire blinked at the special agent and stifled a smile. "On what charges?"

"There's a list."

"Oh, really? I hope you brought handcuffs, Special Agent Cline. You'll need them."

"I did. And these." From behind his back, he produced a pack of Miller's beer.

"You've done your homework, Agent Cline. I could never resist a man with a six-pack."

Rob rushed inside, and Claire pounced on him, wrapping her legs around his waist. They kissed urgently and tore at each other's clothes. Rob swung the door closed behind him, and they tumbled to the floor.

Later, they moved to the king-sized bed in her room upstairs. Claire had created the new expanse by knocking down the wall between her childhood bedroom and Tina's.

Rob handed her a beer and sat beside her in bed. "Here's to your first day back at work."

They clinked the tins together.

"Thank you."

"And the award and promotion, Sergeant Wolfe."

"Don't remind me. I thought you were getting back next week."

"I couldn't stand to be away from you any longer."

"Liar," she teased.

Rob chuckled. "And the Milwaukee case came together faster than expected. But I did miss you."

"Same here."

Claire meant that. The few weeks apart had seemed like months.

Claire gulped her drink. "Where are the rest of the beers?"

"In the fridge."

"Remind me to hide them before Diane gets up. She started AA meetings today."

"That's great. How is she?"

Claire sighed. "The same."

"Mm-hm."

Rob knew not to go there. Her old flame from high school, Rob had arrived in Newburgh with a BAU team to assist with the Middle School Strangler case. Their short but intense reunion had rekindled their relationship as adults.

Rob had believed in her even when Newburgh PD had not. And he'd saved her life. After the case's dramatic conclusion, the FBI had extended his stay in Newburgh to process the evidence of more serial murders Claire had discovered in the basement of a ranch house in the woods. The memory of that basement sent shivers down her spine.

"I almost forgot," Rob said. "I got you something."

He handed her a gift-wrapped package the size of a bulky item of clothing.

"Thank you. You shouldn't have."

"It's to celebrate your first day back. Go on, open it."

Claire tore the wrapping paper to reveal a thick, white, and sleeveless undershirt with Velcro straps around the midsection. The label on the packaging read, "Coolmax Pro covert vest."

"A bulletproof vest?"

"It goes under your clothing. Protection level 3A. Sixty percent survival."

"It's perfect!" Claire kissed him. For an officer who'd recently taken a bullet, the life-saving equipment earned more brownie points than roses. The gift proved Rob wanted her to stay in his life.

"Seriously, though. This time don't get shot. But if you do, wear this."

Claire laughed. "There's little chance of me getting shot. *Sergeant* Wolfe will be spending more quality time behind a desk." The thought dampened her mood. "I didn't want the promotion. Or the award."

"Why not? You deserve them."

"I don't want to gain from the murder of those girls. That's exactly what Bill had wanted."

Claire no longer called him Dad or "my father". She wanted nothing to do with him.

"Your talent and hard work got you that promotion. I'm surprised the department waited so long to make the offer."

Claire turned the conversation away from her father's crimes and her own deadly mistakes. "It's not the only offer I got today. Sarah Malik stopped by the house tonight."

"Do I know her?"

"Sarah 'Drain-the-Swamp' Malik."

"The politician?"

"We had a chat in her fancy SUV. She wants me to join her team as a consultant on public policy."

"Wow. Impressive. What are you going to do?"

"I turned her down. She's using me to beat Mayor Thornton in the election."

Rob shrugged. "Doesn't mean it's a bad move for you."

"I know. But it feels like a betrayal."

"You don't owe Mayor Thornton anything."

"Not Thornton. Chief Emmerso. He's counting on me. The department is short-handed. The timing is terrible. But I might reconsider thanks to my new partner."

"You have a new partner?"

"More of a field trainee. Jessica Long. Fresh from the beat."

"The blonde with blue eyes? She seems nice."

Claire punched his arm.

"Hey! I only remember her because she screwed up the police guard for the girls last year."

Claire grunted. "Let's hope she's a better detective."

"Give her a chance. She might surprise you."

Claire scoffed.

"What?"

"Nothing. She's just...*annoying*."

"What do you mean?"

"Eager to please. Asks too many questions. Where did I graduate and how did I like the academy? Did I always want to be a detective? Isn't it great that we have two female detectives in the Bureau? She writes down everything I say. I feel like I'm under investigation."

Rob chuckled. "She admires you and wants to make a good impression. She's got a lot to learn, and you're the perfect instructor."

"Well, it's embarrassing. I wish she'd just shut up." Claire sighed. "I sound like a jerk, don't I?"

Rob took a swig of his beer but didn't answer. He knew when to hold his tongue. Claire loved that about him.

"I just know she'll get in the way. I don't want to be responsible for her. If anything happens to her like..." She couldn't speak his name.

"Like Jed?"

Claire hugged her knees and avoided his eyes. The Middle School Strangler case loomed in her memory again. Would her deadly mistakes haunt her forever?

Rob touched her shoulder. "That wasn't your fault, Claire. You acted in self-defense, and I'm glad you did. Which reminds me. I have some good news. We found bodies near the ranch house."

Rob had believed the mementos in the ranch house basement meant William Wolfe's murderous pack had claimed more victims. Rob's persistence had paid off. But instead of delighting Claire, the discovery made her sick to her stomach.

Claire stared at him. "How is that good news?"

"We'll uncover the extent of the pack's crimes and give the victims' families closure."

"Victims William Wolfe put in the ground?"

Rob's breakthrough proved her father had devastated more lives than Claire had imagined.

Rob grinned sheepishly. "It gives me an excuse to stay in Newburgh longer."

Longer. The word cut both ways. Rob wasn't here to stay. The BAU sent him to law enforcement agencies around the country to analyze homicides too complex and twisted for local detectives. He did important work. But his job meant he'd always be on the move. Did their relationship stand a chance?

Rob lowered his gaze. "I spoke with Captain Washington. We might get to work together again. Tom and I need help processing the bodies."

Claire's disgust overflowed. "I'll pass."

"Claire, these homicides aren't your fault either."

Nothing was ever her fault. But somehow, she didn't feel any better. She thought of the photographs and jewelry in the basement of the ranch house. Each represented an innocent life her father had snuffed out.

"How many?"

"Two so far. We found shallow graves in the woods outside the ranch house. We think there are more."

"He'd been murdering people for years, and I had no idea. I'm some detective, aren't I?"

Maybe Malik was right. Maybe Claire didn't belong in law

enforcement. Her father's blood ran in her veins. She belonged in a padded cell. That way, nobody else would get killed.

"Sorry. I shouldn't have said anything. I should've guessed how you'd feel."

Claire turned away and wiped a tear from her cheek. If Jess could see her now, she'd take Claire off that pedestal.

CHAPTER 10

The killer stood in Claire's kitchen that night. He'd let himself inside the house without making a sound while Claire slept upstairs. In the darkness of the early morning hours, the house was his playground. He breathed in Claire's scent. He ran his gloved fingers over the back of the kitchen chair where, an hour ago, she'd sat. "Home, sweet home."

He admired the framed photo of Tina, Claire's long-dead sister. The killer had studied Claire's personal history. He knew Claire well, perhaps better than she knew herself. He opened the fridge. Claire stored her leftovers in plastic tubs. Chicken and rice. Steamed broccoli and cauliflower. Claire observed a healthy diet. *Good for you, Claire.* She was getting her mother, Diane, back into shape, too. What a model daughter.

The only exception was the beer on the top shelf, the four cans still joined by the plastic rings of the six-pack. That wasn't Claire's fault. Her visitor had brought the alcohol. Claire had welcomed the man inside, and when the lights had gone out, the visitor remained.

Claire had a lover.

An unpleasant sensation tugged at his heart. Was he jealous? Claire belonged to him, and he belonged to her. No other man could compete with the bond they shared. Even so, this wildcard posed a threat to the plan. He'd better take every precaution.

The killer positioned the night vision goggles over his eyes, and the home emerged in shades of green. He climbed the stairs slowly, shifting his weight from foot to padded foot. Soon, he'd enter her bedroom. They'd breathe the same air. The skin of his arms prickled with excitement.

She'd left her bedroom door open. Was she expecting him? He listened to the rise and fall of their breathing, then floated inside. Two prone bodies lay under the covers of the king-sized bed. Claire, his beloved, and the stranger. He touched the knife in the leather scabbard on his thigh. He could easily skewer the wildcard, right here and now. Claire would understand. But he must stick to the plan. He'd make his entrance at the right time. From their first encounter, she'd see him as her equal, not a thief in the night.

He turned his attention to the bundle of clothing on the dresser. He reached his gloved hand into the breast pocket of the man's jacket and found what he sought. Flipping open the stranger's wallet, he read the name on the identification card.

Special Agent Robert Cline. FBI, Behavioral Analysis Unit. *Claire, you sneaky thing.* Agent Cline might help their cause. *Keep your friends close, your enemies closer.*

The FBI agent shifted in his sleep and smacked his lips. Was he waking up? The killer drew the hunting knife from his leather scabbard. He dared the agent to open his eyes. *Go ahead, make me do this.* But the agent turned over, exhaled a deep breath, and resumed his slumber.

Fine. He sheathed his weapon. *We'll meet again soon, Claire.*

He went downstairs. At the foot of the staircase, he paused. Returning to the kitchen, he scooped up the four remaining beers and escaped into the night.

CHAPTER 11

A kiss to the forehead woke Claire on Tuesday morning. Rob had dressed already. "Got to run. I'm picking up Tom at the motel."

Claire frowned. "What about breakfast?"

"I'll grab something on the way. We've got a busy day ahead of us."

"Good luck."

Claire stretched her arms and climbed out of bed. She headed to the bathroom and brushed her teeth. Maybe Rob was right. Jess was just trying to make a good impression. Claire's mentor at Boston PD, Detective Ned Evans, had shown her the ropes with patience and understanding. She should cut Jess some slack, too. Claire resolved to start over and do a better job as an FTO. A good night's sleep worked miracles.

Claire dressed and went downstairs. To her surprise, Diane sat at the breakfast table, nursing a bowl of cereal. No need to henpeck her mother into civilization this morning. The AA meeting was already paying off.

"Morning, Mom."

"Your boyfriend snuck out already."

Rob had helped Claire move homes and stayed over often when he was in town. He was always kind and polite to Diane, but her attitude never softened. Claire held her tongue. New start, she reminded herself.

Claire fixed a mug of instant coffee and a bowl of Special K and opened the fridge for the milk. Something was missing.

"Mom, did Rob take anything from the fridge?"

"Not that I noticed. Why? Do you limit what he eats, too?"

Diane had chosen the wrong moment to try Claire's patience. "There were four beers in the fridge. Where are they?"

"How should I know?"

"Alcohol is your area of expertise."

"If you say so."

Claire counted to five. "Mom, be honest with me. We need to trust each other to make this work."

Diane glared at her. "Then trust me. I didn't take any beers. I haven't had a drink in a day, thanks to you."

Claire returned the glare, then relented. She didn't have time to police her mother. She'd check the trash later, although by now Mom would have learned to dispose of her drinking evidence more discreetly.

Claire poured milk over her cereal, moved her breakfast to the kitchen table, and unfolded the newspaper. Rob must have brought *The Newburgh Herald* indoors on his way out. He was considerate like that.

The upcoming elections hogged the front page. "Mayor Launches Street Camera Initiative." Claire turned to page two and almost choked on toasted grain flakes.

"Hero's Welcome for Newburgh Detective," ran the article title. A photo showed Claire at the podium, wedged between Mayor Thornton and Chief Emmerso. The other photo was a portrait of William "Bill" Wolfe. The caption read, "The Middle School Strangler, Detective Claire Wolfe's father."

Not only had Bella Winters made Chief Emmerso's ceremony all about Claire, but she'd also highlighted Claire's family connection to a serial killer. Claire's blood boiled as she read about her "bizarre and awkward homecoming" and the public's low confidence in Newburgh's police department ever since the arrest and conviction of the former chief, Harry Wallace.

Claire ground her breakfast cereal between her molars. She could strangle the reporter. Claire imagined tomorrow's headline. "Newburgh Detective Joins Family Business." *Ha!*

Mayor Thornton might kill Bella Winters first and save Claire the trouble. Thanks to Bella, his efforts to improve his image through law enforcement had backfired.

Claire's phone rang, and she answered. "Wolfe."

"Claire, where are you?" Claire's favorite field trainee had called her, bright and early.

"Detective Long, I'll be there soon."

"Be where?"

"At the station. Where else?"

"We need to go downtown. The Barnett Inn called in a homicide. Captain Washington assigned the case to us."

Claire carried her half-eaten breakfast to the sink. "Send me the address. I'll pick you up."

The day just kept getting better.

CHAPTER 12

"Are you squeamish?"

Claire pressed the button for the elevator. The lobby of The Barnett Inn needed new carpets and wallpaper. Jess had been unusually quiet during their ride to the seedy hotel. Either Claire's new partner had taken the hint or she was dreading the crime scene. The victim was female, Dispatch had said, and her death brutal.

Jess shrugged. "No more than the next girl. On patrol, I responded to my share of homicides."

The elevator chimed, and they stepped inside. Claire pressed the button for the third floor and dropped her line of questioning.

The life of a homicide detective had its challenges. You came face-to-face with the worst side of humanity and shouldered the responsibility of putting the culprits behind bars. Decades of legislation had made collecting admissible evidence very challenging. And when the stars aligned and you won a conviction, an appeals judge might shed a tear for the convict's troubled childhood and release the killer so he could strike again. Claire kept those pearls of wisdom to herself. Jess had enough frustrations ahead. She didn't need any bullying from her FTO. Rob would be proud.

"I remember my first homicide at Boston PD. I had a great FTO, and his advice has stuck with me ever since."

Jess's eyes widened with surprise at Claire's sudden openness.

"'Look for what you *don't* see.'"

Jess raised a suspicious eyebrow. Was her partner pulling her leg?

Claire explained. "The obvious details are useful. But what you expect to find at the crime scene—but don't—can generate the best leads. Always look for what's missing."

Jess nodded. This time, she didn't pull out her notebook, and Claire felt a small stab of disappointment. *Careful what you wish for.*

"What do you think we'll find?" Claire asked.

Jess swallowed hard but accepted the challenge. "Judging from the location, I'd guess the decedent is a cheating wife, killed in the heat of the moment."

Claire grunted with approval. "Most murderers know their victims. But let's keep our options open. For all we know, she's a prostitute who picked the wrong john."

Jess had brightened at Claire's praise, but now she studied her feet. The elevator chimed, and the doors opened.

"Time to find out."

The furnishings on the third-floor corridor were in no better state of repair than those of the lobby. The detectives made for the patrol officer who stood guard outside a closed door.

"Morning, Officer Santiago. What do we have?"

Officer Richard Santiago, a stocky Latino, handed her the clipboard with shaky hands. "A real mess. Hey, Detective Long. Good luck."

Claire signed the register and scanned the list of names. Brandon Yang, a county forensic tech, had beaten them to the scene along with Captain Washington and a patrol sergeant, George Eckhardt.

The detectives handed the clipboard back to Santiago and helped themselves to latex gloves and booties from a box beside the door.

Claire gestured at the door. "After you, Detective."

She followed Jess inside and instantly regretted sending her in first. The pokey hotel room reeked of blood and raw flesh. The slaughterhouse stench came from the twin beds where the naked remains of a young woman lay faceup, her feet toward the door.

Santiago wasn't kidding about the mess. Blood soaked the sheets red. Multiple stab wounds covered her torso, arms, and legs like gaping little mouths. A square of exposed muscle and bone marked the dead woman's chest where her breasts should be. The killer had spared the woman's face.

Jess slumped toward the floor, and Claire grabbed her under her armpits.

"I'm OK."

Jess wasn't fooling anybody. Captain Washington and Sergeant Eckhardt looked on with concern while Claire guided Jess toward the fresher air of the corridor.

"Santiago," Sergeant Eckhardt called, his voice gruff. "Get her some water."

Claire eased Jess to the floor.

Jess closed her eyes and leaned her head against the wall. "I'm sorry."

Claire thought the detective was going to cry, but she didn't. Collapsing at a crime scene in the presence of two sergeants and her captain was not an ideal way to start her first homicide investigation.

"It's OK, Jess. Take deep breaths and join us when you're ready."

Jess opened her eyes and nodded. Santiago handed her an open plastic bottle of water. Jess took the bottle and drank. Claire returned to the crime scene and nodded at Captain Washington to confirm Jess was OK.

Brandon Yang smiled at Claire. "Welcome back, Detective Wolfe." In full-body scrubs, the Asian forensic tech photographed the corpse. "Who's the fresh meat?"

Claire glared at him for his insensitive choice of metaphor.

"That's *Sergeant* Wolfe to you," Captain Washington said. "And her new partner is Detective Jessica Long." He gave the tech a meaningful glance, a warning to go easy on her.

Brandon raised his voice. "Nice to meet you, Detective Long."

Jess waved her arm in the doorway in response.

Claire turned her attention to the mutilated corpse on the bed. The victim looked to be in her late twenties. Blood spatter and sweat ruined the silky brown hair, which plumed around her shoulders but still hinted at salon treatments. Toned muscles. Healthy skin. Manicured fingernails kept short and unpainted. This wasn't the body of a street hooker.

Claire's detective brain noted other details: bruising on the girl's wrists and ankles; scraps of clothing on the floor; a small, tidy pile of gold jewelry on the bedside table—two earrings and a necklace of thick chain link with no pendant. Brandon had labeled the items with numbered circles for his photographs.

Sergeant Eckhardt aimed his arched eyebrows at the officer outside. "Santiago, catch us up."

"Yes, sir." Santiago entered the hotel room and told them about the Dispatch call and his arrival at the scene. "The manager found the victim. The Do Not Disturb sign remained on the door long after checkout time."

"Who signed for the room?"

Santiago studied his notepad. "Mary Connor. The victim, according to the manager."

"Did anyone arrive with her?"

"No, but the manager said she'd rented rooms before."

Washington grunted and planted his hands on his hips. "Thank you, Officer. Sergeant Wolfe, the scene is all yours."

Claire retrieved her digital recorder and pressed Record. She described the state and position of the victim in broad strokes, then engaged her detective brain again. The crime was a puzzle she needed to solve, and she searched for the edges of the picture.

"From the contusions on her wrists and ankles and the flaking on the bedposts, it seems the decedent was secured to the bed with a stiff medium such as handcuffs or cable ties. Brandon, did we find any restraints?"

"Nope."

"The killer must have taken them with him. Do we have a time of death?"

Brandon placed paper bags over the woman's hands. "Ten to twelve hours. Pending the autopsy."

Claire turned to Santiago. "When did she check in?"

"Two nights ago."

Captain Washington pointed at the pile of gold jewelry on the bedside table. "I guess we can rule out a robbery. What do you make of it, Sergeant? A lover's quarrel or jealous husband?"

Claire stared at the corpse. Something about this murder scene didn't fit.

"This level of violence could indicate anger. But there's no sign of a struggle around the bed." Had the decedent allowed the killer to tie her up during sex? If so, she'd known her murderer. Claire turned to the forensic tech. "Any sign of sexual activity?"

Brandon photographed a green tote bag on a side table.

"Nope. No semen either."

"Ask the ME to test for spermicides."

"Yes, ma'am."

The tote bag snagged Claire's attention. "Is that Kate Spade?"

"Yep."

"That's got to be worth over five hundred dollars."

"Sorry, Sergeant. This one isn't for sale. By the way, many of those wounds show early signs of healing. She was tortured for quite some time, maybe shortly after she arrived."

Again, Claire's gut whispered that this was not a typical murder. She pointed to the satin blouse on the floor. "Her clothes were removed with a sharp implement. Brandon, did you find any knives?"

"Nada. No weapons in the room." He fished inside the tote bag with his gloved hands.

Claire could ignore her gut feeling no longer. "The killer came prepared, and he cleaned up after. This was no crime of passion."

Brandon removed a driver's license from the victim's purse. "Bingo. She lied to the manager. Her name is Carmine Hannover."

The officers exchanged surprised glances.

"Hannover?" The name reminded Claire of a dedication plaque at the entrance to her high school building. "As in Hannover High?"

Captain Washington nodded gravely. "Her parents donated half the city."

"The Cranberry Kings?" Brandon said.

Washington said, "What's a wealthy heiress doing in a craphole like this? And why the false name?"

"There's two hundred dollars in her wallet and a tube of KY Jelly. She was expecting company."

Claire bit her lip. Carmine Hannover had come to The Barnett Inn to meet a secret lover. But instead of sex, she'd found a brutal death. *Look for what's missing.*

"Any prints on the jewelry?"

"Oh, they're covered in prints. Nice and clear."

"Good. Those might lead us to the lover or the killer. Or both. What's the cause of death?"

"It's hard to tell if the cuts damaged her internal organs. Either way, she lost a lot of blood. I'd go for exsanguination for now, but the autopsy will have the final say."

Washington turned to Claire. "Anything else?"

She scanned the room and peered under the bed. Something was definitely missing. "Where are her breasts?"

Brandon shrugged. "The killer must have taken them."

Washington and Eckhardt grimaced.

Claire stopped the recorder.

Captain Washington spoke to the tech. "Let us know ASAP about those prints. Tell the ME to test for date rape drugs, too. This has become a top-priority case."

Claire's shoulders stiffened involuntarily. She was the lead investigator. Washington had stepped on her toes by calling the shots. Apparently, he hadn't adjusted to his new job either.

"Can I move the body now?" Brandon asked.

"Go ahead."

Things were looking up for the case. They might have the killer's prints. But what about his motive?

Claire said, "I assume her family has enemies."

Washington frowned. "You think the killer was sending them a message?"

"Maybe."

Brandon rolled the body over. "Not just the family. Sergeant Wolfe, have a look."

Claire's jaw dropped. The killer had carved a single word into the milky flesh of Carmine Hannover's back. He'd sent a message all right, and this message was for Claire.

CHAPTER 13

Claire returned to the squad room that afternoon, her heart overflowing with dread. Rumors traveled fast in the department, and once again, she'd become the focus of her fellow officers' suspicions. After what she'd seen at the crime scene, there was no way she'd lead this investigation. This time, Claire would pull the plug herself.

Mahoney glanced up from his desk. "There she is. Second day back in the saddle and the sergeant has already landed a high-profile homicide."

Claire faked a smile. "No rest for the wicked."

Jess was not at her desk. Claire had sent her back to the station on the pretext of getting a head start on their report of the crime scene. Jess could do with the fresh air. But had Jess told the other detectives about the word the killer had etched into the victim's body?

"Have you seen Detective Long?"

"Nope. She might be in the captain's office with the others. Which reminds me, I'm supposed to tell you to join them."

"Thanks."

"You're welcome."

Mahoney turned his attention back to his computer screen. He didn't joke about Claire's name appearing on the victim. Maybe that rumor hadn't spread yet, after all?

Claire knocked on Captain Washington's door and entered.

"We're updating the team about the Hannover homicide," Washington said. "I've assigned Detectives Nakamura and Gomez to help out."

The team. Claire's investigation had grown. Was she still welcome on that team? In the visitor chairs, the two male detectives craned their necks toward her. *Where is Jess?*

"Great."

Washington cleared his throat. "The Hannovers are well-connected, so this case demands extra sensitivity. Nobody speaks to the media. Chief Emmerso and I notified the decedent's parents this afternoon. Understandably, they want to keep the details of their daughter's murder out of the papers. The Hannovers employ half of Newburgh, directly or indirectly. We don't want to hurt those livelihoods. A quick resolution will go a long way to calming public fears and speculation."

Nakamura said, "Speculation about what?"

"Everything. Whenever the rich and famous are involved, imaginations run wild. Sergeant Wolfe is leading the investigation. This case is your number one priority. Understood?"

The detectives nodded. Not only was Washington keeping her on the case, but he'd also upped her resources.

"Over to you, Sergeant."

The detectives turned to her for instructions, their notepads out. Claire couldn't recuse herself from the investigation without divulging why. How much had Washington told them about the murder scene?

"Have you seen photos of the crime scene?"

Captain Washington answered for them. "We'll review

those together later, but let's hit the ground running." He gave her a meaningful glance. The detectives didn't need to know about the killer's message, at least not yet.

Claire was stuck with the case.

"We think the victim was meeting someone at the hotel, possibly a lover. She signed for the room under a fake name, Mary Connor, so it seems she wanted to keep the meeting secret. She might have met this lover or others at the hotel before. Nakamura, speak with the manager. He might have details on her earlier visits. Either the killer is her mystery lover or a third party who followed or lured her to the hotel. He tortured her using sharp implements for many hours, but there's no sign of sexual contact. The motive might be to hurt her family, either as revenge or leverage. Gomez, we need CCTV footage of the area from the time the decedent checked in until the body's discovery. The victim's phone is in evidence. We need a list of friends and family she was in touch with, social media interactions, phone records, and a breakdown of her whereabouts for her last forty-eight hours. And we need to search her home. The ME is working on the time and cause of death. Forensics is processing the prints and trace DNA found at the scene. We might get lucky. But let's stay open to all possibilities. That should keep you busy."

Gomez snorted. "That's an understatement."

"Captain, do you want to update me about the parents?"

"Yes. That's all, gentlemen."

The detectives left the room, and Washington dialed an extension on his phone. "Yeah, we're ready for you." He put down the phone.

Claire said, "They don't know about the writing, do they?"

"Chief Emmerso and I want to keep that quiet for now. The detail might help us narrow the list of suspects."

Someone knocked twice on the door, and Chief Emmerso entered.

"Sergeant. Captain."

"We were just talking about the writing."

"If you can call it that." From a folder in his hand, Chief Emmerso produced a color printout of Carmine Hannover's back, which he placed on Washington's desk.

A shiver traced Claire's spine. Even in photo form, the etched word unnerved her. The killer had turned Carmine Hannover's body into parchment, a means for delivering a message. Her violated corpse stained the grizzly crime with an added layer of inhumanity.

The word read, *CLAIRE.*

The writing dragged Claire back to the dark days of the Middle School Strangler case. *For you, Cub.* In the basement of her childhood home, Claire's father had confessed to killing those girls in her name. Now Carmine's murderer had branded her corpse with Claire's name. Claire had no connection to Carmine Hannover. Why had the killer mentioned her? She searched the jagged writing for answers.

Emmerso asked the obvious question. "Who is Claire?"

"Not a Hannover," Washington said. "I Googled them."

"A friend of the decedent?" Claire guessed. "His next target?" They were pretending not to notice the "Claire" before their eyes, and she was happy to play along.

"Why write her name on the body? Is that a threat?"

"Or the killer's name," Claire said.

Washington scoffed. "I don't think the victim carved her murderer's name on her back with her last dying breath."

"That's not what I meant. Maybe the killer signed her name."

"A woman did this?" Washington's eyes widened. He hadn't

been at Newburgh PD during the Middle School Strangler murders.

Claire's cheeks warmed. "It's possible." If she didn't raise that scenario, others would.

"And she wants to get caught?"

"Or the killer chose a name at random to confuse the investigation." Claire didn't believe that for a second. Claire was an uncommon first name around here. The word was no arbitrary detail. But why would the killer use her name?

Emmerso changed course. "What about the writing? The killer could have used blood. Why cut the word into her skin?"

"Because it's freaky as hell?" Washington said.

Emmerso grunted. "The medium is the message? An act of terror?"

Claire pointed at the photo and the detail that had her mind itching. "The bridge of the A is missing."

"Maybe he was in a rush?" Washington suggested.

Emmerso had another explanation. "Or there's a technical reason. Closing the loop might rip the skin and damage the letter."

Claire pointed at the R. "He closed that loop."

They stared at the photograph.

"Sir, I'm not sure I'm the right person to lead this case."

"Do you know the killer?"

"No."

"Did you know the victim?"

"No, sir."

"Then you're good to go."

"Sir, what if the message is for me? My name was in the press recently, and I just returned to work. What if the killer expected me to lead the investigation?"

"Maybe he dropped your name to disqualify our top sleuth and derail the investigation? Should we give him what he wants? I don't think so. Besides, we can't let both of you drop the case."

"Both of us?"

Washington grimaced. "I didn't get a chance to tell you. I assigned Detective Long to another case."

Claire's heart sank. She hadn't enjoyed having a trainee but felt responsible for her loss of the case.

"Sir, if it's about her reaction at the crime scene today, she'll get over it. Please, give her another chance."

Washington raised his hand for her to stop. "I didn't drop her, Sergeant. She asked me to reassign her. Don't take it personally. It was my fault for starting her on such a brutal homicide."

Emmerso turned to Claire. "She'll be fine. Other detectives will assist you with the investigation. But your number one priority today is to meet with the Hannovers."

"Sir, I thought you and Captain Washington already met with them."

"We did, but the Hannovers want to speak with you in person. They asked for you specifically and want you to lead the investigation."

"Me?"

"They were adamant. I know this is unusual, but the Hannovers have done a lot for the city and they're close friends of Mayor Thornton. They asked for you to visit them at your earliest convenience."

Washington chuckled. "That means immediately."

"They also asked to meet with you alone."

"Yes, sir. I'll see them right away."

"Thank you. Keep them informed of the investigation's progress as you would the family of any other victim. But remember, they're still potential suspects."

"I understand, sir."

"Good. And one more thing, Sergeant. When you're there, watch out."

"For what, sir?"

"Anything. The Hannovers might seem like the rest of us, but they're not. They're...different."

CHAPTER 14

"Here's another fine mess you've gotten us into," Special Agent Tom Brown said.

Rob's partner was grumbling again, and Rob didn't blame him. They had spent the morning knee-deep in dirt and dead bodies, and there was no end in sight.

Rob slammed the shovel into the clammy soil with an ominous crunch and stretched his back. The air was thick with the scent of turned earth and decomposing flesh. Over the past few hours, the men had exposed two more shallow graves among the trees of the woods. At least the agents had worn jeans and t-shirts for their digging expedition.

"Is that another Laurel and Hardy quote? You're showing your age, old-timer."

"Takes one to know one."

Rob laughed. "Your grumbling has rubbed off on me."

The sound of two other shovels a hundred feet away echoed among the trees. Two forensic archaeologists had arrived from Boston to extract the buried corpses. The specialists had staked the shallow graves, dividing the plots into squares with string. They brushed dirt from the exposed limbs and shoveled soil

YOU MADE ME   69

with hand trowels into five-gallon buckets, one for each square. When they'd completely exposed the bodies, they transferred the corpses to body bags and padlocked the zippers. Then, they sifted the collected soil using a screen propped between two sawhorses to search for bone fragments and bits of clothing. They documented and photographed everything. A half hour ago, they had spread out to join the hunt for more unmarked graves.

Rob had requested extra manpower from the Newburgh Police Department, too. Captain Washington had said he'd see what he could do but made no promises. Rob had expected him to send Claire, considering the key role she'd played in discovering the ranch house and its serial murder den. But Sergeant Claire Wolfe had better things to do than digging up dead bodies. That was probably for the best. Rob would find more romantic ways to spend their time together.

Tom's shovel hit something that didn't crunch. "I've got another one. How many is that now?"

"Five."

Rob owed that coyote a big thank you. The severed human forearm had led the agents to the rest of the woman's body, which had protruded from the earth. Despite the advanced state of decomposition, Rob recognized the remains of Anabelle Mervis, the owner of the ranch house, from her picture on file. The second body would be harder to identify. The man had neither hands nor a head. That morning had produced another decapitated body—this time a woman—and a naked, middle-aged man with a bullet hole in the back of his skull. The backlog of forensic work on their hands multiplied by the minute.

Rob resumed his digging. He understood Captain Washington's reluctance to spread his meager resources too thin. The perpetrators of these murders were dead. The landscape of their crimes had taken shape, and Rob searched only for the final missing pieces to complete the picture. But Rob's gut insisted that this puzzle was larger than anyone thought. They had only scratched the surface, so to speak.

"Special Agent Cline?" The young woman's voice came from the ranch house.

Rob straightened and waved his arm. "Over here."

The attractive blonde in the plain brown suit spotted him, waved back, and trotted over, her heeled shoes crunching on the gravel driveway.

"Here comes the cavalry," Tom muttered.

Rob stuck his shovel in the soil. "Be nice. We can use all the help we can get."

The woman arrived, breathless, and stuck out her hand. "Detective Jessica Long. Call me Jess."

Rob suppressed a grin. Of all people, the department had sent him Claire's field trainee. If the mention of her name had made Claire jealous, she'd just *love* the idea of Jess and Rob working together.

He wiped his palm on his jeans and shook her hand. "Call me Rob. This is Special Agent Tom Brown."

Tom deadpanned, "You can call me sir."

"Don't mind him. He's always grumpy before his tenth coffee."

Jess glanced at the two agents eagerly. "Captain Emmerso said you needed help."

Tom scoffed. "Did you bring a shovel?"

Her smile faltered. "I'll get one right away."

Rob glared at Tom. "Don't bother. There's plenty to do besides digging. This way."

He stepped out of his ditch and poured a plastic cup of Kool-Aid from the bottle on a foldable table.

"Want a drink?"

"No, thank you."

She cast a wary eye at the row of occupied body bags on the ground.

Rob gulped down his juice. "I take it you're familiar with the Middle School Strangler case?"

"I worked that case as a patrol officer."

Rob said nothing of her mix-up of the patrol schedule that had left a potential victim without police protection for an entire day.

"Then you know the investigation uncovered a serial killer team—a middle-aged man and a younger woman."

Jess nodded. "William Wolfe and Lisa Evans. William was Sergeant Claire Wolfe's father. She'd been investigating the case."

"Very good. William Wolfe referred to the killing team as a *pack*, as in a wolf pack."

Jess laughed, and the joy in her eyes amplified her beauty. "He must be the corniest serial killer ever."

Rob gazed at the body bags. "And a busy one."

Jess bunched her eyebrows. "I thought serial killers worked alone."

Rob produced a dry grin. "Lone wolves?"

She laughed again. "Nice!"

At least Jess had an upbeat sense of humor. *Look and learn, Tom.*

"Most work alone, but serial killer couples aren't uncommon. Usually, the male partner is dominant and more active in the killing. The female partner assists by luring the victims, but with time she might take part in the murders. A typical example is the so-called Ken and Barbie Killers, Paul Bernardo and Karla Homolka, a young married couple who raped and killed three teenage girls."

Jess narrowed her eyes. "Were the Middle School murderers in a sexual relationship?"

"Not as far as we know. Wolfe and Evans were more like a father-and-daughter team. They were extremely sophisticated, too. They set up the Middle School Murders to frame a police detective for their crimes, including the murder of Wolfe's daughter, Tina."

"To tie up all the loose ends?"

"Exactly. They also leveraged the murders to boost the career of Wolfe's other daughter, Claire, at Newburgh PD. Williams had assumed Claire was a psychopath like him and would join his pack. In that sense, William's pack resembled Charles Manson's murderous 'family' more than typical serial killers."

Jess shuddered. "And I thought my family was messed up."

"Anyway," Rob said. He'd better wrap things up before Tom called him out for shirking his digging responsibilities. "At the end of the case, we discovered the ranch house and its stash of mementos—jewelry and photos of the victims."

"Why did they keep mementos?"

"To relive their crimes later and..."

He trailed off. Dr. Sally Fleischer, the FBI's forensic psychiatrist on the case, had talked about serial killers using mementos and souvenirs to masturbate. Maybe Rob didn't have to share every detail with the young detective?

"The point is, the evidence hinted at other, yet unknown, victims of the pack. But without their corpses, it was all just a theory."

"And now you've found the bodies, you'll be able to identify the victims?"

"Right."

Rob hesitated. His goal was more ambitious than finding

closure. But how could he present his theory without sounding OCD?

Obsessive-compulsive. That's how Unit Chief Alda had described Rob's interest in the case. He glanced at Tom, who studied the new grave he'd discovered. That old cynic hadn't taken him seriously either. He'd dismissed Rob's theory as an excuse to spend more time with Claire in Newburgh. *What the hell.*

Rob lowered his voice. "I think there's more to this than meets the eye. We divide serial killers into categories according to their motivations. Some want to torture and control, others to take possession of a human body or derive some other personal gain from the murders. These motivations influence their MO, victim selection, and their signature—the activities they perform that aren't essential to the execution of the crime. And here's the problem. The mementos we found here cross the boundaries of those categories."

Detective Long wrinkled her nose. "So, you've discovered a new serial killer category?"

"Maybe?"

She stared into the woods as she considered his words. Did she think he was crazy, too?

"That makes sense."

"It does?"

"To cover their tracks, Wolfe and Evans disguised the Middle School Murders as the work of many serial killers." She blinked. "Like a chameleon."

Rob liked the sound of that. "A chameleon serial killer?"

"Yeah. But what do I know? I'm no expert."

She was right. They needed an expert to help piece this together. The Bureau had refused Rob's request to send Dr. Sally Fleischer back to Newburgh. But the new corpses might justify the forensic psychiatrist's time.

"So where do I fit in?"

The question snapped Rob out of his reverie. "We need to identify the bodies. We'll start with fingerprints, then test for DNA matches if necessary. The fingerprinting poses a challenge. Many of the bodies show signs of advanced decomposition. But once we have the prints and DNA samples, it's desk work. Are you up for it?"

"Count me in."

Rob gave in to his curiosity.

"No offense, Jess, but I'd assumed Captain Washington would send Sergeant Wolfe, seeing as she led the Middle School investigation."

Jess studied her feet. Had he touched a raw nerve?

"Sergeant Wolfe is working on a new homicide."

"Oh." Claire hadn't mentioned that. The case must be fresh.

"Agent Cline!" A man in plastic forensic scrubs marched toward them. "You'll want to see this."

The agents had sent the forensic archaeologists deeper into the woods to dig exploratory pits. So far, they'd found nothing.

"What is it? Another body?"

The tech paused to catch his breath. "Make that a dozen."

CHAPTER 15

Too late, Diane realized her mistake. The taxicab had deposited her on a filthy street corner in downtown Newburgh. She double-checked the scrap of paper with the address. The cabbie hadn't lost his way, and she'd jotted down the information exactly as the investment broker on the phone had dictated. She had arrived at her destination. But the dilapidated building carried no sign for Riddle and Ember Investments. The caller had lured her to a decaying tenement block in a rough neighborhood, not the offices of a respectable establishment. But here she was—a lone middle-aged widow on the seedier side of Newburgh. What had she been thinking?

Diane knew the answer. She'd been thinking about money. Ever since her marriage, Diane had stopped worrying about her finances. She and Bill weren't rich. They never would be. But her husband's sales job had covered their expenses, and Diane had focused on running the household. After Tina's murder, Diane had lost interest in life, never mind wealth. But Bill's death had forced her to get a handle on her finances.

Her crash course on money taught Diane one thing—she had none. If Claire hadn't moved in with her, Diane would have wound up on the street. But Claire's financial support came at a price. Her daughter had turned her home into a prison complete with a curfew, an alcohol ban, and an exercise program. Claire paid the bills, and she made the rules. To escape her daughter's prison, Diane needed money.

Last night, Diane told Claire nothing of her mysterious phone call. While Claire was in the tub, Diane had slipped two twenties from her daughter's purse and hid them under her mattress. If Claire found out about the telephone call, she'd prevent her from attending the meeting. So, Diane had gone to bed early and, the next morning, Claire had rushed out without saying a word about the missing cash. Her daughter was not much of a detective.

Instead of going to the gym, Diane had dressed in her best clothes and called a cab. She'd obsessed about keeping her secret from Claire but failed to consider what exactly she was getting herself into. Until now.

A black man in a grimy trench coat stumbled toward her. "Hey, lady, got a dollar?"

He smacked his lips and shuttered his eyelids. The stench of alcohol and pee overwhelmed her. Diane hurried up the steps of the building. Her mysterious meeting couldn't be worse than dodging homeless drunks on the street. For the first time in years, her thirst for alcohol subsided.

The elevator, a rickety box with a sliding trellis gate, lurched sickeningly to the third floor. Diane knocked on the door labeled thirty-three. No sign graced the door either. She prayed nobody was home so she could leave.

But the door opened. A gangly young man fixed her with a searching look. His suit seemed one size too large, and his tie hung off-center. Diane opened her mouth to apologize and say she'd gotten the wrong address, but he spoke first.

"Mrs. Wolfe, you're right on time." He glanced up and down the corridor. "Please come in."

Diane mustered a quick, faltering smile and stepped inside. The interior reminded her of a shoebox—a plain, empty rectangle with a desk to one bare wall and a single guest chair. The office had no other furnishings. *This was a mistake. A terrible mistake.*

The man took his seat behind the desk and tapped his laptop. Diane lingered near the door.

"Mr. Manson..."

"Please, call me Mark."

"Mark, there's no sign outside."

"Oh, don't worry about that. We like to keep our overheads low." He'd said "we" even though he seemed to be the only employee in the office. He smiled at her reassuringly. "Please, have a seat."

Diane did as she was told and clutched her handbag. *Manson.* The name registered disturbing associations. Charles Manson's cult had murdered that lovely young actress. What was her name?

Diane swallowed hard. Coming down here alone was foolish. Her husband had deceived her for years, drugging her and loosening her grip on reality. This young man could easily overpower her and slit her throat.

Mark Manson seemed to find what he was searching for on the laptop. "I'm sorry about your husband's passing."

"Did you know William?"

"We never met in person. Our clients value their time and their privacy, so we invest their money without any fuss. Your husband opened his account a year ago, and so regrettably, we had little time to produce a significant return on his initial deposit."

Diane sagged in her chair. "Oh."

Last night, fever dreams of instant wealth had disturbed her sleep. She should have known better. Bill had been a cruel and selfish man. He'd saved little money and left no will. He hadn't provided for her well-being after his death. On the contrary, he'd planned to outlive her and had devoted his life to making her suffer. With luck, she'd leave this office with beer money, nothing more. Diane could do with a cold beer now. The shock of the homeless drunk had faded, and the prison walls closed around her. She'd never escape her miserable life. She could only dull the pain.

"We learned of his passing incidentally. The policy specifies no beneficiaries in case of death, so we reached out to you as his legal heir."

Mark opened the drawer of the desk, and Diane flinched, expecting him to pull a gun on her. Instead, he attached a square pad to the laptop and handed her a plastic stylus.

"Sign now. And again. One last time. Perfect."

A name popped into Diane's head. Sharon Tate—the poor actress the Manson Family had murdered.

The Manson opposite her retrieved the stylus from her hand and packed away the touch pad. "Shall I transfer the funds to your bank account?"

"Um, yes."

"You haven't changed your account in the last year, have you?"

"No."

"Great."

A bank transfer. So, Bob had unintentionally left her with more than beer money.

"Um, Mark. How much money are we talking about?"

He told her, and her jaw dropped open. The man tapped away at his laptop as if he handled those sums of money every day.

The room swirled around her. *This changes everything.* This was the lucky break Diane had hoped for.

Mark gave his laptop a final tap and straightened, unaware of the emotional fireworks that exploded within her.

"We're done. The funds will appear in your account within a few hours. Again, my condolences on your husband's passing."

Diane let rip a short squawk of joy as her new reality set in.

Mark grinned at her. "And congratulations. What are you going to buy first?"

"Oh my!"

Long-forgotten desires swirled inside. Diane couldn't choose between them. The wide, fertile plain of the future opened before her in crisp, glorious clarity. A broad smile spread over her face. The muscles of her cheeks had atrophied from disuse and hurt at the effort. Then, Diane reverted to a more familiar emotion, and her lips twisted with spite. She knew exactly what she'd buy first.

"Freedom."

CHAPTER 16

C laire drove to Hannover Estate that afternoon. Ten-foot walls enclosed the Cranberry Kings' home of twenty sprawling acres. Security cameras and electrified fencing kept the common folk out. Claire signed in with the armed guard at the double iron gates before driving through a botanical garden of manicured lawns. Chief Emmerso was right. The Hannovers were not like other people. Claire had entered a foreign world.

A uniformed butler waited for her outside the white colonial mansion. Life-sized marble lions flanked the immense front door. Claire's entire house could fit inside the entrance hall. A statue of a single cranberry in the center of the hall towered over her. The Hannovers didn't impress their guests, they intimidated them.

Her shoes clacked on the marble tiles, the hollow sound echoing off the tall walls. Immense oil paintings hung in carved frames decorated with gold leaf. The artworks depicted ancient cavalry battles and portraits of bearded men in frock coats and plump women in frilly ballroom gowns. Hannover Estate was more of a museum than a home—a museum devoted to power.

The butler asked Claire to wait in a drawing room stuffed

with oversized leather couches and armchairs of engraved wood. Family photographs stood on the lacquered credenzas. A teenage Carmine Hannover appeared in two of them. Claire perched beside an embroidered cushion on the edge of a couch, too nervous to touch anything. If she broke something accidentally, the replacement costs would bankrupt her.

Footfalls drew her attention to the trim elderly couple who entered the drawing room. Edward and Cynthia Hannover seemed to have emerged from a museum display case. The husband's plaited cardigan, silky button-down shirt, and comfortable leather loafers radiated money, as did his wife's sporty cashmere turtleneck and designer slacks. Mrs. Hannover's face glowed, her skin as wrinkle-free as her husband's shirt. Only her halting gait betrayed the advanced age of this poster child for high-end cosmetic surgery.

Claire rose to greet them. "I'm sorry for your loss."

"Thank you for meeting with us, Sergeant Wolfe."

Cynthia Hannover's voice was soft but restrained. She pressed her thin lips together tightly as though to suppress the dark emotions that raged within.

"It's no trouble."

They sat, separated by a glass coffee table covered in glossy magazines on home design and art.

Edward broke the ice. "You're the one who got the Middle School Strangler, aren't you?"

By "got" did he mean "caught" or "killed?" Claire forced a smile. Had they requested that she investigate their daughter's murder because of her track record as a capable detective?

His wife explained. "We followed the case in the papers. Those poor girls. Your sister was a victim, too, wasn't she?"

Claire smiled politely. She hadn't come here to discuss her case history or her dead sister. Pulling out a notepad, she opened her mouth to speak but didn't get a chance.

"That must have been terrible for you," Cynthia Hannover added. "To discover that your father was responsible."

Her husband said, "Sometimes, the apple falls far from the tree. Children aren't responsible for their parents' crimes, and parents aren't to blame for their children's choices. Don't you agree?"

Claire sensed a subtext to their conversation. Were the Hannovers trying to make sense of their daughter's death or to absolve themselves of guilt? Claire shouldn't judge. People grieved in strange ways, especially when they had a complicated relationship with the victim. The Hannovers' relationship with their daughter was one of those.

She guided the conversation back to business. "Did you notice anything unusual in Carmine's behavior during the past few weeks?"

The wife gave a short, amused laugh. "Carmine's behavior was unusual from the day she was born."

"Headstrong," Edward added. "Sometimes, infuriating."

"Always the contrarian," Cynthia said. "Always defiant. It was her signature."

Bereaved parents often emphasized their lost child's good qualities and ignored the bad. The Hannovers seemed unusually critical of their dead daughter. Were they still in denial?

"Still, any changes in her behavior might shed light on her state of mind."

The mother sighed. "The truth is we haven't spoken to her in months. We didn't exactly see eye to eye on a range of topics."

The father gave his head a grim shake. "We always knew she'd come to no good."

Not denial, then. Were they *embarrassed* by their daughter's death? Did her murder reflect poorly on the Hannover family brand?

The wife explained. "We didn't approve of how she spent her time or the people with whom she spent it."

"And who were they?"

"I wish we could tell you. Carmine knew better than to bring them over."

Her words roused Claire's interest. Had Carmine's friends led her to the seedier side of Newburgh? Had Carmine hung out with criminal elements to anger her parents?

"Did she have a drug problem?"

"Probably. Nothing that needed treatment. Only money."

"Only money?"

Claire repeated Mrs. Hannover's last few words, encouraging her to elaborate. She had learned this interview technique from Rob, a former FBI hostage negotiator. As wealthy as the Hannovers were, the psychology of mere mortals still applied to them.

"Carmine withdrew large sums of money from her trust fund over the past few months. I can't imagine her artwork has been selling well." Mrs. Hannover stressed the word "artwork," questioning the artistic merit of her daughter's work.

Claire felt the urge to defend the dead woman's honor. "She was an artist?"

"Or sorts. Pottery and knickknacks."

"I see."

Claire was getting nowhere, so she tried a different angle. "Did she have a boyfriend?"

The mother's lips trembled. "I wouldn't know."

Her voice wavered, and her husband touched her arm. Carmine's love life was another sore point.

Her stern facade had cracked. Denial only got you so far. Had she secretly hoped Carmine would wise up and get her life together? Whatever hopes the Hannovers had nursed for their daughter had died with her.

The husband shook his head again. "Nobody deserves to die like that, Sergeant Wolfe."

Claire's detective brain raised its ears. "Like what?"

How much did the Hannovers know about their daughter's murder scene? The department had divulged little to the press, and only a handful of law enforcement officers were privy to the details of the murder. Besides the murderer.

"The mayor came over earlier along with Chief Emmerso and Captain Washington. Tommy told us Carmine's death was brutal."

Claire's blood boiled. Mayor Thomas "Tommy" Thornton had shared details of the murder with the Hannovers. Most victims died at the hands of people they knew—romantic partners, friends, and family. A suspect's knowledge of the crime scene was an important indicator of guilt. Now Mayor Thornton had muddied Claire's investigation, and Chief Emmerso had been helpless to stop him.

Another possibility made Claire hot in the face. Had Mayor Thornton told the Hannovers the killer had carved Claire's name on their daughter's body? Had the Hannovers wanted to lay eyes on the woman strangely connected to their daughter's death?

She cleared her throat and changed the topic. "Are Carmine's siblings in touch with her?"

On her way over, Claire had mulled over her list of suspects. In a wealthy family, a dead sibling meant a larger share of inheritance for the survivors, providing the Hannover progeny with an obvious motive to dispose of Carmine.

"You'll have to ask *them*," Cynthia said. "But I doubt it. Edward Junior lives in London, and Rosalyn moved to Canada to be with her husband's family."

"I see." The Hannover children had fled from their parents,

all except for Carmine, the rebellious disappointment who had wound up dead.

"Barry will know what Carmine's been up to."

"Barry?" Claire glanced at her notes. Her research of the Hannover family had discovered nobody by that name.

"Barry Cook, her personal assistant. That's how we communicated with her when we needed to."

Claire jotted down his name and number. A personal assistant. She should have guessed. Anyone with a high net worth seemed to have one of those.

"I'll contact him."

Claire hesitated before asking her next question, but after the mayor had tainted her investigation, she had to know for sure.

"Does the name Claire mean anything to you?"

The wife narrowed her eyes. Was Claire pulling her leg? "You're the first Claire that comes to mind, Sergeant. Why do you ask?"

"No reason."

Apparently, the mayor hadn't shared *everything* about the murder scene with the parents. On second thought, Chief Emmerso had surely kept that key detail from Mayor Thornton, too. *Good job.*

"What about you—do you have any enemies, anyone who might want to hurt you through Carmine?"

Edward sounded disappointed. "Sergeant Wolfe, we're businesspeople, not criminals. We don't have enemies, only competitors." He sucked in a wavering breath, and for the first time, he looked devastated. "Did Chief Emmerso tell you about our pledge?"

"No, he didn't."

"We're funding the mayor's new street camera project. That

won't bring Carmine back, but the new system might save somebody else's daughter."

Claire nodded. Maybe Chief Emmerso was wrong. The Hannovers *were* like everybody else. Grieving and helpless, they struggled to find meaning in their loss.

"Sergeant Wolfe," Cynthia said. "Do you think you'll find whoever killed Carmine?"

It was an impossible question to answer. "We have some solid leads, ma'am, so, yes, I think we will." Claire hoped the fingerprints on Carmine's jewelry would hit pay dirt.

"Then promise me one thing, Sergeant." Her eyes sparkled with sudden intensity. "When you find the monster who killed our daughter, make sure he pays for what he did."

"That goes without saying, ma'am. We'll make sure he goes to prison."

"That's not what I meant, Sergeant. You know how the courts work. The right lawyer can get anyone off the hook on a technicality. But this son of a bitch tortured and murdered our daughter. When you find the bastard, kill him!"

CHAPTER 17

Bella Winters stood at her boss's desk and shifted on her feet while he read her new article. Steve Hoffman grimaced at his computer screen. Bella knew that grimace well. In her eight years at *The Newburgh Herald*, she'd gotten to know the editor in chief's quirky mannerisms. The Grimace of Death meant her story wouldn't make tomorrow's paper.

"I don't know," he said.

Steve was being polite. Bella's coverage of the Middle School Strangler had put *The Newburgh Herald* on the state media map. Ever since then, Steve had given his star reporter her choice of stories. Her new in-depth piece revisited the Wolfe family. The father—a serial killer. The daughter—a decorated homicide detective. In the article, Bella had tried—and failed—to recapture last year's success. Steve scratched his unshaven chin. The Grimace of Death had hinted at disaster, and now the Scratch of Doom sealed her fate.

"It needs more...meat."

Bella released the breath she'd been holding and clutched at the shred of positivity. Extra meat wasn't so bad. She'd thought he'd say the piece was too "tabloid."

"I'd have more meat if Sergeant Wolfe made good on her promise for an exclusive. I've had to scrounge for scraps."

The Grimace of Death returned. She was making excuses.

"Which reminds me. We got some nasty emails after your piece on Sergeant Wolfe's award."

"Emails—from Newburgh PD?"

Bella walked a tightrope whenever she wrote about the local police department. The cops were sensitive about their public image, especially this close to mayoral elections. But they had never filed an official complaint.

"From readers. Claire Wolfe is a local celebrity now. Let the people keep their heroes. Besides, we've done the Middle School Strangler to death, so to speak. People want to move on. Write something new."

Bella exhaled her frustration. "I'm trying, but the Strangler is a hard act to follow."

"'If it bleeds, it leads?'"

"Exactly. Nothing sells papers like serial killers."

"Active serial killers. Not dead ones. One more piece on the Middle School Strangler and readers will mistake us for the History Channel."

Bella deflated and admitted defeat. "You're right. I'll find something else. Failing that, I'll kill someone."

Steve smiled. "That's the spirit!"

Bella returned to her cubicle and flopped on her desk chair. *Something else.* Selecting her own subject matter had a downside. She could always write about the upcoming election. To avoid stepping on the toes of the political correspondents, she'd take a personal angle. The new female contender, Sarah Malik, might make a juicy target. Her parents had immigrated to the United States from Egypt, and now their daughter was running for Newburgh's top office. There was a story hiding in there somewhere. The American Dream Lives On. Or, The Plight of

Minorities in Massachusetts? How did Malik feel about the trouble in the Middle East? Bella sighed. She sure missed her serial killers.

Her phone vibrated with an incoming message. Her mole at Newburgh PD had sent two words on WhatsApp. *Hot Cakes.* Bella sat up in her chair.

Deborah Jones worked Dispatch and spoke in codes to avoid detection by her supervisors. Bella rewarded her for timely leaks with a Hershey's hamper and a twenty-four-pack of Diet Dr. Pepper every other month. For two long months, her mole had remained silent. But today she had new information, hot from the oven.

Bella's pulse accelerated as Deborah's status changed to "typing." *Spit it out already, Deb!* Bella couldn't stand the anticipation. The message was longer than usual. In her excitement, Deborah had abandoned their lexicon of code words. No code words could contain this hot new item.

Bella shot to her feet and punched the air. "Yes!" Her cry won amused and annoyed stares from the other cubicles. Bella had her story. This time, Steve wouldn't mind revisiting Sergeant Claire Wolfe. Christmas had come early!

CHAPTER 18

"Bad news," Detective Lucas Gomez said.

Those weren't the words Claire had hoped to hear at the update meeting late that afternoon.

Captain Washington had assembled the team in his office to share their findings. Daylight faded from the Newburgh horizon along with Claire's enthusiasm for the case. The Hannovers had provided little useful information and treated her like their private assassin. Claire desperately needed to improve her public image.

"Always start with the bad news," Nakamura said. "That way things can only get better."

There came a knocking at the door, and Chief Emmerso entered. "Mind if I join you?"

"Get the chief a chair," Washington told the detectives.

"No need. I'll stand. Pretend I'm not here. As you were."

The chief leaned against the wall and folded his arms. Chief Emmerso was following the investigation closely thanks, no doubt, to the Hannovers' involvement.

Claire said, "Detective Gomez was about to share some bad news."

"Don't shoot the messenger," Gomez said. "Forensics sent preliminary results. The fingerprints on the jewelry match the victim."

"All the prints?"

"Yep."

Claire's hopes for a quick resolution died.

"Any trace evidence—DNA or semen?"

"Nada. The trace evidence found seems to belong to the victim. The perp was careful. But the ME confirmed the time of death for between seven and nine PM yesterday. Cause of death, exsanguination. And they found adhesive residue around her mouth."

"He taped her mouth shut."

Gomez nodded. "She couldn't cry for help. The DNA testing will take some time. The same goes for the pathology report."

"I'll call them," Chief Emmerso said. "See if they can speed things up."

"Thank you, sir," Claire said.

Technology had let them down. They had to rely on good old-fashioned deductive reasoning.

Claire turned to her team. "We found her jewelry piled on the bedside table. This wasn't a robbery. So why did she take it off?"

Gomez snorted. "For sex. She was meeting a lover, wasn't she?"

Nakamura scoffed. "Since when do women remove their jewelry before sex? Don't answer that, Gomez. It's obviously not your field of expertise."

Captain Washington chuckled and won an annoyed stare from a reddening Gomez.

Claire moved on. "Carmine didn't undress either. The killer cut her clothes from her body, apparently after tying her up. Somehow he restrained her without a struggle."

"Maybe they were into kinky stuff?" Gomez ventured. "An S&M routine that went too far?"

Captain Washington said, "Was the decedent seeing anyone?"

Claire answered. "The parents didn't know of any boyfriends, but they hadn't spoken in months. They disliked her daughter's choice of friends but couldn't say who those friends were. Her siblings live overseas. The only interesting lead the parents gave was about money. Carmine withdrew large sums from her trust fund over the past few months."

"How much?"

"They didn't say." She spoke to the detectives. "We'll need to check Carmine's financials and contact the siblings. What turned up in her social media?"

Nakamura spoke up. "Two names show promise. Victoria McAdams and Kitty Tucker."

A chill passed through Claire, and Captain Emmerso met her gaze. Kitty Tucker had died before Claire's eyes six months ago. Emmerso's meaningful look reflected her own suspicions. Was this a coincidence or was Carmine's murder connected to the Middle School Strangler? *No.* That couldn't be true. Claire had closed the door on that chapter of her life for good.

Nakamura seemed oblivious to Claire and Emmerso's silent exchange. "Kitty Tucker died last year. I'm meeting Victoria McAdams tomorrow."

Victoria. Kitty. But still no Claire.

"Did you find their names on the victim's phone?"

"An old Twitter account. Carmine left social media two years ago. Her iPhone 11 is a dead end. Since iOS 8, Apple no longer stores the encryption keys on their servers. The phones are uncrackable. We'll need to subpoena Apple for an Emergency Request."

Captain Washington sighed. "I thought we were done with the bad news."

Claire said, "We need to figure out her last forty-eight hours. Maybe we can get that from her home computer? We might access her phone from there as well. Do we have a search warrant yet?"

"Getting it signed tonight," Gomez said.

"Good. I'm meeting with the victim's personal assistant, Barry Cook, bright and early tomorrow morning at her art studio. He might have a key to her home and save us from breaking down the door. What about street camera footage?"

"Nada."

"Nothing?"

"Nothing interesting. A camera outside a Seven-Eleven caught her walking toward the hotel alone at eight PM on Monday. There's a lot of street traffic but no red flags. Our coverage downtown is patchy."

Claire grunted. The bad news kept flowing. The Hannovers were funding more street cameras, but they'd arrive too late to assist their daughter's murder investigation. Claire searched the information for connections. *Why did Carmine take off her jewelry?*

"The lover did it," Gomez said. "The hotel room showed no sign of forced entry. There were no defensive wounds or hints of a struggle. She let him in, let him tie her up, and then— boom! Otherwise, her lover would have walked in on them."

"Not necessarily," Washington said. "When she didn't answer the door, he figured she'd stood him up and left."

The details clicked in Claire's mind. "It was a stranger."

Her declaration drew the room's attention.

Gomez said, "Why'd she let him in?"

"He found an excuse. Once inside, he pretended to rob her."

Nakamura caught on. "'Hand over your jewelry, and I'll

leave you alone.' If she thought he was robbing her, she'd play along to avoid a violent confrontation. Especially if she thought her lover was on his way."

Claire nodded. "Then, he tied her up and taped her mouth shut, so he could get away before she called the cops."

Gomez's eyes popped with understanding. "By the time she realized he was lying, it was too late."

Nakamura glanced at Captain Washington. "Her lover might have come knocking but never heard a thing. One moan and he'd cut her throat."

"That's a good working theory, Sergeant," Washington said.

Claire shrugged. "It's how I would have done it, sir."

"Remind me never to cross you. Anything else?"

"Nothing from the hotel manager," Nakamura said.

A name floated to the surface of Claire's mind. *Kitty Tucker.* Carmine had known Kitty. Claire didn't want to dredge up the past, but her conscience wouldn't let up.

"Captain, if we're dealing with a stranger, there's another possibility we should consider in light of the brutality of the murder."

"What's that?"

"Maybe he's done this before?"

Washington scoffed. "A serial killer? Do you think that's likely, Sergeant?"

"No, sir. Two serial killers within a year is highly unlikely. But the Hannovers claim they have no enemies, and it seems likely Carmine didn't know her murderer. We should eliminate that possibility."

Gomez said, "You mean maybe Carmine was in the wrong place at the wrong time?"

Washington frowned. "Don't go there yet, Sergeant. We still have leads to follow, and the decedent's house might provide more. Don't start rumors about serial killers just yet, OK? This city has barely recovered from the last one."

The team dispersed. At her desk, Claire reviewed the reports from the ME and the other detectives. After ten PM, she headed home, images of Kitty Tucker's exploding head looping in her mind. She'd have trouble getting to sleep tonight. Perfect timing. She had an early meeting tomorrow and a killer to catch.

Rob had texted her two hours ago, asking whether she had plans tonight. Caught up with meetings and reports, she'd only seen the message now. She texted him an apology. What she needed was a hot shower, a good night's sleep, and a suspect.

She drove home and got out of the car. On the sidewalk, she froze. A night breeze rose and fell as the car keys tinkled in her hand. She sensed eyes watching her from the shadows. An image of the morning's crime scene flashed in her mind—a single word carved into human flesh. *CLAIRE.* Was the killer's message intended for her? Was he observing her right now?

Claire touched the grip of her Glock 22 while she turned slowly to scan the street. Nobody was there. The case was messing with her mind, making her paranoid. Either way, Claire was an experienced officer and a crack shot. She could protect herself.

Exhaling a deep breath, she locked the car and continued toward the house, fishing for her house key in her bag. Then, she stopped dead in her tracks.

Three large packing boxes blocked the front door, the cardboard flaps unsealed. This was no Amazon delivery. Claire stepped closer and studied the packages. The sleeve of a shirt peeked out from the first box, a high-heeled shoe from another. She recognized the clothing. This was her stuff. *What the hell?*

She swore under her breath. Her mother had dumped her stuff on the street. What a stupid little stunt. Was Mom drunk again? Claire jammed her key in the door, but the lock didn't turn. She double-checked the key and tried again, twisting the metal with all her might. She swore again.

"Mom!" she yelled. "Open up. It's me."

A dog barked down the street. She was waking the neighbors, but she was too tired to care.

The window of the main bedroom slid open overhead, and Diane's smug face smiled down at her. "I changed the locks. You're not welcome here anymore."

"Not welcome?"

Her mother's ingratitude knew no bounds.

"I'm your daughter."

"You're not my daughter. You're your father's girl."

That did it.

"Not your daughter?" Claire yelled. "I moved in to help you. I pay your bills. And this is how you thank me?"

"I don't need your help. Thank you very much."

Claire laughed, a short, mirthless gasp of frustration and disbelief. "You need water and electricity. You need food to eat. All those require money."

This was an empty display of rejection and contempt. Mom was too bitter and vindictive to admit she needed her. She was acting like a rebellious teenager. But instead of backing down and grudgingly letting her in, her mother cackled.

"I have all the money I need."

The day had come. Mom had gone insane. "No, you don't, Mom. You're broke. We checked your account together, remember?"

Still, her mother refused to listen to reason. "As it happens, Bob opened a retirement account last year, and I'm his legal heir."

Retirement account? What was she talking about? The search their estate attorney had run for Bob's financial assets had found nothing.

"Mom, that's impossible."

"Oh, yeah? The money came in this morning."

Mom smirked at her. She'd finally won.

Was she bluffing? Diane could be petty and hateful, but she wasn't stupid or suicidal. Had she suffered a psychotic break or received a bizarre stroke of good luck?

Claire said, "How much money?"

CHAPTER 19

Johnny liked to watch her. Her body mesmerized him. She was beautiful and she knew it.

Emily flicked her silky blonde hair at every opportunity. The short denim cutoffs she chose showed off her ass, and her tank tops pressed her breasts together like ripe, juicy melons.

He looked away quickly whenever she caught him staring. But tonight, he'd be invisible to her. Tonight, he'd see every inch of her perfect female form. Johnny trembled with anticipation.

This is wrong. Emily was his big sister, even if she was a total jerk. She called him Dipshit and Asswipe and teased him about having no friends. Still, he shouldn't sneak into her room and bury his nose in her panties. He shouldn't fantasize about touching her body. And he definitely shouldn't be hiding in the service balcony with the noisy washing machine and dryer, peeking through the gap of the sliding door, waiting for Emily to take her nightly shower. The temptation overpowered him.

Johnny had planned the operation to the last detail. He'd camped on the balcony a half hour ago with a jar of Vaseline and a box of Kleenex. Their mother was out, as usual, getting stoned with her boyfriend of the week. The rumble of the washing machine drowned out any sound Johnny might accidentally make. And Emily was too self-absorbed to notice anything besides herself. This time, nobody would catch him.

Emily was right, though. Something was wrong with him. Only freaks did this. But he couldn't help himself. A fire raged in his bones. When he lay awake in bed, all he could think about was the body underneath his sister's clothes. Maybe if he saw her in all her glory just this once, the blaze inside him would die down?

The bathroom door opened, and Johnny straightened on the step stool. Emily breezed into the bathroom, tossed her pajamas onto the toilet seat cover, and latched the door. She turned on the shower tap and hummed to herself while she gazed at her reflection in the medicine cabinet mirror.

Then, she began to undress. She removed her shirt, kicked off her flip-flops, and slipped out of her denim shorts. Emily faced sideways to admire her profile in the mirror, gracing Johnny with an unobstructed view of her lingerie-model body. She stretched her arms behind her back and searched for the clasp of her bra.

When her breasts sprang free from their restraints, Johnny could contain himself no longer. He shot to his feet and dropped his trunks. He dipped his hand in Vaseline and worked furiously to relieve the tension between his legs. Emily leaned over to remove her panties, and her breasts dangled. Johnny groaned with pleasure and closed his eyes.

Whoosh! The balcony door slid open so fast, the panel banged against the casing. Emily glared at him with murder in her eyes.

"You little pervert!"

"Wait! I can explain!"

But with his trousers around his ankles and a greasy hand clutching his penis, he wasn't talking his way out of this one. He didn't get the chance.

Emily punched him in the solar plexus. Johnny bent over, winded. She slammed her elbow into his spine, and he collapsed on *the bathroom floor. Emily towered over him. She didn't bother to cover her chest.*

"Wait until Mom hears about this."

"Please, don't tell her!"

She kicked him hard in the belly. "That'll teach you to perv on me, Asswipe." She kicked him again. "You're the reason Dad left us. He took off the day you were born, and I don't blame him."

Johnny writhed, his hands over his aching stomach. The third kick connected with his exposed crotch, and white stars exploded before his eyes.

"You're nothing. You're a worthless piece of crap!"

Johnny struggled to breathe.

Emily grabbed the toilet brush. "I'll show you what we do with crap. Who's a piece of crap?"

She raised the brush over his defenseless body, and Johnny flinched. But she didn't hit him. Not yet. Emily stamped on his shoulder and shoved him facedown on the floor. She sat on his back, pinning him down with the full weight of her body. Then, she whipped his naked ass. The stiff, filthy bristles stung his delicate skin, and Johnny cried out in pain.

"Who's a stinky piece of crap?"

Johnny gasped. "I am."

"I can't hear you!"

He sucked in air. "I am!"

She whipped him again. "Who's the boss?"

Another blow. Blood trickled down his ass cheek.

"Who's the boss around here?"

Tears flooded Johnny's eyes. His body shuddered. "You are. You are!"

CHAPTER 20

Rob raised his eyebrows at Claire. "A million dollars? A million US dollars?"

"That's what she said."

Claire still fumed at her mother. She wanted to slap Diane's face for throwing her out. Mom had favored Tina since her birth. For over a decade, she had blamed Claire for her little sister's murder. But somehow, this last rejection hurt the most. After all Claire had done for her, Diane had kicked her out on the street at the first opportunity.

Claire had shoved the packing boxes into the back of her car and turned up at Rob's motel room. "I'm sorry," she had said. Her knocking had woken him. "I literally have nowhere else to go."

Rob had welcomed her inside and told her to stay the night.

"Are you sure? I can get a room."

"No need. There's a spare bed for you. Tom flew home this afternoon. Some family emergency."

"Is everything OK?"

"Yeah, nothing life-threatening. I think he's just sick of digging up bodies. Please stay."

Claire accepted the offer gladly. The thought of spending the night alone in a motel room depressed her. She needed a warm hug and a sympathetic ear. Rob was a reliable supplier of both. He helped her carry all her worldly possessions into the motel room. Claire was definitely not a Hannover. She showered, they made love, and, resting comfortably in Rob's arms, Claire shared the details of her bad day.

She pictured her mother bathing in hundred-dollar bills like a maniacal Scrooge and cursing her daughter behind her back.

"It makes no sense. William was a traveling salesman. Where'd he get that kind of money?"

"Maybe he saved over the years and invested wisely. You'd be surprised what compound interest can do."

"He wasn't a big spender," Claire admitted, "but a million dollars? Diane said he'd opened the account only last year. That's not enough time to grow an investment. And the account didn't turn up in the search the estate attorney ran."

Rob's chest rose as he inhaled. "New accounts might not appear in a search."

"No, this stinks to high heaven. Her *inheritance* is blood money. I just need to prove it."

"And take away your mother's financial freedom? That won't build any bridges."

He was right. "Why do I care so much? Why can't I just ditch her and get on with my life?"

"Because you're a good person, Claire. Look on the bright side. Now I get to see you every day."

"I'll rent a new place as soon as possible."

"There's no rush."

"I can't live off the FBI forever."

Rob grinned. "I wonder if your old place is still available."

"There is no way I'm going back there. Too many bad memories."

Newburgh PD had broken into her old rental house and turned the place upside down. Claire had almost blown her brains out on the couch. She preferred to keep both those memories buried.

"Not all of them were bad." Rob was right. He'd cooked her dinner in her old kitchen, and in her old bed, they had made love for the first time.

"True. But sometimes the bad outweighs the good."

Wasn't that the story of her life? She thought of Kitty Tucker and the message the killer had cut into Carmine Hannover's dead flesh. The Hannovers thought Claire was a cold-blooded killer, too, and now Mom had inherited her father's blood money. When would it all end?

"Hey," Rob whispered. He stroked her head.

Claire was sobbing. She wanted to tell Rob about her new homicide case and all she'd experienced today, but she had no right to discuss an ongoing investigation with an outsider.

"Hey," he repeated. "It'll be OK."

Claire wiped her tears with her fingers. "Sometimes I think I'll never leave him behind. His crimes—his legacy—will follow me around forever. His blood runs in my veins—"

Rob hushed her. "Claire, you are not your father."

"But I think like him. I think like a sociopath."

"That makes you a great detective."

"Or evil."

"Nope. Not evil. Empathic. You can immerse yourself in other perspectives."

Claire wanted to believe that. She needed to.

"Thanks, Rob. What would I do without you?"

He chuckled. "You'd be a mess. Is this about your new homicide?"

"How do you know about that?"

"Detective Long mentioned it."

"Detective Long?"

"The department sent her to help with our investigation."

"Oh, I see. And when exactly were you going to tell me?"

"I just did. Didn't Captain Washington tell you? Long is your detective."

Claire slipped a teasing note into her voice. "And what exactly is she doing for you?"

"You know. Identifying corpses. The fun stuff. I won't see much of her. Jess will spend most of her time at the morgue."

"So, it's Jess now, not Detective Long?"

Rob played along. "Digging up dead bodies is a powerful bonding experience."

Claire laughed. "Good luck with that. Judging by her reaction at our crime scene, I don't think she'll last long at the morgue."

"Why, what happened?"

"She almost fainted."

Rob bunched his eyebrows. "She had no problem with our corpses."

The talk of corpses dampened her mood. Despite her disgust for her father's murderous pack, curiosity got the better of her.

"How many more did you find?"

"A few." He was evading a full answer.

"Rob, how many more people did the pack kill?"

"Twenty-eight."

The number shocked her into silence. Claire had expected one or two more. Counting the Middle School dead, her father was responsible for over thirty murders. His evil deeds had mushroomed beyond her imagining. And Claire shared half of his genetic material. "You're not my daughter," her mother had said. "You're your father's girl."

In her mind's eye, Kitty Tucker's head exploded, and Carmine Hannover's mutilated corpse stared at her. A giant rolling boulder of guilt and pain threatened to run Claire down. Her and the people close to her.

"Sally is flying in from Quantico tomorrow morning," Rob continued. "It'll be good to have her back on the team. We want to figure out how the pack—"

"Enough!" Claire hadn't intended to shout. "I'm sorry, Rob, but—enough!" She massaged her temples. "I don't want to know."

CHAPTER 21

From his truck, the killer watched the motel room. The lights went out. Claire was spending the night with Special Agent Robert Cline. He clenched his fists. This was not a part of the plan.

He'd surveilled the Wolfe home for weeks and made preparations. But now, just as the plan gained momentum, Claire had moved out of the house and shacked up with the FBI agent. The changes had rendered his long hours of painstaking research worthless. *Not cool, Claire.*

He shouldn't judge her. The mother had kicked Claire out, and she needed a place to sleep. In a perfect world, Claire would turn to him. For now, that was impossible. They'd be together later. Until then, he needed to bide his time.

The plan rolled on. There was no stopping now. He'd maneuver around this...inconvenience. He needed more time, that was all. Fate had extended the hunt, and the hunt was his favorite part.

That morning, Claire had visited The Barnett Inn. She'd received his message. His *first* message. There'd be more.

Had she smiled when she'd read her name on Carmine

Hannover's body? She would've noticed the subtle marking that identified his work. Did she experience the same thrill of anticipation?

Claire sensed his presence now. She knew he was watching. And yet she'd run to the FBI agent. What did Claire see in Robert Cline? Was she taunting him—playing hard to get? Or had she replied to his message? *Keep an eye on Robert Cline. He means trouble.*

"Your wish is my command, Claire."

He'd give Special Agent Robert Cline special attention. There was no cause for jealousy. No man could compete with the bond he shared with Claire. They were soul mates, cut from the same cloth, destined for each other. Nobody could understand her as he did.

He'd win her heart with a gift. A gift like no other. One she'd never forget. He'd earn her respect and her love. *Soon. Yes.* And this time, he'd deliver his message in person.

CHAPTER 22

Wednesday morning, Claire stared at the display shelves in Carmine Hannover's workshop, and her mouth fell open. She'd never seen so many pairs of boobs in one room.

"Fabulous, aren't they?" Barry Cook spoke with a lisp.

The morning chill frosted the air of Newburgh's fashionable East District when Carmine Hannover's pudgy but well-groomed personal assistant had let Claire into his late employer's store. The neighboring trendy cafés and designer clothing boutiques had yet to open their doors for the day.

Claire struggled to find an appropriate response. Her eyes refused to budge from the shiny collection of ceramic human breasts. They had an almost hypnotic effect. The sheer variety amazed her. There were pink boobs and red boobs, ebony black and ivory white—even yellow boobs with blue polka dots. The breasts shared the same voluptuous curves and lifelike, grainy areolas. Carmine had used a single model for all her artwork and, judging from the pronounced nipples, she'd taken her measurements on a chilly day. "Knickknacks," Cynthia Hannover had said. Knickknacks indeed. Give a girl a trust fund, and this is what you got.

Barry blew his nose on a Kleenex. "I'm so proud of Carmine's work." His chin-puff goatee jiggled up and down with each lisped word. "I can't believe she's gone!"

Claire glanced at the price tags on the artwork and almost gagged. Hannover boobs didn't come cheap. Claire had to tell Rob about this place. Maybe she'd bring him here one day without warning. She'd love to see his expression when a hundred pairs of perfect breasts stared him down. A smile threatened to crack Claire's face in two.

"The radio said she was murdered," Barry continued. "Who'd dream of hurting Carmine?"

Claire wanted to ask him the same question. "Were you and Carmine close?"

"Very close. Carmine wasn't just my boss. We were friends. She trusted me. I run the store whenever she's out."

"Were you and Carmine ever in a romantic relationship?"

Barry laughed. "Me and Carmine? No way! She wasn't my type. I wasn't hers either."

Claire sensed Barry preferred men. "Did she have a boyfriend?"

"Not that I know."

"Any violent exes or enemies?"

"Carmine was a very private and honest person. She had no enemies and she never spoke about her love life. Not even to me. She was afraid of her parents. They disapproved of every-thing she did. Horrible people, her parents."

"I see."

Carmine hadn't shared her love life with her PA. Had a blackmailer threatened to reveal her secrets to her parents?

"Barry, did you notice any changes in her behavior lately?"

He searched the rows of boobs for an answer. "She spent less time at the workshop." Fresh tears welled in his eyes. "I never dreamed anybody could kill her."

"As you said, she had no enemies."

"That's not what I meant. Even if she had enemies, Carmine could handle herself. Don't let the slim outer shell mislead you. She knew how to defend herself. She had a brown belt in karate."

"No kidding?"

"She started training when she was six years old. I wouldn't dare take her on. I guess a brown belt doesn't make you bulletproof."

Barry raised an eyebrow at Claire, and her Spidey-sense tingled. The killer had done many things to Carmine, but shooting her was not one of them. Was Barry fishing for details of his employer's death or was he planting disinformation?

"Where were you Sunday night?" Claire held her pen and notebook at the ready. The old-fashioned writing implements intimidated interviewees less than her digital recorder.

"At a birthday party for an old friend."

"How long were you there?"

"From eight until late. I left around twelve."

The party eliminated him as a suspect. Claire jotted down the friend's details to verify Barry's alibi.

"When did you know something was wrong?"

"Monday morning, when she didn't answer her phone."

"But you didn't report her missing."

"I thought little of it at first. She was a free spirit, and as I said, she hadn't come to the shop lately. I figured she was sleeping in after a busy weekend. She had nothing scheduled for Monday." Barry teared up again. "I had no idea she was already gone!"

"You managed her schedule?"

"Hello," he waved at her. "Personal assistant?"

"I need to see her schedule for the last few weeks."

"Fine by me. Her work calendar synchronizes to her iCloud on her phone and laptop. But she had nothing going on these past few weeks."

Claire would examine Carmine's calendar later. Right now, she needed to explore her financial situation and the possibility of blackmail.

"Did Carmine sell a lot of her...artwork?"

"Not as many as she deserved. Few people truly appreciated her vision."

Claire raised her eyebrows at his evasive language, and he relented.

"One or two a week. The workshop was more of a passion project for Carmine. She didn't need the money."

"Did she experience any financial issues lately?"

He laughed. "You can't be serious. Carmine was a Hannover."

"An art studio in East District isn't cheap. Was she ever late in paying rent or your salary?"

Barry seemed insulted at the question. "Never."

"I see. Do you have a key to her home?"

He gave her a suspicious glance.

"I'd prefer not to break down the door."

"Yes, of course." He fished for a key chain in his pocket, handed over the house key along with the code for her alarm system.

Claire cast a last glance at the collection of clay breasts. The killer had removed Carmine's. Had he visited her workshop? Was her murder a bizarre attack on femininity? Did the crime contain an element of religious extremism?

"What's going to happen to her creations?"

Barry gave the display shelves a forlorn look. "I guess her family will decide."

Claire's phone rang. The name Bella Winters appeared on the display. Claire had saved the reporter's number so she could screen her calls. Bella had a lot of nerve calling her after her shameless questions at Monday's press conference, and Claire was not in a sharing mood.

"I need to take this." She handed Barry a business card. "Please call me if you think of anything else that might help our investigation."

"I will."

Claire exited the workshop and answered her phone on the sidewalk. "Ms. Winters."

"Sergeant Wolfe."

"Are you calling to apologize?"

"Do *you* apologize for doing your job?"

Claire scoffed. "Chief Emmerso deserved better. You made his ceremony about me."

"Mayor Thornton did that. I just followed his lead. And if you'd given me the exclusive you promised, we could've skipped those questions." The newshound had her there. "I'm calling about a new story. I want to get your response before we go to press."

Claire's heart sank. Newburgh PD had notified the media about Carmine Hannover's murder. But the reporter wouldn't have called Claire to rehash the official account of the homicide. How much did Bella know about the crime scene?

Claire played stupid. "What story?"

"The Hannover murder. The department's Public Information Officer has been tight-lipped about this one."

"Not all homicides are newsworthy."

"Not all homicides involve a Hannover. How well did you know Carmine?"

Stay calm, Claire. She's only fishing.

"I didn't know her. Why do I get the feeling you're trying to make me the focus of this story, too?"

A knowing smile slithered into the reporter's voice. "Because this murder has your name written all over it. Or should I say, carved into the victim's back?"

CHAPTER 23

W hen Jessica Long had applied to become a detective, she'd imagined herself solving crime using brilliant deductions and sly interrogations. She hadn't expected to spend her days in a cold room full of decomposing human bodies. Her Sherlock Holmes dream job had turned into a Dr. Frankenstein nightmare.

Truth be told, she didn't mind the dead bodies. The corpses were the most interesting people in the room. The medical examiner's assistant was a different story. Currently, he poured noxious chemicals from a jerry can into a shallow plastic tub.

"Mm, don't you just love that smell?"

He laughed. At least she thought he was laughing. The halting, breathy convulsions made him sound like a hyena with hiccups.

His name was Daryl Holt, but Jess thought of the gangly pathologist simply as Igor. Like Frankenstein's assistant, he probably exhumed dead bodies for fun in his free time.

Daryl put down the jerry can and sealed the lid. Chemicals bubbled in the plastic tub.

Jess wrinkled her nose. "What is that?"

"A mixture of formaldehyde, alcohol, and acetic acid. It helps the tissue swell and harden so we can take fingerprints. Here, you do it."

Jess desired to handle neither corpses nor noxious chemicals. But she pulled on a pair of rubber gloves and accepted the challenge. A morgue-load of victims were counting on her to tell their story.

A woman lay on the gurney beside the plastic tub, one of the many corpses the FBI had dug up at the ranch house. Jess grasped the dead woman's shriveled arm and guided her hand into the tub of chemicals, submerging the fingers.

"Good," Igor said. "Let her soak for five minutes, then you can do the printing." He spoke as though handling the semi-decomposed corpse was a special treat. Did he bring his dates here, too? On second thought, Igor probably dated little. His social skills catered better to the dead.

While they waited for the chemicals to do their work on the dead woman's wrinkled skin, Jess and Daryl got started on the other corpses. They took turns pouring the liquid into plastic tubs and rehydrating the victims' fingertips. Jess shut her mouth tightly against the nauseating fumes. She kept her eyes on the dead and ignored the assistant's furtive glances at her.

Igor cleared his throat and leaned his elbow on a steel dissection table. *Here it comes.* "So, um, Detective Long. Do you like camping?"

"Camping?"

"You know, the great outdoors?" The hyena hiccupped again.

"Um, I guess." Did his ideal date involve exhuming corpses or hunting for roadkill?

"Did you ever try those dehydrated snacks—you know, just add water?"

"I think so."

"Well, this is the same idea. Just add formaldehyde."
Hiccup.

Jess forced a polite smile.

"So, Jess..." He slurred his speech as he struggled to find the words to ask her out.

Please, don't!

"You don't mind if I call you, Jess, do you? So, I was thinking—"

"What about her?" Jess pointed at the handless and headless body on the dissection table behind him.

Igor gazed at the decapitated corpse. "What about her?" The distraction was working.

"We can't fingerprint her, obviously. How do we identify her?"

Igor jumped at the opportunity to show off his expertise. "We'll send a DNA sample to the county forensics lab for testing."

"That will take time, won't it?"

"Yeah, months."

Jess focused on the woman's headless body. If Jess was stuck here, she might as well try to be useful. After her embarrassing performance at the crime scene, she resolved to make a better impression on Agent Rob Cline and his team. They were counting on her to identify the victims as soon as possible. There must be a way to short-circuit the identification process.

A purple patch of skin on the woman's right thigh snagged her attention. "Is that liver..."

She searched for the right word. Jess had studied textbooks on crime scene investigation techniques to prepare herself for her new job. The pooling of blood in a dead body often presented itself as a purple coloration, which indicated the position in which the body had remained in the first hours after death.

"Livor mortis? No, that's a port-wine stain." He answered her confused stare. "You know, a birthmark." Igor tapped his forehead. "Like Gorbachev?"

Jess studied the birthmark. Its shape resembled the state of Florida. An idea struck.

"Can we use that to identify her?"

"I don't think so. There's no database of birthmarks. Fingerprints and dental records are our best bet. DNA is a crapshoot. The databases are patchy. To find a match, you'd need to get lucky."

He wobbled his head and grinned. *Get lucky*. Was that a not-so-subtle innuendo? *Ugh*. Jess turned away in disgust.

"Hey!" Igor whispered as though offering her a joint behind the school bleachers. He tipped his head toward the hive of metal doors in the cool storage section. "Carmine Hannover's in the cooler. Do you want to see her?"

Carmine Hannover. Jess's insides twisted into a knot. Igor seemed to think she'd jump at the opportunity to see the dead celebrity in the flesh. Nothing could be further from the truth.

The sight of Carmine had devastated her yesterday morning, and the mention of her name made her queasy. Jess preferred the anonymous corpses. With them, it was easy to maintain a professional distance. In her mind, Carmine Hannover smiled at her. Beautiful Carmine. Tough-as-nails Carmine.

"No, thanks," Jess told Igor.

The murders had just become personal again.

CHAPTER 24

"Thank you for meeting with me," Detective Haruto Nakamura said. He'd almost opened with, "Nice place!" then changed his mind when he saw his hostess's expression.

Victoria McAdams was not in the mood to talk about her mansion in the upmarket suburb of Seven Oaks. Tears had smeared her mascara in black smudges beneath her eyes, giving her a gothic look. But instead of tight leather and metal studs, she'd selected a white satin blouse and matching slacks for the interview.

"I'm glad you called, Detective." Grief had lent her voice a deep, rough edge. "I'll do anything to help catch the bastard who murdered Carmine."

She led him through an entrance hall of large shiny floor tiles and modern-art paintings in white frames—originals, he assumed, but he was no expert—to a lounge of leather couches and armchairs in earth-brown tones and leopard print. Like her dead friend, Victoria came from old Newburgh money. He hadn't expected her to answer the door herself.

They sat, and Nakamura offered his condolences.

"It seems you and Carmine were good friends."

Victoria grimaced and pressed both hands to her chest as though to massage her aching heart. "Like sisters."

Was her dramatic display of emotion genuine? Sometimes Nakamura missed the old days before he'd become a cop. People had told the truth, and he'd suspected no one of anything. Those days—and his faith in humanity—were long gone.

"When did you see her last?"

"Thursday. We met for dinner at Mon Ami."

Nakamura had heard of the French gourmet restaurant. He enjoyed eating out with his wife and kids, but that restaurant was far above his pay grade. Besides, he doubted Mon Ami served cheeseburgers and French fries.

"Did you meet often?"

"Every week. We were a tight group of friends."

"A group?"

"There were three of us. My two best friends were murdered within six months. I'm the only survivor."

She shuddered. This was no act. Senseless violence had destroyed her inner circle. Her loss saddened him.

"Was Kitty Tucker the other friend?"

Victoria nodded and stroked her arm. "Kitty was gunned down in her home, two streets down from here. She was a good friend. Carmine, too. I can't believe they're gone."

Nakamura digested the information. According to Sergeant Wolfe, Carmine's parents had disapproved of their daughter's choice of company. But Carmine had hung out with Victoria McAdams and Kitty Tucker, two seemingly fortunate young women like herself. What fault could her parents have found with them? Or had Carmine kept other, less socially acceptable, company?

"Did Carmine have enemies—anyone who might want to harm her?"

Victoria shook her head.

"What about boyfriends—was she seeing anyone?"

Victoria hesitated, a sadness in her eyes. "Not that I knew of."

"Did she suffer from addiction?"

"No, nothing like that."

Victoria had painted a squeaky-clean picture of her late friends. Was she whitewashing their flaws or hiding their troubles? Nakamura headed to well-charted territory to test the reliability of his witness.

"Did Carmine get along with her parents?"

"Not at all. Her parents are mean, small-minded people. Carmine wanted nothing to do with them." She gave him a quick, worried look. "They wouldn't have had her killed. At least not like that."

Nakamura's ears tingled. "Like what?"

"You know...so brutally."

Nakamura studied her closely. Victoria seemed to know a lot about her friend's death. Too much.

"How so?"

"I heard she was tortured."

Nakamura tried to sound surprised. "Where did you hear that?"

"Just rumors. I know people in the media. Word gets around."

"What else did you hear?"

Victoria straightened on the couch and fixed him with an icy stare. "That Newburgh's police department might be involved."

Nakamura pretended not to take offense. "How so? We'll leave no stone unturned until we bring her killer to justice. He won't get away."

"He or *she*?"

Nakamura returned her stare. "What are you trying to say?" His sympathy ended at baseless accusations against the men and women who risked their lives every day to keep citizens like Victoria McAdams safe.

She scoffed. "You know very well what I'm saying, Detective."

"No, ma'am, I don't."

"You're not here to investigate her death, are you? You're here to cover it up."

Nakamura had to laugh. Victoria McAdams had a head full of wild speculation and a lot of nerve. "I'm here to do my job and serve the community."

"Like you did for Kitty?"

"Kitty Tucker's death was an accident."

"You call a bullet to the brain an accident? She had a closed-casket funeral service!"

"She was in the wrong place at the wrong time."

"No, Detective. She was at her home in the middle of the day. But one of your fellow officers got to her."

Nakamura tore open his emergency store of empathy. Victoria was grieving two tragic losses back-to-back. Terrible coincidences spawned conspiracy theories.

"Ms. McAdams, that was a hostage situation. We investigated the shooting thoroughly. The officers involved followed standard operating procedures."

"Save it, Detective. I know the story the police fed the media. But I also know the truth. Your police department covered up her death. Claire Wolfe killed Kitty Tucker."

Nakamura blinked at her. This conspiracy theory had become a self-reinforcing delusion. "Ma'am, you're mistaken. I was at the department during the Middle School Murders and I know all the details. I assure you, a sniper killed Kitty Tucker by accident. Nothing was covered up."

"Officer Wolfe appeared on the department's most wanted list that day. Hours later, she shot her partner dead, too. Why wasn't she brought to trial?"

"A full internal investigation was conducted. No charges were filed against Officer Wolfe."

"That doesn't make her innocent."

"There was no evidence of wrongdoing."

Victoria laughed again. "*No evidence*. I don't want to get you into trouble, Detective. But if you really want to find Carmine's killer, investigate Claire Wolfe."

Nakamura drew a deep breath. He needed to tread carefully. Victoria McAdams had connections, and she might interpret anything he said as corroboration of her crackpot speculations. He needed to poke holes in her theory.

"Why would Sergeant Wolfe kill your friends?"

"Because she's a vicious psychopath? For heaven's sake, her father was a serial killer. He murdered his little daughter, and Claire probably helped. What do you expect? It's in her blood."

Nakamura pressed his lips together. "I'm sorry for your loss, ma'am, but there's no evidence connecting Sergeant Wolfe to Carmine's murder."

Victoria flashed her eyes in disbelief. "No evidence? Ha! Allow me to enlighten you, Detective. If Claire Wolfe has no connection to the murder, why was her name written on Carmine's body?"

CHAPTER 25

An alarm beeped softly when Claire unlocked the door of Carmine Hannover's art deco house. She punched a code on a keypad to disable the security system, flipped a light switch, and almost collided with a naked woman.

Carmine had inherited her parents' love of sculpture. But instead of a gigantic cranberry, she'd selected a life-size statue of the unadorned female form to welcome her guests. With her white arms stretched over her head and one leg bent, the likeness left nothing to the imagination. The message was clear. "Leave your inhibitions at the door."

Detective Lucas Gomez let loose a wolf whistle. "Looks just like her."

He was right. The face belonged to Carmine. She had modeled the statue on her own body, capturing her physical form in every detail. Claire recognized the ample breasts from the workshop. The statue wasn't the only artwork Carmine had based on her perfect figure.

Gomez stood transfixed. "Ms. Hannover sure wasn't shy about her femininity."

"You should see her workshop. C'mon, we've got work to do."

Carmine had furnished the large, airy interior in shades of white and cream. Wearing plastic booties and latex gloves, Claire and Gomez split up to explore Carmine's home. She saw no signs of forced entry or hurried searches. The house remained as Carmine had left it on Sunday evening.

Claire followed a corridor lit by LED sconces.

Carmine Hannover had no romantic entanglements. She and her parents had no violent enemies. Either she'd carried dark secrets or she'd stumbled into the wrong place at the wrong time. The writing on the corpse favored the latter theory. But Captain Washington was right. Two serial killers within a year was highly unlikely.

Had the Middle School Strangler inspired a copycat? If so, the killer should have targeted young girls, not grown women. The copycat theory only explained the killer's use of Claire's name at the murder scene. Claire had appeared prominently in the media's coverage of the Middle School Murders. Again, she had to agree with Captain Washington. The writing on the body could be a weak attempt to confuse law enforcement. Still, the detail gnawed at Claire's conscience. Wherever she went, her father's ghost followed at her heels.

A blouse and two pairs of faded jeans lay on Carmine's king-sized bed. A cupboard door stood open in the walk-in closet. Carmine had deliberated about what to wear. She'd wanted to look perfect for her meeting at The Barnett Inn. She'd counted down the minutes and rushed to meet her death.

Carmine had obsessed over the female form. The killer had destroyed her femininity by amputating her breasts. Was the murderer familiar with her artwork? How well did he know her?

"Over here," Gomez called. "I found her computer."

Claire located the detective in a computer room staring at a MacBook.

"Perfect. It'll have the work calendar her PA mentioned and her list of contacts."

"I'll get the Faraday bag."

She nodded. Faraday forensic bags blocked wireless access to devices in case criminals attempted to wipe or alter data remotely.

Claire scanned Carmine's workspace. There were no signs of sculpting implements or raw materials in the room. Carmine had confined her creative side to her workshop. At home, she'd turned to other obsessions. A thick manila folder lay on the far edge of the desk. Claire opened the cover, and a chill spread down her spine.

Gomez returned with the Faraday bag. "What've you got there?"

He drew near and glanced at the photo within the folder. Tall skeletal office buildings rose from an enormous construction site.

Claire said, "I know this place. It's Silicon Towers."

"The project in SouthPark?"

In her mind, a memory flashed. A fourteen-year-old girl lay on the ground beneath a thick layer of white powder.

"The Middle School Strangler dumped his second victim there."

Gomez grunted with surprise.

A premonition gathered in Claire's chest. The postcard from last year's traumatic homicides didn't bode well. The folder was a dark abyss. Once she stepped over the edge, she'd never find solid ground again. But staying put was not an option. Duty urged her onward.

Claire moved the photograph aside. The next item in the

folder was a newspaper clipping. The article's image showed the same construction site, but the buildings had more flesh on their bones. "Middle School Strangler Strikes Again" ran the title, and Bella Winters wrote about the discovery of Karla Smith's body.

Carmine Hannover had followed the case. No surprises there. Media outlets like *The Newburgh Herald* had ensured that Newburgh's citizens lived in fear of the Middle School Strangler. But the folder didn't focus purely on that serial killer.

Claire paged through the next clippings, and her breath caught in her throat. She spread the items on the desk, side by side.

Gomez emitted his second wolf whistle of the day. The folder's unifying theme centered not on the Middle School Strangler...but on Claire Wolfe.

CHAPTER 26

"God, I hate this place." Dr. Sally Fleischer dropped her travel bag at Rob's feet.

He'd been discussing the case with Jess in the squad room when the tall woman with the wavy hair had marched in. Sally's deep, sensitive eyes filled with dread.

Rob gave her a commiserating grin. "Welcome back." Knowing how unpleasant this trip was for her, he reached for a distraction. "This is Detective Jessica Long. Detective Long, meet Dr. Sally Fleischer, our favorite FBI forensic psychiatrist."

Jess sprang to her feet and offered her hand. "Call me Jess."

Sally summoned a smile. "You're new here, aren't you?" She turned to Rob. "Where's Detective Wolfe?"

"*Sergeant* Wolfe is working another homicide."

"Oh."

Rob felt the need to explain his colleague's lack of enthusiasm to the young detective. "Sally created the profile for the Middle School Strangler."

Sally sniggered. "You mean *profiles*, plural."

"There was a profile for each of the killers?" Jess said.

"If only. We didn't realize we were dealing with a serial

killer couple until the end. I updated my analysis every day as events unfolded. The case was a profiler's nightmare."

"But the outcome," Rob said, "proved your original profile right."

Sally narrowed her eyes, frisking the compliment for insincerity. "Special Agent Cline is being kind." Then, with a shrug, she discarded her insecurities and got to business. "You found more bodies."

Rob glanced around the squad room. This was not the ideal place to begin their analysis of the corpses. "Let's continue our discussion in the conference room."

"The same as last time?"

"Yep. Just like the good old days."

"Perfect."

Rob and Jess had arranged the photos of the corpses on the conference room table and written notes on the whiteboard. Sally scanned the materials, assessing the big picture.

"Jess did some great work putting the pieces together."

Rob nodded at Jess, a signal for her to take over, and her eyes brightened with a mixture of surprise and gratitude.

"We exhumed twenty-eight bodies in total and fingerprinted all except for two."

Sally pored over the photos of the corpses. Some showed the bodies partially buried. Others displayed the full human remains on metal dissection tables.

"Were they too badly decomposed for printing?"

"No. Their hands are missing. And their heads. A man and a woman, both in their mid-twenties."

Sally nodded, her expression tightening as she scrutinized the photos. "Were body parts removed from any of the other victims?"

Jess turned to Rob for reassurance before answering. "We think some of the women are missing chunks of flesh, but it's hard to tell because of the advanced state of decomposition. So far, we've identified five victims using the fingerprints, and we're waiting on DNA analysis for the rest. Anabelle Mervis, the owner of the ranch house. We have little information on her. The other four were reported missing over the past year."

Jess read from a printout. "Michael Anderson, from Boston. Mellissa Goodman of Albany, New York. Steven Lefebvre from Hartford, Connecticut. And Andrea Brent from Manchester, New Hampshire."

"That's quite a spread. Why travel so far from home?"

Rob answered. "William Wolfe worked as a salesperson. Maybe he killed wherever his work took him?"

"Four victims in four different states," Jess said. "That made the crimes harder to connect."

Sally nodded, her attention still on the photos. "Then, suddenly, he killed three girls in Newburgh?"

Rob said, "He had a specific goal in mind—to frame Jed Wallace and tie up the murder of his daughter, Tina."

"Anything else?"

"Yeah. Two of the victims went missing on the same day. In two different states."

"How long before the Middle School Murders?"

"A few months."

Sally grunted. "The pack was already active. William Wolfe killed the one, Lisa Evans killed the other. We know they were working together at least since Evans started teaching at the Middle School. But this means she'd started killing earlier."

Rob pointed at the photos on the table. "That might explain another detail. We've grouped the victims according to MO. Half were shot in the back of the head, execution-style. Some show signs of asphyxiation. For many, the cause of death is unclear. Some display multiple stab wounds and contusions, but we can't rule out drowning or poisoning. And then there's the two decapitated victims."

Sally's gaze roved over the photos. "Multiple MOs."

"Exactly."

"What's the spread between male and female?"

"About even."

"Do they match the photos in the basement?"

"Two of the women and three of the men. With the others, it's unclear."

"Sexual assault?"

"Some show signs of sexual assault before and/or after death."

Sally straightened and aired her thoughts. "A serial killer couple. Sometimes they killed together, sometimes apart. They experimented with different techniques. What did the victims do for a living?"

Jess conferred with her notes again. "We have an investment banker, a partner in a law firm, and two housewives."

"High net worth?"

Rob glanced at Jess. They hadn't considered that angle. "It seems so. You think they were on an anti-capitalist crusade?"

"Maybe. But mission-oriented serial killers usually attack prostitutes, specific racial groups, or homosexuals. These are high-profile targets. Why risk exposure?"

Jess spoke up. "Maybe they were homosexuals?"

"It's worth checking." Sally didn't sound optimistic.

Jess tried again. "Maybe they grew bored with easy targets? They chose these victims for the challenge—to raise the stakes."

The psychiatrist shook her head. "Again, possible but unlikely. Serial killer couples are usually romantically involved. They choose specific victim profiles. The male takes the lead, and the female follows. This is too...atypical." She contemplated the photos in gloomy silence. "What do we know about Lisa Evans?"

Rob said, "Not much. Her parents live nearby, in Springfield."

Sally perked up. "Are they still married?"

"Yep."

"Was she adopted?"

"No."

"And she had no history of delinquency or abuse?"

"Not as far as we know."

Sally folded her arms. "Most serial killers have a history of early childhood neglect and abuse and an emotionally distant mother."

"Most, but not all. Karla Homolka had a clean record and pampered life until she met Paul Bernardo."

Jess said, "The Ken and Barbie Killers?"

Rob nodded at Jess, the excellent student. "Bernardo triggered her capacity for murder."

"Homolka was different," Sally countered. "She mostly recruited the victims and looked the other way. She might have been a sociopath, but she didn't kill independently with an individual MO. The same goes for Gerald and Charlene Gallego."

Jess said, "Maybe we've discovered a new type of killer couple?"

The psychiatrist sighed again. "I don't know. I need time to study the data. Meanwhile, speak with the parents. We need to find out more about Lisa's childhood, and how she came to know Wolfe."

Rob beamed at the psychiatrist. "That's a good idea. We'll do that." Five minutes back in town and she'd already added value. "It's good to have you back, Sally."

She snorted. "Something tells me I'm going to regret this."

CHAPTER 27

"This time give me some good news," Captain Washington said.

The investigation team had assembled in his office for an update Wednesday afternoon. Once again, Chief Emmerso joined the meeting, his shoulder to the wall and his arms crossed. Claire had more bad news than good, but she delayed the inevitable and led with the only positive development in the case.

"We found the victim's computer and had a forensic copy made of the hard disk."

"And?"

"Her personal calendar had the evening of her death blocked out."

"Don't keep us in suspense. What did she have planned?"

"She labeled the appointment with a single letter, M. That's all there is."

"Was she secretive about all her appointments?"

"Not at all. Detective Gomez has the full schedule."

Gomez read from his notes. "She went to a cosmetic clinic

that morning and had a massage the day before. Either she got lazy or she kept this meeting secret."

Washington said, "Could this M be McAdams? Nakamura, where was Victoria McAdams that evening?"

Nakamura clicked his tongue. "Not with Carmine Hannover. Her alibi checks out. She claims Carmine was her best friend."

"Any other ideas?" Washington glanced at Gomez and Nakamura, who both shrugged. "What's with the single-letter monikers? What is this—James Bond?"

Gomez snorted.

Claire continued. "There are appointments labeled M every week or two going back six months. Then, the letters switch to L."

Washington snorted. "So, she was having an affair with the alphabet."

Gomez chuckled. Nakamura didn't. His eyes met Claire's for a long, serious moment, then he looked away. Nakamura had acted cool toward her since she and Gomez had got back from searching Carmine's home.

"What about the personal assistant?" Captain Washington asked, snapping her back to the discussion.

"Barry Cook gave us the key to the victim's home. He claims to have no idea about any romantic relationships or financial difficulties. He shared her low opinion of her parents. And he was at a birthday dinner the night of her murder. His alibi checks out, too."

Washington wasn't giving up on the PA. "That doesn't rule him out as an accomplice."

Gomez gazed at Claire. The time had arrived to tell their captain about Carmine's folder. Sweat beaded on her forehead. The file would force Captain Washington to share the details they'd kept secret, and Claire expected unpleasant reactions from the detectives they'd left in the dark.

Thankfully, Washington changed the subject. "How much money did she withdraw from her trust fund?"

Nakamura answered. "Fifty grand a few weeks ago. Another fifty grand five months before that. Each time, she transferred the money out of her account immediately."

"Where did it go?"

"We're still working on that."

Washington sighed. "Follow the money, Detective. This homicide is starting to feel like a DEA operation."

Follow the money. That was timely advice. Claire still had no idea how her father had left her mother a million dollars. His victims wouldn't have carried that kind of cash on their person. Had he extorted money before taking their lives? *Not your problem anymore.* Claire had shut the door on her father and his crimes. She was glad Diane had thrown her out. Otherwise, Claire's conscience would torture her for living off his blood money. *Thanks, Mom. You did me a solid.*

"Talking of money," Captain Washington continued. "What did the siblings have to say for themselves?"

Gomez answered. "Dead end. They hadn't spoken to Carmine in months. They seemed annoyed about having to return for her funeral."

Washington shook his head at rich people and their weird family relations. "What about the pathology report?"

"The results show no sign of date-rape drugs. The attacker must have disabled her some other way. Sergeant Wolfe's idea about the fake robbery is still our best working theory."

Washington turned to the other detective. "Nakamura, what else did Victoria McAdams have to say for herself?"

"She seems pretty torn up by Carmine's death. They were both close with Kitty Tucker." Nakamura shot Claire a glance.

"And? Did she provide us with any new leads?"

Nakamura studied his hands. "Nah, just conspiracy theories."

Captain Washington gave Claire a meaningful look. She knew what he was thinking—had their secret leaked?

"What kind of conspiracy theories?"

"McAdams thinks Carmine's death is related to Kitty's."

Washington shrugged. "That's understandable from her point of view, but not much of a conspiracy."

Nakamura hesitated. "She has this crazy idea that Sergeant Wolfe is responsible for both."

Washington straightened in his seat. "And why would she think Carmine's murder has anything to do with Sergeant Wolfe?"

"Because, apparently, Sergeant Wolfe's name appeared on the victim's body."

Gomez snickered incredulously. When he saw Captain Washington's expression, he sobered up. The temperature in the office dropped.

Nakamura continued, deadpan. "Of course, I told her that wasn't true."

His voice had gained a blunt, accusatory edge. Claire groaned inwardly while the detectives realized their commanding officers had kept them out of the loop.

Chief Emmerso broke the awkward silence. "She's right. The killer carved the word 'Claire' on the victim's back. We assumed that was a diversion. I withheld that detail in the hope it would help isolate the killer. I apologize for the lack of transparency, but the tactic seems to have paid off. How did Ms. McAdams come by that information?"

"From her contacts in the media."

Claire swore under her breath. "Bella Winters called me this morning asking for my comment. I thought she was fishing for information, but somebody must have leaked to her, and then the rumor spread to McAdams."

Gomez scoffed. "Well, Nakamura and I didn't leak it, that's for sure."

Captain Washington sighed. "It must have been a forensic tech or the ME's staff."

Chief Emmerso spoke up again. "Wonderful. *The Newburgh Herald* is going to have a field day."

"There's more." Claire's comment won her more annoyed glances. "We found a folder of photographs and newspaper clippings at Carmine's home. The Silicon Towers project. The Middle School Strangler murders. All the items have one common theme—me." Claire swallowed hard. "The writing on the body might be more than a diversion."

Washington had more questions. "The file was just sitting on her desk?"

"Yes."

"Somebody wanted you to find it. Who else had access to the victim's home besides Barry Cook?" Captain Washington hadn't given up on his PA theory.

"Nobody, as far as we know."

"Fingerprint the folder. Call Cook in for questioning. If he had access to her lawyers and bank accounts, he might have helped himself to Carmine's money, killed her, and—I don't know—cooked up this obsession with Claire to muddy the investigation. It's a long shot, but let's eliminate that angle."

"Yes, sir."

Relief filled her. The emotional burden of keeping that secret from her team members had lifted from her shoulders. And the investigation had identified a person of interest. Claire had feared that, like last year, the homicide investigation would turn on her once the detectives learned of her involvement. Captain Washington had laid those fears to rest.

"And, Nakamura, see what you can find on McAdams. She probably had access to her friend's home. If she and Carmine fell out, she might be behind the folder and the writing on the body. That would explain her accusations against Sergeant Wolfe, too."

"Yes, sir."

"Let me guess," Gomez said. "It's a long shot but what the hell?"

"You're getting the hang of things, Gomez. Good for you."

The meeting concluded, and the detectives exited Captain Washington's office.

Chief Emmerso motioned for Claire to stick around. "How are you holding up?"

Did he know she'd been kicked out of her mom's house?

"Good. Getting used to people dropping my name to further their private agendas, but I guess you were right about the price of celebrity."

He frowned. "It's the way things are."

Claire nodded at her chief and her captain and returned to the squad room. She approached Nakamura and Gomez at their desks. "I'm sorry about that. I didn't feel comfortable keeping you in the dark either."

Nakamura smiled. "We'll get over it. Need to know and all that."

"Exactly."

Gomez raised his eyebrows. "Any other secrets we should know about?"

"Let a girl keep some of her secrets. Nakamura, we need surveillance on Cook."

"I'm on it."

"And the prints—"

"Already handling it," Gomez said.

"Great. I'll just sit on my hands and pretend to be useful."

Nakamura snorted. "See—you've gotten used to command already."

Claire enjoyed the chuckle at her own expense and returned to her desk. She opened the murder book for the homicide and started her report on her interview with Barry Cook.

The murky homicide had transformed into a typical murder-for-profit. Barry Cook hadn't struck Claire as a murderer. But as Claire had learned only too well, cold-blooded killers were good at hiding in plain sight—even within her own family. Still, Claire's gut instinct wouldn't leave her in peace.

She logged into the ViCAP Internet site. ViCAP, the FBI's Violent Criminal Apprehension Program, kept a searchable database of unsolved murders and sexual crimes. Claire ran a search for homicides of females with multiple stab wounds. A circle icon spun on the screen while the system searched the FBI databases. Captain Washington wouldn't appreciate her pursuing the serial killer angle, but what her boss didn't know couldn't hurt.

Unsurprisingly, the results displayed several hits, each with an image of the unlucky victim of the unsolved homicide. Claire clicked the links and reviewed the PDF posters summarizing the location and state of the corpse. ViCAP was a miserable place to hang out. She filtered the results by the past few months and scanned for indications of torture. Two recent cases in Albany, NY, caught her eye. Albany was a two-hour drive by car. Claire clicked the entries and skimmed the details, her gaze pouncing on the word "mutilation." Within a month, two women in their early twenties had turned up dead in public locations, their bodies covered in dozens of shallow stab wounds and signs of mutilation. Claire's pulse thumped in her ears.

What if her gut instinct was on target? If these homicides matched Carmine's, their investigation was focusing its efforts in the wrong direction. Unlikely or not, Claire had to know if Newburgh had spawned another serial killer. She found the number for Detective Paine at the local Investigations Bureau. He answered on the second ring. "Paine here."

Claire introduced herself, keeping her voice low so as not to be overheard by the surrounding officers. "I'm calling about the two homicides last month in Albany. Females, early twenties, multiple stab wounds, and mutilation. I was wondering—"

"The hookers? Yeah, what about them? You got something for me?"

Hookers. Even with her limited exposure to forensic profiling, Claire knew that a major difference in victim profile made linking the crimes unlikely.

"Never mind. Our homicide is probably unrelated. The MO is—"

"I'd appreciate any help you can give." He'd cut her off again. Detective Paine was not a man she'd enjoy working with. "We're out of leads and, hookers or not, these crimes were pretty disturbing."

Claire had to ask. "Did the killer remove their breasts?"

"Among other parts, yeah."

The receiver chilled Claire's hand. That detail changed everything. Was that form of mutilation the killer's signature?

Detective Pain blabbered on. "The bastard let them bleed out. I was hoping ViCAP would trigger something. And now—"

"Sarge," Nakamura called.

Sarge. She'd have to get used to that word. Claire ignored him. She had to get the information she needed, fast. She cut Detective Pain off mid-sentence.

"Did he remove the breasts from the scene?"

"What? No. Why would he do that?"

Nakamura raised his voice. "Sarge?"

"I have to go," she told Paine. "I'll call again if it's relevant."

She put down the phone. "What is it, Nakamura?"

"The call list for Carmine's phone arrived. One number shows up often, both incoming and outgoing."

"And?"

"It's registered to Sarah Malik."

Gomez butted in. "Malik—the politician?"

Claire's insides lurched again. Sarah Malik had shown up at Claire's home Monday evening around the time of Carmine's death to offer Claire a job. Now it seemed Malik knew the victim and had called her often. Claire cringed. Once again, a web of unlikely coincidences ensnared her personal life in an ongoing homicide investigation.

She glanced at Gomez, and his eyes widened. Like Claire, he'd made the connection to Carmine Hannover's last appointment.

He said, "I guess we've found our M."

CHAPTER 28

Bella Winters had died and gone to Heaven. The sun sank toward the horizon, but Bella still stooped over her keyboard in her cubicle, her fingers dancing over the letters as though animated by dark magic. The words flowed. Adrenaline intoxicated her. This was why she'd become a journalist!

A Neil Gaiman quote surfaced in her mind. "Tomorrow may be hell, but today was a good writing day, and on the good writing days nothing else matters." The quote had an ominous overtone. *Tomorrow may be hell.* But that hell was reserved for a certain police detective who had snubbed Bella.

Her conscience twinged only a little at the pleasure she derived from Claire Wolfe's imminent discomfort. There was a word for that. *Schadenfreude*—the enjoyment experienced from another person's misfortune. Bella was in the mood for long, snobbish words. After this story hit the street corners, she'd win a Pulitzer for her investigative journalism. She'd become an official member of the literary elite. Or was that *literati*?

CLAIRE. The moment Bella had learned about the gruesome message the killer had left on Carmine Hannover's dead body, her reporter's brain had flown into overdrive. Claire *Who*?

The answer "Claire Wolfe" was almost too convenient to be true. But not unlikely. Thanks to Bella's news coverage, Claire Wolfe was a household name in these parts. But why would the killer connect his crime to Newburgh's favorite homicide detective? Bella shouldn't jump to hasty conclusions.

A familiar, juicy angle beckoned. Perhaps this murder wasn't a typical homicide? Torture and gruesome messages were the hallmarks of deranged psychopaths, and these clues raised another question. Had he killed before?

Bella threw herself into research mode. A dozen internet searches and a handful of telephone calls later, she'd discovered the answer. Her hands trembled with excitement as she began her new article. The killer had struck before—twice within the past month—in Albany, New York State, only a couple of hours away. The victims were young women. Both had suffered multiple shallow stab wounds and vicious mastectomies. The details were too similar to Carmine Hannover's murder to be a coincidence. Bella had found her serial killer. No—much better than that. She'd found her Jack the Ripper!

When she had submitted her article that afternoon, Steve had loved the title. He'd even approved of the feminist angle she'd slipped into the copy and asked for more.

Right away, Bella had started work on a feature for Sunday's expanded edition. The killer built on the work of the Middle School Strangler. His crimes attacked the victims' femininity. An epidemic of violence against women had infected Newburgh. No girl or woman was safe.

She couldn't resist adding another poke at Newburgh PD. *You heard it here first, folks.* A crazed killer stalked the streets of Newburgh while the city's finest buried their heads in the sand. Bella even dropped Sarah Malik's name and hinted that the need for long-overdue changes would topple Newburgh's old white patriarchy. Steve would be proud. God, Bella loved serial killers!

Bella left empty paragraphs for later victims. It was only a matter of time until the killer struck again. She doubted he'd add another victim to his list by Sunday's publishing deadline. But it didn't hurt to be prepared.

A coffee mug hovered over the cubicle divider, but Bella didn't look up for fear of breaking her rhythm. "Steve, you're going to love Sunday's feature."

The editor in chief cleared his throat. "Bella, I'm holding your piece on the Hannover murder."

Bella's fingers froze on the plastic keys. The black spell had broken. "What?"

Anger had slipped into her voice. She shouldn't yell at the editor in chief, but Jack the Ripper didn't come along every day —or every century—and Bella needed this story.

Steve raised a hand to calm her. "I'm not dropping it. But there's something you should hear before we go to print."

Bella's hands balled into fists. He was going to pull her story, she could feel it. Had Newburgh PD intervened again? Had the mayor threatened to punish their business? They were journalists, for crying out loud. Their job was to speak truth to power, and Bella pledged to keep her readers informed ahead of the elections.

Steve gestured with his coffee mug. "C'mon. She's in my office."

Bella released her fists. *She?* Had Claire Wolfe descended on the news desk to plead for favorable coverage? Bella would use the opportunity to grill her about the message on Carmine's corpse.

Bella abandoned her keyboard and followed her editor in chief. Steve was her boss, and she had to toe the line. But if he blocked her story, she'd use her lungs' full capacity, and every *Herald* employee would know she had stood by her principles.

She halted at the glass door of Steve's office. The young woman in the visitor's seat modeled a Gucci suit and Louis Vuitton bag. This was not Sergeant Claire Wolfe. The woman rose when Bella entered, and she offered her hand. Steve made the introductions.

"Bella, meet Victoria McAdams. Victoria was a close friend of Carmine Hannover."

McAdams. The heiress of the second most powerful Newburgh family had summoned her to Steve's office.

The unsmiling woman skipped all the usual pleasantries. "We need to talk."

Bella folded her arms over her chest. "About what?"

Did Victoria oppose the paper exposing the gory details of her friend's death? Bella knew little about *The Herald*'s finances, but the name McAdams appeared at the top of the list of shareholders. Had the bankroller come to silence her? But Bella's fears were groundless.

Victoria McAdams cracked a conspiratorial grin. "About Claire Wolfe."

CHAPTER 29

Diane Wolfe nursed her drink at the bar of The Red Keg that evening. Soft eighties music played on the speakers. The murmur of friendly conversation surrounded her. She felt good, better than she had in decades. Diane had won! She'd liberated herself from Claire's tyranny. And tonight, she'd celebrate her new life. Fifty-dollar notes stuffed her pockets, and Jack Daniels lined her stomach. She was on top of the world.

"Can I buy you a drink?"

A man had materialized on the stool beside her. Beneath his peaked cap and rounded nose, a bushy mustache dominated his liver-spotted face. He wasn't exactly handsome, but his smile radiated warmth. And he had noticed her.

"I've already had four."

A giggle slipped into her voice. It was good to speak to someone besides Claire, someone who didn't know about her past. Someone who didn't see her as just an alcoholic.

The man laughed. "Why stop when you're on a roll?" His voice was rough but soothing, the voice of an old cowboy.

Uncouth. That's what her mother would've called him. She'd said the same about Bill, but Diane had married him anyway. Mom had been right about him. Dead right. But Diane hadn't come here tonight to think about Bill or her mother. To hell with them both. To hell with Claire, too. Diane was old enough—and rich enough—to make her own bad decisions. What was the opposite of uncouth anyway—*couth*? Who in their right mind wanted a couth man?

Tonight, Diane had two goals on her mind: to get drunk and to get laid. She was on target to achieve goal number one. Now, she'd focus on goal number two.

"OK," she said.

The stranger grinned. "George, two more of whatever our mystery lady is having."

Mystery lady. Nobody had ever called Diane a mystery lady before. And tonight, she was not in a ladylike mood. The bartender, a bald man with a t-shirt that read, "Trust me, I'm a bartender," poured two whiskeys.

The stranger raised his glass. "Cheers!"

They clinked their drinks together and drank.

His grin widened. "Are we drinking to remember or to forget?"

Diane considered the question. "Both."

"I'm Frank."

"Diane."

He repeated the word, savoring each syllable. "That's a lovely name."

Diane giggled. When had she last received a compliment? She couldn't remember. Frank didn't see her as an overweight drunk. He saw a mysterious and available woman at a bar.

His eyes brightened. "Now I remember you. Planet Fitness! Your daughter drops you off every other day, am I right?"

The mention of her daughter soured Diane's mood. "Yep, that was me."

Tina Turner was playing on the speakers, and Diane used the opportunity to change the subject.

"God, I love this song!" She crooned the words. "A dancer for money, do what you want me to do." The whiskey was doing its thing.

"You like Tina Turner?"

"She's my favorite. I even named my daughter after her." At the thought of her darling Tina, Diane teared up. This was not the way she'd wanted to spend the evening.

"Are you OK?"

She wiped the tears from her eyes. "It's nothing."

"Go on, sing some more. 'Any old music will do,'" he sang, painfully off-key. "On second thought, I think I'll leave the singing to you." Again, he'd made her laugh.

Diane accepted the challenge and sang the next line.

"You've got a pretty voice."

"I used to sing in a band."

"No kidding? Why'd you stop?"

"Life got in the way. Marriage. Kids. Now the kids are gone, and I'm single again."

Diane was being too forward, but she didn't care.

"Why don't you sing for us?"

"What, here, now?"

"Why not?"

Diane shook her head. She wasn't *that* drunk. Was she?

"Hey, George," Frank said. "Play some more Tina Turner. We've got a singer."

Before she knew what was happening, Frank placed a microphone in her hand and pulled her to her feet. A roomful of smiling drinkers waited for her with expectant glances. *What the hell.*

The first song began, "What's Love Got to Do with It?" Diane started soft but quickly got into her stride. Hands clapped, and heads nodded. *This isn't so bad.* Two older men in baseball caps sent her drinks. The crowd loved her.

Five minutes and three tequilas later, a miracle happened. Her hurt melted away, and her inhibitions weren't far behind. She was nineteen again, her entire life ahead of her. Diane stepped onto a small wobbly table, swinging her hips and stretching her lungs to the tune of "Simply the Best." She gestured with her free arm. Diane ruled the bar. She was its queen.

"We love you!" one of the baseball caps yelled.

"Show us your titties!" said his friend.

Drunk on her newfound power, Diane weighed the suggestion.

Yeah, what the hell.

CHAPTER 30

"How can I help you, sir?"

The bald man in the orange Home Depot uniform stared at him, but Johnny didn't fall for his fake smile. *Nobody noticed Johnny and nobody ever called him "sir." The man was old enough to be his father. For all Johnny knew, the attendant was his father. Dad didn't care about Johnny either. Johnny didn't want the attendant's help. Tonight, he was going to kill Emily, and nobody could know about his plan.*

Johnny wheeled his shopping cart past the old man toward the Tools department.

"Rude kid," the attendant grumbled.

Johnny had been right about him. Nobody cared. He tossed a roll of thick black duct tape into the cart and added a jumbo pack of zip ties.

Johnny had waited over a year for this day. After Emily had caught him with his pants down on the service balcony, her teasing had gotten worse. Much worse. Johnny retreated to the safety of his inner world. His fantasy evolved. He still wanted to see her naked. But instead of watching her strip, he tore the clothes from her body.

And he no longer wanted to touch her. The idea of hurting her aroused him more.

The fantasy looped in his mind, day and night. With each iteration, he added details and adjusted the sequence of events. Johnny would surprise Emily in the middle of the night. He'd grown four inches since his bathroom humiliation and packed on five pounds of muscle. She wouldn't overpower him so easily. He'd tie her to the bedposts, seal her mouth, and hurt her. Nobody would hear her screams, even if their junkie mother was home and conscious.

Johnny halted before a display of long, sharp knives. He lifted one from the rack. Even within the plastic packaging, the blade's heavy solid form radiated power. He'd like to use the serrated blade on Emily. The fear in her eyes would be priceless. Who's the boss now? He'd make her call him "sir." Johnny sniggered at the idea.

A little girl with bangs passed by and gave him dirty looks. He read her thoughts. Freak. Asswipe. Nothing. He stuck his tongue out at her, and she scooted to catch up with her mother.

Johnny returned the blade to the rack. He couldn't afford the two-hundred-dollar Camillus knife. He'd taken two twenties from Mom's wallet. She was always low on cash but never seemed to notice the missing bills. She never paid him any attention either. The tight budget meant he'd probably get caught. He had no money for vats of acid to dissolve Emily's bones.

Johnny dropped a ten-dollar utility knife into the cart. His plan was worth the risk. He'd make Emily pay for the years of abuse, and everybody would know his name. Everybody would know that Johnny Norton, the quiet loner, was a badass killer.

He waited in line at the checkout counter. The beeping of the barcode scanner sounded like a security alarm. The closer he drew to the cash register, the quicker and shallower his breathing became. This was actually happening. His fantasy was seeping into real life. What if something went wrong? What if Emily survived his attack?

He'd spend the rest of his life in prison. Beads of sweat formed on his forehead.

The cash register attendant asked for his loyalty card. The girl was about his age and pretty, with short hair and a nose ring hole. The edge of a tattoo peeked out of the collar of her uniform shirt. Johnny shook his head.

While she swiped his items, the truth hit him. Johnny wouldn't sneak up on Emily tonight. He wasn't going to murder her. Even the cash register attendant was more badass than him.

The girl smirked. Did she despise him, too? You're nothing. You're a worthless piece of crap.

"That'll be nineteen dollars and ninety-one cents."

She made eye contact, the smirk still on her lips. Johnny tossed a twenty on the counter. He was burning up under his shirt. He needed to get out of there.

The till opened, and she collected his change. "Is this for your red room?"

Red room? *He blinked at her in confusion.* "What?"

"You know—duct tape and cable ties?" She slipped a hardcover novel from under the counter. The knot of a gray necktie dominated the cover. "Fifty Shades?"

Johnny's face must have turned bright red. He'd heard about the book, which dealt with kinky sex.

"Oh. No, I haven't read it."

"Yeah, right."

She sounded doubtful. Was she calling him a liar? He was about to say something mean, but she held out her hand and grinned.

"I'm April."

CHAPTER 31

"Nice to see you again."

Alexandro "Al" Menendez, Sarah Malik's flamboyant personal assistant, grinned at Claire through the gate when Claire rang the bell that evening. Once again, Al sported a designer suit and fancy shoes, but today he'd opted for a peach color instead of lime. The PA cultivated an expensive orchard in his bedroom closet.

The mansion in Seven Oaks was modest by Hannover standards but still impressive with gray stucco walls and low roofs tiled with curved red ceramic in the style of a Spanish villa. Claire was developing expensive taste.

Al's smile exposed a gold-capped tooth. "I'm glad we're working together."

"Don't get your hopes up."

Claire had asked for a private audience with the mayoral candidate without explaining why. From experience, people cooperated with law enforcement better when blissfully unaware they were persons of interest. Had the politician assumed Claire had called to accept her job offer? Let Sarah Malik think what she wanted to.

"Claire!" Sarah strode through the courtyard to greet her, all smiles. They shook hands, and Malik embraced her.

Claire didn't fall for the overwhelming display of affection. Political theorists called this a charm offensive. Was Malik closing the deal with her new political adviser or painting over her guilt in Carmine's death?

"Thank you for seeing me so late."

"No rest for the wicked. Please come inside."

Claire followed her host down a windowed corridor that flanked a large lighted swimming pool. A uniformed servant fished leaves from the waters with a net on a long pole.

Malik's office had an enormous desk, a thin laptop, and a row of colored squares of paper with to-do lists scribbled in curly freehand. Framed campaign posters dominated the walls with photos of Sarah and her pledge to "drain the swamp." Claire turned down the offer for a drink.

"You work from home?"

From behind the desk, Sarah spread her hands in defeat. "Trying to cut expenses. We'll run a lean administration after we win the election, too."

"I'm glad to hear it."

Malik opened the drawer of her desk and slid a bundle of stapled pages toward Claire. "Your salary is on page two."

"You prepared a contract?"

Malik placed a silver ballpoint pen beside the documents. "I'm an optimist. You choose the start date. Take off a few days to decompress. You'll be very busy once you start."

Claire paged through the document. The salary was four times what she currently earned. Tempting. But Claire wouldn't abandon a homicide mid-case.

She put the pages down. "I didn't come here because of your offer."

"Then how may I help you, Sergeant?"

"How well did you know Carmine Hannover?"

Malik stiffened. "Carmine was a good friend."

"That's...surprising. Her parents are strong supporters of Mayor Thornton."

"Carmine is nothing like her parents. *Was.*" Her cool and confident facade wavered for a moment. She sucked in a deep breath. "I'm having trouble coming to terms with her death."

"When did you last see her?"

"We had lunch on Wednesday, I think."

Wednesday. Carmine's diary placed her with M on Sunday evening, when her ordeal with the killer had begun.

"Where were you Sunday evening?"

Malik swiped the screen of her new iPhone and tapped her finger to navigate to her calendar. "I was in a strategy meeting with an outside consultant."

"All evening?"

"From seven until ten. But we ended at eleven-thirty. Voter polls don't analyze themselves."

"Are you sure you didn't have plans to see Carmine on Sunday?"

"Absolutely. Al can confirm my whereabouts. We were together the whole time."

"But you called her on Sunday."

"We spoke often. As I said, she was a good friend."

"Did her behavior change lately?"

"How so?"

"Did she seem concerned?"

"About what?"

"Anything. Financial troubles?"

"Not that I noticed."

"Did she have any enemies?"

"Carmine could be blunt sometimes, but she didn't hold

grudges. She was a kind and generous person. I can't imagine who would want to hurt her."

"Hurt her?"

"I've heard the rumors, Sergeant. She was tortured. Maybe you should speak with her parents."

Malik's cheek twitched. She hid a lot of pain beneath the surface. Claire didn't doubt the sincerity of her words. But had the politician told her the whole truth?

"I'll do that."

"I know it's a cliché, Sergeant, but this swamp is far from dry. When the people at the top are corrupt, their evil trickles down. You of all people should understand that."

As a well-connected politician, Malik received inside information on major events. Was she hinting at the way Claire's father had manipulated Newburgh PD thanks to dirty cops? Claire didn't appreciate the reminder.

"I do."

Claire drove her white Ford hatchback down the darkened streets of suburban Newburgh, her mind afloat with conflicting theories. If not Malik, who was the "M" in Carmine's diary? Was Malik aware of Carmine's obsession with Claire? She'd given no indication. Maybe Washington was right about the killer planting the documents in Carmine's home? And if so, why was the killer determined to connect Claire, specifically, to the victim?

Barry Cook had access to Carmine's home. If he'd blackmailed her and emptied her trust fund, he'd want to implicate somebody else in the crime. But was he capable of torturing his boss and leaving her to die? The violence of the attack indicated intense anger and hatred. Was Barry secretly in love with her? Had she spurned his advances?

Claire parked on the curb, then realized she'd driven to her mother's home by force of habit. The lights were out. Mom was probably in bed, snoring. Or on the floor, unconscious after self-medicating with a bottle of red. *Again, not my problem.*

Parting ways with her mother was for the best. Claire had wanted Diane to get back on her own two feet and she'd done so. It hurt that she'd used her new independence to kick Claire out, but maybe Claire had pushed her too hard? Maybe they both needed a space to recalibrate their relationship and reconnect as adults? Claire shook her head at her own neediness. She just couldn't let go, could she?

Claire started the engine and drove to Rob's motel. The ghosts of the past drifted through her mind. She'd investigated brutal homicides before. The Middle School Murders had also involved mutilation. But anger and hatred had contributed little to those deaths. They were the work of disturbed minds, psychopathic killers who had murdered the girls for their own cool and calculating purposes.

The profile photos of the dead prostitutes in Albany floated before her eyes. Had Carmine Hannover fallen prey to the same twisted predator? Was this killer now toying with Claire, taunting her with his message? And if so, would this killer stop with Carmine?

Claire let herself into the motel room. This time she caught Rob in the shower. She shed her clothes and snuck into the bathroom. He jumped when a naked woman materialized in the shower stall but overcame his surprise admirably.

Later, Claire lay in bed, still damp under the covers, and the ghosts returned.

"Do stranger killings always involve mutilation?"

Rob stirred beside her, half asleep. "Claire, we need to work on our pillow talk."

"I'm serious."

"So am I."

"Answer the question, smart-ass."

"No, not always. But sometimes the mutilation is more important than the actual killing."

"Do they ever change their target selection?"

"Drastically? No. Most organized serial killers look for easy targets. Vulnerable people who won't be missed."

Claire had suspected that much. Carmine Hannover was a high-risk target. Her death was probably unrelated to the Albany murders.

"Is this about Carmine Hannover?"

"Yeah." There was no point in denying it. He read the newspapers along with the rest of the city.

"Dr. Fleischer is back in town. She'd be happy to assist."

"Maybe later. Captain Washington is trying to steer clear of serial killers."

"I don't blame him."

"How are things going with your case?"

Rob exhaled a deep, frustrated breath. "Slowly. Every answer leads to another five questions."

"I know the feeling."

Claire's phone rang, and she groaned. She longed for sleep. *Who can that be now?* She reached for her phone on the bedside table. Dispatch was calling. Her heart skipped a beat. Had another body turned up?

"Wolfe here."

The operator chewed gum while she spoke. "Sergeant Wolfe, we received a call about an indecent exposure incident. The subject is in the main holding cell."

Indecent exposure. Was she kidding? "You've got the wrong number. I'm with the Investigations Bureau."

"No mistake, Sergeant. This one's for you. The subject is Diane Wolfe, your mother."

CHAPTER 32

Diane Wolfe leaned over the metal toilet bowl and puked her guts out. Minutes ago, she had ruled the world. Now her universe had shrunk to the jail cell's seatless crapper. Even in her nauseating, drunken state, the symbolism wasn't lost on her. Her entire life was a toilet bowl.

She heaved again, emptying her stomach until nothing remained inside. Then, she wiped her mouth on her arm, rolled to the side, and leaned against the cement wall. The holding cell stank of puke and urine. Or was that her smell? It didn't matter.

Get drunk—check. Get laid—not happening. After her performance and subsequent arrest, she'd never see her date again. What was his name? Frank. He'd been nice.

"Goodbye, Frank. So long. Have a nice life." Diane puffed, her head spinning with alcohol and shame. She wanted to crawl into a dark hole and die.

With a start, she noticed the man on the other side of the cell. Sitting on the floor with his legs crossed, he gave her his familiar smirk. Diane's surprise turned to rage.

"This is all your fault," she said.

Bill Wolfe stared at her, unimpressed. "How is this my fault, Diane? I'm dead. Claire's gone, too. And yet here you are. There's nobody left to blame."

Her husband wasn't really there. Diane was hallucinating. Waves of relief washed over her, and a tsunami of panic overtook them. She was losing her mind. Where Bill had failed, she'd succeeded and without outside help. Except for whoever had called the cops on her tonight. A wife of one of her new fans at the bar? Typical. Women always cut each other down, didn't they? And Bill was wrong. He *was* to blame!

"If you hadn't left me that money..." She cut her complaint short. Bill's ghost had evaporated. Diane was alone in the cell and talking to the wall. She wanted to get out of this place. She needed to go home!

Claire worked as a detective at this police department. She could pull strings to release her. But she wouldn't. Diane had thrown Claire out. Why should Claire drag herself there in the middle of the night and call in favors? In her shoes, Diane wouldn't. And she didn't have the guts to beg.

There's nobody left to blame.

Diane should never have treated her daughter that way. Claire had only wanted to help. She'd tried to save Diane from herself, but Diane had resisted her with every fiber of her being.

No, Diane would spend the night in jail. She deserved this. Diane had made a lot of mistakes in her life. Some of them were unfixable.

Hinges squeaked as the barred door swung open. A uniformed officer entered the cell. Was he the one who'd arrested her? Diane couldn't remember. But the question fled her addled mind when a woman in jeans and a sweater followed him into the cell. Claire's eyes brimmed with embarrassment.

Diane looked away, the shame sobering her up. She hadn't wanted Claire to see her like this. But her daughter hadn't come to gloat.

Claire held out her hand. "C'mon, Mom. I'm taking you home."

CHAPTER 33

Thursday morning, Claire woke up in her own bed. Daylight poured through the gap in the curtains. She'd overslept. The night was a blur of awkward memories summed up in two words, "Indecent exposure."

Claire climbed out of bed and rummaged in her overnight bag for a fresh set of clothes. *Indecent exposure!* After hearing about Diane's behavior, a part of Claire had wanted to let her mother spend the night in jail. *Serves her right!* But the rest of her knew she'd post bail and take her home.

True to form, Mom had sabotaged herself. She'd used her newfound cash and freedom to get plastered out of her mind. Only this time, she'd hit rock bottom.

The patrol officer who had responded to the 911 call had found her mother dancing topless on a table at The Red Keg and singing at the top of her voice. It had taken the officer and two onlookers five minutes to remove her forcibly from the table and bundle her into the patrol cruiser. Try as she might, Claire couldn't erase from her mind the image of an enthusiastic crowd of drunks ogling Mom's naked breasts.

Claire helped herself to a bowl of the Special K in the

kitchen using the last of the milk. Her mother hadn't done the grocery shopping. *Typical.*

She ate quickly and prepared to leave. Diane might not remember last night's scandalous events once she emerged from her drunken coma, but she'd definitely not want to find Claire in her kitchen this morning.

Claire washed her bowl and spoon. There was no point in sticking around. Six months of henpecking hadn't changed Mom's behavior. An angry rebuke would only give her mother another excuse to hate her.

The trash can under the kitchen sink was full. Did Diane even know where to dump the garbage? Claire tied the strings together, removed the bag, and installed a fresh lining in the can. Then, she heaved the trash to the front door. The morning's edition of *The Newburgh Herald* lay on the welcome mat. Carmine Hannover's face appeared on the front page again. Claire bent down and picked up the newspaper. She made a mental note to call *The Newburgh Herald* and change her delivery address.

When she unfolded the paper, her own face stared back at her. An unflattering portrait photo of Claire appeared beside that of Carmine. She read the title, and her heart sank. As she scanned the content of the article, her blood boiled.

She cursed Bella Winters under her breath. The reporter had broken every journalistic code, mixing fact with fantasy for maximum shock effect. Add to the witches' brew one conspiracy theory courtesy of Victoria McAdams, and Bella shoved Claire once again into the rogue's gallery of public opinion.

Claire rolled up the paper and marched to her car. She'd make Bella Winters answer for her reckless words. This time, the bitch had gone too far.

CHAPTER 34

The newspaper landed on Charlie Emmerso's desk with an angry thump and sent waves of déjà vu through his mind. Emmerso had assumed that his promotion to chief of police would end his days as a human punching bag. In his line of work, media crap storms were inevitable. But with him at the helm, he'd expected to weather those storms with his dignity intact. That morning, Mayor Thomas Thornton had burst into Emmerso's office to prove him wrong.

"This is a catastrophe!" Mayor Thornton bellowed, thumping the newspaper on Emmerso's desk with his fat hand. "Can you believe this?"

Emmerso had read the morning's edition of *The Newburgh Herald* already, and he agreed with the mayor's assessment. The front-page headline read, "Newburgh Slasher's Trail of Blood." From the article, one might think the city morgue was overflowing. The story might be a death blow for the mayor's campaign and, possibly, Emmerso's career, too.

"Another serial killer? Are they serious?"

Emmerso kept his voice calm and reasonable. "The

evidence fits a standard homicide so far, but it's not impossible."

"Then what are you waiting for—share the evidence."

"It's too early. We've identified a few persons of interest but have nothing solid on them yet."

"Well, Bella Winters has got it all figured out. She claims her slasher killed two women in Albany last month, and that Sergeant Wolfe inspired his crimes. He even carved her name into Carmine Hannover's back! Did Bella Winters make that up?"

"Most of the article is wild speculation. Sergeant Wolfe had nothing to do with Carmine's death. She didn't kill Kitty Tucker either."

"But did her name appear on the victim's body?"

When Emmerso nodded, the mayor swore and adjusted his comb-over.

"We kept that detail under wraps, hoping it would narrow our list of suspects. For all we know, the killer left the writing to mislead our investigation. There are precedents, and Sergeant Wolfe is a public figure."

The mayor was no longer listening. "Winters makes it sound like we're encouraging crime, not fighting it." He pointed at a paragraph. "She says it right here. 'An epidemic of violence against women triggered by systemic sexism.'" He scoffed. "That's us! We just promoted two women but somehow, we're women-haters? Explain that one to me, Charlie."

Emmerso shrugged. "You're right, Tom. *The Herald* has no shame. They'll do anything to sell papers."

Mayor Thornton pointed at the wall and continued his rant. "But Sarah Malik is a hero simply because she has no balls. She'd kill for this kind of coverage. Ha! You should investigate her."

Emmerso used his poker face. Sarah Malik was also a

person of interest in their investigation, but he couldn't share that detail with her rival.

"We need to close this case pronto, Charlie. How hard can that be? Carmine Hannover was found naked in The Barnet Inn, for heaven's sake. Maybe she took her kinky sex too far?"

Emmerso winced. "Her death was no accident."

Thornton threw his hands up in defeat. "Then arrest somebody. I'd like to see the look on Bella's face when she finds out there's no serial killer. I'll make sure *The Herald* issues an apology. Meanwhile, Sergeant Wolfe has become a liability. I think you should put somebody else on the case."

Emmerso had imagined the mayor would suggest that. "She's a top investigator, and she's already immersed in the evidence. Pulling her now will only delay an arrest."

"Then call in the feds. If *The Herald* wants a serial killer, let the experts say she's got her head up her ass."

"BAU agents are assisting with another case. We can ask for their professional opinion on the Hannover homicide, too." Emmerso picked up his phone. "I'll get right on that."

"Good. Let the FBI take the heat. We'll smell like roses no matter how this turns out."

Mayor Thornton left, and that rush of déjà vu returned. Emmerso had called in the FBI last year, too. Again, the Hannover homicide recalled the manic days of the Middle School Murders. Emmerso hoped that this time they'd wrap up the case without bloodshed.

CHAPTER 35

When the killer entered the Newburgh Police Department, the uniformed officer at the front desk waved him in. She didn't ask for identification. She didn't even question him about the box under his arm. He'd prepared for both scenarios. He'd expected more from the cops. But police officers were just human, and human beings were fools. They were in for a big surprise. And so was Claire Wolfe.

He followed the signs to the Investigations Bureau, keeping his head down, the peaked cap shielding his eyes. The officers he passed in the corridors didn't give him a second look. The secret to his invisibility was a UPS uniform and a clipboard. But he wasn't overconfident. He'd taken precautions. People would ask questions once his bomb detonated, so to speak. An alert officer might remember his face. A camera might capture his likeness. Some daring feats were worth the risk.

The anticipation put a spring in his step. Today, he'd meet Claire Wolfe up close and personal. And his gift would bind them together forever.

He stepped into the squad room and scanned the desks in the open space for his target. The clock read nine AM, but only two detectives hunched over their computers. His heart sank. *Where is Claire?*

"Can I help you?" said the suit with the mop of tawny hair.

The killer glanced at his clipboard. "I'm looking for Claire Wolfe."

The detective pointed at the desk diagonally opposite him. "Leave it over there. I'll make sure she gets it."

The killer's lip spasmed. He wanted to see Claire, to gaze into her eyes, but he had to remain in character. He walked over to Claire's desk. She'd draped her suit jacket over the back of her chair. The screensaver of her computer displayed the Newburgh PD emblem. She sat here every day. He inhaled the air she had breathed, savoring the hint of her scent. If he lingered, he might meet her, speak with her, brush his hand against hers as he handed her his pen.

"Do you need a signature?" Hair Mop asked.

"No, we're good." He placed the box on Claire's desk beside the folded newspaper.

The detective leaned back in his chair and eyed the clipboard. "I thought everything was digital these days?"

The killer swallowed. This detective was more observant than the other officers. "Our servers are down, so we're back to the Stone Age."

Hair Mop chuckled and turned back to his screen. This was easy. Too easy. Carmine Hannover smiled at him from the newspaper on the desk. A giddy sense of power energized him. He'd put her face on the front page. He controlled what people thought and what they talked about. They feared him. *The Newburgh Slasher.* He liked the name. What else had they written about him?

With one eye on the detective, he unfolded the newspaper. A second photo showed Claire Wolfe. He'd done that, too. The article mentioned the message he'd left for Claire on Carmine's body. *Finally*. The plan was coming together.

The reporter had interviewed Victoria McAdams, too. He smiled to himself. Now there was a familiar name. But when he read further, his excitement flagged. They were getting it all wrong. They accused Claire of involvement in Carmine's death and called for the police to investigate her. Anger flared in his core. He'd wanted the media to connect him with Claire, but how dare they implicate her in the murder. Hannover's death was his creation, not hers! Their amateur guesswork was jeopardizing the plan.

"Anything else?" Hair Mop asked.

The killer dropped the newspaper on the desk. He'd lingered too long.

"Nope. I'm done here."

He flashed a smile and hurried toward the exit, a new purpose animating his body. He'd speed things up. The article had forced his hand. He'd correct the paper's false portrayal of events. Victoria McAdams had spoken against Claire, and she'd pay the price.

CHAPTER 36

"Can we sue them?" Captain Washington asked Chief Emmerso. "They've accused us of complicity in a homicide."

Claire wished she could sink into the chair and disappear. He'd said "us," but every officer in the captain's room that morning knew he meant "her." They had all read the newspaper article's theory about Claire. As far as *The Herald* was concerned, Claire Wolfe was Public Enemy Number One.

She could thank Victoria McAdams for that. McAdams didn't know Claire. They had never even met. But that didn't stop her from dragging Claire's name through the mud. Once again, total strangers had assassinated Claire's character, and she felt sick to her stomach.

Chief Emmerso answered from his usual perch by the wall. "The wording is vague. I don't think even *The Herald* knows what, exactly, they're claiming. And even if we had the budget for a libel case, what would a lawsuit accomplish?"

"They'd think twice before pointing fingers."

Detective Gomez raised his hand. "And a lawsuit could

generate revenue for the department. McAdams is loaded, and we could do with another coffee machine."

Nakamura snickered. Gomez's jokes were improving, but Claire found no humor in her predicament.

"The First Amendment protects our right to spout nonsense," Emmerso said, "and Sergeant Wolfe is a public figure. Fighting the media will only reinforce their claims. We're better off ignoring them."

Claire spoke up for the first time at that meeting. "Sir, maybe I should step away from the case, for the sake of appearances. We need to be above suspicion."

"Sergeant Wolfe, I appreciate your willingness to take one for the team, but this isn't the time to give in to media pressure."

"Sir, considering my history—"

Emmerso cut her short. "All the more reason to set the record straight. If we pull you from the case, we'll give credence to their accusations. Don't let *The Herald* get to you. The best way to prove them wrong is to solve the case."

Claire nodded. Emmerso was no fool. The media-induced panic reflected badly on the department, and he was probably under immense pressure from Mayor Thornton to sacrifice her on the altar of public opinion. But if he had the guts to shield her, she could at least cooperate.

Captain Washington got back to business. "Sergeant, I understand you met with Sarah Malik last night."

"She and Carmine were close friends, but she claims she only saw her last week. Her alibi holds for the evening Carmine was attacked. Malik was in a campaign meeting with her PA, Alexandro Menendez, and an outside consultant."

Washington grunted, unimpressed. "Politicians like Malik let other people do their dirty work. Did she have a fallout with Carmine?"

Claire's gut itched again. "There's no sign of bad blood between them. Malik claims she knew nothing of any financial troubles. But she's hiding something."

"Course she is," Gomez said. "She's a politician."

The detective drew Captain Washington's fire. "What's our friend Barry Cook up to?"

"He's minding Carmine's store. And his golf handicap has improved."

This time, Washington did seem impressed. "I didn't peg him as a golfer."

Gomez shrugged. "Hang out with the rich and famous long enough and their lifestyle rubs off."

"What about the prints on those newspaper clippings at Carmine's house?"

"Most of the prints are Carmine's. There's a second set we couldn't match."

Washington sighed. "To sum up, Carmine Hannover had an unhealthy obsession with Sergeant Wolfe, and the killer wrote her name at the scene. Coincidence? Maybe. The murder was no robbery gone wrong. Carmine didn't get along with her parents, but she had no known enemies. Everything else is murky. The mysterious M she met that night might be Malik or it might be misinformation planted by her PA. We have no motive, no murder weapon, no camera footage, and zero useful trace evidence. Anything to add?"

The room fell silent. Claire had raised the possibility of a serial killer before. Since then, she'd discovered a striking similarity between Carmine's death and the prostitute murders in Albany. But despite *The Herald*'s enthusiasm for serial killers, the change of victim profile meant the homicides were unrelated. The investigation had run out of leads.

Captain Washington gazed at Chief Emmerso, who nodded

meaningfully. They had coordinated their next move. *What were they planning?*

Washington's eyelids drooped with displeasure. "We're still assuming we have a regular homicide on our hands. But seeing that the city is fixated on serial killers, we've asked the FBI to assist."

The tension in the room eased. Reinforcements were on the way.

The captain continued. "Dr. Sally Fleischer, a forensic psychiatrist with the FBI's Behavioral Analysis Unit, is here already. Sergeant Wolfe worked with her on the Middle School Strangler case. We've asked her to review the files for the Hannover homicide, too. Let's hope she'll have some new ideas." He waggled a finger at the investigators. "This isn't a signal for you to slack off. This is still our homicide investigation, and I expect us to solve this before Dr. Fleischer can say Ted Bundy. Gomez, you still owe me answers about the DNA and bank transfers."

"I'm still on it," Gomez said.

"Good. Go through that camera footage again with a fine-tooth comb. The killer got there somehow. Nakamura, learn The Barnett Inn guest list by heart. Look for patterns. Sniff around. Speak to people. Somebody must've seen or heard something." He glanced at Claire. "Sergeant Wolfe, you'll liaise with the forensic psychiatrist. She's set up shop in the main conference room. Let's hope she finds an ace up our sleeve."

"Yes, sir."

Claire left the office. When she cut through the squad room to visit Dr. Fleischer, Mahoney called her name.

"Hey, Sergeant Wolfe! You've got a secret admirer."

She stopped in her tracks. A white box had materialized on her desk, tied with a red ribbon. Had Rob sent a gift to cheer her up?

Gomez smirked. "If it's chocolate, you know the rules, Sarge. Sharing is caring."

"Forget chocolate," Mahoney said. "I bet it's something kinky. Agent Cline seems the type to me."

Claire's face burned. If Rob had sent lingerie to her work desk, she'd mail a set of Carmine Hannover's designer boobs to his office in Quantico. That'd teach him.

"C'mon, open it already. The suspense is killing me."

Claire gave in to peer pressure and walked over to her desk. There was no card with the gift. She lifted the box into the air. The package was cool to the touch...and heavy. She gave the box a shake, and something shifted inside.

Nakamura laughed nervously. "Let us know if it ticks so we can clear the room."

The detectives ignored the warning and gathered around her. Claire untied the ribbon and removed the lid. And the smile dropped from her face.

Mahoney swore. Gomez groaned.

"Oh, man!" Nakamura said. "I think I'm gonna puke."

CHAPTER 37

"It still doesn't seem real," Mrs. Jean Evans said. Her hand shook as she poured two glasses of lemonade for her guests. She didn't entertain FBI agents in her home every day.

"That's understandable," Rob said. He rarely met with the mother of a serial killer either.

The BAU had developed its serial killer profiling system in the seventies by interviewing the killers in prison. But as far as he knew, the Bureau had never undertaken a systematic study of the killers' family members. The house in Springfield was a typical middle-class suburban home. Despite their homey surroundings, he hoped Lisa Evans's mother would provide critical insights into William Wolfe's murderous pack.

Mrs. Evans handed Rob and Jess their drinks. "I don't mean her death. That devastated us." Her emerald eyes narrowed at the painful memories. "But the things they said she did... That wasn't the Lisa we knew. She wouldn't hurt a soul."

Rob gave Jess a meaningful glance. On the drive there, he'd explained that Lisa's childhood might provide the key to unraveling her later behavior. Was she a willing accomplice in the killings—just as cruel and bloodthirsty as William Wolfe—or had she fallen under the spell of the older man and committed crimes that ran against her nature?

Jess had asked what to look for, and Rob had rattled off the list of a serial killer's typical early childhood experiences: a distant and critical mother; an absentee father; social isolation; and cruelty to animals and peers. The big red flags included arson, promiscuity, and early exposure to sexual abuse. This was their opportunity to learn about Lisa's formative years.

"How was Lisa as a child?"

"She was...normal. Her grades were better than average. She wasn't popular, but she had a few close friends."

"Do you remember any unusual incidents during her teenage years? Did she ever get into trouble with other children or injure them?"

"No, nothing like that. She had a gentle nature."

"Did she have any pets?"

"Only Dotty, a Dalmatian. She died five years ago. Lisa was very attached to her."

"How did Dotty die?"

"Peacefully in her sleep. Old age."

"What about boyfriends?"

Mrs. Evans tittered. "She was in no danger of a shotgun marriage if that's what you mean. She was shy around boys. Maybe she had a boyfriend but nothing intense."

Jess glanced at Rob. According to the mother, Lisa Evans matched none of the criteria. How had William Wolfe ensnared her in his murderous web?

Mrs. Evans looked from Rob to Jess, her eyes full of hurt and confusion. "What did we do wrong?"

"Mrs. Evans, where is your husband?"

"At work. Ryan runs an accounting practice in the city."

"Does he know we're here?"

"I told him. He didn't want to join us. This whole story

broke his heart. We were both very close to Lisa until a year ago."

"What happened?"

"She finished her teaching degree and left home."

"If she was so close to you both, why did she leave town?"

"That surprised us, too. It all happened so suddenly. She found a job at a school in California and had to start right away. She didn't even say goodbye, which was highly unusual. We never saw her again."

She shook her head and laughed dryly. "*California!* We'd always joked she'd land up in Florida someday. But California? We didn't see that coming."

"She never came home to visit?"

"No. She emailed us a few times to say she was doing well. We were happy for her."

"When did she last make contact?"

"Let's see. Her last email was August last year, I think."

"She never called?"

"Never."

"Did you call her?"

"We tried a few times, but her number was disconnected. She must have gotten a new phone number from a local carrier. Then, when the police called, we learned that all this time she'd been living only a few miles away in Newburgh. She'd lied to us all along."

Rob and Jess exchanged another glance. Not only did Lisa Evans's childhood not match that of a serial killer, but her sudden disappearance and erratic behavior also drew large question marks over their assumptions about the pack. Dr. Fleischer's guidance had paid off in spades, and Rob had a new hunch that needed testing.

He leaned forward on his chair. "Mrs. Evans, was Lisa buried or cremated?"

"Buried, here in Springfield."

"Did you see her body?"

Mrs. Evans shook her head. "The funeral home suggested a closed-casket ceremony. Considering the circumstances of her death, Ryan and I didn't want to see her again."

Rob scanned the living room for hints of their daughter and found none. "Do you have any photos of Lisa?"

The mother reached for a brown envelope on the table. "I thought you'd want to see this. Ryan threw out the framed pictures we had of her in the house, but I saved one from when she was young.

She handed Rob and Jess a photograph. "That's how I like to remember her. Our gentle little Lisa, long before she did those terrible things."

The teenager stood between her parents, their arms interlocking, a rosy smile spreading over her rounded cheeks. Rob had seen Lisa Evans's corpse, and he'd reviewed the case files for the Middle School Murders with Jess ahead of their visit.

The Lisa Evans he knew was a beautiful blonde with blue eyes and shoulder-length hair. The girl in the photo had long black tresses and green eyes like her mother. Jess shot him a quick, alarmed look. The girl was not William Wolfe's accomplice.

Rob held Jess's gaze but said nothing. "May I take a photo of this?"

"Sure."

Rob snapped a photo of the image with his phone.

"Do you still have Lisa's old things—a hairbrush?"

The mother gaped in confusion, so he explained.

"A strand of Lisa's hair might help our investigation." Rob held his breath while Mrs. Evans processed the question. The woman the Evans parents had buried was not their daughter. Rob had a theory about what had happened to their daughter, but he'd need a sample of her DNA to confirm his theory.

"I'm sorry, but Ryan cleared out all of Lisa's things soon after the funeral. As I said, she broke our hearts."

Rob sighed. "I see."

He had no DNA sample to match with that of the murderer. His theory would remain just that—a theory. The photo of a teenage Lisa was helpful but inconclusive. Lisa might have dyed her hair and had cosmetic surgery. And exhuming their daughter in Springfield on a hunch would be a bureaucratic nightmare.

Rob got to his feet. "Thank you for your time, Mrs. Evans."

"One more question," Jess said.

Rob sat again. Had Jess thought of another angle?

"Mrs. Evans, you said you'd thought Lisa would land up in Florida."

"Yes, it was a running joke for years."

"How did that joke start?"

Rob gave Jess a quizzical look, but she focused on the mother. *Where is she going with this?*

"That's simple. Lisa was born with a birthmark shaped like the state of Florida."

"And where was this birthmark?"

"On her right thigh."

"I see. Thank you." Jess got to her feet.

What was that about? Rob handed Mrs. Evans his business card, and they left the house.

He led Jess to the Bureau car. "Her daughter didn't kill those girls. William Wolfe's accomplice stole her identity."

Jess nodded, a knowing smile spreading over her lips. She'd come to the same conclusion.

Rob got into the driver's seat. "We need to locate the real Lisa Evans. I doubt she made her way to California."

Jess remained silent. Her mysterious smile was driving him nuts.

"What?"

Jess beamed at him. "You're right. She didn't land up in California."

For once, Jess was one step ahead of him, and she savored the moment by keeping him in suspense.

"And how can you be so sure?"

Jess shrugged as though the answer was obvious. "Because I've already found her."

CHAPTER 38

Ten minutes later, Claire sat in Captain Washington's office, her stomach churning with disgust.

Detective Gomez looked a green around the gills. "What a sick, sick bastard."

"You got that right," Captain Washington said. The gift box sat on his desk, the lid firmly in place. The detectives eyed the object with concern like queasy travelers. "I wish I could erase that image from my mind."

"Yeah," Gomez said. "I'll be celibate for life after this."

Detective Nakamura managed a weak chuckle. "That's the status quo for you."

Claire shared their sense of revulsion. Inside the box, on a bed of ice cubes, a pair of shapely human breasts had stared at her.

"I'm assuming those belong to Carmine Hannover," Washington said.

He turned to Mahoney in disbelief. "The psycho just walked in and dropped them on her desk?"

Mahoney gave them a sheepish grin. "Pretty much."

"And then he just walked out?"

"Not right away. We had a little chat."

"Geez! He has balls of steel, I'll give him that. What did he look like?"

"Mustache. Glasses. Peaked cap. UPS uniform from head to toe."

"Get me an identikit right away."

"Yes, sir." Mahoney fled the room and its box of horrors.

Washington glanced at the remaining detectives. "The perp cleaned up the murder scene well. He's no amateur. We can assume he came here in disguise and Mahoney's identikit will be worthless. Gomez, check the CCTV footage. Maybe he has a thing for limited-edition sneakers we can use to track him down."

"Yes, sir."

Nakamura said, "Why would he risk coming here?"

"Delivery services leave a paper trail."

"Yeah, but he could have delivered his...gift to Claire's home."

Claire weighed the question in silence. Did the killer know Diane had kicked her out? Was that why he'd tried her at work? She shuddered. How long had he been following her?

Gomez said, "Because he's a sicko, that's why. And he's giving us all the finger."

Two knocks sounded, and the door opened. Chief Emmerso entered, trailed by Dr. Sally Fleischer.

"Gentlemen, this is Dr. Sally Fleischer of the BAU. Dr. Fleischer, this is Captain Washington and Detective Gomez. You already know the others." Sally nodded at Claire and Nakamura. ""

"Thank you for joining us," Captain Washington said. "You arrived just in time."

"I hope I can help. I've reviewed the files for the Hannover homicide. What's this recent development?"

The captain pointed at the box on his desk. "The perp delivered this to Sergeant Wolfe's desk an hour ago. I won't ask you to look inside but—"

"The breasts?" Sally said.

Captain Washington blinked at her. "Yes."

A glimmer of hope warmed Claire's core. With the talented forensic psychiatrist on their side, they'd make sense of the crime in no time.

"What does this mean, Doctor?"

Sally raised an eyebrow. "The unsub doesn't lack confidence, for starters."

Nakamura chuckled.

"Excuse my ignorance, Doc," Gomez said. "The *unsub*."

"Unknown subject. That's how we refer to the unidentified serial killers at the BAU."

"Yeah, but this isn't a serial killer. He's only killed once."

"I doubt that. He planned the murder ahead of time and left no forensic traces at the crime scene. He's what we'd call an organized killer. Binding the victim, the shallow stab wounds, and the mutilation are consistent with a Hedonist/Lust or Power/Control serial killer. The lengthy amount of time he spent at the scene is a sign of confidence. He's likely killed before."

"You said he's a Lust killer. But the scene showed no sign of rape."

"The unsub might derive sexual gratification from torturing his victim. Sexual intercourse isn't always necessary, especially if the Power/Control motivation is dominant."

"What about the writing on the corpse and the breasts," Washington said, "Are those threats?"

"I don't think so. If he wanted to attack Sergeant Wolfe, he would have. The writing and the breasts both serve a different function. He's stalking her."

Claire's skin crawled. For days, she'd sensed malevolent eyes watching her from the shadows, and now Sally had vindicated her suspicions. *She had a stalker.* But this Peeping Tom was also a serial killer. Why was this happening to her?

"I don't understand," Washington said. "If he's stalking her, why isn't she in danger?"

"Stalkers don't want to hurt their targets. They desire a relationship."

Gomez scoffed. "This is his idea of foreplay?"

"In a sense. He wants to get Claire's attention by doing something...exceptional. There's a well-known example. John Hinckley Jr. shot President Reagan to impress an actress, Jodie Foster. He almost killed him. Our unsub wants Sergeant Wolfe to respect him, to treat him as an equal, someone worthy of her attention and admiration."

Claire spoke up. "But why did he think killing Carmine Hannover would impress me?"

"What's your connection to her?"

"Nothing. I'd never heard about her until her death. But she'd taken an interest in me. In her home, we found a file of photos and newspaper clippings about me and the Middle School Murders."

"Was the killer in Carmine's home?"

"Not that we can tell. We found no sign of forced entry."

Sally chewed her lip. "You're a public figure. The file might not be significant."

Captain Washington said, "Or the whole stalker theory might be wrong?"

Sally didn't flinch. "Maybe. Nothing in Newburgh is ever what it seems."

"Gomez, get elimination prints from the PA, Barry Cook. He had access to Hannover's home. I bet he knows about the files and the second set of prints belongs to him. Maybe he used

Claire's name to throw us off his track? And check if he fits Mahoney's identikit of the UPS guy."

"Yes, sir."

Nakamura cleared his throat. "There's another connection between the victim and Sergeant Wolfe. Carmine Hannover was a close friend of Kitty Tucker."

Sally said, "The woman the sniper killed last year?"

"The same. Now another friend of the two women, Victoria McAdams, is spreading a conspiracy theory that Sergeant Wolfe killed her friends." Nakamura's eyes widened with a sudden idea. "For all we know, McAdams had Carmine murdered and is working with the UPS guy to frame Sergeant Wolfe."

"Does McAdams have a motive for killing Carmine Hannover?"

"Not as far as we know. Her grief seemed genuine."

"Then the stalker hypothesis might be the simpler explanation. The news reports of a rogue cop lured him to Newburgh. If he believes the same conspiracy theory as McAdams, he might see Sergeant Wolfe as a celebrity murderer and a kindred spirit. To gain her attention, he's continuing what she started and going after Kitty's friends."

Claire folded her arms and hugged her body. She'd become a magnet for homicidal creeps. This was the Middle School Strangler all over again.

"What?" Gomez blurted, angry and confused. "You're saying this guy killed Carmine Hannover to get into Sergeant Wolfe's good books? No offense, Sergeant."

"None taken."

"Sorry, Doc, but that makes no sense."

"Congratulations, Detective Gomez," Dr. Fleischer said. "You're not a psychopath."

"That's a relief," Nakamura said. "I had my doubts about him."

"Psychopathic thought patterns are difficult to understand but easy to test." Sally grinned playfully. "Thank you for volunteering, Detective Gomez."

Gomez paled and seemed to realize he'd become the psychiatrist's lab rat. "Volunteering for what?"

"Here's a quick test for sociopathic thinking. Consider the following scenario. A young woman loses her father. At the funeral, she meets the love of her life. The next day, she murders her sister. Why?"

The detectives looked at each other in confusion.

Gomez chewed his lip. "She thought the stranger liked her sister. She was jealous."

"Nope. All the facts you need are in the story. There's no missing information."

Nakamura tried his luck. "She blamed her sister for her father's death?"

"Wrong again. Any other ideas?"

A warm flush spread over Claire's cheeks. The answer had come to her easily. What did that say about her thought patterns?

"OK, we give up," Washington said.

Sally turned to Claire. "Sergeant Wolfe, you've dealt with psychopaths before. Want to give it a go?"

Claire swallowed hard. Sally had sensed she knew the answer. But what would her coworkers think of her if she got it right?

"She wanted to meet the man again. At her sister's funeral."

Nakamura and Gomez frowned. Then, understanding bloomed in their eyes.

Sally grinned. "Remove your moral restraints and voilà. You too can think like a psychopath."

"I would never have guessed that," Nakamura said.

"That's why I'm here."

Captain Washington redirected the discussion to their case. "Let me get this straight. By killing Carmine Hannover and delivering her breasts to Sergeant Wolfe, the killer was acting like a cat bringing a dead mouse home to its owner?"

"That's one way of putting it."

Washington raised his eyebrows and sucked in a deep breath. Clearly, he placed little faith in the psychiatrist's new angle.

"So how does this help us catch him?"

"He'll try to impress her again. Each time, he'll risk exposing himself." She nodded toward the white box. "Maybe he screwed up already. You'll want to test that box for finger-prints and trace DNA. Sergeant Wolfe, has he contacted you directly?"

"No."

"He will. I'm surprised he hasn't already. Make sure your contact details are readily available online. Set up a new email account and phone number you can monitor easily. Publish them on the department website. Mention them to the press. He won't be able to resist."

Gomez said, "If this guy's in love with Sergeant Wolfe, maybe she can get him to turn himself in?"

"He won't fall for that. But he'll watch her compulsively. I'd post plainclothes officers on Sergeant Wolfe's street. They might get lucky."

Claire's pulse accelerated. She didn't want the department to learn that her mother had kicked her out of the house and she'd shacked up in Rob's motel room. There must be another way.

"I doubt he'll risk that," Claire said. "After today, he'll expect me to be under surveillance. He'll keep his distance.

The gift box might be a diversion. Maybe he wants us to focus on me?"

Sally considered Claire with her dark, mesmerizing eyes. Could she read Claire's thoughts?

"That's possible," she conceded. "He might use this opportunity to kill Kitty Tucker's other friends. What was the name of the conspiracy theorist?"

"Victoria McAdams."

"You'll want to put her under police protection, too. But be discreet. He's probably surveilling her right now. We need to catch him in the act."

"Nakamura," Washington said. "You interviewed McAdams earlier. Make sure she stays put until we send reinforcements."

"Yes, sir." Nakamura got busy on his mobile phone.

"The profile for a Power/Control killer can be useful here, too," Sally said. "The unsub is most likely a white male in his mid-twenties to late thirties. He might have a wife and kids and a stable job. But he leads a double life. Beneath the superficial charm, he's sly and deceptive. Once he's gained access to his victim, Dr. Jekyll turns into Mr. Hyde and he shows no mercy. I'll try to track down his other victims."

"If there are any," Washington said. "We don't want to add fuel to the media's serial killer scare."

"Of course not."

"Good. OK, everybody. Back to work."

On the way out, Claire touched Sally's arm. "It's good to have you back."

"Thanks. I hope I'll be more helpful this time."

Claire lowered her voice. "I might have a lead on his earlier murders. But it's not clear-cut."

"It never is. Let's talk."

"Holy crap," Nakamura said. He stood in the middle of the squad room, staring at his mobile phone. "Sergeant Wolfe, I think I found the source of Victoria McAdams's conspiracy theory."

He handed her his phone. One glance was enough to send another shudder down Claire's spine.

Detective Gomez looked over her shoulder at the screen and chuckled. "Congratulations, Sarge. You've got a fan club."

CHAPTER 39

Sweat soaked Diane's gym shirt that afternoon. Her legs burned, and her brain still throbbed. But no matter how fast she pedaled, the exercise bike never moved an inch. That was the story of her life.

She'd felt like death when she woke up an hour ago. The mother of all hangovers pounded her temples. But far worse than the headache was the cocktail of nauseating memories, and Diane wished she'd blacked out. She'd danced on a table in The Red Keg and flashed her breasts at a roomful of strangers.

"Get your hands off me!" she'd yelled at the black police officer who'd asked her to leave the bar. "My daughter is a cop!"

But while she'd sat in the back of the squad car, Diane had recalled burning that bridge. She'd kicked her daughter out of her home for the crime of cleaning up her alcoholic mother. And without Claire around, Diane's self-restraint had turned to dust. Sitting on the floor of a jail cell that reeked of pee and vomit, she'd had a revelation. No amount of money could solve her problems. She had to change.

And then, in her darkest hour, the angels sent her a miracle.

The jail door opened, and her daughter held out her hand. Without a word of reproach, Claire had bailed her out and took her home. Too ashamed to even speak, Diane obeyed her daughter's directions. She'd stripped, climbed into the bathtub, and let Claire hose her down. Dry and in a clean set of pajamas, Diane had passed out the moment her head touched the soft pillow.

In the morning, a burning sense of shame pulled her out of bed and dragged her downstairs. Claire had left already. Diane had wanted to thank her daughter for coming to the police station in the middle of the night to save her. But a part of her was glad she didn't have to face her. She flushed with self-loathing at that undeserved kindness. After last night, Claire would probably never want to see her again. And neither would Frank.

Diane had stared at her reflection in the bathroom mirror and slapped her face. "You better shape up, Diane. Next time, you won't land up in jail—you'll die."

A new resolve had flowered in her throbbing head. She'd freshened up, ate a light breakfast, dumped her secret stash of wine and beer in the trash, and hit the gym. Ignoring the pain —no, *savoring* the pain—she spun the pedals with all her might. She imagined the alcohol seeping out of her pores along with her sweat. Maybe her stupidity would seep out, too.

"Diane!" The man's voice rang with amused surprise. "I'm glad to see you're back on your feet already."

Frank stood beside her exercise bike. He wore a different peaked cap but the same cowboy smile. Diane didn't want him to see her like this—hungover and drenched in sweat. She looked repulsive.

"It's me—Frank. We met last night at The Red Keg."

Diane wanted to hide her face in shame. "Yes, I remember. I'm so sorry about last night."

"Are you kidding me? You were great! I should apologize to you. I had no idea somebody called the cops."

"Well, if I hadn't taken my shirt off..."

He chuckled. "Never mind that. You're a wonderful singer."

"You're...very kind."

"Sing for us again."

She gave him a cynical glance.

"I'm serious. Tina Turner never sounded so good."

"Thank you, but I don't think that's a good idea. And after last night, the owners won't let me near the place."

"Well, you're wrong. I should know. I'm the owner."

"You own The Red Keg?"

"Yes, ma'am, and I'm officially inviting you back. We used to do live music events years ago. Had a band and everything. We're not Vegas, but we put on a good show. What do you say?"

A hot flush burned her cheeks. "Oh. I don't know."

"Is that a yes?"

Was he serious? Through the fog of shame and regret, the thrill of the stage flared. "Maybe."

"It's a deal—you're on Monday night."

"Thank you for the offer, Frank, but I don't think anybody will show up."

"Are you kidding me?" He flashed his mischievous cowboy grin. "After last night? You bet they will!"

CHAPTER 40

April took a long drag on her cigarette and passed it to Johnny. "You don't talk much, do you?"

The sun set over the lake to the croaking of a hundred frogs. April had spread her picnic blanket on a secluded hill with a magnificent view.

Johnny put the cigarette to his lips and shook his head. They both laughed.

He enjoyed spending time with her. Over the past week, they'd gone to a movie and strolled together in the park. She did most of the talking. Correction—all the talking.

Being with her felt great...and strange. In her presence, he became someone else, someone fun and good. Johnny had wanted to speak his mind. But he knew that if he did, April would realize he didn't measure up to the man she imagined. She'd reject him, and he'd never see her again.

April stubbed out the cigarette and shifted closer. Her body warmed his shoulder, and a thrill passed through him. They had touched before—fingers brushing as they'd walked—and he'd sensed she wanted more. Johnny had stolen a condom from Mom's bedside *drawer that morning and shoved it in the back pocket of his jeans, hoping to get lucky. He'd slipped a few other items into his pockets, just in case. April's physical closeness injected him with confidence. Tonight, his life would change.*

She leaned her head on his shoulder and placed her hand on his thigh. Then, she closed her eyes and pressed her lips to his. The kiss was warm and wet. Her nose ring tickled his skin, but he didn't care. He closed his eyes, too. With the frogs cheering him on, he reached under her shirt. She didn't brush his hands away. She wanted him! Her breasts were smaller than Emily's, but they were real and soft above the edge of her bra. April rose to her knees, and he followed her. He struggled with the clasp at her back but couldn't unfasten her bra. Why did he make a mess of everything?

But it didn't matter. April pulled her shirt and bra over her head. Johnny gazed at her breasts, then took his shirt off, too. She ran her fingers over his smooth chest, and before he could stop her, she slipped her hand into his jeans.

The spell broke. April leaned back as though he'd poured a bucket of cold water on her head. Even in the soft light, he saw the disappointment in her eyes.

"Is...everything OK?"

"Yeah. Just a second."

Johnny never had trouble getting an erection. His fantasies aroused him without fail. He closed his eyes and imagined she was Emily—bare-chested and ready for him. Nothing happened downstairs. What was wrong with him?

April reached for her shirt. "It's OK. We don't have to—"

"Wait! I've got an idea."

He shoved his hand into his pocket and retrieved the other items.

April raised an eyebrow at the zip ties. "Seriously?"

"You like this kind of stuff, don't you?"

"Um. OK." She giggled nervously and held out her hands.

"Behind your back."

He shuffled on his knees and looped the cable around her wrists. His flesh stirred in his pants. Yes! This was better. He was calling the shots.

"Ow! That's too tight."

"Now your legs." He was playing out his fantasy, step by step. If they stopped, he'd lose his momentum. "Here, I'll help you." He eased her backward onto her elbows. "That's it. Lie flat on the ground."

"I can't, Silly. You tied my hands behind my back."

Johnny hadn't taken that into account. He'd have to adjust his fantasy. "Never mind."

He unbuttoned her jeans and peeled them off along with her panties. There she was. He had a naked woman all to himself.

"I brought protection," she said.

"Me, too."

April seemed to relax. She stared at his swollen crotch and grinned. "Now it's your turn."

Johnny touched his belt, then stopped. He was so close to fulfilling his fantasy. If he deviated from the script now, he'd go limp.

She spread her legs to encourage him. "I want you, Johnny."

No. He was the boss. He told her what to do.

"Put your legs together."

"How are we going to—?"

"Just...trust me."

She closed her legs. He grabbed another cable tie and bound her ankles.

"Hey, not so rough. What's our safe word?"

Johnny faced away from her, his heartbeat racing. He unwrapped the strip of duct tape he'd folded into his pocket, then spun around and covered her mouth.

April stared at him, her face a mask of shock...and fear. Yes! This is what Emily deserved. Suffer, bitch! *Johnny wasn't a nobody. He held her life in his hands. He didn't want to sleep with her anymore. Hurting her was better than sex.*

With the frogs baying for blood in his ears, Johnny drew the utility knife from his pocket and extended the blade. And April screamed.

CHAPTER 41

"So, you're with the FBI, huh?"

The gangly medical examiner's assistant stared at Rob doubtfully. Daryl Holt was far creepier than the dead bodies on the dissection tables of the county morgue. But the unsettling encounter was a small price to pay if the visit would ease the conscience of two bereaved parents and help identify a killer.

Daryl leaned on a metal gurney, which drifted away and almost floored the assistant. This young man needed to spend more time in sunlight and less in the company of corpses. But the awkward posturing had little to do with Rob and everything to do with the pretty blonde detective at his side.

Jess answered for him. "Special Agent Cline is with the Behavioral Analysis Unit."

Daryl snapped his fingers at Rob. "The serial killer guys. The mind hunters." He was referring to a popular Netflix series based on the agents who had pioneered the psychological study of "stranger killers" in the seventies.

Rob nodded. "That's us."

"Awesome!" The assistant's eyes widened with awe, and he

shot jealous glances at the two visitors. Did he think Rob had stolen Jess from him?

"Ig—um, Daryl," Jess said. "We need to examine one of the ranch house corpses."

"Which one? We have gunshot wounds, mutilations, decapitations—you name it!" He sounded like a waiter reciting the specials of the day.

"The decapitated female."

Daryl winked at Jess and threw in a knowing smile. "You've got a soft spot for her, haven't you? Coming right up."

While he sauntered off to find the corpse, Rob and Jess exchanged amused looks.

Jess leaned closer to Rob and whispered, "I almost called him Igor."

Rob snorted. "Frankenstein's assistant?"

Jess stifled a giggle. "I can't help it."

The nickname was spot on.

"All he needs is a hunchback."

"Give him time."

Despite the weird antics, Rob pitied the assistant. "I hope you're right about this. The Evans parents could use some good news."

Rob wasn't sure this qualified as good news. Good news would be the return of their sweet daughter, alive and well. But Lisa Evans's parents would have to settle for the knowledge that they hadn't raised a psychopathic child-murderer. Everything depended on what Igor had to show them today.

Wheels squeaked as Daryl pushed a gurney toward them, the sound effects complementing his "mad scientist assistant" performance.

"Here you go!" He unzipped the black body bag. "One female, sans head, hands, and feet."

Jess pulled back the plastic body bag to expose the

deceased woman's right thigh. *Bingo.* Rob photographed the patch of wrinkled skin with his phone. Despite the effects of decomposition, the dark-purple birthmark stood out clearly—a port-wine stain shaped like the state of Florida.

"Thanks," he told Daryl. "You've been a great help."

The assistant shrugged and returned the body to cold storage.

"It's her," Rob told Jess. "That's Lisa Evans. Good job."

Jess beamed at him. "Then who did her parents bury?"

"That's what we have to find out. We'll need to exhume the killer's body and hope the fingerprints, dental records, or DNA find a match."

Jess's shoulders sank at the mention of another exhumation. "That sounds like a lot of red tape."

"Not with the parents' support, which I'm sure they'll provide once they know this will clear their daughter's name." He reached for his phone again. "I'll tell Dr. Fleischer."

They stepped out of the morgue and into the afternoon sunlight and fresh air.

"You were right," he told Dr. Fleischer when she answered the call. "Evans is the key. Wolfe's accomplice used a false identity. The real Lisa Evans is the decapitated woman from the ranch house. Jess identified her using a birthmark."

"Good. We'll need to exhume the accomplice and follow the trail."

"We're on it. Any progress with your analysis?"

"Not much. Chief Emmerso commandeered me to work on the Hannover homicide."

The news jolted Rob. That was Claire's case. Last night, she'd asked him questions about serial killers, and today the department had co-opted Dr. Fleischer to examine their case. "Another serial killer?"

"Captain Washington doesn't like to use the S-word. PR issues."

Rob grunted. "It's election season."

"Yeah. And it seems Claire has a stalker."

Rob took a moment to digest the news. "A stalker— Hannover's murderer?"

"It seems so. The unsub delivered Carmine Hannover's breasts to her desk."

"I'll be right over." He hung up. "Jess, I need to check on another case. Can you move this forward without me?"

Her lips parted in surprise and disappointment, but she recovered quickly. "Sure. I'll take my car once we get back to the department."

They marched to the Bureau car.

"Is everything OK?"

"Yeah." Rob got into the driver's seat and fastened his seat-belt. "Everything's fine." An ominous cramp in his abdomen disagreed. "For now."

CHAPTER 42

"Are these people for real?" Gomez said.

Claire had wondered the same thing. She and the other detectives had returned to Captain Washington's office, their gazes glued to their smartphones. A surreal sensation enveloped Claire as she browsed the website Nakamura had discovered. She'd stepped into an alternate universe—a universe that revolved around her.

KillerWolfe.com displayed photographs of the Middle School Strangler crime scenes, the victims, and their homes. But mostly, the website promoted images of Claire. The photos depicted Claire from every angle. The site runners had lifted media photos from news sites and snapped candid images of Claire in public without her knowledge. But the most visible images were Photoshop creations cobbled together, it seemed, by hormonal teenagers with an obsession with cleavage and graphic violence. The website had turned Claire's traumatic homicide case into a cottage industry that spawned merchandise and rambling articles claiming to expose a diabolical police cover-up.

"I want a T-shirt," Nakamura said.

"The anime one is nice," Gomez said.

"There's an anime shirt?" Claire asked.

"Yeah, check it out."

Gomez offered her his phone. The cartoon figure on the white T-shirt had Claire's face, a porn star's body, and a heavy-duty revolver aimed at the viewer. The word "bizarre" didn't do the image justice.

"This is crazy. Somebody, arrest these people."

"Yeah," Nakamura said. "The prices are criminal. They want forty bucks for a T-shirt!"

"That's not what I meant."

"You should at least get a royalty cut."

"Who'd buy this stuff?"

"The same people who buy art prints of violent films. If Tarantino can, why can't you?"

"I'm not in the entertainment industry."

"You are now," Gomez said. "Today everybody's a product, even criminals. Billy the Kid, Buffalo Bill."

"So, now I'm a criminal?"

Gomez backtracked quickly. "No. You're a hero. A dark hero. Or is that *heroine*?"

Claire rejected the positive spin. "They're saying I'm a rogue cop!"

"Newburgh PD did put out a BOLO for you."

Chief Emmerso cut in from his perch at the wall. "That was a mistake. But this website explains the conspiracy theories. I doubt Victoria McAdams is involved, but they're all pushing the same nonsense. Which reminds me—Nakamura, did you get hold of McAdams?"

"She's not answering her phone."

Captain Washington said, "Go there if you have to. If she disappears mysteriously, it'll only feed the crazies. Gomez, find out who operates this website. Our stalker might be the owner or a customer. Review their list of subscribers. I'm betting Barry Cook is a regular."

"Yes, sir."

"OK, enough Internet time. Let's take this sicko down."

The team dispersed, and Claire made for her desk. She requested a second Newburgh PD telephone number and email address from IT and installed a call recorder app on her phone.

Then, after a momentary hesitation, she browsed Killer-Wolfe.com on her computer. An entire community of strangers believed she was a cold-blooded murderer. They'd never let her forget her father's crimes. She'd send the website a cease and desist letter *after* they released their customer list. The conspiracy theorists might have encouraged her stalker. They could at least help Claire catch the killer.

"Sergeant Wolfe." Rob stood by her desk. Concern lined his face.

"Special Agent Cline, what brings you to our humble squad room."

At the station, she and Rob always used their formal titles, although the other detectives probably knew they were dating. The titles helped keep their relationship professional.

He pulled up a chair and lowered his voice. "I just heard about the stalker."

Claire put on a brave face. "Comes with the territory."

Rob didn't fall for her act. "Has he made contact?"

Claire told him about the writing on Carmine Hannover's corpse and the gift box containing the victim's breasts.

Rob swore under his breath. "Has the department arranged protection?"

"Unnecessary. Dr. Fleischer said I'm not in danger."

Rob didn't look so sure of that. "Did he make contact before this?"

"I'd have told you if he had."

"Tell me if he does. This doesn't feel right."

"That's the understatement of the year. How's your case going?" Claire didn't care to know the details of the ranch house victims, but she needed a change of subject.

"We've made progress. Lisa Evans isn't who we thought she was. She'd stolen that identity from one of the victims. We identified her using a birthmark. Jess made the connection."

Claire shot him a playful smile. "It sounds like you and Jess work well together."

"She's a talented detective."

Claire gave in to curiosity. "Who was William Wolfe's accomplice?"

"We're still working on that. We'll need to—"

Claire's mobile phone rang. The incoming call came from an unlisted number. Was her stalker reaching out to her as Sally had predicted?

"I should take this. It might be him."

With Rob watching her closely, she answered.

"Sergeant Wolfe?"

Claire relaxed. The male voice belonged to Edward Hannover.

"Mr. Hannover, how are you?" Claire raised her eyebrows at Rob. False alarm.

Sensing that Claire needed privacy, Rob waved goodbye and walked off. Had Hannover called to keep an eye on his hired gun, or did he have new information for her?

"As well as expected. The medical examiner's office is finally releasing Carmine's body."

"I'm glad to hear that."

For a moment, Edward Hannover was no longer a meddling billionaire but simply a bereaved father. In homicides, an autopsy often delayed burial, adding to the family's grief. This time, the ME had returned the victim's corpse quickly.

"We'll be conducting a private ceremony for Carmine at Hannover Estate on Tuesday. Cynthia and I would be grateful if you could join us—that is, if your attendance doesn't hamper your investigation."

There it was. Hannover had deftly turned the conversation to Claire's hunt for Carmine's killer. Was the invitation to the private funeral simply an excuse to keep tabs on Claire?

"Thank you, Mr. Hannover. I'd be honored to attend if I can."

Did the Hannovers expect her to have dispatched Carmine's murderer by then? Often, the victim's funeral was an opportunity to examine suspects and analyze the family's body language, but in this case, Claire would be glad to stay away.

Seeing that Claire had offered no information, Edward attacked the subject head-on. "How is the investigation progressing?"

"We're exploring every lead."

"Have you discovered who killed her?"

"We're getting closer."

Claire couldn't share the specifics of an ongoing homicide investigation with a citizen, even the parent of the victim. But she didn't point that out. A confrontation would only prompt the Hannovers to pull strings and, possibly, remove Claire from the case.

"Remember our agreement."

Claire rolled her eyes. Were the Hannovers patrons of KillerWolfe.com? That wouldn't surprise her. The website should add "contract killing" to the list of merchandise. Claire hadn't agreed to dispose of the murderer, but again she held her tongue. The less said, the better. Her new app was recording this call.

"Have a good day, sir."

She disconnected the call. Claire understood his need for justice. Tina's murder had aroused the same emotions in her. But her mental feelers detected a subtle vibration. Did the Hannovers' demand for a vigilante solution stem from a parent's impulse to avenge a daughter's death or a conspirator's desire to silence an accomplice?

"Got 'em," Gomez said.

"Who?"

"Your fan site. The domain belongs to a Peter Knowles. He didn't bother to hide his name or physical address. He lives downtown. It's as though he wanted us to find him. I'll send a squad car to pick him up."

"Wait."

His comment gave Claire an idea. The huckster might be her stalker. If they hauled him in for questioning, he might flee or raise his defenses. Was there a smarter way to lure him to the department building?

"Dr. Fleischer said the stalker craves my attention, right?"

Gomez shrugged. "Yeah."

Claire grinned. "Then let's give him what he wants."

CHAPTER 43

The alarm system was unarmed when Victoria McAdams arrived home. She always activated the alarm on her way out. She'd upgraded the system after Kitty's murder, and ever since Carmine's horrific death she checked the video console compulsively. Her two best friends were dead, and sure as hell, Victoria would not be next.

She reached into her handbag and closed her fingers around the cool, hard form of the Sig Sauer. The handgun had been Carmine's idea.

Carmine had teased her about her new home security system. "What's next, Vic—guns?"

Victoria had taken her friend's joke seriously. She'd bought the handgun and learned how to use it. *You're not laughing now, Carmine, are you?*

For years, Kitty Tucker had warned her friends about the corruption in Newburgh's police department. But she'd stopped short of revealing the source of her knowledge and carried that secret to the grave. Then, shortly before her death, Carmine had developed an obsession with Detective Claire Wolfe, the only person present during Kitty's murder.

Victoria still couldn't believe Carmine was gone. Her friend had been too confident—too indestructible—to end her life as a crime statistic. Victoria had no brown belt in karate like Carmine, but she had a healthy survival instinct. And now she possessed a gun.

As she stepped through the door of the garage and into the hall, anxiety filled her heart. Her parents had raised Victoria to speak her mind, but had she been wise to share her suspicions with the press? Thanks to the article in *The Newburgh Herald* that morning, Claire Wolfe knew Victoria was onto her. Had the dirty cop broken into her home to settle the score? So much for Victoria's survival instinct. She gripped the gun and prepared to use it.

"Miss McAdams?"

Victoria almost cried with relief. "Maria!" She shoved the gun back into her handbag. "You scared the bejesus out of me. I thought you'd left already."

Maria cast a worried glance at Victoria's bag. *Had she seen the gun?* "Sorry, Miss McAdams. I wanted to explain about the food."

Maria took off every other weekend to visit her ailing mother in New Mexico. Victoria covered the plane ticket. She was happy to help her longtime live-in housekeeper with the expense. But now she regretted letting Maria leave her alone in the house for the weekend.

Maria detailed the meals she'd prepared and frozen. To avoid starvation over the next two days, all Victoria had to do was toss a precooked Vegan dish in the microwave and press a button. Victoria was no culinary wizard, but she could operate the microwave. And there was no way she'd hang out in restaurants with a crazed killer after her.

Victoria thanked Maria and, as an afterthought, hugged her. "Goodbye, Maria."

"Goodbye, Miss McAdams." The housekeeper's raised eyebrows implied she feared more for her employer's sanity than her safety.

Victoria locked the front door after Maria left and poured herself a glass of dry red. *To Kitty Tucker.* Kitty had loved her wine.

Victoria's phone buzzed, and the screen displayed the caller's name. She'd stored Detective Nakamura's number on her phone, confident that with more evidence she'd convince him of Claire Wolfe's guilt. The detective had called her twice in the past thirty minutes, and Victoria had refused to answer. Did he want to vent his annoyance on her after reading the piece in *The Herald*? Was the detective in league with Claire Wolfe? Probably. Cops were notorious for closing ranks. But after her recent scare with her home alarm system, Victoria considered another possibility. Did the detective have new information that might impact her safety?

She answered. "Hello, Detective."

"Ms. McAdams, I was getting worried about you."

"Why—what's happened?"

He hadn't mentioned the article. "We believe you might be in danger."

Victoria sniggered at his incompetence. "That's what I've been telling you all along. I was wondering when you'd start taking me seriously."

"We take your safety very seriously. I'm sending a patrol officer to watch over your property."

A patrol officer? Victoria had just exposed a serial killer in the ranks of Newburgh's finest, and their solution was to send an officer to her home? No, thank you! For all she knew, she'd find Claire Wolfe on her doorstep.

"Why the sudden concern for my well-being?"

"We believe the article in *The Newburgh Herald* might have put you on the killer's radar."

There—he'd mentioned the paper. The detective's transparency was pathetic.

"Is this your idea of intimidation? Scare tactics? So I won't dare speak out again?"

"No, ma'am. We're doing everything possible to solve Ms. Hannover's murder. I can't go into the details of the investigation, but what you said might agitate the killer. We want to protect—"

"I don't think so, Detective. My good friend, Kitty Tucker, let one of your colleagues into her home, and I won't make the same mistake."

"Ma'am—"

"I don't need your protection. I've got a state-of-the-art alarm system and a private security company on call. I can take care of myself. Good evening, Detective."

She hung up. The nerve! Detective Nakamura had gotten one thing right. Victoria was in the killer's crosshairs now. Thankfully, she'd prepared her fortress ahead of time. She wouldn't leave home until this nightmare was over and Claire Wolfe was behind bars. Maria had cooked provisions for the weekend. And if the siege lasted longer, she'd order in. Thank goodness for online shopping.

Victoria selected a single-serving cashew and tofu casserole from the freezer and tossed the contents into the microwave. As the machine hummed, she downed another glass of red.

The microwave beeped. She opened the door, releasing a cloud of steam. Like an idiot, she touched the plate without oven mittens, burning her fingers.

The front gate buzzed. Victoria swore under her breath. Detective Nakamura had sent his foot soldier all the same.

She'd tell the officer to piss off and leave her alone or else... Or else what—she'd call the police?

She walked over to the security console and studied the camera feeds. Instead of a uniform, the man at the gate wore gray trousers and a white button-down shirt. He held a black duffel bag in one hand. His thick mustache and glasses fish-eyed comically on the screen. Had Nakamura sent a detective instead of a patrol officer?

"Who is it?"

"Jeffrey Reaver, from *The Boston Globe*. We spoke earlier about your story concerning the Newburgh Police Department."

Victoria had forgotten about him. The reporter had called, hoping to interview her and bring her story before the state-wide media.

"I'm sorry to show up here like this. But I'm leaving town in the morning, and people need to hear your story."

Victoria hesitated. Something about the man made her skin crawl. He didn't have a Bostonian accent. This was no cause for suspicion. Many people relocated for job opportunities, and *The Boston Globe*'s reputation extended beyond state lines.

The McAdams family had a controlling interest in *The Newburgh Herald*, but Victoria disliked news people. Reporters reminded her of scavenging creatures, and this Jeffrey Reaver was no exception. And what was with the bag? He didn't expect her to invite him to spend the night, did he?

She sighed. If she wanted the truth to reach a wider audi-ence, she'd have to suffer a few more scavengers. With all the security cameras around, he wouldn't try anything funny. She buzzed him in.

CHAPTER 44

L ater that night, Claire drove to her mother's home. Her neck ached. She'd had a long day, and tomorrow promised to be longer. Claire was in no mood for another confrontation with Diane, but she had no choice.

She parked outside, walked up to the front door, and pressed the buzzer. Inside, she'd probably find a pile of empty beer cans and wine bottles. Or did Diane drink more expensive stuff now she had money? Blood money. *What do you care, Claire? She's not your problem anymore.*

Claire glanced over her shoulder. Beyond the streetlights, the neighborhood sank into shadow. Was the killer watching her right now? The sooner she got back to Rob's motel room, the better.

Footsteps sounded inside. Surprise, surprise. Mom was still conscious and sober enough to answer the door.

"I've just come to pick up my stuff," Claire said as the door opened, preempting her mother's angry response.

But she found no anger in her mother's eyes, only sadness. Did she remember last night? Standing there in her pajamas and a pink bathrobe, she looked disappointed.

"I rushed out this morning and forgot my bag upstairs. May I come in?"

Diane seemed to snap out of a trance. "Sure."

She stepped aside to let Claire in. Claire had never seen Diane like this. Was she drunk or high? With money in her pocket, the next logical step was to expand her addiction horizons and experiment with stronger substances—methamphetamines and opioids. Within a few months, she'd discover cocaine. How much money would she burn through before she overdosed?

Whatever. Claire tried to shrug off her concern but failed. One day she'd learn to stop caring. She trudged up the stairs, collected her overnight bag, and made for the exit.

"Wait," Mom said.

Claire paused at the front door and turned around. What parting shot had her mother prepared for her tonight? Would she call her a murderer and blame her for ruining her life or had she invented new accusations?

Mom stared at her, a vulnerable glint in her eyes.

"I didn't thank you."

Claire scoffed. "Don't worry. I'm used to that."

"Claire... You could have left me in that jail cell. Why didn't you?"

Good question. Leaving her mother to sober up in the holding cell would have raised questions in the department about the new sergeant's moral fiber. But concerns for her career hadn't motivated her actions. Why had Claire rescued her despite all the abuse and anger Diane had piled on her over the years?

Claire shrugged. "Because you're my mother?"

She fixed Diane with an accusatory stare. Diane's words from two nights ago rang in her ears. *You're not my daughter.*

Mom must have remembered, too, because she lowered her gaze to the floor.

Was that regret? All her life, Claire had showered Diane with opportunities to treat her like a daughter. Every time, Diane had broken her heart. Would tonight be different?

Diane pulled her hand from her pocket, and Claire flinched at the sudden movement. But her mother hadn't drawn a weapon. She offered Claire a key.

"For the new locks. You can stay if you like. I'll understand if you don't want to."

Claire studied her mother's eyes. Was she finally ready to make amends or did she just need a Get Out of Jail Free card? Was Claire willing to give her one last chance?

Claire reached out and accepted the key. "OK." She hooked her thumb toward her car. "I'll go get the rest of my things."

Diane smiled gratefully, then she turned away and climbed the stairs.

Claire stood on the welcome mat a while longer. She examined the key. Would the object—the work of cruel genies—evaporate into thin air? She closed the door and inserted the key in the lock. It worked. Claire got in her car and drove to Rob's motel room, her mind in a daze.

"What did I tell you?" he said after Claire told him what had happened. "People are full of surprises." He lounged on his single bed, while Claire sat on Tom's.

"This isn't people, Rob. This is my mother."

"She's a person, too. And this is great news."

"Are you trying to get rid of me?"

"Not at all. I'm coming with you. You didn't think I'd leave you alone at night with a serial killer stalking you, did you?"

"I told you. Sally said I'm not in danger."

Claire wasn't sure she believed that. Judging by his worried frown, neither did Rob.

"Sally's only human. This unsub picks high-risk targets. I'll sleep better knowing you're safe."

His suggestion made sense. Claire could fend off the average criminal, but Carmine Hannover's martial arts training hadn't saved her. This stalker was no average criminal.

Another concern weighed on Claire's mind. The killer had murdered innocent people to gain her affection. What would he do if he discovered she had a boyfriend? Was she endangering Rob's life, too?

Claire masked her fear with humor. "You can't guard me day and night."

He grinned. "Why not? And your bed is bigger and more comfortable. It provides so many more...uh, possibilities."

"Not tonight, Rob. Tonight belongs to me and my mom." Claire climbed onto Rob's bed and kissed him on the lips. "But soon we'll explore all those possibilities."

She packed clothes for a few days and drove back to her mom's place. The day had started crappy but ended surprisingly well. She had big plans for tomorrow, too. Things were looking up.

CHAPTER 45

The scent of tofu casserole roused Victoria McAdams from her slumber. Her casserole. Her mouth watered. She was hungry. Starving. And the back of her head throbbed. She lay spread-eagled on her bed. The circular LED light fixture glowed yellow on the ceiling. But when Victoria tried to get off the bed, she couldn't. Thin, hard wires tied her arms and legs to the bed frame. What had happened to her?

The reporter! She'd let him into her home and then...a black void in her memory. Pain pulsed in her skull. He must have knocked her unconscious the moment she turned her back. And the truth hit her even harder. The reporter wasn't from *The Boston Globe*. His name was not Jeffrey Reaver. *Reaver.* Was that even a name? The word meant someone who stole and plundered. The barbarian had tricked his way into her home, and his intentions were clear. He'd destroy her.

Terror brought tears to her eyes and involuntary sobs to her throat. After all the precautions she'd taken, how could she have been so stupid? She had to wise up fast, or he'd swipe more than her jewelry. He'd rob her of her life as he'd done to Carmine.

Victoria craned her neck. Lengths of rope extended from the cable ties on her wrists and ankles and disappeared beneath the bed. Her attacker had secured the ropes to the legs of her bed. She yanked with all her strength. The plastic strips bit into her tender flesh, but the ropes held.

She panted. *Think! Think!* A chair leg squeaked. Her attacker was in the kitchen. Victoria was lucky. She'd come to when he was out of the room. She was fully clothed and unhurt. This was her chance to escape a terrible death. If only she could think!

Help. She needed to call for help. Where was her phone? She'd spoken with Detective Nakamura on it in the kitchen. If he called again, the killer wouldn't answer. Victoria had screened the detective's calls before. Nakamura would think she was avoiding him.

Forget the police! When her attacker returned, she'd shoot the son of a bitch dead. She'd do it for Carmine and Kitty. *Crap!* She'd left her gun in her bag, also in the kitchen.

Wait—the panic button! Of course! Fear had frozen her brain. She'd placed several of the little remotes around the house. On the kitchen wall. At her bathroom sink. And on her bedside table!

Victoria strained her neck to search for the button. On her bedside table, the white plastic case of the panic button glinted in the bright LED light. *Yes!* She stretched her arm. If she could close her fingers on the remote, a response team of armed guards would arrive within minutes.

"You're awake."

The voice startled her. The killer stood over her and chewed, a smile on his lips. He'd removed the thick mustache.

"Thanks for dinner. Not bad for tofu."

He spoke to her like an old friend who had stopped by for a social call. Neither handsome nor ugly, the man was unremarkable in every way. His face wouldn't stand out in a crowd. He might have served her in a restaurant. He was her age, perhaps a few years younger. Just a man. She could get the better of him.

"There's more in the freezer. Help yourself."

"Maybe later. There's no rush."

The words unsettled her. If Victoria had attacked a stranger in his home and tied him up, she'd be pretty eager to finish what she'd gone there to do and get out. The creep must be stupid.

He sat beside her on the edge of the bed. She flinched when he reached out to touch her. But he only stroked her hair, his hand in a blue latex glove.

"Life is funny, isn't it? You're rich and beautiful. Out of my league, that's for sure. But here we are—just the two of us."

Victoria willed herself to look away from the panic button. Her fingers had been so close! Let him talk. Let him think she had no way of fighting him. When he wasn't watching, she'd act.

"I read what you said in the article. You shouldn't speak that way about people you don't know. Words can hurt. Imagine how your words made Claire feel."

"You're working with her, aren't you?"

He smiled. *She knew it!* Victoria had been right about Sergeant Claire Wolfe. Her father was a serial killer. He'd killed four young girls, and Claire had investigated those murders. She must have known. She'd got away with killing Kitty. Whatever happened to Victoria today, she took pride in knowing that she'd blown Claire Wolfe's cover. But that fact didn't seem to upset the killer.

"Not in the way you think. I don't expect you to understand. You're not like us. We're...a different species. Claire and I are predators, and you...you're our prey. It's the way of the world."

He stood and walked over to the black duffel bag on the

chaise lounge at the foot of the bed. Victoria stole a glance at the little white box on the bedside table. When she turned back, she almost peed her pants. The killer held a long, sharp cleaving knife—a butcher knife.

He grinned at her. "This won't hurt."

He placed a gloved hand on her ankle, and her breathing became fast and shallow. *Don't believe a word he says.* She had to press that panic button before it was too late.

He slid the knife into her trouser leg and ran the blade along the length of her slacks. Her clothes fell away like tissue paper. Victoria closed her eyes and held her breath, afraid that her slightest movement would cut her flesh on the razor-sharp edge. The blade slipped beneath the straps of her panties, and her underwear disappeared, too. Her bra followed.

"That wasn't so bad, was it? Open your eyes."

She released a pent-up breath and obeyed his command. He'd stripped her completely naked. Her legs and arms retracted instinctively but failed to cover her intimate areas. She was completely vulnerable and at his mercy.

He feasted his eyes on her body, a maniacal glint in his eyes. His jeans bulged at his crotch.

"You've taken good care of your body, Victoria. Good for you."

He was going to kill her. Slowly. Like Carmine. If only Victoria could have saved Carmine. She'd do anything to save herself from that fate now.

Desperate pleas poured from her mouth. "Please, don't hurt me. I have money. You can have it all."

He laughed. "I don't want your money, Victoria."

"Please! Take what you want and go. I won't tell anybody. Nobody has to know."

"What about your security cameras?"

"I'll turn them off. I'll delete everything. Please."

"You're not so powerful now, are you? Not in control. What good is all that money if it can't save you from me?" He chuckled. "Underneath it all, we're all the same. I'll show you. Like I showed Carmine. Pretty Carmine. I enjoyed working with her. Together, we created a masterpiece. Now it's your turn."

The mention of Carmine's name snapped Victoria from her delusions of a happy ending. There was no reasoning with this twisted sadist. He'd come here to kill her.

She lunged sideways and stretched her arm, the cable ties biting into her skin. Her fingertips closed around the white box, and she squeezed the panic button for all she was worth. *Yes! She'd done it!* The security team would be at her house soon. She'd won. Her attacker had better flee if he didn't want to get caught.

But the killer didn't run. He didn't budge. Instead, he smiled. Why was he smiling? Something was wrong. And then she realized what it was. She didn't hear the electronic beeping of the alarm. Were the batteries of the remote dead? No, the small light in the corner had lit up when she'd pressed the button. What had happened?

"Good for you, Victoria." The killer's voice was patronizing. "You're a fighter. I like that."

"It's a silent alarm," she lied. "The armed response team will be here any second."

"Really?" His eyes widened—not with fear or surprise but delight. "I don't think so. Let's do a little experiment." He snatched the remote from her hand and jabbed the button with his gloved finger. He pressed the button over and over, then cupped his hand to his ear.

"Do you hear them coming? I don't. Oh, right!" He palmed his face. "Silly me. I disabled the alarm." He stared at her, drinking in her distress. "I wiped the cameras, too. And Maria is on a plane by now."

Victoria went numb at the mention of Maria. He knew her by name. The killer had been watching her. He knew everything about her life. He'd planned this attack to the last detail. Victoria was going to die here.

His voice softened. "It's just you and me, Vic. Let's get started."

He sprang into action with demonic speed. Digging around in his duffel bag, he found another, longer knife. Frenzied excitement sparkled in his eyes.

"We're going to send a message."

Victoria understood what that meant. He was going to torture her to death and carve Claire Wolfe's name on her corpse. Her body trembled with shock. Tears flooded her eyes. A warm, wet sensation spread between her legs as her bladder emptied and soaked the bedding.

He raised the blade over her helpless body. "This is going to hurt, Vic. This'll hurt a lot."

CHAPTER 46

"Is that him?" Claire asked, Friday morning. Detective Brendan Mahoney squinted at the computer monitor in the observation room. On the screen, a plump, balding man sat at the table in the interview room. Peter Knowles, the owner of KillerWolfe.com had come willingly to the station at the invitation of none other than Sergeant Claire Wolfe. The temptation had been too great for him to pass up. But instead of a cozy chat with the object of his obsession, he waited under the imposing stare of Detective Lucas Gomez.

Mahoney shook his head. "I don't think so."

"Are you sure?" Captain Washington said. "Should we stick a mustache on him?"

The officers had squeezed into the cozy observation room along with Chief Emmerso and Dr. Sally Fleischer to study their new person of interest.

"Don't bother. This guy's shorter and fatter."

On the monitor, Peter Knowles lost his patience. "Where's my stuff?"

"You'll get it back soon," Gomez said.

They had searched Knowles for weapons when he'd arrived

at the station and confiscated his backpack before leading him
to the interview room.

Chief Emmerso asked, "What did he have on him?"

Captain Washington answered. "Posters of Sergeant Wolfe."

"Posters?"

"Pictures of her with a gun."

"And fewer clothes," Mahoney added, helpfully.

Chief Emmerso raised his eyebrows at Claire. "Sergeant
Wolfe, have you been moonlighting?"

Her cheeks warmed. "It's Photoshop, sir. They superim-
posed my face on some kind of...action hero."

"Lara Croft," Mahoney said and won surprised looks from
the others. "What? Don't tell me you haven't played Tomb
Raider?"

Washington ignored him. "A Magnum Forty-Four isn't our
standard service weapon. They should have done their
homework."

"Can I have a poster?" Mahoney said. "You don't mind, do
you, Sarge?"

Claire gave him a glare that could freeze water.

"You'll have to ask our guest," Captain Washington said.
"The posters are his property."

On the screen, Peter Knowles wiped the sweat on his brow
with a handkerchief. Did people still use handkerchiefs?

"Where's Sergeant Wolfe? She invited me here to meet with
her."

In the observation room, all eyes focused on Claire.

"I'll see what he knows."

"Are you sure you want to do this?" Washington said. "He
might be our perp."

She nodded. "I'll have a better chance of getting his coop-
eration."

Mahoney said, "Don't forget to ask about your royalty. Don't leave all that money on the table."

Claire snickered. Cashing in on her notoriety was the last thing she wanted. The fan site made her feel dirty and violated. The racketeer in the interview room had trampled on her privacy and dragged her name through the muck to make a quick buck. Claire hoped she didn't slap him before he shared his secrets.

She left the officers, knocked on the door of the interview room, and entered. Their guest's eyes lit up, and he shot to his feet.

"Sergeant Wolfe, I'm so glad to meet you finally."

Peter Knowles behaved like a teenager meeting his pop idol. Did posters of her Photoshopped likeness cover his bedroom walls? Did he still live with his mother?

Claire managed a warm smile. She walked past Detective Gomez, stuck out her hand, and shook the civilian's sweaty paw. Was he excited to meet her or did he think she'd pull a Magnum .44 on him?

An idea struck. Her bad-cop persona could work to her advantage. Claire turned the vacant chair around and sat facing Knowles, leaning her arms on the backrest. Her badass act might loosen his tongue.

"Want to help me catch a killer?"

He bobbed his head eagerly. "I sure do!"

Claire smiled within. The one-two combo of posturing and flattery had knocked Knowles into compliance.

He leaned in for a conspiratorial whisper. "Carmine Hannover's killer, right? It's all over the news. What a mess, right?"

Peter Knowles enjoyed the gruesome details. Claire wanted to drag him to a crime scene and shove his face in the full horror of a recent murder. He'd quickly lose his appetite for stylized violence.

"Wait a minute," Gomez said. "Don't you believe Sergeant Wolfe is behind the crime?"

"No, of course not."

"But that conspiracy theory is all over your website."

"C'mon, Detective. That bullshit sells merchandise. Nobody actually believes it."

"*The Newburgh Herald* disagrees. It's front-page news."

Peter Knowles laughed. "Don't tell me you believe what you read in the papers, too. Trust me, I used to be a journalist. All those articles about miracle drugs and multivitamins? They're paid placements. It's all a big money-making racket."

"Unlike your website."

Peter didn't seem to take offense. "At least my website is obviously for entertainment."

Claire steered the conversation back to their investigation. "Peter, the killer seems to have fallen for the hype. He might be a customer of yours. You can help us track him down."

The huckster looked scandalized. "You want my customer list? Sergeant, these people trust me with their data. Sharing their personal information would be unethical. I'd need a search warrant, and for that, you'd need probable cause, which I'm guessing you don't have. Any judge would consider that a flagrant breach of their constitutional rights."

"Now you're a criminal lawyer, too?" Gomez's voice dripped with contempt for the man's self-serving ethics.

"Nope. But reporters pick up many interesting tidbits."

Claire's smile faded. They had hit a brick wall. Knowles had no sense of civic duty.

The hawker leered at her. "But I'd be more flexible if you made it worth my while."

Claire was ready to slap the brazen opportunist. "What do you have in mind?"

"If you were to, say, autograph a few posters, I'd be very grateful."

"How many?"

Peter's smile widened. "I have a dozen in my bag, which the officers took." He glared at Gomez. "And fifty more in the car."

Claire got to her feet. "I'll see what I can do. But we need the data first."

Peter Knowles smiled smugly. This was what he'd wanted all along. The man worshipped money, not Claire. Taking the moral high ground was merely a negotiation technique, and he'd gladly turn a profit from murder porn.

Claire's conscience twinged. Did she have a right to point fingers? She'd moved back home with Diane. Did their cease-fire justify living off her father's blood money? Maybe she and Peter Knowles weren't so different, after all?

"Detective Gomez, let's get Mr. Knowles to a computer and cross-reference his customer list with known criminals. We'll start with those who purchased the more graphic prints—the crime scene photos, for example."

Gomez stood. "C'mon, Mr. Knowles. Time to earn those autographs."

Claire returned to the observation room.

"Good job, Sergeant," Captain Washington said.

"Thank you, sir."

Chief Emmerso gave her a bemused smile.

"What?"

"Is that the first time somebody's asked for your autograph?"

"It feels icky."

"Nobody said fame was fun."

"I didn't sign up for this, sir."

The door opened, and Detective Nakamura burst in, his face drawn. Something bad had happened.

"We found another body."

All the positive vibes in the room died.

"Who is it?" Washington asked, but Claire had already guessed the answer.

"Victoria McAdams."

CHAPTER 47

J ess knocked meekly on the door of Newburgh PD's main conference room. She'd hoped to join Rob in Springfield to exhume the body of William Wolfe's accomplice. But Rob had called that morning to reassign her to Dr. Sally Fleischer. Jess had thought she'd made a good impression on the special agent with her brilliant deduction. But ever since, Rob had sidelined her in the investigation. Had Jess accidentally stepped on his toes?

When Jess opened the door, the forensic psychologist lifted her gaze from the groups of photographs on the conference table and smiled.

"Congratulations."

"Congratulations?"

"For identifying the real Lisa Evans. That's our first actual sign of progress since Rob discovered the bodies. Finally, we have something positive to report to our unit chief."

Jess brightened at the compliment. "I guess I was in the right place at the right time."

"Don't sell yourself short, Detective Long."

"Please, call me Jess."

The doctor's dark-pool eyes lingered on her with concern. "Are you OK?"

Could the psychiatrist read her thoughts? "Sure. I'd just assumed I'd go to Springfield today with Agent Cline."

"Don't take that the wrong way, Jess. Rob didn't want to waste your time. We both thought you'd be more valuable here. Maybe you can give us a fresh opinion on the data?"

Jess flushed with pleasure. Rob hadn't snubbed her. He'd promoted her. Both Rob and Dr. Fleischer valued her opinion.

She turned to the groups of photographs on the conference table, determined to justify the confidence they had placed in her. But the mass of corpses daunted her. Jess was out of her depth. Yesterday was a fluke. Dr. Fleischer and Rob were the experts. Did they expect Jess to pull another rabbit from her hat?

While Jess studied the photos, Dr. Fleischer explained. "We've failed to identify a consistent victim profile no matter how we categorize the corpses. As you know, the victims differ in age, sex, and race. Currently, I've arranged them by MO. Thirteen shot in the back of the head at close range. Six strangled. Seven mutilated. Two decapitated, one of whom you identified yesterday. Two murderers, four MOs. The mutilations are all women. Some were buried naked, others clothed. Most appear to be over thirty years of age. That's all we've got so far."

Jess leaned over the table, willing the photos to reveal their secrets, but the corpses refused to help.

"Strange, isn't it?" Dr. Fleischer added. "People can live full, meaningful lives, but posterity will only remember how long they lived and how they died. Lisa Evans, twenty-five, murdered by the Middle School Strangler. John Doe, sixty-five, heart attack. Most people never learn how they die. Many are aware of their imminent death for only a few seconds. How they died is insignificant compared with how they lived. But that's what we'll remember."

Jess had never thought about death that way, but the psychiatrist was right. "That is strange. I guess we focus on our own mortality even when we should be thinking about others. We can't help it."

Dr. Fleischer smiled at her. "Are you sure you didn't study psychology?"

Jess snorted. "I'm sure I'd remember that."

She stared at the photos. Her thoughts drifted to their first conversation about the bodies the day Dr. Fleischer had arrived.

"We thought the pack changed their MO over time, experimenting with new techniques."

The psychiatrist shook her head. "If that were so, we'd expect to find the same degree of decomposition within each group. We don't. Their *experiments* overlapped and extended over a long time."

"Oh. Back to the drawing board."

Jess scanned the photos for clues.

Dr. Fleischer shifted the smallest group to the side. "The decapitations stand on their own. As you discovered, Wolfe's accomplice stole the female victim's identity. The pack removed her head and hands to make identification difficult if the body was ever found. They didn't expect the birthmark to be significant. Wolfe probably assumed the identity of the male decapitation victim to gain access to the other targets."

"Right."

Jess hadn't taken that extra but obvious mental step, but she didn't want to highlight her deductive failings. She glanced at Dr. Fleischer from the corner of her eye. Jess hoped her more experienced companion would say something soon because all she saw was a random collection of dead bodies. She remembered Carmine Hannover's murder scene and the advice Claire had shared with her. *Look for what's missing.*

Jess's lips parted in surprise. Something *was* missing.

"What about the girls?" In answer to Dr. Fleischer's questioning gaze, Jess added, "The Middle School girls and Tina Wolfe. The pack killed them, too."

Dr. Fleischer grinned. "Good idea."

Maybe Jess had something useful to contribute, after all? The psychiatrist opened her leather carry bag, withdrew a manila folder, and soon four photographs of the dead girls formed a fifth group on the table.

She hesitated. "Do they belong to the strangulation group or mutilation?"

"Maybe they're an independent group?"

Dr. Fleischer kept the photos separate, and Jess's mind tingled with delight. The psychiatrist was rolling with her theory.

"They're the only children among the victims," she said, thinking aloud. "This group has a clearly defined victim profile and MO. William Wolfe had a specific purpose in mind for these murders, which they dressed up as the work of an organized serial killer. Every detail was intentional from the choice of victims to the mutila…"

Had Dr. Fleischer discovered something?

"What is it?"

Jess held her breath, like a Dr. Watson, eager to witness Sherlock Holmes's deductive genius.

Dr. Fleischer pointed at the ax wounds on the dead girls' faces. "The damage is extensive. But the injuries form the same shape. The killer had to change his position to create this effect. Blows from one side of the corpse, then from the other."

Jess stared at the photos. All she saw was red pulp.

"What shape?"

Dr. Fleischer's voice was distant now. She seemed lost in thought. "Narrow at the top, wide at the bottom. A chevron. An A without the bridge. Or an upturned V."

Now Jess saw the pattern. But what did the symbol mean?

The doctor's phone rang, and Dr. Fleischer answered.

"Good morning to you, too, Rob. A match for what?" She glanced at Jess, and an excited smile animated her face. "That's wonderful. I'm putting you on speaker. Jess, Rob found a match for the body's fingerprints."

A thrill passed through Jess.

The excitement in Rob's voice was audible on the phone's speaker. "Her name is Rachel Morris."

"Does this mean she had a criminal record?" Dr. Fleischer sounded hopeful.

"Oh, yeah. You're gonna love this."

CHAPTER 48

Diane shouldn't follow strange men to unfamiliar, isolated places. But Frank wasn't a stranger, was he? His gruff-yet-gentle cowboy manner told her she could trust him. He wasn't a creep. He wouldn't take advantage of her in broad daylight, would he?

A rolling metal gate covered the entrance to The Red Keg. Frank dropped to his haunches, slipped a key in the lock, and pulled the gate upward. Why had he brought her here after hours?

"Why are we here, Frank?"

He found another key on his chain and unlocked the bar's front door. "I don't want to ruin the surprise."

"I don't like surprises."

He grinned. "You'll like this one."

Diane had a poor track record with mysterious men, and she didn't want to repeat the nightmare that had stolen the best years of her life. Frank had called Diane and convinced her to meet so they could discuss her next performance. Diane hadn't committed to the gig, but the longer she sat at home alone, the more she thought about her next drink. And Frank had seemed interested in her. But in the bright morning light, Diane second-guessed her decision to meet with the stranger on the deserted backstreet lined with shuttered bars. What were his true intentions?

The darkened bar reeked of alcohol and regret. The memory of Wednesday night's embarrassment haunted her every step as she revisited the scene of the crime. She recognized the stool where she'd ordered her first drinks and the table she had turned into a makeshift stage. Had Frank brought her there to rub her nose in her misbehavior? Would he ply her with alcohol again and tell her to strip as she'd done that night? Her face burned with shame and suspicion. Frank's good first impression was wearing thin.

"Can I get you a beer?"

"I've quit drinking."

"Good for you." The bar owner didn't seem upset to have lost a reliable customer. "Alcohol isn't for everybody. Would you like a soda?"

Was he trying to slip her a date-rape pill? "No, thank you."

"Suit yourself." He opened a door behind the counter and stepped aside. "After you, ma'am."

Diane clutched her handbag and entered, against her better judgment. They followed a narrow corridor. Passersby on the street would neither see her nor hear her cries for help if Frank cornered her.

"Almost there," Frank said, nudging her onward.

He opened the second door and flipped a light switch. Diane peered inside from the corridor. The small room contained a tall closet and a dressing table. Light bulbs traced the edges of a large mirror. In her dreams of a successful career as a solo artist, Diane had imagined preparing for concerts in backstage dressing rooms like this. But that was a lifetime ago.

"What do you think?"

"It's lovely."

"We used to have a live music act every other week."

"Frank, thank you for the offer. But as I told you already, my singing days are over."

Frank didn't seem to hear her. He opened the closet and fished around inside.

"There she is."

He pulled a hanger from the closet. The fabric of the dress shimmered with silver sequins—a minidress worthy of Tina Turner. Without asking her brain for permission, her arm reached out, and her fingers caressed the sparkling material.

"What are you waiting for? Try it on."

Was this his sneaky way of convincing her to undress? The thought both frightened and confused her. What sane and sober man would want to see her naked?

"I can't."

"Go on. I'll wait outside."

He handed her the hanger, left the room, and closed the door behind him. She faced the mirror and held the dress to her body. The designer had created the outfit for a woman with a full body. A few months ago, the dress would never have fit, but thanks to Claire's military regimen, Diane had lost twenty pounds. Could she wear this dress? Could she step onto a stage again—without alcohol to dull her nerves?

She opened the door and handed back the dress. "I'm sorry, Frank. I know you mean well, but Wednesday night proved to me that my singing days are over."

Frank opened his mouth to protest, but a metallic noise interrupted him. Diane cocked her head in the sound's direction. There it was again—the familiar clatter of cymbals preceded by a percussion beat. Someone was warming up a set of drums. A dormant emotion fluttered in Diane's heart.

"What was that?"

Frank grinned, and his mustache shifted to a rakish angle. "It's time our singer met her band."

CHAPTER 49

The stench of congealed blood and raw flesh triggered a sickening wave of déjà vu. Claire had witnessed this scene before. The bed was larger and more comfortable than that of The Barnett Inn, and the human remains that stained the covers red belonged to Victoria McAdams.

"Where's the blonde?" The question had come from Brandon Yang, the forensic tech in full-body scrubs, who photographed the corpse.

"Excuse me?"

"The new detective."

"Detective Long is working another case."

Brandon looked disappointed. "Too bad. I brought a barf bag especially for her."

Detective Gomez grunted. "Thanks, Brandon. You're a stand-up guy."

The tech snapped another photo. "I get the feeling we're dealing with the same perp."

"You think?" The sight of another butchered young woman had soured Gomez's mood, too.

"Just sayin'. Can I turn her over now?"

Claire swallowed hard. Victoria lay faceup on the bed, her eyes open, her wrists and ankles secured to the bed by cable ties and lengths of rope. Claire shared the forensic tech's curiosity. Had the killer carved Claire's name on Victoria's back, too, or had he chosen a new message, something that might shed light on his identity?

"Not yet."

She'd run this investigation by the book. The Hannovers needn't worry. This killer wouldn't get off on a legal technicality.

Captain Washington entered the bedroom. Like the other officers, he'd covered his hands and shoes with disposable plastic baggies.

"Nice place. Pity about the owner. I guess we can remove her from our list of suspects."

"How did her parents react to the news?"

"No answer yet. They're in Hawaii. I'll try them again later. Where's Detective Nakamura?"

"Behind you, sir."

Washington was quick to point fingers. "Didn't we have her under police guard?"

"Not in time to save her. She refused police protection."

Washington shook his head. "Who said conspiracy theories didn't hurt anybody? Morning, Sergeant Eckhardt."

Patrol Sergeant George Eckhardt had walked in, his eyebrows raised higher than usual.

"Your men discovered the body?" Washington asked him.

"Yes, sir. Detective Nakamura requested a squad car to check up on her this morning when she didn't answer her phone. Officer Hackett found the front gate unlocked and the front door open. We've called the security service to assist. There are cameras all over the property. They should tell us something."

Washington grunted, doubtfully. Like Claire, he probably suspected the killer knew about the cameras and prepared accordingly.

"Sergeant Wolfe, let's walk the scene."

Claire hit the button on her digital recorder and described the details of the murder in the usual matter-of-fact language. The killer had tortured and slaughtered Victoria in the same way as Carmine.

"Unlike the first murder," Claire said, "the killer left the victim's breasts at the scene—between her feet on the bed. And unlike the first victim, her wrists and ankles remain bound using a combination of cable ties and nylon cord."

"What do you make of that, Sergeant?"

"Maybe he rushed this job? Detective Nakamura, when did you last speak with her?"

"Yesterday around seven PM."

She turned to the forensic tech. "Brandon, what's the estimated time of death?"

He took a break from photographing the corpse. "Ten-to-twelve hours ago. Around ten PM. But that's a rough estimate—"

"We know," Claire interrupted, "pending the autopsy. The killer spent three to five hours with the victim—much less than last time. He must have figured we'd check on her after she appeared in that newspaper article."

Gomez spoke up. "If he was reacting to *The Herald*'s article, he moved pretty quickly. With less time to prepare, there's more chance he messed up."

"Let's hope you're right," Captain Washington said. "Did she live alone?"

"As far as we can tell," Claire said. "Nakamura, check with the neighbors. Gomez, ask the security company about the cameras."

The detectives hurried to their tasks.

"Hello!" Brandon said. "There's a panic button on the floor." He placed a numbered card beside the small white remote on the pale parquet and snapped another photo.

Victoria's traumatic last hours took shape in Claire's mind. "She must have tried to call for help."

"Maybe she did," Sergeant Eckhardt said. "But the security company screwed up."

Claire wrapped up her description of the murder scene. "There are no signs of forced entry. The decedent might have let the killer inside."

"She knew him," Washington said. "She wouldn't have let a stranger into her home. Not in her state of mind. Where was Hannover's PA last night?"

Claire had asked the same question. "Home all night. I spoke with the patrol squad we assigned to him. Brandon, are there any prints?"

The forensic tech cut the cable ties from the victim's wrists. "Nothing yet, but I'll keep looking. If the last crime scene is any indication, I wouldn't get my hopes up."

Washington sighed. "Well, Dr. Fleischer's got her serial killer. The media are in for a feeding frenzy." He glanced at Claire, and his Adam's apple bobbed. "Let's turn her over."

"One second." Brandon removed the cable ties from Victoria's ankles. "OK. Give me a hand."

Claire helped the forensic tech place the victim's arms and legs alongside her body, and they rolled her onto her belly.

"So much for originality," Brandon said.

Claire agreed. The killer had incised Victoria's back with the word "CLAIRE", exactly as he'd done to Carmine, including the same broken A.

"Post-mortem," Brandon continued. "Note the lack of bleeding."

"I don't get it," Claire said. "If this was revenge for speaking to *The Herald*, why didn't he write something more relevant?"

"You mean, 'Lying bitch?' or 'Serves you right?'"

Claire stared at Brandon. "You're scary."

"Comes with the job."

Washington shrugged. "The killer isn't much of a poet?"

Claire's gut disagreed with her captain's assessment. The writing was intentional. Something didn't fit.

Nakamura returned. "I spoke with the patrol officers. The neighbors heard nothing. McAdams had a live-in housekeeper, Maria Pérez. She left yesterday afternoon to visit her mother in New Mexico. She's away the entire weekend."

Washington met Claire's glance. "Coincidence? Nakamura, get hold of Ms. Pérez. Let's see what she has to say."

Gomez returned, too, breathless. "The security guys are here, but check this out. There's no camera footage. Not for the past month."

"Are the cameras out of order?"

"That's the thing. Victoria called them this week to check the system. But all the cameras are offline, and the footage is gone. The killer must have known about her security system and wiped the memory clean."

Again, Washington met Claire's eyes. "That's one too many coincidences."

Claire agreed. "He knew her routine. He'd researched her security system. This wasn't a spontaneous crime. He'd planned her murder for weeks."

CHAPTER 50

"What's the matter with you, Johnny?" His mother had cornered him on the torn living room couch and stared at him as though he were a giant bug. "I thought you were done with all that."

So had he. Johnny hung his head in shame and felt sick to his stomach. He was broken and twisted—an animal, not a human being.

"I'm sorry, Mom. I didn't mean to."

"You didn't mean to?" She scoffed. "This isn't something a person does by accident."

How could he make her understand? The fantasy had taken over. Every day, the urges inside him grew until they spilled into the outer world. Once he'd tasted absolute control, he was hooked. Of all people, his addict mother should understand.

She ran her hand through her matted hair. Mom had more age lines on her neck. The rings under her bloodshot eyes had darkened since Emily had left home. His big sister had walked out on them, just like his father, and now his mom had to deal with him alone. She'd figured Emily had helped take care of him while she was roaming for her next fix. She was wrong.

A shameful part of Johnny enjoyed this moment. Mom was here, sitting with him on the couch—talking *to him. When Johnny was in trouble, he wasn't invisible to her.*

"You're lucky she isn't pressing charges. You're eighteen now. They can try you as an adult. You could go to prison."

Johnny nodded solemnly. April had been his first, and he hadn't hurt her much. He'd hooked up with three others since. Each time he followed the script of his fantasy further. Johnny grew impatient, too. He no longer bothered with foreplay. Johnny observed them, following them and learning their routines without making contact. Then, he pounced.

He was practicing for Emily, or so he told himself. Once he'd perfected his routine, he'd take his sister all the way. He'd tower over her while she begged for mercy and he'd watch the life force seep from her body. But Emily had left home six months ago. And even if he tracked her down, did he have the guts to follow through? Freak. Asswipe. Piece of crap.

Mom was right. This had to stop. He needed to get professional help before things went too far and he threw his life away.

The doorbell buzzed.

"I'll get it," he said.

He left his mom on the couch with her tears and answered the door. The stranger in the brown suit smiled at him.

"What is it?"

"John Norton?"

Johnny's heart skipped a beat, and he folded his arms. Was it too late? Had the cops caught up with him already? Would the man drag him to prison in handcuffs? But the man didn't seem threatening.

"Yeah?"

"I was hoping you'd be home."

He looked at Johnny the way April had once—with appreciation. Hope sprouted in Johnny's breast. Was this man his father? Had Dad come home to reclaim him?

"*Do I know you?*"

"*No, Johnny, you don't.*" The man opened his wallet and flashed an identity card with his portrait photo and an official seal. "*I'm from the Federal Bureau of Investigation.*"

CHAPTER 51

"You were right," Captain Morris Washington told Dr. Sally Fleischer.

"I wish I wasn't."

So did Claire. The investigation team had assembled in the captain's office, but the sights and smells of Victoria McAdams's murder scene still lingered in Claire's mind. The unsub had killed twice. Carmine Hannover's murder was no isolated homicide. They couldn't deny this chilling, brutal fact. Newburgh had another serial killer, a stalker who branded his victims with Claire's name. The gruesome crimes joined the long line of homicides that marked Claire's bloodstained path through the world.

Was Claire cursed? Was she doomed to incite violence and death wherever she went? When would it all end? Or would the body count rise until Claire joined the list of victims?

"He's killed before," Sally continued.

Washington groaned. "Isn't two enough?"

"He's too confident and professional to be new to this. He's honed his technique. His sexual fantasy is highly specific. And we've already identified two of his earlier victims."

"How long ago?"

"Last month. Two prostitutes in Albany, New York, were found dead and mutilated, two weeks apart."

Washington folded his arms over his chest. "You're siding with *The Newburgh Herald?*"

Sally glanced at Claire but said nothing of her earlier tip-off. The tabloid reporters would claim they had bested Newburgh's finest, and Captain Washington had a powerful incentive to prove them wrong. But Sally let him vent his frustration on *The Herald* instead of his sergeant.

"Siding with the truth is the surest way to catch the killer."

"How can we be sure it's the same perp?"

"The stab wounds, mutilations, and cause of death match those of Hannover and McAdams."

"But our victims are high-society women, not prostitutes."

"You're right. But we can't ignore the other similarities and the proximity in time and location. News of the Middle School Strangler lured him to Newburgh. The subsequent conspiracy theories about Sergeant Wolfe induced him to adjust his victim profile. But he stays within the framework of his Power/Control fantasy. He dominates his victims and takes his time to follow his fantasy script of torture and control. The multiple shallow stab wounds are a replacement for sexual intercourse. He might be impotent or he's compensating for past rejection by the women he desired. He might have taken trophies from the crime scene—hair cuttings, jewelry, or identity cards."

"So, the breasts were trophies?"

"No. In the Albany murders, he left the breasts at the scene of the crime, as he did with McAdams. The Hannover homicide was different. He used the breasts to get Sergeant Wolfe's attention. Now that she knows he's doing this for her, he can dispense with that added risk."

"This guy is a stalker *and* a serial killer?"

Sally hesitated. "I admit, we're on shaky ground. Serial killers usually stalk their victims, but stalkers rarely murder the object of their obsession. Most stalkers are motivated by feelings of rejection, revenge for perceived wrongdoing, or they're simply interested in a relationship. Most aren't physically violent. This unsub fits the literature for both."

"I don't know, Doc," Gomez said. "Wasn't our stalker supposed to have asked Sergeant Wolfe on a date? Either he hasn't stepped up or Sergeant Wolfe is keeping him all to herself."

The detectives shared a nervous laugh, releasing some of the tension in the room.

"You're right. I expected more direct communication. But this is the only theory that explains his use of Claire's name and the change in victim selection. His actions speak louder than his words."

Captain Washington folded his arms. "Practically speaking, what are we looking for?"

"I stand by my original profile. White male. Superficial charm. Medium intelligence or above. Based on his recent murder, he has intimate knowledge of security systems, too. He might work in a technical field—an electrician or engineer. And he probably has a criminal record for rape or other violent crimes."

"Gomez, how many of Peter Knowles's customers have a record?"

Gomez consulted his notepad. "Of his eight-hundred customers, only twenty appeared on the sex offender lists."

Nakamura's jaw dropped. "Eight hundred?" His reaction mirrored Claire's dismay.

"That's just the paying customers. Many live out of state, too. Sergeant Wolfe is a national celebrity now." He turned to Claire. "Don't let it go to your head, Sarge. We knew you before you became rich and famous. Which reminds me. Peter Knowles is still here, and he wants his autographs."

Claire grimaced. "No rest for the wicked."

Washington said, "Track down every sex offender on the list. We need to tighten the net before the perp kills again." He turned to Dr. Fleischer. "Any idea who he might attack next?"

"Anyone connected to Kitty Tucker."

"What about the reporter?" Nakamura said. "Bella Winters. She wrote the article that got McAdams killed. Wouldn't the killer target her, too?"

"I doubt that. The unsub planned these murders. Their friendship with Kitty Tucker made them targets, not the recent article. He might even approve of the article. Remember, he wants a relationship with Sergeant Wolfe, and *The Newburgh Herald* has connected him to her in the public's mind."

"All Kitty Tucker's close friends are dead. Will he stop now?"

"That's possible. But he's also driven by a compulsion to kill. We should assume he'll expand his victim pool. Family members of Kitty and the other victims might qualify, too."

"Anything else?" Washington asked.

Sally made to speak but held back. "That's it for now. He'll try to contact Sergeant Wolfe again. It's a matter of time. Be ready for him."

"OK, then. Back to work."

Chair legs scraped as the detectives got to their feet, but Claire simmered in thought. The investigation was playing catch-up with the killer, always lagging two steps behind. The helplessness was eating her from inside.

"Sir, we can try a proactive approach." The others faced her. "If I'm the focus of his obsession, maybe we can leverage that?"

"What do you have in mind?"

Sally said, "Contacting him won't help. He'll suspect the

department is setting a trap for him. And he's delusional. He'll interpret anything Claire says as a disguised sign of her approval."

"I have something else in mind."

Claire weighed her words carefully. Her plan was dangerous and might backfire horribly. But she'd gladly accept the extra risk to stop her stalker's murder streak.

"We can't tell him to quit or surrender," she said. "But maybe we can select his next target?"

CHAPTER 52

B ella Winters stormed toward her boss's office as though her life depended on it. Today, it did.

Steve was talking on the phone, his ankles crossed on his desk, when she barged through his door. "I'll call you back." He put down the phone, returned to a sitting position, and smiled at his star reporter. "Good news! We hit a new mid-week sales record. Readers loved yesterday's piece."

"You mean they're scared shitless?"

Steve shrugged. "Same thing. Your follow-up article is tomorrow's cover story."

"I'm withdrawing it."

"What? Are you kidding me? The Newburgh Slasher is a hit. People can't get enough."

"Well, I have. Victoria McAdams is dead. She spoke out, and he killed her. What if he comes after me next?"

She was crying now, her mascara probably spreading down her cheeks, but she didn't care.

"I'd call in Newburgh PD for protection, but after my last few articles, they probably want me dead, too."

Steve's voice softened. "Close the door. Have a seat."

He opened a drawer, pulled out a bottle of Jack Daniels, and filled two shot glasses.

"Cheers."

Bella knocked hers back, and her throat stung.

"To be clear," Steve said, "we're celebrating. This story is exactly what you've been waiting for. A serial killer in Newburgh. Fear and high drama. Incompetent police officers. We're having a field day!"

Bella shook her head. "The Middle School Murders were different. The killer was after little girls. I wasn't in danger." Her words sounded callous and selfish. Bella *had* been callous and selfish. But the threat of torture followed by a violent death had shown her the error of her ways. "I should never have written about those girls. I'm paying for that now because this time the killer's coming after me!"

"Nobody's coming after you, Bella."

"Oh, yeah? Victoria McAdams sat right here—in this chair —two days ago. Now she's dead. My name is on that article, Steve. You know what he did to her and Carmine Hannover. He'll do the same to me!"

Steve raised both hands to calm her down. "Firstly—and don't take this personally—you're neither a Hannover nor a McAdams."

"Thank God for small mercies."

He topped up her shot glass. "Your net worth alone elimi-nates you from their exclusive club, OK?"

Bella nodded, wanting to believe his words. She'd never been thankful for her rocky financial situation until now.

"And secondly, this weirdo kills people for notoriety. Who's going to care if he kills a reporter?"

Bella glared at him. "This reporter will."

But his arguments made sense. Sort of.

She reached for her second shot. "I don't know, Steve. Serial killers aren't reasonable. Reasonable people don't run around murdering and mutilating innocent women."

A knock on the door startled her. Bella spun around in her seat, spilling whiskey on her hand. Sergeant Claire Wolfe stood in the doorway with Captain Morris Washington looming beside her. Wolfe fixed Bella with a stern look. Had the officers shown up to complain against her in person? Did they want to get her fired? Would Claire Wolfe accuse Bella of contributing to Victoria's savage murder? Bella did.

Steve rose from his chair. "Captain Washington, Sergeant Wolfe. I'd offer you a drink, but it seems you're on duty." His voice rose an octave, betraying his anxiety.

Bella broke down. "I'm sorry. Truly, I am. I should never have written those articles."

They had to understand that she'd changed her ways and needed their help.

"We're not here to assign blame," Washington said.

Steve crossed his arms over his chest. "Then what brings you here today?"

"I hear the pen is mightier than the sword. Let's hope that's true."

They need a favor, Bella thought. Perfect! She needed a favor from them in return. She needed them to keep her alive. But what could the officers possibly want from *The Newburgh Herald*?

Steve cleared his throat. "How can we help?"

Sergeant Claire Wolfe answered this one. "Let's catch a serial killer."

CHAPTER 53

A female police officer was waiting in Diane's living room when she got home Friday evening. Diane was hot and sweaty, but the rehearsal had invigorated her, and she was looking forward to sharing the news with her daughter. Claire had pestered her to get out of the house and make her way in the world, and Diane was doing just that. She'd concluded a marathon session of Tina Turner hits with Frank's band, and tomorrow night, she'd perform onstage—fully clothed. She wanted Claire to be there. But at the sight of the uniformed officer, Diane traded her excitement for concern. Were the cops pressing charges for her drunken misconduct?

Claire whispered something to the policewoman as Diane entered, and another suspicion popped into her brain. Had Claire called the police? Had she told them about the inheritance Diane had received from Bill's retirement annuity? Claire had claimed the money was dirty and somehow tied to her late husband's criminal activity. But he'd murdered Tina and those schoolgirls out of cruelty. He'd wanted Diane to suffer and others to take the blame. He'd made no money from his crimes. The retirement funds were legal until proven otherwise. Had

Claire found proof? Was she kicking Diane's financial legs out from under her?

"Claire, what's going on?"

"Mom, this is Officer Wendy Dunn."

The short, pixie-faced officer nodded at her. "Evening, ma'am."

"She'll escort you to a hotel."

A hotel? "I don't need a hotel. This is my home."

Claire pointed to a black suitcase, Bill's old travel bag. "I packed clothes for the next few days. I'll send more if necessary."

Anger ignited in Diane's breast. Was Claire throwing her out of her home in revenge for what she'd done to her?

"I'm not going anywhere."

Claire glanced at the officer. "Give us a moment."

Officer Dunn nodded. "I'll be in the car." She wheeled the travel bag past Diane and outside, and closed the front door behind her.

Diane's temper exploded. She'd extended an olive branch by inviting Claire back home, and this was how she repaid her?

"This is my home. You can't kick me out."

"It's for your protection, Mom."

"The hell it is!"

"You don't understand—"

"I know exactly what's going on here." The years of suspicion Diane had cast away snapped back into place. "You preach about sobering up and fending for myself. But you can't bear to see me stand on my own two feet. The moment I get control of my life, you want to take it away."

"It's not like that, Mom. I'm working a double homicide. The killer has mentioned my name, and there's a good chance he'll come after me tomorrow."

A splash of doubt dampened the flames. Claire was in

danger. Then the flames rose again. "Tomorrow? Did he make an appointment?"

"I can't go into detail—"

"If you're in danger, *you* should leave. Why should I have to go?"

"He's stalking me. For all we know, he's broken into the house before. Remember the beers that Rob had left in the fridge?"

"The beers you accused me of drinking and lying about?"

For a moment, Claire seemed contrite. "Yes. The killer might have taken them."

"So now you believe me? And the killer—what—just stopped by for a drink?"

"I don't know. It doesn't matter. But he'll expect to find me here tomorrow, and you can't be here when he arrives."

Diane placed her hands on her hips. She wasn't buying the martyr story. "Admit it—this is about the money."

Claire hesitated. "It's not about the money, but you'll have to deal with that eventually."

"Deal with what—me not needing you anymore?"

Claire's eyelid twitched. "William *stole* that money."

"William? You mean your father?"

Claire's jaw muscles bulged. "He's not my father."

"He is, Claire. And guess what. You're exactly like him."

"I am *not* like him!"

"Neither of you could stand to see me happy. You want to control me and watch me suffer."

Claire opened her mouth to argue, then sighed. "We don't have time for this. Officer Dunn will take you to a hotel. You'll be safe there and under police surveillance. Newburgh PD will cover the costs."

"I'm not going anywhere."

Claire raised her voice. "For once, just do as I say or..."

"Or what...you'll freeze my bank account?"

Claire glared at her as if Diane was stupid. "Do I need to cuff you? This is for your protection. We've reserved a hotel room, but the station's holding cell will do fine. Maybe you'll feel more comfortable there seeing that you know the place so well."

Claire was reminding Diane of her darkest hour. Claire couldn't imprison her, could she? But she could rat her out about the money, and Claire had the weight of local law enforcement behind her.

"Fine, have your revenge. I hope you choke on it."

"Don't you read the news?" Claire's voice broke with frustration. *Good.* "He tortured and killed two women this week. Do you want to end up like them? Do you want *your daughter* to die?"

Diane turned her back on Claire. "You're not my daughter."

She left the house. Claire had won this battle, but the war had just begun.

CHAPTER 54

Claire had just screwed a security chain onto the kitchen backdoor when the sound of urgent knocking startled her. The knocking had come from the front hall. Despite the Glock 22 in her holster and the two plainclothes police officers staking out her street, Claire had bought the security chains from Walmart as an extra precaution. This killer had a special talent for gaining access to his victim's homes, and Claire wouldn't make his task any easier. But she hadn't expected him to arrive before *The Newburgh Herald* hit the city's doorsteps tomorrow morning. Had her stalker discovered her plan already?

She drew her service weapon and padded into the hall, her rapid heartbeat drumming in her ears. He'd gotten past the officers outside. Claire pictured the occupants of the unmarked sedans hunched over, their throats slit. The knocking came again, more urgent. She stepped to the side of the door in case her mystery visitor fired through the wood.

Leaning forward, Claire put her eye to the peephole. Then she unlatched the security chain and opened the door.

"You should have called before coming over."

Rob stepped inside. "Are you crazy or suicidal?"

Claire had never seen him so angry. She closed the door and secured the chain. Claire understood his reaction, but after clashing with her mother and playing cat and mouse with a brutal serial killer, her frayed nerves could handle no more conflict.

"Sally told you?"

Claire had consulted with Dr. Fleischer about her plan, and the FBI profiler must have told Rob about the upcoming article in *The Newburgh Herald*.

"She told me the important bits. Calling your stalker an impotent coward in the newspapers will light his fuse."

"That's the point, Rob. I'm counting on him getting angry and coming over here."

"So you're the bait?"

"Sally thinks it might work."

"It might get you killed."

"I can handle myself. And I have backup on the street."

"Yeah, Tweedledum and Tweedledee have made themselves pretty obvious."

"I can ask them to leave. They can join the small army at Bella Winters's home."

Rob shook his head at her, hurt glimmering in his eyes. "Why are you doing this?"

"You know why—to catch the son of a bitch."

"Do you want him to kill you?"

"If it'll end this, maybe? If it'll break the curse."

"You're not cursed, Claire."

"That's strange because wherever I go, people die. If I'm gone, the killer will lose interest. End of story. Nothing to see here, folks. Move along."

Rob stepped closer and held her. "People care about you, too."

Claire shifted away. "You shouldn't be here. If he knows we're seeing each other, he'll come after you, too." She thought of the missing beers. Rob had brought her the drinks. "He probably knows already."

"Then let's face him together."

"You've got other things to do. Any progress on the pack?"

"Don't change the subject."

"No, really, I'm interested." She was shouting now. "How many people did my father kill and exactly how did he kill them? I should want to know. He did it for me, didn't he? Tell me all the gory details. Please! They're so fascinating, aren't they?"

She had shamed Rob into silence.

"I'm not investigating out of morbid curiosity. We're trying to understand what happened so we can save lives."

"We? You mean, you and Jess?" With her defenses weakened, Claire's latent jealousy had seeped out.

Rob rolled his eyes at the veiled accusation of infidelity. "And Sally and Tom and the entire BAU. We've just made a breakthrough. The accomplice's name was Rachel Morris. She lived in Springfield."

Despite her anger, his words had stoked Claire's interest. "Why her?"

"That's what we want to find out. We're going to visit her father tomorrow morning."

Claire swallowed. "Then we should both get an early night."

His shoulders sank. Rob had thought he could talk her out of this. But the newspapers were printed and the publicity scheduled. Claire couldn't slam on the brakes even if she wanted to.

Rob threw up his hands in defeat. He would respect her decision.

"Be careful, Claire. I love you."

"I love you, too."

What remained of her defenses crumbled, and she sobbed. He held her again.

"I...had a fight with my mom. Whatever bridges we built went up in smoke."

"She'll get over it."

"This is my fight, Rob. I don't want you to get hurt, too."

"I know. I won't."

Claire collected herself. "Good luck with tomorrow."

"I'll delay the trip."

"Don't."

"I can't leave town now. He could show up here any minute."

He had her there. She could ask many things of Rob, but she couldn't demand that he stop caring.

"OK."

"Promise me you'll wear the vest."

Claire grinned at the memory of the Coolmax Pro Rob had bought her.

"I promise."

"Call me right away if he shows up. Text me or leave a missed call."

"I will." They kissed, and Claire pulled away. "You should go."

When he left, she locked the door and engaged the security chain. She glanced at her watch. Ten-thirty PM, Friday night. The waiting game had begun. She hoped she'd get some sleep tonight. What the hell had she gotten herself into?

CHAPTER 55

Sunday morning, Rob gunned down I-90 West. Blue skies stretched overhead. The sun played in the tall trees along the highway. At long last, he and Jess were heading for Rachel Morris's last known address. The farm outside Springfield was registered to Leonard Morris, her father. The surprise visit might reveal how Rachel had become William Wolfe's protégé and shed light on other key questions. Or they might find nothing at all. Either way, it was a beautiful day for a road trip. But Rob's mind drifted to Claire.

He'd delayed this outing a full day, staying within two minutes' drive of Claire's home and checking his cellular phone reception every few seconds. Her murderous stalker was only one of his concerns. The homicides were getting to Claire. Her childhood traumas had weakened her sense of reality and wounded her self-confidence. Over the past six months, while her physical injuries had healed, Rob had tried to soothe her mental injuries, too. Now the guilt had returned. Overwhelmed with shame, Claire was risking her life to snare a merciless killer. Her sense of self-worth was slipping. And in her line of work, psychological wounds were deadly, too.

But perhaps the danger had passed? Saturday had come and gone, and still, the killer hadn't shown up. Claire was crawling the walls at home, and Rob had relaxed his vigil. Their unsub hadn't fallen for the trap. This relieved Rob, but the killer's unpredictability disturbed him, too. A typical stalker would have reacted strongly to humiliation from the object of his obsession. Either the unsub was smarter than they had thought, or they had completely misdiagnosed the killer.

"Rob?" Jess asked him from the passenger seat. It was the second time she'd spoken his name.

"Sorry. I was somewhere else."

"That's OK. I was wondering. Even if Rachel Morris displayed the typical characteristics we'd expect in the childhood of a serial killer, will that help us understand the pack's unusual MO?"

"Yes and no."

A white Toyota Tundra appeared in the rearview mirror. Rob had seen a similar pickup truck down the street from the motel yesterday. Was the vehicle following him or had the news of Claire's stalker made him paranoid?

Rob hadn't planned on sharing his suspicions about Rachel Morris with Jess just yet. But he'd roped the young detective into working on the weekend. The least he could do was turn their fishing expedition into a worthwhile educational experience.

"In the seventies, the BAU interviewed convicted serial killers in prisons. The analysis of that data produced the set of categories and characteristics we use to guide the search for unknown subjects."

"Dr. Fleischer's profiles?"

"Exactly. We've expanded and honed our techniques over the decades, but the field is still not an exact science."

"I guess people are hard to predict."

"That's true. But the patterns are surprisingly reliable."

Jess jumped on the opportunity to show her knowledge. "Serial killers usually kill within their own race. They prefer certain MOs and signatures. They are mostly male, had cold and critical mothers, and were often exposed to sexual abuse at a young age. Early on, they develop violent sexual fantasies, which become more detailed and obsessive with time."

"Very good. But what if all of that is wrong?"

Jess gave him a sharp look and a cautious smile. Was that a trick question? She made a stab at an answer. "The pack broke the mold?"

"Yes and no. At first, the Middle School Strangler seemed to fit the pattern perfectly. But later we discovered the killer had done this on purpose. William Wolfe had read the serial killer literature. He designed the murders to frame somebody else, Detective Jed Wallace, as a standard serial killer."

"Life imitating art?"

Rob grinned. "Killers imitating psychology textbooks. He would have gotten away with it, too. We only discovered the deception because William Wolfe confessed. But the number of victims and MOs we've discovered now means we need to rethink everything."

"To adjust profiling theory for the new data?"

"I'm not sure that's enough. This case has exposed a major gap in our knowledge of serial murder. We based our theories on the killers we've caught. But many murders go unsolved. What if the successful killers have a different profile altogether? Or worse —no reliable profile at all. Our profiling system might have a huge blind spot that allows these killers to operate undetected."

"Wow!" Jess had grasped the enormity of the problem.

Rob checked his mirrors again. The white truck had fallen two cars behind.

"Exactly."

With Tom in Quantico, Sally away for the weekend, and Claire in no mood to analyze her father's murders, the young detective was the first sympathetic ear his theory had found. *How ironic.* "In the best-case scenario, our research into criminal psychology has helped serial killers up their game. But if we can figure out how William Wolfe operated, we might open a window onto a whole new subfield in criminology."

"To eliminate the blind spot?"

"That's our goal."

Rob turned onto a dirt road. Dust clouds rose in the rearview mirror as they approached the farm. The white truck sped by without slowing. *Paranoia, it is.*

White cedars traced the edge of a marsh, but the parched earth seemed unable to support crops or herds. Had Rachel Morris traded the barren landscape of her childhood for a thrilling world of violent crime?

Rob parked beside a rusting Chevy pickup on the gravel lot. The visitors got out and walked toward the farmhouse. Stretches of sun-bleached wood outnumbered the strips of peeling paint. The owners had despaired of maintaining the structure and let nature take its course. Did anyone still live there?

A few knocks on the screen door produced the answer—a thin, bent man with a jaw of white stubble and wary, pale-blue eyes.

"You took a wrong turn," he said by way of a welcome.

"Leonard Morris?"

He studied their faces, his eyes filling with suspicion. "People call me Lenny."

Rob produced his badge. "I'm Special Agent Cline, and this

is Detective Long of the Newburgh Police Department. Can we speak? It's about Rachel."

"Rachel?" The word seemed foreign to him, as though he hadn't heard his daughter's name in some time. "Is she in trouble?"

CHAPTER 56

The killer cruised along I-90, following the brown sedan at a safe distance. He drained the last drops from his Starbucks and settled in for a long drive. He should feel calm and collected. The plan was proceeding without a hitch. Only one last step remained. Even the newspapers had fallen into line. But ever since he'd discovered the FBI agent in Claire's bed, he'd known Robert Cline spelled trouble. And the more he observed the agent, the stronger his premonitions grew.

For the past two days, he'd staked out the motel and monitored Agent Cline's movements. This was the agent's second trip to Springfield. The first had taken him to the cemetery, where he'd spent a half hour in the main building before leaving in a hurry. What had he discovered?

Not much, it seemed. Agent Cline had spent Saturday kicking his heels in Newburgh. If the agent had picked up a scent, he would've followed the trail. But he didn't. *False alarm.*

The killer had bought a copy of Saturday morning's *The Newburgh Herald*. He'd liked the paper's coverage of his work, especially the moniker Bella Winters had created for him, *The*

Newburgh Slasher. The reporter had connected the murders to the hookers in Albany, too. *Good work, Ms. Winters.* The interview with Victoria McAdams had rubbed him the wrong way, but on second thought, her accusations were harmless. In fact, her cheap shot at Claire dovetailed nicely with the plan.

But Saturday's article had riled his feathers. In a sudden flip-flop, Winters had interviewed Claire and, ignoring McAdams's theory, she'd printed Claire's side of the story. And Claire had used harsh words against her stalker. Claire was only playing a role. Even so, a man had his pride. *That's no way to treat family, Claire.* He'd have a word with her about that. *Soon, Claire. Very* soon. But first, he'd complete the plan.

Well-trained in caution, he'd continued his vigil of the FBI agent. Robert Cline had eaten breakfast with the forensic psychiatrist, Dr. Sally Fleischer, who was staying at the same cheap motel. *Tut-tut.* The FBI's budget didn't go far. Then, Agent Cline had hit the road, and this time he'd taken the younger blonde detective along. But instead of driving to the police station or even the ranch house, they had turned onto I-90 East.

The killer eased his foot off the accelerator and fell two cars behind the brown sedan. Observation and preparation were the fundamental tools of his trade. But too much observation could give the game away.

The sedan exited the highway at Springfield, and the killer followed. Sweat prickled on his forehead, despite the AC. How much did Cline know? When the sedan turned onto the dirt road, he had his answer. Special Agent Robert Cline had picked up the scent.

This was bad. A catastrophe. And with the plan so close to completion, he couldn't afford any risks. He stepped on the accelerator and flew past the farmhouse. If Cline had come this far, soon he'd piece things together. Agent Cline had to be stopped.

A smile cracked his lips. An idea had struck. *Yes.* He knew just how to silence the FBI agent. The step would require only a small deviation from the plan. But the pivot was worth the risk. He'd kill two birds with one stone.

CHAPTER 57

"Dead?" Lenny Morris said.

Rob nodded solemnly, clasping his hands as he sat on the stained covers of the sagging sofa in the old man's living room. News of his daughter's death seemed to have aged him another decade.

Lenny's lips trembled. "How?"

Rob considered how to present the devastating information. Lenny surely knew about his daughter's juvenile record and, possibly, her other clashes with the law. But no father expects to outlive his children, and Lenny was no exception.

"There was a confrontation with law enforcement officers. Rachel was involved in some criminal activity."

"Criminal activity?"

The news seemed to surprise him. Rob and Jess shared a meaningful glance. Was Lenny in denial of his daughter's criminal behavior? Rob needed more context.

"When did you see her last?"

"About a year ago."

"You weren't in touch often?"

"Not since she left home."

"How long ago did she leave?"

Lenny rubbed the white stubble on his jaw while he made a mental calculation. "Seven years ago."

"How old was she then?"

"Eighteen. She'd been itching to leave for years. I didn't blame her. Rachel never got along with her mother." Lenny shook his head in disbelief. "Died six months ago? Where is she buried?"

"Here, in Springfield. Mr. Morris, where is your wife? We were hoping to speak with her, too."

His boney shoulders rose as he sucked in a deep tremulous breath. "Ruth left a year after Rachel." He gave a dry, bitter laugh. "She'd been so happy to get rid of Rachel, but then she took off, too. Just upped and left. Didn't take any of her clothes or nothing. This place has a way of driving folks off."

Jess caught his eye again. Knowing what they did of Rachel's adult crimes, her mother's sudden disappearance sounded highly suspicious.

"I had always worried she'd come to no good."

"Why is that?"

Lenny hesitated, reluctant to bad-mouth his dead daughter. "She'd gotten into trouble as a kid."

"The arson incident?"

"There was that. I never believed she set fire to O'Reilly's barn. That was just another rumor their son, Dale, spread."

"There were other rumors?"

"Nasty stories. He'd always had his eye on Rachel, but she didn't want him. So, he tried to ruin her reputation. Maybe if nobody else would take her, he'd win her over."

Lenny rubbed the liver mark on his arm. "There were other signs, I suppose. Money disappeared from my wallet. Not a lot. She swore she'd taken nothing. But deep down, I knew."

He turned to Rob as if for reassurance. "Kids do stupid

things they regret later, don't they? That's what I thought about Doris, too."

"Doris?"

"Our dog." He winced at the memory. "She was a beauty. A Pomeranian. Ruth loved that dog. I found her hanging from that big cedar out front, drawn and quartered. Ruth blamed Rachel, of course. I refused to believe her. But whenever we talked about Doris, Rachel would smile. It wasn't a kind smile if you know what I mean."

Rob nodded. Arson. Theft. Cruelty to animals. Lenny's description of Rachel's childhood behavior checked many of the early indicators for psychopathy.

"Mr. Morris, you said that deep down you suspected Rachel was responsible for those incidents. But when we mentioned her later criminal activity, you seemed surprised."

"I thought she'd turned over a new leaf ever since she joined you."

"Joined who?"

Until now, Lenny's story had made sense. Now, he'd thrown Rob for a loop.

"You're with the FBI, aren't you?"

"Yes. But I still don't understand."

Lenny looked him squarely in the eye. "Rachel went to work for the FBI. That's the reason you're here, isn't it?"

Jess's eyes widened. Whatever they had expected to learn about Rachel's past, a career at the Bureau was not on the list.

"How did that happen?"

"They recruited her. A few months after the arson incident, an FBI agent showed up asking about Rachel. He said she was in a high-risk group for future criminal activity. The FBI had a program, The FBI Youth League, to bring kids like her back to the straight and narrow. They offered board and lodging, as well as training. And if she played her cards right, she'd get a job at the FBI."

Rob had never heard of such a program, and he sincerely doubted the Bureau would draw future agents from a pool of criminally inclined youths.

"That's why she left home," Lenny continued. "To join the FBI."

"But you saw her after that?"

"She'd drop by every few months, but only after Ruth left. Sometimes she'd bring along a friend from the Youth League."

Rob reached for his notepad and pen. "What was her friend's name?"

"Jerry? Johnny? I don't remember. He was about Rachel's age. She seemed happy. I thought she'd found her place in this world. A safe place."

"Did you see the recruiter again?"

"A few times."

A thought occurred to Rob. He pulled his phone from his pocket, his heart thumping, and located a photo.

"Mr. Morris, is this the FBI recruiter?"

The father glanced at the photo and frowned. "He looked younger then, but yeah, that's him."

Rob showed Jess his phone, and her mouth opened in shock. They had identified the FBI recruiter.

CHAPTER 58

"We need a new strategy," Captain Morris Washington said on Sunday evening.

On the square video feed of Claire's phone, he munched potato chips and dropped crumbs on his casual gray T-shirt. Grudgingly, Claire agreed.

As the sun set on the weekend, her captain had scheduled a Zoom video conference to discuss their progress—or lack of progress—in the Newburgh Slasher case. Claire took the call on her phone as she paced her mother's living room. She hadn't left the house in two days, and her stalker still refused to show up. Her tension and frustration had reached boiling point.

Captain Washington took a swig from a bottle of beer. "Any ideas why he didn't bite?"

"Maybe her police guard scared him off?" Sally's face appeared on the screen when she spoke. Her black tank top exposed the clear, milky skin of her shoulders, a result of endless hours studying crime scene photos indoors. The wall behind her had the same cheap brown wallpaper of Rob's motel room.

"I told Patrol to be discreet," Detective Lucas Gomez said.

His video camera was off, and Claire didn't speculate about the detective's weekend clothing choices.

"What do you think, Sergeant Wolfe?" Washington asked.

"Are they that obvious?"

Rob had mentioned the plainclothes officers when he'd dropped by on Friday. That seemed a lifetime ago.

"Probably. Especially if our perp is expecting a trap. Any action at Bella's?"

"We almost shot a pizza delivery guy."

"Fair enough." Detective Haruto Nakamura's disembodied head blocked a shelf packed with books. "Junk food kills."

"Yeah, well, he won't be returning to that address."

"He's blown us off," Claire said. "We can send the officers home."

Washington took another sip of beer and swished the beverage in his cheeks while he thought. "Let's keep them until morning. If the killer doesn't show his face by then, we're back to good old-fashioned detective work. We'll regroup then."

"Yes, sir."

The call ended. Claire groaned. She'd spent the last forty-eight hours watching detective shows on Netflix and munching Fritos. If she didn't change her lifestyle soon, she'd transform into one large, paranoid corn chip.

She changed into her running clothes and hit the street. Too late, she remembered the bulletproof vest Rob had given her. She didn't need the extra layer of protection. Her stalker had stood her up, and Claire had better things to do. When she turned into the next street, an unmarked police car pulled up alongside her.

Through the open window, Officer Del Freeman smiled at her. "Making things easy for him?"

Claire tapped the Glock she'd stuffed into the pocket of her sweatshirt. "The opposite. I don't take rejection well."

"Hell hath no fury like a woman scorned?"

Claire chuckled. "An armed woman—for sure!"

The officer shadowed her for the rest of her run. He was clearly bored out of his mind and worried he'd be blamed if the killer intercepted her during her exercise routine.

The rhythmic padding of Claire's running shoes on the sidewalk filled her mind. She wanted to kick herself. While she'd languished at home, the killer was probably scouting his next victim.

Claire slowed to a walk as she returned to the house. The failed plan had cost her more than wasted time.

You're not my daughter. Claire hadn't spoken to Mom since their fight. Diane was convinced Claire had evicted her out of spite. But Claire had only wanted to protect her, not pay her back in kind. The fallout was partly Claire's fault. She could have packaged the news better. But her mother's knee-jerk reflex reaction of hatred and suspicion had triggered Claire's defenses, and she'd been too tired and edgy to restrain her mouth.

A figure emerged from the shadows and headed for the house. Claire's heart skipped a beat. She reached for her gun, then relaxed her grip.

"Gomez?"

Detective Lucas Gomez spun around. "Sergeant Wolfe. You snuck up on me." He looked different in jeans and a dark sweater.

"I didn't mean to." *What is he doing here?* She glanced at the takeaway bag from New Burgher.

"I got you some dinner, figured you'd be stir-crazy by now." He laughed nervously.

"Thanks." This was awkward. Gomez had gone above and beyond the call of duty, and the selfless act seemed out of character. His aftershave carried on the breeze. Was he trying to hit on her? Claire was his commanding officer. Didn't he know she and Rob were dating?

Officer Freeman's car cruised by, and they watched him pass.

She pointed at the door. "I should freshen up and get some sleep. The waiting has drained me."

"Right. No problem. Here." He held out the takeaway bag. "I'll see you at the department."

Claire accepted the food. "Yeah. Thanks again, Lucas."

"No problem."

Back inside, Claire locked the door behind her and latched the chain. She added mayo to the burger and took a few bites. *That was weird.* But appreciated. Nakamura was right about Gomez's communication issues with women. The New Burgher delivery reminded Claire of her first unofficial date with Rob. He'd remembered her preference for mayo with her burgers from her teenage years. What was Rob having for dinner tonight?

Claire ran the bath upstairs, peeled off her wet running clothes, and eased into the scalding water. Immersed in a fog of rising steam, she closed her eyes and breathed in the lavender scent of the bubbles. The heat soothed her muscles, and the tension faded.

Rob had called to check up on her a few times. That morning, she'd told him not to delay his trip to Springfield any longer.

Rachel Morris. William Wolfe's accomplice had killed a young teacher and stolen her identity to gain access to Newburgh Middle School. Rob was retracing her father's footsteps and unraveling his complex criminal plot. What new abominations had Rob discovered today?

Claire thought of her mother's million-dollar payout. The

money was dirty. It must be. But how had William Wolfe leveraged his criminal genius to get rich?

"Nothing like a hot bath to ease your bones," a man said.

Water surged and splashed as Claire nearly jumped out of
her skin. Thinking she was alone in the house, she hadn't
closed the bathroom door. Now a man stared down at her from
the threshold while she lay naked in the tub. An evil grin
twisted his lips, and in his hand he held a butcher knife.

CHAPTER 59

D r. Sally Fleischer's eyes widened. "The FBI?"

Rob sat with her and Jess in the Newburgh PD conference room that evening. Lenny Morris's revelation had floored him that morning, and now Sally experienced the same slap of surprise. The forensic psychiatrist had traveled to Boston for the day, but Rob had mobilized her to discuss their discovery. Because if he and Jess weren't mistaken, William Wolfe's murderous pack hadn't died with him.

"That's what he said. An FBI agent recruited Rachel for a program designed to rehabilitate criminal youth. The so-called FBI Youth League was supposed to lead to a career at the Bureau."

Dr. Fleischer snorted. "The FBI headhunting psychopaths —that's highly unlikely. And that would mean the FBI is partly responsible for this." She jerked her head at the crime scene photos on the conference room table.

Jess leaned forward, her elbows on the table. "We thought his story sounded fishy, too. Lenny Morris didn't remember the name of the FBI recruiter, but he identified him from a photo."

Rob showed Sally the photo on his phone, and she raised her eyebrows.

"The recruiter was William Wolfe?"

"He's certain it was him."

"I called Chief Alda," Rob said.

"On a Sunday? You're a brave man."

"She never stops working. Alda said there's no FBI Youth League or similar program by another name. William Wolfe impersonated an FBI agent and invented the program to recruit criminal youth to his pack."

Sally stared at the wall while she processed the information. "He'd be able to mold them to his way of thinking and turn them into his foot soldiers. Juvenile criminal records are usually sealed. With his training, they'd operate freely under the radar of law enforcement. It's ingenious." She sighed. "So now we know how he roped Rachel Morris into his pack. Couldn't this wait until morning?"

"There's more."

Rob nodded at Jess to continue the discussion. She'd pieced important parts of the discovery together and deserved the limelight.

"Lenny said Rachel sometimes brought a friend along on her visits—a colleague from the fabricated FBI program. He was about her age and called Jerry or Johnny—Lenny couldn't remember."

Sally's eyes widened. "Another man? The pack isn't dead."

"And we've identified another victim. Lenny said his wife, Ruth, didn't get along with Rachel and had accused her of killing their dog. A year after Rachel's recruitment, Ruth disappeared into thin air. He thought she'd left him. Then, Rachel started to visit him on the farm."

"Rachel murdered her mother?"

"That seemed likely. When we found fingerprints on the

mother's hairbrush at the farmhouse, we stopped by the medical examiner's office to confirm our theory."

"They consult on Sundays, too?"

Jess blushed. "The assistant made an exception. He's a... friend of ours. We compared the prints with those of the buried corpses."

"And?"

"We found a match. Ruth Morris is one of the pack's victims."

"Good work. But you didn't have to go to the morgue for that. We have the fingerprints on file."

"There was another reason for our visit." Jess eyed Rob, handing back control of the conversation.

"Jess discovered Rachel's true identity using the birthmark on the decapitated female victim. But there was a second decapitation victim, a male. We'd assumed William Wolfe had used that victim's identity to pursue other targets. But now we know there was another male member of the pack. What if the stolen identity was meant not for William, but another accomplice—Rachel's friend?"

Sally's chest rose as her breathing sped up. "Did you identify him?"

"We got nothing more from the body. No birthmarks. But I'll ask the FBI lab to speed up the DNA work."

"Good." Sally turned to the photos on the desk. "Which one is Ruth Morris?"

Jess pointed at a photo in a group of thirteen. "That's her."

Sally chewed her lip. "Shot in the back of the head. Lisa Evans—I mean, Rachel Morris—killed the last Middle School victim by gunshot. That was her preferred MO. That's it!"

Rob and Jess traded confused looks. "What?"

The psychiatrist shifted the groups of photos on the conference room table. "We thought we had a serial killer couple with multiple MOs. But the pack contained three killers, each with a personal MO. Rachel used guns. William strangled his victims. So, the third member of the pack..." She trailed off, her mouth hanging open.

"What is it, Sally?" Rob asked.

Sally extracted a manila folder from her leather carry bag. "I didn't say anything before. The investigation had resisted considering serial murder, and I didn't want to rock the boat by broadening the scope of the murders. But now this is more than conjecture."

From the folder, she retrieved two crime scene photos. Both depicted the naked back of a murder victim, the word "Claire" cut into the dead skin.

"These are the two new homicides, Carmine Hannover and Victoria McAdams." She pointed at the writing on the bodies. "Note the malformed A."

Rob looked closer. Missing its bridge, the A resembled an upturned V or chevron. The symbol triggered a vague memory. "We've seen this before, haven't we?"

Sally slid another group of crime scene photos closer. Rob recognized the victims of the Middle School Strangler. Sally pointed at the ax marks on three of the victim's faces. Despite the severe damage to them, the mutilation marks thickened into a shape resembling a broken A.

Rob met Sally's gaze. "It's the same symbol."

"The cases are connected, Rob. The pack—or whatever remains of it—is behind these homicides, too."

She moved the two recent crime scene photographs with Claire's name toward the group of stabbing victims he'd unearthed at the ranch house.

"The forensics on the older corpses isn't certain, but the MOs seem to match. Shallow stab wounds and exsanguination.

Mutilation. The so-called Newburgh Slasher is the missing member of the pack."

Rob stared at the photographs. "William Wolfe wanted Claire to join his pack."

"That would explain the killer's fixation with her."

"I don't know. That's a strange way to recruit her to his murder club."

"Not to recruit her. Maybe he believes the rumors. Maybe he thinks she's already with the pack?"

"Then why draw attention to her? Why leave a marking that could connect the crimes?"

He'd raised solid objections, and Sally took her time answering. "The symbol must serve another purpose. But a connection to the pack explains why he didn't fall for Claire's trap. He's not a stalker—not a typical stalker."

Rob sighed. "One step forward, two steps back."

"Welcome to Newburgh. Something tells me Captain Washington won't like this new direction either."

"I don't blame him. Excuse me, I need to make a call."

Rob stepped outside the room and called Claire. Her number rang. Claire didn't want to hear about her father's crimes, but now she had no choice. If her stalker belonged to William Wolfe's pack, she might be the key to catching him. Did the killer crave her attention or—aware of her rejection of the pack—did he seek revenge?

By the fifth ring, Claire still hadn't answered. A dark cloud descended on Rob's mind. Why wasn't she answering? He pressed the phone to his ear, willing Claire to be alive and well.

"C'mon, Claire. Pick up."

CHAPTER 60

D iane stepped into the spotlight, and butterflies flitted about in her stomach. Alone on the stage, she'd walked into a dream. This *was* her dream, after all. But tonight, she was wide awake and as sober as a judge.

The microphone trembled in her hands, and her knees wobbled. She shielded her eyes against the bright light. Silhouettes shifted in the crowd of The Red Keg. Frank hadn't lied. A large crowd of people had turned out, and they expected a good show. But could Diane deliver? She'd never needed a drink more than now.

"Are you ready?" she said into the microphone.

"Yeah!" a woman yelled.

A man whooped. The audience was in a great mood, and the good vibes were catchy. She wouldn't let them down. What did she have to lose?

"Show us your titties!" a man cried, and a woman swatted him on the head. His wife, probably.

Diane tittered. "Not tonight, folks. Been there. Done my jail time."

People chuckled. They were laughing with her this time,

not at her. She was funny. Maybe she could pull this off.

"I'm staying dry now. I just hit a personal record." Hands clapped, and she bowed. "Two days sober."

More laughter.

She glanced at the drummer behind her. Jimmy gave her a thumbs-up. On the electric guitar and keyboards, Mike and Barry nodded at her. After two intense days of rehearsals, the band was ready to rock 'n' roll. Diane turned back to the waiting crowd. She wasn't perfect, but she got better every day.

"All right. Let's do this."

Jimmy tapped his drumsticks together four times, and the music played, nice and slow at first. They started with her favorite, "Proud Mary".

Diane sang of leaving a good job in the city. Her fingers still trembled, but her knees didn't buckle. Heads in the crowd swayed to the tune. She sang of false starts and rebirth. The lyrics told the story of Diane's life. When she reached the chorus, the audience joined in and put their hands together. They were rolling on a river. The story strummed Diane's heartstrings and, she sensed, those of the crowd.

Then the band dialed up the tempo and volume. Diane belted out Tina Turner's greatest hits, the songs she'd sung that first, infamous night at the bar. The band slowed for "We Don't Need Another Hero." Diane had heard the songs a thousand times, but they'd never spoken to her like tonight. By the time she reached "I Don't Want to Lose You," tears welled in her eyes. She knew who she was singing for. She sang for the one person who should be at the bar but wasn't.

If only Claire could see her now, she'd find an apology in her mother's eyes. Diane would take back her angry, hurtful words. Claire *was* her daughter. She always would be. They needed to bury the past to clear a path to the future.

Diane sang of people who'd made mistakes. She sang about

the fear of taking chances on somebody she'd just met. In the crowd, Frank met her gaze and nodded. He understood.

When the last song ended, Diane didn't want to leave the stage. She was born for this. Why had she wasted all those years on drink and despair?

Diane headed for Frank when she stepped off the stage. "How'd we do?"

"Perfect. Just...perfect."

Diane wiped a tear from her eye. "I don't want this night to end."

Frank hooked his arm in hers. "Darlin', the night has just begun."

CHAPTER 61

The killer stared at Claire, and she stared back. She cursed her carelessness. Lulled into a false sense of security, she'd left her Glock in her sweatshirt, which now lay in a pile of clothes on the bathroom floor and out of reach. By the time she'd lay hands on her weapon, he'd skewer her with his long blade. Her pulse raced. She had to think fast, or she'd share the fate of Carmine Hannover and Victoria McAdams.

In his mid-twenties, the killer's thin, wiry body sported dark jeans and a sweater. He stole a glance at her naked body in the water. Most of the bubbles had disappeared, and Claire covered her nakedness with her hands.

"Don't be embarrassed, Claire. We're family."

Family? The stalker was delusional. How had he slipped past the two police guards and snuck inside without a sound? Unarmed and alone with a killer, Claire needed to call for backup. But if she made one wrong move, he'd murder her.

Claire's phone rang. The killer followed the sound with his eyes to the pile of clothes.

"Aren't you going to get that?"

To answer the phone, she'd have to climb out of the bath

and expose her naked body. The move would also reunite her with her gun. Was that what he wanted—an excuse to gut her on the bathroom floor?

"It can wait."

The ringing phone bought her time. Watching him closely, she compiled a mental inventory of her potential weapons. A squirt of shampoo to his eyes might buy her a few seconds while she used the shower cord to disarm him. In hand-to-hand combat, she'd have a fighting chance, and her soapy, wet skin would slip through his grip.

But he'd caught her in an unfavorable position. The odds in a physical confrontation worked against her. Words offered a better alternative. In this negotiation, she was both the negotiator and the captive—and the stakes were her life.

What had Rob taught her about negotiation? *Understand your opponent.* Learn about his goals and constraints. Did this killer consider himself a master strategist? Did the murders serve a bizarre grand plan? She had to keep him talking.

The phone fell silent. Her time was up.

We're family. The killer's words gave her an opening. If they were family, she'd treat him like an equal despite the power imbalance.

"What are you doing here?"

"I know. We weren't supposed to meet like this in Phase Two, but plans change."

"Phase Two?"

She repeated his words, using strategic empathy, the negotiation technique Rob had taught her to encourage him to elaborate.

The man narrowed his eyes. "Didn't Bill tell you?"

The stranger might have poured a bucket of cold water on Claire's head. *Didn't Bill tell you?* This killer was no stalker.

And Claire understood. Bill hadn't fathered a bastard son

during his many travels. The man with the knife belonged to her father's murderous pack.

Soon this city will be ours. Her father's words rang in her mind. Bill had almost gotten away with the Middle School Murders. The recent homicides formed a part of another complex criminal plot. Her father's plot. He'd set the wheels in motion but hadn't lived to see its fulfillment. Claire was neither this killer's target nor his love interest. She was his collaborator. And if Claire wanted to survive this meeting, she needed to preserve that mistaken belief. And she'd better be convincing.

"Bill said he had big plans for the city. But he didn't get a chance to share the details."

The killer frowned. "That explains a lot." He ran his fingernail along the sharp blade of the butcher knife. "You said some hurtful things in the paper. That was...unsisterly. I was starting to think you'd forgotten who you are."

"I thought the pack was gone. I didn't know this was our work."

He narrowed his eyes again. "I left you a sign."

Claire swallowed. Was this a test? "What sign?"

He scoffed. "Bill told you nothing. Maybe he thought you didn't need to know?"

"He didn't tell me I had a brother either. Maybe he thought you weren't worth mentioning?"

He scowled at her. Had she pushed back too hard?

"Not a brother. A kindred spirit. Our bond is deeper than mere DNA."

Then, he sniggered.

"What's so funny?" Had he lied to her? Had he come there to kill her? Was he toying with his prey before delivering the death blow?

He shrugged. "Bill spoke about you all the time. He idolized you. But you know nothing about the pack. Isn't it ironic?"

Her tactic was working. For the moment, her life was not in danger. But what was the purpose of Bill's Phase Two? She had to learn more to stop the next murder.

"He died before he could tell me everything."

The mention of Bill's death sobered him up.

"And you avenged his death. Jed Wallace got what was coming to him, and for that I'm grateful."

Claire kept a poker face while her brain filled in the blanks. A popular theory on KillerWolfe.com claimed Claire had killed Wallace in cold blood in revenge for killing her father. The story confused the sequence of events and misidentified the active parties. But the killer must never learn the truth. If he did, he'd go after Rob.

"What's my role in Phase Two?"

"The less you know, the better. Bill wanted to keep you out of Phase Two."

"Then why leave my name on the bodies?"

The killer smirked. "There's a reason for everything, Claire. You'll understand when the plan has run its course. It's brilliant."

He wasn't giving her anything.

"What's your name?"

"I go by many. You can call me Johnny."

"How many more will die?"

"Just one. The cherry on the top. We've been building up to this for a long time. Everything is in place. It's beautiful. We're going to make Bill proud."

"Who's the target?"

He smirked. "You don't want me to ruin the surprise, do you?"

"How will this give the pack control of the city?"

"You're a good detective, sis. Figure it out. But I need you to do one thing for me."

"What?"

"Special Agent Robert Cline."

Claire's heart skipped a beat. How much did he know about Rob?

"What about him?"

"You've become close, haven't you?"

A tremor entered his voice. He disapproved of her relationship with Rob. Was he jealous? Or did he think dating an FBI agent could jeopardize his plan?

Claire raised her chin. "Keep your friends close, your enemies closer."

"I prefer to bury them. To each his own. But Agent Cline has been poking his nose where it doesn't belong. He might know too much already. If he figures us out before we're done, he could ruin everything."

"I'll keep an eye on him and find out what he's learned."

"That's not good enough, Claire. We can't risk screwing this up. This is Bill's legacy—your father's legacy. The Apex reputation is on the line."

"Apex?" Was that the pack's name?

Johnny scoffed. "Wow, Claire. You really do know nothing. I can help with that. I'll leave you a little surprise on my way out. But you need to stop Agent Cline's investigation."

Claire held his gaze. "I'll take care of it."

"Good. Because if you don't, I'll handle him myself." He bowed his head. "It's been a pleasure to meet you, Claire. We'll meet again soon." He made to leave, then turned back and grinned. "Oh, I almost forgot. Thanks for the beer."

CHAPTER 62

"Dinner's on me," Rob told Jess. The cozy booths at Eddie's Bistro in Newburgh's trendy East District had comfortable seats of rugged leather and tables of thick, lacquered oak. After wrapping up their brainstorming session with Sally, Rob and Jess realized they hadn't eaten since breakfast, so Rob asked Jess to recommend a nice local restaurant. The old-fashioned steakhouse did not disappoint, and Rob's mouth watered from the ambient aromas of sizzling beef.

Jess furrowed her brow. "Are you sure?"

Rob perused the leather-bound menu. "Definitely. My treat. We're celebrating, remember? We made a huge breakthrough today."

Jess gave her shoulders a youthful, elated shrug, and her face beamed with a broad smile. "We did!"

Rob believed in recognizing the victories in life, and Jess had sacrificed her weekend to the case without complaint. She deserved this. They ordered steaks and beers and enjoyed the soft country tunes on the speakers. At the end of an intense and stressful weekend, Rob seized this opportunity to unwind.

Claire had scared him by not answering her phone earlier that evening. Rob had called Newburgh PD Dispatch, and the call center had put him in touch with Officer Del Freeman, who assured him that Claire had just returned from a run and was probably in the tub. Rob had overreacted. No stalker would approach the house with two poorly concealed police officers watching. Claire was in no real danger. He'd share their discoveries with her tomorrow morning. If Rachel Morris's criminal friend was the Newburgh Slasher, the decapitated man's DNA might lead them to Claire's stalker in short order.

Jess leaned forward and rested her elbows on the table. "Is Dr. Fleischer right—are the chevrons the pack's secret symbol?" Her eyes sparkled. The day's adventures hadn't put a dent in her energy levels.

Rob leaned back on the padded upholstery. He'd deliberated the question ever since Sally had pointed out the chevrons.

"I don't know. The signs seem real enough. But we can't rule out apophenia."

"Don't make me Google that."

"Apophenia is our tendency to see meaningful connections between unrelated things. Evolution has hardwired our brains to find patterns. Is that rustling in the bushes a hungry tiger or just a breeze? Paranoid early humans survived better. Today, they litter the Internet with conspiracy theories. Finding meaningful connections is Sally's job. But maybe the chevrons exist only in our minds?"

A waiter delivered the beer bottles.

Rob played devil's advocate. "Why would the pack leave markings that could connect the Middle School Strangler with the Newburgh Slasher? These killers thrived on secrecy and misdirection."

"Maybe it's their signature—or a kind of ritual?"

"Then why didn't they mark the buried bodies? They're the pack's work, too."

Jess brushed a lock of blonde hair from her eyes. "I guess they only marked the bodies they wanted people to discover."

Rob took a swig of his beer. "I think you're onto something."

Jess had an uncanny way of finding a handle on a problem —the telling detail that cleared a path to the solution. The more time he spent with Jess, the more he realized Claire had underestimated her.

Jess sipped her beer and smiled self-consciously. "What?"

He'd been staring at her. "You're a good detective."

She snorted, unconvinced.

"I'm serious."

"I almost fainted at my first crime scene."

Claire had told Rob about the Hannover murder scene. "Carmine Hannover was different, wasn't she?"

Jess tensed up and tried to mask her discomfort with another gulp of beer. Was she embarrassed about her reaction at the crime scene or had something else made her squirm?

Rob let the subject go. This was no time to dwell on murdered women. "Forget about that. We're celebrating, right?" He raised his bottle. "To us."

Jess smiled. "To us."

Their bottles clinked together, and the steaks arrived.

Rob sliced into the steaming chunk of meat and chewed. "Mm. This is *good*."

Jess groaned in agreement.

Rob's conscience pinched. He should celebrate with Claire, too. He'd wanted to share more details of the case with her. Claire had a sharp mind and knew the cases by heart. But she hated hearing about her father's criminal past. And without Tom around to act as a sounding board, Rob had turned to Jess.

Claire's father wasn't the only source of friction in their relationship. Claire was under a lot of pressure to catch the new serial killer. He'd carved her name into the dead women's bodies and delivered their body parts to her desk. Most people would respond with shock and horror. But Claire's reaction included a double serving of guilt.

The shame of her family history made her reckless. She'd used herself as bait to lure her stalker to her home. And when Rob tried to protect her, she pushed him away.

His phone rang, and Rob hurried to answer. But the caller wasn't Claire.

"Sorry," he told Jess. "I should take this. It's Tom."

Jess swallowed a mouthful of steak. "Sure. Go ahead."

"Nice to hear from you, old-timer."

"Don't remind me about my age, Rob. How are you holding up on your own?"

"Who said I was alone? I traded you in for a newer model." Rob winked at Jess, who blushed at the compliment. "And we've made progress."

Tom grunted. "Don't be greedy now. Leave something for me to do."

"How's the family?"

"All good. I'm heading back tomorrow morning."

"Glad to hear it." Rob made a mental note to move Claire's stuff out of the motel room. "See you then."

Rob put away his phone and sliced another chunk from his steak. "Tom is getting back tomorrow. I hope we find a match for the second decapitation victim. If this investigation helps us catch the Newburgh Slasher, too, my boss will have to agree that the trip to Newburgh wasn't a waste of Bureau resources."

Jess took a long chug of her beer, and a mischievous smile curled her lips. "I don't think your trip was a waste at all."

CHAPTER 63

Claire remained perfectly still in the bath and listened, straining her ears over the deafening beating of her heart. The steps creaked as the killer went downstairs. A door closed. The killer—Johnny, if that was his real name—had left the house.

Claire lunged over the side of the tub, and the bath water surged and splashed. She pulled her phone from her sweat-soaked clothes and, fingers trembling, selected the number of Officer Del Freeman.

"What up, Sergeant?"

"He's here!"

"Who is?"

Claire stepped out of the bath, cradled the phone to her ear, and grabbed a towel.

"The killer. He just left the house."

"Nobody's there. I'm looking at the front door right now."

"He has to be. I heard a door close downstairs. He's on the street."

"Slow down, Sergeant. I've had my eyes on the house the whole time. Nobody left."

Claire blinked, water dripping from her body onto the bathroom tiles. "He must have gone out the back. Go through the yard, I'll meet you there."

"I'm on my way! Calling for backup."

Claire wrapped the towel around her body and found her Glock. Barefoot, she padded downstairs, her weapon aimed at the floor. Johnny's short visit had swamped her mind with revelations. The pack survived and it had a name—Apex. Her father had planned the recent murders. And the killer believed she was on his side.

Thanks for the beer. Claire had accused her mother of taking the beer cans Rob had left in their fridge. But Mom had told the truth. As Claire had suspected, the killer had been here that night, in her home, walking around while she and Rob slept in her bed. She shivered. He'd violated her home, helping himself to the contents of her fridge. Had he known she was his enemy, he would have murdered her in her sleep.

A sudden doubt gnawed at her mind. She could arrest Johnny for breaking and entering, but did she have enough evidence to charge him with Carmine Hannover's murder? He'd left no forensic traces at the crime scenes. Claire had no record of their conversation. If she arrested him now, he'd know she was working against the pack, and she'd lose her only advantage.

Claire glanced at the front door. The security chain was still latched. Del was right—the killer hadn't used the main entrance. Noticing the police surveillance, he must've entered through the kitchen's back door. But she would've heard him break in. She'd soaked quietly in the tub with the bathroom door open. Had he forced his way inside while she'd run the water?

She stepped into the kitchen, gun at the ready, the tiles cold beneath her bare feet. And her breath caught in her throat. The security latch of the backdoor was fastened, too. That made no sense. She'd heard a door closing when he'd left. Without breaking the windowpanes, he couldn't attach the security chain from outside. Icy fingers of uncertainty curled around her heart.

The kitchen door rattled, startling her. A hand knocked on the wood from outside. Claire inched the window curtain aside with the barrel of her gun, then unlatched and opened the door. Officers Del Freeman and Adam Jenkins stood on the threshold.

"No sign of him," Officer Freeman said. "No footprints in the dirt either."

Claire shuddered in the chilly air. "The door was chained."

The redheaded Jenkins rubbed his bulbous nose. "He must have climbed out a window."

Freeman shook his head. "We didn't see him on our way around the house. Maybe he already jumped the wall or..."

His eyes flashed as the realization struck.

Claire mouthed the words. "He's still inside."

Freeman raised his eyebrows at Jenkins. "Did you call it in?" He spoke louder than necessary. They were putting on a show for the hidden stalker.

"Yeah. Another squad should be here any second."

"Good."

Freeman closed the door, secured the latch, and motioned with his finger for Jenkins to stay put and watch both exits while he and Claire explored the house.

She rubbed her arms and shoulders to warm them from her short exposure to the chilly night air. Claire followed Freeman to the basement door beneath the staircase. Was this the door she'd heard the killer use? Had he overheard Claire's discussion with the officers? Did he know she wasn't his willing collaborator?

Freeman aimed his gun in both hands and gestured for Claire to open the door for him. She nodded and steeled herself with a deep breath. The last time she'd entered the basement, her father had almost strangled her. She'd been lucky to survive. This time, the killer would be waiting for her and doubly deadly. Claire shoved her fears aside, turned the handle, and swung the door inward.

The basement was dark and silent. Freeman hit the light switch. He swept his gun sideways, scanning the room for intruders. Then he descended the steps. The hairs on the back of Claire's neck bristled.

The basement was empty. The officer opened the built-in closet at the end and peered inside. Except for an old hangar on a horizontal pole, the closet contained nothing. Freeman turned to her and shook his head. Johnny wasn't there. That left the bedrooms upstairs. They climbed up the stairs, Claire expecting the door to slam shut and lock them within, but they emerged into the entrance hall without incident.

They were running out of places to search. As silently as possible, Claire led Freeman upstairs, their weapons at the ready, and Claire's heart thumping.

Steam still hung in the bathroom air. Claire's running clothes lay beside the full bath. She tried the door to her bedroom, Diane's room, and her mother's en suite bathroom. Nothing.

They returned to ground level.

"He's not here," Freeman told Jenkins. "The windows are all locked from the inside, too. False alarm."

Jenkins whipped out his phone. "I'll call Dispatch."

Claire gaped at Officer Freeman. "This is not a false alarm. The killer was here, in my house. He had a knife. I spoke to him while I was having a..."

"When you were in the tub?" A note of humor had entered his voice.

Claire folded her arms. "Yes."

"Are you sure you didn't doze off? I drift off in the tub all the time."

"I didn't dream him up, Officer." Claire didn't mean to snap at him, but his patronizing tone had severed her frayed nerves.

"Just saying. Happens to the best of us. Mind if I make some coffee?"

"No, go ahead."

Jenkins put away his phone. "Make that two." The redhead looked Claire up and down. "It's all the same to me, but you can get dressed now."

Claire went upstairs. What was happening to her? She'd seen the killer. He'd spoken to her. But how the hell had he left the house without a trace? Was Officer Freeman right—had she imagined the whole encounter? Was she losing her mind?

She came downstairs in her winter pajamas, half expecting the killer to be there, holding the officers at knifepoint. Instead, Freeman handed Jenkins a steaming mug.

"Thanks for the coffee, Sergeant."

"Don't mention it."

Claire let the officers out and locked her fortress again. Outside, they chuckled. Tomorrow, she'd be the laughingstock of the department. *Crazy old Sergeant Wolfe in the tub with her imaginary serial killer. What a nutjob!*

Claire pressed her back to the door and slid to the floor. Her body trembled. *What the hell just happened?*

CHAPTER 64

"This is me," Jess said.

Rob pulled up outside her apartment building, but the pretty young detective made no move to leave the Bureau car. A pleasant buzz tickled Rob's mind. He wasn't ready for the day to end either. The beers and steak had hit their mark, and their recent breakthroughs in their case had put them in a good mood. He and Jess had fallen into a comfortable working rhythm. But with Tom returning tomorrow, he'd see less of her in future.

"I'm sorry for making you work this weekend."

She giggled. "Are you kidding me? This was the most fun I've had in years." The beers had loosened her tongue, too.

"Even the trip to the morgue?"

"Maybe not the morgue." Her eyes sparkled in the dim glow of streetlamps and apartment windows. "Thank you, Rob."

"For what?"

"For believing in me. Taking me seriously. Most people in the department don't. All they see is a blonde. They think I made detective because the chief had to fill a diversity quota." She grinned ironically. "Maybe I should dye my hair?"

"Don't change a thing. You're a great detective. People will understand that once they get to know you."

Jess grinned like the Cheshire cat. She deserved to feel proud of herself. Rob had only pointed out the obvious.

"Do you want to...come upstairs for a drink?"

Rob's pulse sped up. His body was saying yes. Jess was attractive and fun, and their work partnership was ending. If he wasn't in a relationship, he'd take her up on her offer. He'd thought everyone at Newburgh PD knew he and Claire were together. Jess, it seemed, was out of the loop.

"I'd love to, but I'm dating someone."

"Oh. I'm sorry!" Even in the soft light, a red flush spread over her cheeks. "I had no idea you had someone back home."

Nope, the rumors hadn't reached her. Rob had to tell her the truth.

"Actually, she's here, in Newburgh. Claire."

"Claire Wolfe?"

"Mm-hm."

Her mouth dropped open. She'd been hitting on her superior's boyfriend.

Rob broke the shocked silence. "We met in high school but lost touch when her family moved to Newburgh. Last year, I came here to work on the Middle School Murders, and we reconnected. I thought that was public knowledge. I'm sorry if I misled you."

An uncomfortable thought passed over her face. "I, um—"

"Claire doesn't have to know about this. I know you'll be working together again soon."

"Yes, we will. Thank you! And thanks for dinner." She opened the passenger door, eager to flee the awkward situation.

"Jess."

She turned back.

"I had a good time today."

She smiled. "Me, too."

"See you tomorrow?"

"Yep."

She entered her apartment building, and Rob exhaled. Had he created false expectations by buying her dinner? He didn't think so. Rob was just being nice. But he'd avoid these situations in the future. Next time, he'd invite Sally to join them. And Claire, too!

His phone rang. Claire was returning his call. Had her female senses detected his close encounter with another woman? He chuckled at his superstition.

"Claire, I tried to reach you earlier. Are you OK?"

"He was here."

Claire's voice sounded nasal as though she'd been crying. Rob understood immediately. The stalker had shown up at the house.

"Are you OK?"

"Yeah. But he got away."

Rob breathed a sigh of relief. Claire was unharmed. But something had gone wrong.

"Rob, I need you."

He shifted the transmission into Drive. "I'm on my way."

CHAPTER 65

C laire sat on the entrance hall floor and shivered. She hugged her legs in a fetal position and rocked back and forth, still clutching her Glock. Her world was imploding. Again.

A question buzzed in her head, the question in Officer Freeman's eyes. Was she losing her grip on reality?

No! Claire had seen and heard the killer in her house. He revealed details about the case of which she had no prior knowledge. But how had he entered without a sound? And how had he vanished into thin air, leaving the doors and windows locked from the inside?

Her detective's brain audited her memory of the event. The killer claimed to belong to her father's pack. He said William Wolfe had planned the recent homicides. But no shred of evidence connected the Newburgh Slasher deaths to the Middle School Strangler murders. Had Claire's guilt over her father's homicidal legacy bled into her present-day life and caused a psychotic break with reality?

The sound of knocking on the front door jolted her from

her dark thoughts. Claire wiped her teary face on her pajama sleeve, picked herself off the hard floor, and peered through the peephole. Like a frightened little girl, she had begged Rob to come over right away, and he'd answered her call. She fell into his arms the moment he stepped inside.

"He was here." She blabbered into his chest and held him tight. "But nobody believes me."

He shushed her. "I believe you."

His words should've sounded ridiculous. He hadn't heard what she had to say yet. But his declaration of unconditional trust calmed her. Rob always knew the right thing to say.

"I'll fix us a hot drink, and you can tell me everything. OK?"

Claire nodded. She sat at the kitchen table while he heated the kettle and mixed two mugs of hot chocolate. While the steam rose from their drinks, Claire told Rob about the killer's surprise visit, his revelations about Phase Two and Apex, and his concerns about Rob's investigation. Rob nodded and gave her his undivided attention. He listened without interrupting, even when she told him how the killer had baffled the officers by disappearing without a trace.

Tears threatened to flow again. "I'm losing my mind."

"You're not. Everything you told me makes perfect sense."

Claire scoffed. He was patronizing her, too, playing along with her mad story until the men in white coats arrived with a straitjacket. They'd lock her in a padded cell and throw away the key.

"I mean it. The Middle School Murders are related to your current case. I wanted to tell you earlier, but I couldn't reach you."

Claire perked up. "Seriously?"

"To be honest, I wasn't sure you'd want to hear that news. You wanted to put your father's crimes behind you, and I don't blame you. But today we found evidence that the pack is still active."

Rob told her about his visit to Rachel Morris's father, Sally's insight into the markings on the victims' bodies, and their deduction that the pack comprised three killers, not two.

"Lenny Morris said Rachel's friend was called Jerry or Johnny. That's too close to be a coincidence. The Newburgh Slasher is the last surviving member of Apex. William planned these murders, too. Thanks to you, we know Phase Two calls for one last murder and Johnny still thinks you're with the pack. This is great news, Claire. We have a good chance at stopping him."

Claire released a brief burst of pent-up breath. She hadn't lost her mind. She'd made a breakthrough.

"But how did he get in and out of the house? You should've seen the way the officers stared at me—like I was batshit crazy. Dispatch notified Captain Washington when the officers called for backup, and he called me to follow up. He thinks I'm wacko, too."

"Then we'll prove them all wrong, Claire, like we did before. There must be a rational explanation. The officers must have overlooked something."

Claire nodded and sipped her hot cocoa.

Rob raised his mug to his lips, then paused. "What if he got inside before you used the chain?"

"Before?"

"When you went for a run."

"How did you know I went for a run?"

"I called Officer Freeman. He said he tailed you in his car. That means only one officer remained at the house. Johnny could've slipped inside unnoticed while you were out."

"But how did he leave?"

Rob froze. "Maybe he didn't?"

"We thought of that, too. We searched everywhere. He's not here."

"Let's have another look."

They abandoned their drinks and drew their guns. Claire stayed close behind Rob. Could Johnny still be in her home? If so, she'd spent the last half hour cowering on the floor, alone with a serial killer. He would have overheard every word they'd said. But if Claire had blown her cover, why hadn't Johnny attacked her once the officers had left? Was he waiting to catch her unarmed? Or would her premature death spoil her father's carefully laid murderous plans?

They went upstairs and checked the house room by room. Rob opened closets and poked around inside. He tapped the walls and panels and listened for hidden crawl spaces. He tested the windows for loose panes. Again, they found nothing.

Only the basement remained. Rob opened the door and turned on the light. The hollow shell of the underground chamber resonated with menace. Claire followed Rob down the stairs. Terrifying memories flashed in her mind with every step. Her father's confession. The weight of his body on her back, pinning her to the floor. The deadly cord tightening around her neck. William Wolfe had murdered and mutilated his victims in this basement. And Claire had almost joined them.

Steel shelves lined one wall. William Wolfe had stored his murder trophies there, along with the collection of oversized, hairy spiders he'd used to torment Diane. Now the shelves stood empty. A forensics team had cleared out the contents. The only furnishing was the empty built-in closet at the end of the room.

Rob opened the doors of the closet. An unused clothes

hanger hung from the horizontal pole. They had searched the entire house but discovered no secret hiding places and no concealed means of escape.

"I told you—" Claire began, but Rob put his finger to his lips.

He pointed with his gun. A thin black line separated the board at the back of the closet from the wall. The plywood panel concealed not bedrock but a dark opening.

Rob holstered his gun and stepped into the closet. The wooden base creaked under his feet.

"Careful," Claire whispered.

She trained her weapon on the black line. Rob had discovered a hidden compartment, and the killer might be inside, ready to pounce.

Rob placed his fingers along the edge of the panel. The plywood board shifted sideways under his touch and glided noiselessly on hidden tracks.

Claire held her breath. Within the closet, a narrow room faded into darkness. No murderers lurked within, only a desk with a laptop and a small wheeled stool.

Rob flipped a switch on the wall, and a naked bulb ignited overhead. A thick layer of dust coated the desk and laptop. Rob drew his gun again and stepped into the room. No, not a room —a tunnel with bare cement walls.

I'll leave you a little surprise on my way out. Johnny had left the house using a hidden tunnel, and he'd left the secret doorway open for her to find.

Claire followed Rob inside. The smell of wet rot hung in the dank air. Cobwebs filled the corners but didn't obstruct the tunnel. The killer had passed this way.

Rob turned on his phone's flashlight, and Claire did the same. The tunnel stretched on and on. Claire followed as if in a dream. For years, she'd lived upstairs, unaware of the hidden access space beneath her feet. Her father had used this tunnel to commit his crimes unnoticed, and now Claire was walking in his footsteps. William Wolfe had more secrets than she'd imagined, and her gut whispered that she'd only scratched the surface.

Rob stopped abruptly at the far wall. Then, the beam of his flashlight rose toward the ceiling. Metal rungs in the cement led upward, forming a ladder. Rob climbed the rungs and disappeared into a vertical shaft.

Claire grasped a cold metal bar with one hand and ascended after him. The hard metal rungs pressed into the arches of her slippered feet. They were stumbling blindly into the unknown beyond enemy lines.

Rob halted. "There's a hatch."

He groaned with effort, and cold air blew into the tunnel. Rob continued upward and stepped into a dark circle of stary sky.

Claire waited on the ladder. She aimed her gun at the opening and braced for the sound of gunshots. None came. Seconds later, she poked her head out of the tunnel. Walls hemmed the narrow patch of dirt on three sides. Rob approached her from the far end of the strip between neighboring properties. His breath frosted in the chilly night air.

"It ends in a bush facing the street. Johnny must have come and gone using the tunnel." He smiled at her. "You're not crazy, Claire."

A lump of gratitude lodged in her throat. But her newborn relief died quickly. The killer had easy access to her home. She needed to seal that gaping hole in her security. Or did she?

"Johnny said he'd leave me a surprise. He knew William hadn't told me much. He left the panel open on purpose."

Rob nodded. "Let's see what other surprises he left us."

They returned the way they had come, down the shaft and

along the tunnel to the small desk and laptop. Dust coated everything except for the laptop's keyboard and stool. Claire sat at the desk.

"We should let Forensics handle the computer," Rob said.

Under normal circumstances, Claire would agree. Forensic technicians routinely created forensic clones of hard drives under investigation. The procedure left the computer in its original state and eliminated the possibility of tampering with evidence. But these were not normal circumstances.

"He wanted me to find this. He'll be expecting me to open it. If I don't or the computer goes offline, he'll know something is wrong."

Rob handed her a pair of latex gloves. Fingerprints on the secret laptop might help identify and locate Johnny.

Claire donned the gloves and stared at the laptop. What horrors lay hidden within?

"This is where he planned it all. The Middle School Murders. The bodies at the ranch house. Carmine Hannover and Victoria McAdams. It's all in here."

A part of her didn't want to know the details. That part wanted to bury her father's gruesome deeds forever. But Phase Two called for one last murder—a life Claire might save.

Rob laid his warm hand on her shoulder. "Are you ready?"

Claire nodded. She placed her finger on the touch pad and nudged the computer out of hibernation. A log-on screen appeared. The username read "william."

Claire swore under her breath. Access required a password. A crime lab might take hours to break into the computer, but Claire needed answers now.

"Johnny didn't mention the password, did he?"

"No, he didn't."

What good was Johnny's "surprise" without the password? Was he toying with her or had he assumed she'd figure it out?

Most people used predictable passwords, but her father wasn't most people. Still, he'd use something meaningful to him. Claire tried his telephone number. *Invalid password.* She tried his birth year. *Invalid password.* How many log-in attempts would she get before the computer locked her out?

Rob hovered over her shoulder. "Try your mom's details."

"He'd never use those. He hated her with a passion." The suggestion sparked an idea. He hated Diane. But he loved Claire. He'd seen her as his protégé and expected her to join his murderous pack. She tried her name and birth date. She tried the word "Apex." No luck.

Rob straightened. "I guess we should call in that forensics team first thing tomorrow morning."

Claire wasn't ready to give up. She was a Wolfe. Her father's daughter. She should be able to figure this out.

"Claire?"

"Give me one more shot."

"It could lock us out."

"I know."

He idolized you. And Claire understood. She typed three letters, hit Enter, and the screen unlocked.

She punched the air. "Yes!"

"Cub?"

"It's a pet name he gave me. William wanted me to find this."

Rob leaned over her shoulder, and they studied the screen. A browser window displayed a log-on screen. There were no explanatory texts or links, only a single-word title in block letters. APEX.

The pack had an online portal, and William Wolfe had logged in before his death. He'd wanted Claire to unlock his secrets. Or had Johnny done her this favor, too?

Rob spoke softly in her ear. "This is the mother lode, Claire."

Claire had come too far to stop now. She entered "william" for the username. In the password field, she typed the word "cub." A table of data appeared—a list of names. This was the missing piece she'd searched for. Now, everything made sense.

CHAPTER 66

" A pex?" Detective Gomez repeated the word Claire had used, and it seemed to taste bitter on his tongue. Monday morning, Claire met with the investigative team in the Newburgh PD conference room. The two cases had merged into one, and Captain Washington's office was too small to host the discussion. Claire, Rob, and Dr. Sally Fleisher had stitched the strands of new information into a coherent theory last night and were ready to unveil their conclusions to the rest of the team. Despite the psychological strain and sleep deprivation, the turn of events energized Claire. For the first time since Carmine Hannover's murder, a solution to the case appeared within reach.

"As in 'Apex predator,'" Sally explained. "The top of the food chain. This fits the wolf pack metaphor William Wolfe used for his group. An individual serial killer is vulnerable. But a pack of psychopaths—sharing information and coordinating activity—is much more formidable."

Rob had told the detectives about Lisa Evans's stolen identity, William Wolfe's recruitment strategy, and the evidence pointing to a third member of the pack. Sally explained how the chevrons connected the Middle School Strangler victims to those of the Newburgh Slasher. Finally, Claire described the killer's visit last night, his connection to the pack, and his concern about Rob's investigation, as well as the secret tunnel and laptop she and Rob had discovered.

"The chevron represents the A of Apex."

Claire continued where Sally left off. "We found a list of names on the Apex darknet website."

As the detectives knew, the darknet consisted of websites inaccessible to regular search engines such as Google. This hidden underbelly of the Internet served as a haven for illicit activity. The laptop's browser, Tor, allowed the user to explore the darknet anonymously.

"The names—aliases really—match the victims we unearthed at the ranch house. Last on the list are two names: C.H. and V.M."

"Carmine Hannover and Victoria McAdams," Captain Washington said. "They're all connected—the recent homicides and the Middle School Murders. As we suspected, the McAdams murder wasn't a reaction to *The Herald*'s article. We're in Phase Two of the pack's grand plan."

Nakamura raised his hand. "Why keep a list of victims? Doesn't that incriminate the pack?"

Claire answered. "This is a management interface that Apex used to coordinate the pack's activity. Each name has a dollar amount, ranging from fifty grand to a few hundred thousand. From what we can tell, the entries are dated weeks or months before the victims' deaths. It seems Apex operated an assassination ring. Dr. Fleischer?"

Sally took over. "This is a criminal operation unlike any I've encountered. Apex has generated millions of dollars in revenue from the murders. By staging the crimes as serial killings, they sent law enforcement in the wrong direction. Don't get me wrong—the assassinations *are* the work of serial killers. Apex located young psychopaths using the insights of forensic behavioral psychology. But the group channeled their murderous compulsions to serve the pack."

Gomez chuckled. "If you're going to kill somebody anyway, you might as well make a buck?"

"In return, the killers got a new family. Support. Acceptance. We found more details on the laptop. Clients ordered the hits online and deposited money in numbered accounts. This explains the killer's choice of high-risk victims."

"What about the chevrons?" Washington asked. "Did they sign their work—like artists?"

Sally hesitated. "We're still unsure about the symbol's significance. None of the ranch house bodies bear the Apex mark."

Nakamura raised his hand again. "Coming back to the Middle School Murders, why would anyone pay top dollar to knock off little girls?"

"The girls don't appear on the hit list. Their murders were an internal project. As William Wolfe confessed, he'd planned those crimes to frame Detective Wallace for Tina Wolfe's murder and to advance Sergeant Wolfe's career."

All eyes focused on Claire. This time she didn't flinch. She'd emerged from her near breakdown last night with a new resolve. She was done running from her father and his crimes. Claire was going to undo his work and root out Apex. Her family connection to the criminal group had helped crack the case, and she'd leverage her inside information to destroy Apex. She'd turn her curse into a blessing.

Jess had lingered in the corner and spoke up for the first time. "So, who paid for the murders of Hannover and McAdams?"

Claire had wondered the same thing. "The clients on the

Apex site used monikers instead of their real names. Some are single characters. Only one moniker appears in the list twice, the client who ordered the last two hits—Hannover and McAdams."

"What's the moniker?"

"A single letter, M."

Gomez said, "Hannover was going to meet an M the night she died. Didn't we think M stood for Malik?"

Claire shrugged. "That's possible. But we learned something else from Johnny. Phase Two calls for one last murder. He called the third murder 'the cherry on the top'—the climax of the other homicides."

Nakamura had a third question. "I thought Hannover and McAdams were the last names on the list. How can there be one more?"

Claire exchanged a glance with Rob and Sally. They had debated this point into the early hours of the morning.

"You're right. We're not sure."

Gomez sighed. "So, we have no idea who this next target is —or even if there is another target?"

Captain Washington took over. "We can explore two angles. First, the killer. If we find him before he strikes again, we'll shut down Apex for good. Forensics is at the house now, dusting for prints. The FBI lab is processing the DNA from the male decapitation victim as a top priority, and Sergeant Wolfe has created an identikit of Johnny. Sergeant, add that to the murder book."

"Yes, sir."

"Gomez, search the camera footage of the hotel and the vicinity of the McAdams house for the perp."

Gomez groaned. "Again? I know that camera footage by heart."

"Quit grumbling. Connect him to a vehicle registration, and we'll have him for sure. We're so close." Washington turned to

Nakamura. "Find out what you can on Apex. Help Gomez with the financials. For all we know, Hannover's PA paid for the hit with her trust fund money. Agent Cline, see if the FBI has a file on Apex. They must have turned up on their criminal radar."

Rob nodded. "Will do."

"Where's Agent Brown?"

"Back in town later today."

"Good. What now, Nakamura?"

Nakamura lowered his hand. "What's the second angle?"

"The mysterious letter M. The client who hired Apex to whack Hannover and McAdams might lead us to the third target—directly or indirectly. When the killer strikes again, we'll be waiting for him. Sergeant Wolfe and Detective Long will follow that lead. Any more questions?" He raised his eyebrows at Nakamura, daring him to ask another. "OK. Let's get moving. Somebody's life depends on us."

The team dispersed. Claire went to the bathroom, then returned to her desk and attached the image of the computer-generated identikit to the case files. Her vision doubled over her computer monitor. She'd slept two hours last night. Rob had jammed the door of the basement closet shut with a kitchen chair and locked the basement door for good measure. She'd need an oil tanker of coffee to survive the day.

"Sergeant?" Jess had materialized at her desk. "Where should we start?"

"Start?" Claire's exhausted mind drew a blank.

"Our mysterious friend, M?"

"Right. Sorry, I'm running on fumes." Claire had gotten used to flying solo. Now she had to keep her field trainee occupied. "Um, review the reports. There's a lot of new information. Draw up a list of suspects, anyone with a motive to kill both Hannover and Victoria."

Claire yawned. Fatigue had misaligned the cogs of her

brain, and her mental wheels spun uselessly. She needed fresh air. During her lockdown weekend, personal chores had piled up, too. She needed to collect Diane from the motel. And Tom was getting back today. *Crap.* She had to clear her things out of Rob's room before his partner returned. At the climax of her investigation, she'd become a moving service. Claire hoped she wouldn't fall asleep at the wheel.

She reached for her suit jacket. "Start with Sarah Malik. I need to run a few errands. I'll be back later."

The morning sunlight seemed too bright when she emerged from the station. As Claire got into her car, her phone rang. *Private number.* Edward Hannover, probably, checking up on his hired gun. She answered, despite having zero patience for her wealthy shadow.

"Yes?"

"Sergeant Wolfe?" The fragile female voice on the line belonged neither to Carmine Hannover's father nor her mother.

"Who is this?" Had the unknown third victim contacted her? Was Johnny already at her door?

"This is Sarah Malik."

M is for Malik. Talk of the devil.

"I'm sorry. I didn't recognize your voice. How can I help you?"

"I need to speak with you."

"If this is about your offer—"

"It's not. This is about Carmine Hannover and Victoria McAdams. Can you come over now?"

CHAPTER 67

Diane woke with a start. She lay in a strange bed...and she was naked. Memories of last night arose in her mind, and she relaxed. A contented smile spread across her lips.

After the gig at The Red Keg, she'd gone home with Frank. They'd made love—and she didn't even know his last name! She giggled. *Diane Wolfe, you're behaving like a reckless teenager.* Thankfully, Frank wasn't in bed with her now or he'd think she'd lost her mind.

She lingered in the warm bed and savored the thrill of her new life. A few months ago, she'd given up on the future. What man would ever look her way, never mind seduce her with kindness? She'd never dreamed she'd appear onstage again either. Not while sober! Her heart burst with gratitude.

The door swung open. Wrapped in a wooly, white bathrobe, Frank entered the bedroom sideways and balanced a crowded tray in his hands.

"Breakfast in bed for our new star."

Diane shifted into a sitting position, leaned against the headboard, and clutched the sheet to her breasts. The scent of fresh toast and crispy bacon got her juices flowing.

"Mm. That smells good. So, you cook, too?"

He grinned beneath his thick mustache. "Only on special occasions."

As he placed the tray on her lap, Diane pecked him on the cheek.

"Thank you."

Last night, Frank had proved to be a considerate lover, too. What had she done to deserve this gentle cowboy?

"What about you, Frank? Where's your breakfast?"

"On its way. How do you like your coffee?"

Two minutes later, they sat side by side in his bed and ate with gusto. Diane freshened up in his enormous bathroom and found him in the kitchen by the sunlit window, reading a newspaper through dark sunglasses. He was in no rush this Monday morning. The bar only opened in the evening.

"Another coffee?"

"Sure. I'll help myself." She turned on the kettle and found a fresh mug. "Thank you for a perfect night."

"I should thank you. The Red Keg rarely gets such talent. We'll do it again if you're up for it."

Diane was about to say "maybe" but caught herself in time. In her old life, Diane had been afraid to get her hopes up in case the genie's spell broke and all the good things in her life evaporated.

"Yeah. Why not?"

"That's the spirit."

A phone rang on the kitchen counter. Diane's phone. Frank had plugged her device into a charger while she'd slept. She glanced at the screen. Claire was calling. Was she going to follow through with her threat to take away Diane's inheritance? True to form, her daughter was trying to spoil a perfect morning. Diane let it ring.

"Go on," Frank said. "Don't be shy."

Not wanting to raise uncomfortable questions, Diane answered. "Hello."

"Where are you?" Traffic hummed in the background. Claire was calling from her car.

"Does it matter?" Diane didn't want to give away any details. With luck, Frank would never meet her daughter.

Claire sighed with frustration. Or concern? "Yes, Mom, it matters. I told you—there's a killer on the loose. The officers said you blew them off."

"I'm with a friend."

"What friend?"

Diane's shoulders tensed. Was Claire implying she had no friends—that she was incapable of friendship?

"A new friend."

Frank looked over his shoulder at her and grinned. Would Frank take her tight-lipped response the wrong way and think he embarrassed her?

"His name is Frank. Don't worry about me." Then, not to sound cold, she added, "Are you OK?"

"Yeah. For now." *What did that mean?* Claire sounded exhausted. "Anyway, it's safe to return home now. Things can go back to normal."

Did Diane want life to go back to normal? She wanted to stay here with Frank. Was she being too hard on her daughter? If Claire hadn't badgered her into sobriety and better health, Diane would never have met Frank. Did Diane still need Bill's dirty money?

"Mom?"

"I heard you." *Perfect.* Now she had to leave Frank to check out of the motel.

"I can pick up your things from the motel if you like."

The considerate offer surprised Diane. Claire was

extending an olive branch. "Thank you. That would be a big help."

"OK. I'm on my way to a meeting, but I'll stop by a bit later. I'm glad you're OK."

"Me, too. Bye, Claire."

Diane carried the two mugs of fresh coffee over to Frank and sat beside him. The French windows of the kitchen faced a small garden with pretty flowers in blue and red.

"Was that your daughter?"

"Who?"

"On the phone. The daughter who drops you at the gym?"

"Oh, yes." Diane had forgotten that Frank had seen Claire already. She sipped her coffee and stared at the flowers outside, trying to avoid further questions.

"You're lucky to have a daughter like that."

"Yes, I suppose I am."

"What does she do for a living?"

"She's a police officer."

"No kidding?"

"A detective, actually. Make that sergeant. They promoted her last week."

"Congratulations. You must be proud."

Diane snorted coffee.

"Are you OK?"

She nodded. Pride was not a concept she'd applied to Claire. Diane longed for Tina, not Claire. But she felt a stab of guilt for the hateful things she'd said on Friday. Claire *was* her daughter. Diane had even wanted Claire to see her onstage. She'd started a new life. Maybe she could find a place in her heart for Claire?

She changed the subject. "Do you have children?"

Frank's grin waned. "I had a son."

"I'm sorry. We don't have to talk about him."

"It's OK. When he was alive, I pretended he didn't exist. Now he's gone, and I can't seem to stop thinking about him."

Diane too had lost a child. She had no idea Frank had suffered the same tragedy. "What happened?"

"Overdose. We were never on good terms, especially after his mother died. I was tough on him, kicked him out, thinking that a wake-up call would make him change his ways. But he didn't." Frank sighed. "The truth is, I was embarrassed to have him around. My son, an addict? No way! I poured him his first beer at The Red Keg. He was just weak or lazy. When he'd finally sober up, we'd talk. I'd tell him how much I love him. He'd understand that all I had done was for his own good. But he never sobered up. He graduated from alcohol to marijuana. Then his so-called friends introduced him to heroin." Frank grimaced. Her cowboy was hurting. "I'm sorry. I didn't mean to dump that on you."

"I'm glad you told me." She needed to confide in him as well. "I haven't been on the best terms with my daughter either."

"At least you're talking."

"After the things I've said to her, I think shutting up might have been better."

She chuckled. He put his arm around her and found his cowboy grin again.

"It's not too late to fix that."

CHAPTER 68

"Third time lucky?"

Alexandro "Al" Menendez smirked at Claire and buzzed open the security gate at Malik's home that morning. Did the PA think she'd returned to accept—at long last—his employer's job offer? Claire didn't let the effeminate lisp and tidy goatee deceive her. Beneath the designer suit, Menendez packed a lot of muscle. He never seemed to leave his employer's side. Did he double as Malik's head of security? If the politician had hired Apex to kill Hannover and McAdams, Claire was stepping into the lion's den.

"I told you not to get your hopes up."

Menendez grinned, exposing his golden tooth. "This way. Ms. Malik is waiting for you."

She followed him down the windowed corridor alongside the swimming pool. The pool guy was nowhere in sight. Had Malik cleared out her staff ahead of Claire's visit?

Sarah Malik didn't get up to shake Claire's hand this time when she entered the office. The politician seemed to take refuge behind her oversized desk. With her shoulders hunched, her dark eyes flitted to Claire, her face transformed by a hunted look. What had shaken her so much over the weekend?

"What I'm about to tell you cannot become public knowledge. I need your word that this will remain between the two of us."

Claire shrugged. "That depends on what you have to say."

After a momentary hesitation, Malik relented. "At first, I thought Carmine's murder was a coincidence. Now I'm not so sure." She turned to Menendez. "Give us the room."

Menendez bowed his head and exited, closing the door behind him.

"They approached me two years ago."

"Who did?"

"The three of them: Kitty Tucker, Carmine Hannover, and Victoria McAdams. They were a tight-knit group of friends and they shared dark views about Newburgh's future. Kitty claimed the police were corrupt. Together, they dug around and found more shady operations in government. Newburgh was broken, and they'd fix it. That's when Carmine approached me to run for mayor."

"That was Carmine's idea?"

"Carmine and I met through my law offices. I had a successful practice. A political career was a vague option for later in life but not something I'd considered seriously. When Kitty died because of police corruption, the need for change became urgent. Her friends made that their mission in life. Carmine and Victoria became my major campaign donors. But hiring you was Carmine's idea."

Claire suppressed her surprise. "Why did Carmine want to hire me?"

"She'd followed your career. She even compiled a file on you. Newspaper clippings and photos." Malik chuckled wistfully. "Carmine had an artist's heart but an analytical head. You brought down Chief Wallace, the man whose corruption had led to Kitty's death. Our campaign needed someone with your talent and integrity."

Claire studied Malik's expression. The investigation had searched for a connection between Claire and Carmine Hannover. They had wondered why Carmine had withdrawn money from her trust fund. Malik's story answered both questions. But Forensics had found a second set of prints on Carmine's file of clippings, and Claire would bet a month's salary they belonged to Malik. Was the politician coming clean to aid the investigation or to explain away her presence in Carmine's home?

Claire wasn't falling for the charm offensive this time. "You mean, you needed someone with my celebrity."

Malik shrugged. "It didn't hurt that you were already a public figure."

"And with me on your side, Mayor Thornton couldn't use me in his campaign."

"You were his fig leaf," Malik said sharply. She regained her composure. "But not everybody was on board with that idea. Victoria thought you were a part of the corruption. She was convinced that *you* had killed Kitty. But Carmine didn't believe that. It's because of her I offered you that job."

"The night before she died?"

Malik shuddered. "Her death devastated Victoria and me. First Kitty, now Carmine. When we heard they found your name on her body, Victoria felt vindicated. She vowed to share her suspicions with the world."

"Are those your suspicions as well?"

"I wouldn't have called you here if they were. Now Victoria is dead, too. All three of my primary donors are dead—two of them murdered in the past week. This isn't some crazed killer, Sergeant. Somebody is trying to destroy my campaign."

Claire sized up Malik in silence. Her distress seemed genuine. She was right—the murders were not the work of a stalker, despite what the papers claimed. But only a few law enforcement officers knew about the Apex assassin ring. Had Malik reached the same conclusion by coincidence or was she backpedaling furiously to cover her tracks? Claire dismissed that theory. Malik had no motive to send hitmen after her greatest supporters. If she was telling the truth.

"You could have told me this when we discussed Carmine's death. Why the secrecy?"

Malik coughed. "The state limits the amount of money I can receive from a single donor. Carmine and Victoria found creative ways around that."

Claire smiled. "You bent the rules to save the city from corruption—the end justifies the means?"

Malik fixed her with an angry stare. "This might surprise you, but people aren't falling over each other to support an unknown female candidate with an Islamic-sounding name. A little campaign irregularity is nothing compared to what Thornton and his friends get up to. At least we didn't kill anybody."

"But Thornton did? Have the donors of his other rivals disappeared, too?"

"I'm Thornton's main contender. I'm the only one who can unseat him."

"Why attack your donors if he could just kill you?"

"And derail the elections? If I turn up dead, Thornton would be a prime suspect."

Claire had to laugh. "So, Thornton is the Devil? Don't get me wrong—I'm not his greatest fan. But where's the evidence of his corruption?"

Malik didn't answer right away. Did she think Claire was in

Thornton's pocket, too, or was she keeping some cards to herself?

"Carmine found something on Thornton."

"What?"

"I don't know, but it proved he was dirty, and the scandal would bring him down. Carmine didn't get a chance to share the details with me before her death, but it involves permits."

"What kind of permits?"

"I don't know."

"Anything else?"

"That's it."

Claire nodded. Malik had added some important threads to the tapestry, but Claire had yet to see the design in the chaos of details.

"I'll dig deeper."

"Please do, Sergeant. Three good women lost their lives over this. Don't let their deaths count for nothing."

Claire returned to the station, a storm brewing in her gut. Besides two unsolved and high-priority homicides by a complex assassination ring, now she had to contend with a conspiracy theory involving Mayor Thornton. Chief Emmerso was going to love this. Claire despised Thornton for using her to boost his reelection campaign. But she didn't think him capable of murder. Would he do anything to hold on to his position or did he stand to lose more than his political career? Had Carmine found evidence that could land him in prison?

Malik's claims soared high above Claire's pay grade, so she'd play it safe. She'd report to her commanding officer and let him sweat it out. Captain Washington wasn't in his office, so she tried Chief Emmerso. The chief responded to Malik's theory better than Claire had expected, considering that the mayor was his boss.

"That explains Carmine's withdrawals from her trust fund. Political campaigns aren't cheap."

"What should we do?"

This was not a simple question. If Thornton discovered they were exploring allegations against him, he could get them both fired.

"Do your job. Investigate. But keep it quiet. We don't want to start rumors, especially if they're baseless. Maybe that's exactly what Malik wants. If Thornton's dirty secrets could impact these homicides, we need to know."

"How do I investigate him without creating a storm? Who'd speak out against him if he's assassinated his opponents?"

Emmerso's eyes twinkled. "Somebody with nothing left to lose."

CHAPTER 69

Claire's heart pounded as she drove north in her white Ford hatchback that afternoon. The road cut through thick forests under gloomy skies. The scenery mirrored the dread that circulated in her body and gnawed on her mind. With every bend in the road, the boxes of her belongings and her mother's bags shifted on the back seats and in the trunk. Today, Claire had taken her baggage along for the ride. After cleaning out the two motel rooms, she had run out of excuses to delay the trip to Gardner. She'd wanted to turn back many times, but she pressed on. Today, she'd stare her past square in the eyes.

With its low, wide buildings and electrified fencing, the North Central Correctional Institution looked like a heavily guarded warehouse. A guard at the gate checked Claire's name off his clipboard and waved her in. Chief Emmerso had called ahead to expedite the meeting. Claire parked in the visitors' lot, locked her service weapon in the trunk, and entered the main building with the triangular blue roof.

North Central was a minimum- and medium-security

prison. Claire had seen worse. But the tightness in her chest resulted from the purpose of her visit, not the venue.

She passed through a series of locked gates and waited in a visitation cell for the guards to fetch the inmate. When the door opened, she straightened on the chair of hard plastic. The prisoner in blue overalls had lost some belly weight and shaved his hair to a salt-and-pepper stubble, but the bulldog's jowls and short mustache remained unchanged since she'd last seen him six months ago. He saw Claire sitting at the table and halted. For a moment, she thought he'd turn around and walk out. But he didn't. He sat in the chair across the table from her.

Claire glanced at the corrections officer, who lingered at the door. "Can we have some privacy?"

He exited the room, leaving her alone with the inmate.

Harry Wallace, Newburgh's former chief of police, considered Claire with undisguised contempt.

"If I'd known it was you, I would've stayed in my cell."

"I understand why you feel that way."

Claire had killed Jed, his son. Jed had given her no choice. But could Claire have acted differently and avoided that outcome? Either way, his father, Harry, would've gone to prison.

"What do you want?"

"Information."

"About what?"

"Two homicides I'm working on."

Curiosity sparkled in his eyes. "Hannover and McAdams?"

Harry Wallace may be corrupt, but he was still a cop at heart.

Claire nodded.

He sneered. "Are you trying to pin those on me, too? Or on Jed? Oh shucks, you can't do that anymore. You already killed him."

The words stung, but Claire stood her ground. "In self-defense."

"He didn't deserve to die."

"Neither did I."

"Are you sure?"

Claire clenched her teeth. "The FBI is assisting the case. If you cooperate, we can ask them to reduce your sentence."

Claire had called Rob on the way over. The FBI couldn't make any promises. But assisting an investigation would reflect favorably on him at his parole hearings.

Wallace sniggered. "So I can—what—resume my position as chief of police?"

Rage twisted his face, and Claire regretted leaving her service weapon in the car. But the moment passed, and his fury faded to dejection.

"I gave Newburgh the best years of my life. Now all they'll remember is Harry Wallace, the dirty cop."

Claire said nothing. Decades of community service didn't entitle him to tamper with evidence and cover up homicides. Harry Wallace was more likely to resurrect his son than restore his public image, and he knew it. But maybe Claire could speak to the disgraced officer's dormant inner detective?

"We found more bodies at the ranch house."

His eyes glimmered again. "How many?"

"Twenty-eight."

"What's that got to do with Hannover and McAdams?"

"The Middle School murderers ran an assassination service. The bodies we dug up appear on their list of targets along with Hannover and McAdams. A member of the pack is still out there, and he'll go on killing until we stop him."

"We?" He leaned over the table. "There is no we. My son was innocent, but you put him in the ground, and then you put me in here. Your daddy killed those people, *Sergeant* Wolfe. How does that make you feel?"

He'd jabbed his fingers into her open wound and was beginning to enjoy this visit.

Claire ignored his taunts. "Carmine Hannover and Victoria McAdams were major donors to Sarah Malik's campaign. Now they're both dead. Somebody put their names on the assassin's list."

Wallace's smile widened. "I get it now. You've already destroyed a chief of police, so now you're going after the mayor?"

"This isn't about me."

"Are you sure? Because Tommy Thornton is as clean as they come."

"And how clean is that?"

He shifted sideways, resting his forearm on the table. "Tommy is a friend. He made me the chief of police. You want me to turn on him?"

"He didn't keep you out of prison."

"Why should he stick out his neck for a dirty cop?"

"Exactly."

Wallace shut his mouth. She'd found *his* wound.

"Thomas Thornton didn't stand up for you. If he's corrupt, he should pay, too. There's another target on the list. We don't know who. If you have information on Thornton, he might give us that name. You could save a life and catch a killer."

Wallace scoffed. "I'll be a hero?"

"Not a hero—a father. These are the people who set Jed up. We can't bring him back. I wish we could. But sure as hell, we can shut these bastards down."

Claire hadn't wanted to mention Jed. She'd balked at using his memory to serve her agenda. But an innocent life was at stake. If anything could motivate the former police chief, it was his love for his dead son.

Wallace spread his hands in defeat. "I have nothing on Thornton. Like I said, he's clean."

Claire deflated. She'd driven all this way and faced her ghosts only to learn she'd been chasing hot air. Thornton was the type who colored outside the lines. Surely Wallace knew *something*?

"What about permits?"

He frowned. "Nothing that could lead to jail time." Harry's eyes shifted. "There was one thing. It's probably just a rumor."

"I'll take it."

Wallace rose from his chair and called for the guard. Claire swore under her breath. He'd teased her, leading her on only to screw her. The door opened, and the guard appeared in the doorway. Harry Wallace walked out.

At the door, he turned back. "Two words," he said. "Silicon Towers."

CHAPTER 70

Claire paused on the threshold of the squad room like an outsider. Phones rang and keyboards clattered as the detectives of the Investigations Bureau worked their cases. Visible through the open door of his office, Captain Washington spoke with Detective Gomez. The captain owed his recent promotion to Mayor Thornton. How would he react when Claire made Thornton a suspect in the double homicide? She should tread carefully.

She headed for her desk. Her report on her visit to Harry Wallace and Malik's theory would have to wait while she gathered more evidence.

Jess looked up from her computer screen. "Everything OK?"

Claire had left to "run errands" at the height of the homicide investigation and reappeared hours later. Even a newbie detective would suspect Claire was hiding something.

She dodged the question. "Did Gomez find anything on the street camera footage?"

"Not as far as I know."

"What about you—any luck with our mysterious M?"

"I went through the reports. Hannover and McAdams met

at a private school, but their career paths split after graduation. I'm making a list of their known associates besides Kitty Tucker. Maybe they shared an enemy."

Claire grunted. The investigation was firing in every direction and hoping something fell from the trees. She needed Jess's help to explore her new leads. But how could she do that without exposing her secret meeting with Harry Wallace?

"What do we know about Silicon Towers?"

The detective's eyebrows shot up. "Silicon Towers?" Was Claire testing her knowledge of the case files or was this a trick question? "It's a new technology park at the southern edge of Newburgh. The Middle School Strangler deposited his second victim at the construction site."

"Why leave the body at a construction site?"

"It's a public space. Busy during the day but empty at night. A perfect drop-off spot."

"What else?"

"The site appears in the photos from Carmine Hannover's place."

"Why was Carmine so interested in that project?"

"She wasn't. The clippings and photos all have a connection to you. Silicon Towers just happened to feature in an investigation you handled."

"What if there's more to Silicon Towers than meets the eye? Let's review the photos again."

Claire joined Jess behind her desk and peered over her shoulder. Jess opened the murder book for the case and clicked through the scanned items from Carmine's folder. An early photo of the construction site appeared on the carousel.

Claire pointed to an empty patch of earth beside the skeleton of a tower. "Over there. They hadn't started building the second tower yet."

Jess's eyes widened. "This photo was taken before the

Middle School Murders. Carmine had scouted the site before it
became a crime scene."

"Exactly."

Jess grinned. "'Look for what's missing.'"

The sparkle of admiration in her eyes needled Claire's
conscience. She'd only made the deduction thanks to Harry
Wallace's tip-off. Claire had deceived Jess, and she was far too
good at lying for her liking.

"What's so special about Silicon Towers?"

"There were huge protests when the building started last
year. We had to secure the construction site in case the demon-
strations got violent. Captain Rodriguez almost blew a fuse."

"Why were they protesting?"

"The land was earmarked for a recreational park and artifi-
cial lake. Instead of grass and ducks, they were getting
skyscrapers. The environmentalists declared war on the city
planners."

Permits. Had Thornton bent zoning laws to advance the
project? And if so, who benefited from his underhand dealings?

"Find out everything you can about Silicon Towers. Who
owns the project? Who bankrolled it? Everything. Maybe
Carmine and her green friends messed with the wrong
people."

Jess turned back to her computer with renewed purpose
and energy.

Claire walked over to the messy-haired detective's desk.
"Mahoney, how does zoning work in Newburgh?"

"Who said it works?"

She laughed. "Who do I have to sleep with to change
zoning regulations?"

He brightened. "Me."

"You're in charge of zoning?"

"Nope, but it can't hurt to try."

"And if the applicant is a three-hundred-pound gorilla with a venereal disease?"

"In that case, I'd refer Ms. Kong to the Zoning Board of Appeal. The board's eight honorable members deal with all exceptions or 'variances.' And good luck with that."

"Mahoney, you're a treasure trove of useful information."

"That's what we call experience, Sarge. It comes with age and good looks."

And a taste for whisky. Claire headed to the conference room. Questioning the Zoning Board of Appeal would alert Mayor Thornton to her investigation. She hoped Rob and Sally had made better progress with finding the killer.

Claire found them poring over the crime scene photos and case file printouts. This time, Special Agent Tom Brown joined them. All three gazed at her when she walked in.

"Welcome back, Agent Brown."

"I leave town for a week, and Rob makes more progress than we did over the past six months. I'm starting to think I just slow him down."

"I doubt that."

"Congratulations on your promotion, by the way."

"Thank you." She turned to the others. "Any luck tracking down Johnny?"

Rob and Sally exchanged mysterious glances. They were onto something.

"Not yet," Sally said. "The FBI databases have nothing on Apex. But our psychological models might be useful. The Apex client who ordered the assassinations may have selected the victims for Johnny, but he's still a serial killer in other respects. He probably had a juvenile record, which allowed William Wolfe to locate him. That leads to the next question—how did Wolfe obtain that information? We know he impersonated an

FBI agent, but maybe he also had connections within law enforcement?"

"Or social services," Rob said. "Either would give him access to young offenders."

Claire said, "What about the fingerprints in my basement?"

"Forensics found nothing interesting."

"And the DNA of the decapitated man?"

"Any day now."

Claire ground her teeth. Any day now, Johnny would strike his final victim, and the team still had no solid leads.

The door opened behind her, and Jess walked in. "Sergeant, I think you'll want to see this."

Claire apologized to the FBI agents and stepped into the corridor with Jess.

"The project is owned by Silicon Towers Corporation."

"A holding company?"

"That's what I figured, so I dug deeper. Silicon Towers Corporation is owned by Hannover Group."

"As in Edward and Cynthia Hannover?"

"Exactly. Carmine's parents."

CHAPTER 71

S arah Malik chewed her nails and stared at her desk phone. *Don't do it, Sarah.* She'd promised herself she wouldn't stoop that low, no matter what. But like a true politician, she'd break that promise.

A knock on the door shook her from her dark thoughts, and she hid her destroyed fingernails beneath the desk.

Al poked his head into the office. "I spoke with the staff."

"How did they take it?" Too ashamed to fire her house-keepers in person, she'd delegated the dirty task to her personal assistant.

Al shrugged. "They were surprised and disappointed, I guess. But they all wish you good luck. I said we'd rehire them as soon as we can."

"Thank you, Al."

He gave her a brave smile. "Hang tight. Things will work out, Sarah. I'm heading home for the night."

"G'night."

Sarah leaned back in her chair and exhaled a tense breath. Before long, she'd have to dismiss Al, too. She glanced at the telephone again.

Sarah had dipped into her personal savings and borrowed an extra fifty thousand from her 401k. Used to a steady stream of money, she hadn't scaled back her expenses fast enough when the tap had unexpectedly run dry. She'd met with the banks, hoping for a break, but their bean counters considered political campaigns to be highly unprofitable ventures. And they were on the money.

If Sarah didn't take immediate and drastic action, her campaign would go bankrupt, and Thornton would win. How was she supposed to run the city if she couldn't balance her campaign finances? Serves her right for relying on a few wealthy individual donors. An ironic laugh escaped her lips. Newburgh's diversity candidate had failed to diversify her donor pool.

Blood simmered in her veins again. Thornton hadn't beaten her at the polls. He'd sabotaged her campaign by murdering her sources of income. Thornton played dirty. If Sarah wanted to survive, she'd have to get her hands dirty, too.

She opened her black pocketbook and found a telephone number. This was not a number she'd ever store on an electronic device. This was a number nobody should ever associate with her. But today she'd use it, hoping and praying the decision didn't come back to haunt her. She had no choice. She'd run out of options.

With trembling fingers, she dialed the number and waited for the call to connect.

"Salaam," an old Arab man said. No nosy secretaries. This was his direct line.

"It's Sarah." She spoke English. Despite her mother's best attempts at educating her in the ways of tradition, Sarah couldn't speak Arabic to save her life.

"Ah, Sarah!"

His voice rang with joy. Or was that smug satisfaction? He

humored her with his halting English. The Egyptian accent grated on her nerves. The ethnic card was useful up to a point, but the man on the phone was a part of her background she'd hidden well. She had almost convinced herself he didn't exist—that she'd popped into existence from thin air.

"I wondered when you would call for help."

The condescending tone shredded her resolve, and she almost slammed down the phone. *Of course, you'd come running to me. How could you possibly succeed on your own?*

"Who said I needed your help?"

He chuckled. "Politics is an expensive game, no?"

"Politics is not a game."

"Said like a true politician. How much do you need? One hundred thousand US dollars? Two hundred?"

When Sarah's mother had emigrated to the United States forty years ago, she'd stopped speaking to her brother. But Uncle Fara had weaseled his way into Sarah's life with lavish gifts on her birthdays, joyous reunions at family events in Egypt, and a strangely coincidental meeting while she'd visited Paris as a student. Over the years, he'd invested wisely in his American-born niece, expecting his investment to yield dividends when the time was ripe. The old crocodile made his fortune providing security services to oil sheiks. Wikipedia tied him to the Muslim Brotherhood, a major player in global Islamic terrorism.

Sarah could name her amount, and the money would appear magically in a numbered account. He was her genie of the lamp. But what would he demand in return? Fara might be her uncle, but first and foremost he was a businessman. He didn't serve free lunches. One day, he'd call in the favor. *This is a bad idea.*

"Never mind. I'll manage. Send my regards to Nasim."

She hung up before she changed her mind. *That's it, Sarah.*

You're screwed. She'd admit defeat and crawl back to the world of contracts, mergers, and litigation. *Newburgh, you're on your own.*

Carmine's beautiful face arose in her mind's eye. *Dear Carmine.* She'd been a fighter. So had Victoria. Both were dead now, Malik's memories of them already fading. How could she give up knowing her friends had sacrificed their lives to save their city?

The phone rang, startling her. Fara hadn't given up on her so easily. *Screw it.* Nobody won at politics by being squeaky clean. Nobody ever drained a swamp without wading knee-deep into the muck.

"Fine," she said into the receiver.

"Ms. Malik?" a male caller spoke with an American accent.

"I'm sorry. I was expecting another call."

"Then I'm glad I got to you first. Ms. Malik, we haven't met yet, but our group has admired your campaign for some time."

The cold call knocked the words out of her. Was this the answer to her prayers? She recovered her ability to speak.

"I'm glad to hear that."

"We'd like to make a humble contribution to your campaign."

Sarah had played this game long enough to know that "humble contribution" meant a significant amount of money. This windfall could save her.

"That sounds good."

"We'd like to meet face-to-face to move things forward. Are you available tomorrow morning?"

Sarah almost blurted that she was available right now but held back. There was no need to appear desperate. Her lucky break had arrived.

"Tomorrow should be fine. To whom am I speaking?"

"Call me Jim."

CHAPTER 72

"I never expected to see you again." Janet, the black counselor, did a double take when Diane entered the basement of the Second Presbyterian Church. But she delivered the words with warmth.

Diane gave her an apologetic smile. "I never expected to see you either."

Her previous visit to the Alcoholics Anonymous group had been memorable but bitter. She'd do better this time.

"Make yourself at home."

"Thank you."

The other participants helped themselves to disposable cups of Kool-Aid and cookies on the refreshment tables, but Diane made for the nearest empty chair in the circle. She hadn't come here to make friends or small talk. Some of the regulars eyed her and whispered among themselves. "The crazy lady is back," she imagined them saying. "This'll be entertaining!"

She deserved that. But she'd changed since last week's meeting, and her transformation had nothing to do with the million-dollar inheritance. Diane had met Frank. She'd performed onstage and enjoyed the warm embrace of a loving audience. Admittedly, her first show had landed her behind bars. But she'd survived. She'd endured experiences far more painful than a smelly jail cell. And many challenges still lay ahead. But today she was taking a step forward. And if she put one foot ahead of the other, day by day, in the future, Diane would look back on her trials and tribulations and laugh. The first step was always the hardest.

The meeting's attendees settled in their seats. One man nodded at her, and she forced a brave smile. At least he wasn't laughing at her. Not yet.

Diane listened to the first three speakers, her heart beating so loudly in her ears that she couldn't concentrate on what they were saying. In her mind, she rehearsed the words she'd come here to say. The words needed to leave her mouth and find a sympathetic ear.

Janet cleared her throat. "Diane, do you want to share something with us today?"

Diane nodded and drew a deep breath. *Here goes.*

"I used to think my life was over." Her voice sounded strange to her own ears. "I thought I was broken. And because of that belief, I hurt people. I hurt the people I should have helped—my family. My daughter."

A calm, attentive silence filled the room. The eyes of her fellow survivors gazed at her without judgment.

"Blaming others became a way of life. I drank to dull the pain, but drinking was also a weapon. Then something happened that forced me to stop and think. People have hurt me. And I have my problems. But that doesn't mean things can't get better. The truth is, I've been running from myself. By hating other people, I could pretend I wasn't a part of the problem. Hating meant I didn't have to change. But I'm done running. I don't need to run anymore. Because I believe I can change. I *want* to change."

Tears welled in her eyes, and she sniffed. Her words had tumbled out all wrong. But maybe that didn't matter either?

"I'm sorry, I almost forgot. My name is Diane Wolfe, and I'm an alcoholic."

CHAPTER 73

B ill Wolfe pointed at the windshield. "Look at them. What do
you see?"

Johnny peered into the neon-lit gloom outside. Across the dark
street, the silhouettes of three long-legged women stalked the sidewalk in high-heels and suggestive clothing unsuited to the late-night
chill. He passed over the words "prostitute" and "hooker." Bill had
high expectations of him for tonight, and Johnny didn't want to
disappoint him.

"Whores?"

In the driver's seat, Bill grinned. "Sheep. Objects for you to use
and discard. You're a wolf. You're higher on the food chain. Never
forget that."

Johnny nodded. He wasn't a freak. He was a superior subspecies
of Homo sapiens—a Power/Control killer. Bill had taught him that.

The FBI agent at the front door had sent Johnny into a panic.
But the agent hadn't come to arrest Johnny for his crimes. He'd taken
the young offender under his wing. Johnny's mom had rejoiced at the
chance to hand him over. He wasn't her problem anymore. Her reaction broke his heart. But what he gained that day more than made up
for the hurt. Johnny had found a new father.

The agent wasn't his biological father. He wasn't even an FBI agent. He was Johnny's twin soul. Bill had asked about his fantasies and listened without judging. The tales of bondage, torture, and murder didn't disgust him—they pleased him. He encouraged Johnny to develop his fantasy further. Johnny needed to fulfill his inner potential, and Bill would guide him on that path.

Bill aimed a finger at the prostitutes across the street. "A wolf cub must learn to kill, and it's important to blood him right. You always remember the first time."

Johnny shifted on the passenger seat. Bill meant well, but this mission didn't excite him.

"I want to kill Emily, not some street hooker. What power is there in destroying the weak?"

"Nobody will miss these women. There's more room for error. Don't worry, we'll get to Emily soon enough. I know what you're feeling." Bill chuckled. "I was young and inexperienced, too, once. I didn't understand what I was, and I had nobody to guide me. So, I made mistakes. You see, the first kill is the one they'll use to find you."

"The FBI?"

"Among others. The first kill is usually unplanned and happens close to home. Law enforcement will connect your crimes and track you down. That's why your first kill must not be personal."

Johnny swallowed his frustration. Bill's words rang true. A wolf must avoid the hunters' traps to reach old age. Bill had let him stay in a secluded ranch house and given him textbooks on forensic science and police procedures. Johnny had enrolled at a technical college to gain the skills he'd need to support his dark habit in anonymity. With Bill's mentoring, Johnny was on the way to maximizing his potential.

"Who was your first?"

Bill's talk of his early mistakes had kindled Johnny's curiosity. His new father never talked about his personal life. But they had earned each other's trust over the past few months, and Johnny was graduating into the next level of predator life. He yearned to learn more about his twin soul.

"Tina." Bill savored the word, no doubt recalling the sensations of his first kill. "I left too many loose ends. But I'll tie everything up soon, with the help of the pack."

"The pack?"

There are others. *The news rankled Johnny.* He'd thought his relationship with Bill was unique. Had Bill adopted other young killers?

"A lone wolf is vulnerable. After your first kill, you'll join the pack. We'll have your back."

Johnny's annoyance subsided. Sharing Bill had advantages. He'd found a new father and a new family. People like him. A home where he belonged. His desire to prove himself—and impress Bill —strengthened.

Across the street, two of the hookers got into the back seat of a car and drove off.

"Perfect," Bill said. "Are you ready?"

"Yeah."

"Remember what I taught you and you'll do fine."

Bill turned the car around and pulled up beside the last remaining hooker. He rolled down the passenger window, and the woman bent over and glanced inside. Not a woman—a girl about Johnny's age.

"You boys looking for a good time?"

She chewed gum and used too much makeup. Bill was right. She was perfect.

"My boy here just turned eighteen. It's time we broke him in."

She grinned at Johnny. "Hey, sweetie." She gazed at Bill. "It's two hundred bucks an hour."

"I'll throw in another fifty if you let me watch."

"You got yourself a deal, Daddy."

The girl got into the back seat and squeezed Johnny's shoulder. "*Don't worry, sweetie. I'll take good care of you. You'll do just fine.*"

CHAPTER 74

C hief of Police Charlie Emmerso was putting on his jacket when Claire knocked on the door of his office Monday evening.

He registered her expression and frowned. "I won't like this, will I?"

"No, sir."

Emmerso was a good man. But even good men had their limits. Would he risk his career for her? He perched on the edge of his desk but kept his jacket on. The chief was an optimist.

"What did Harry Wallace have to say?"

"He wouldn't rat on Thornton, but he pointed me in the right direction. Silicon Towers. The mayor seems to have pushed through zoning changes for the project."

Emmerso shrugged. "That's old news. Many people opposed the project. But zoning changes aren't criminal unless he bribed public officials."

"What if he's the official? Hannover Group owns Silicon Towers Corporation. The Hannovers are contributors to Thornton's campaign. They've donated a new street camera system to help his reelection."

Emmerso ran his tongue over his teeth. "So Carmine Hannover was using her trust fund to replace her parents' puppet in the upcoming elections?"

"Carmine Hannover and Victoria McAdams believed Thornton was corrupt. They poured money into Malik's campaign. Silicon Towers features in the file Carmine compiled for Malik. Carmine was going to expose Mayor Thornton and her parents."

A bemused smile spread over Emmerso's mouth. "And the Hannovers assassinated their daughter to cover their tracks?"

Claire shot him a challenging look. "Fathers have killed their daughters for less."

Her father had killed her sister out of spite. He'd tried to kill Claire as well to hide his crimes. Why was Emmerso playing devil's advocate?

"You told me the Hannovers aren't like us."

"I didn't mean they're psychopaths."

"There's something I haven't told you about them. I guess I was embarrassed."

"OK, Sergeant. Now you have to tell me."

"When I met with them, the Hannovers told me to find their daughter's murderer...and kill him."

Emmerso's smile faded. "They said that?"

"'When you find the bastard, kill him.' I believe those were Mrs. Hannover's exact words."

Emmerso gave his head a slow, surprised shake, but the news didn't spur him to action.

"Sir, some people believe I killed Jed in cold blood. The Hannovers are among them. They're the only suspects with motive, means, and opportunity. Maybe they didn't have their daughter killed. But to rule that out I need surveillance. Wiretaps, for starters."

Emmerso raised his hand. "Slow down, Sergeant. Wiretaps are difficult to approve—impossible without Mayor Thornton finding out. If he's colluding with the Hannovers on this, they'll destroy any evidence we might otherwise have found. Are you sure you've exhausted all other means of investigation?"

"Interviews and search warrants will only tip them off that we're investigating them. But with surveillance in place, I can prod them and see who they turn to for help."

Emmerso focused his compassionate gaze on her for three long seconds. "Not getting much sleep lately, Sergeant?"

"No, sir."

"I'm sure the killer's visit didn't help either. How are things at home?" Emmerso knew about Claire's rocky relationship with her mother.

"Getting better."

Claire didn't like this line of questioning. Was he implying her theory was a fever dream born from stress and sleep deprivation?

Emmerso eased off his desk and onto his feet. "I'm sorry, Sergeant. We'll need more evidence of wrongdoing for a wiretap. Sleep on it. You're a good detective. You'll think of something."

CHAPTER 75

Claire returned to her mother's house late that night. She inserted the key into the lock of the front door, then glanced down the darkened street. Was the killer watching her from the shadows? She clenched her fists, daring Johnny to show himself. *Let's get this over with.* But if she confronted him now, did she have sufficient evidence to charge him with murder?

And Johnny wasn't working alone. The serial killer relied on Mayor Thornton's connections and the Hannovers' deep pockets. What chance did a lone homicide detective stand against the long shadow of power and wealth?

The ruling elites had used Apex to achieve their aims. William Wolfe, the king of misdirection, had planned these murders. He'd disguised the assassinations as the work of a homicidal stalker obsessed with Claire. Was the use of her notoriety another attempt to springboard her up the ranks of law enforcement? No. According to Johnny, Bill had wanted to keep Claire out of this plot. These killings served a different purpose.

Soon this city will be ours. How tightly coupled were Apex and Newburgh's powerbrokers? And who was their third victim —the "cherry on the top?"

Claire turned the key in the lock. Maybe Chief Emmerso was right, and all she needed was a good night's sleep? She'd let the chaos of facts and theories germinate in the fertile soil of her resting brain. By morning, she might discover, to her surprise, the sprout of an inspired solution to the case.

In the house's darkness, she locked the door and engaged the security latch. A wooden stair creaked. Claire reached for her gun, and the intruder halted on the staircase. Had Johnny broken into her home again? Claire's eyes adjusted to the dark. The intruder was not Johnny.

She flipped the light switch. Diane stood on the top stair in her bathrobe. Claire exhaled with relief. She hadn't expected Mom to be awake at this hour.

Diane's weak smile wavered. "You're home." Her voice was matter-of-fact and empty of accusations. "It's late." She seemed to choose her words carefully.

Claire said nothing, unsure how to respond. She'd dropped her mother's bag at home that afternoon. They had spoken that morning, but Claire hadn't seen Mom since Friday. Would a misplaced comment spark another tirade? Claire was tense and overtired. She had no energy to rein in her temper.

Diane descended the remaining stairs, her hands fidgeting as if she didn't know what to do with them. This was uncharted territory for her, too.

Her mother halted at the foot of the stairs. "You look exhausted."

The statement was not an insult. Was Mom expressing genuine empathy or simply filling the awkward silence?

Claire found her tongue. "It comes with the job."

"Bad day?"

"I've had better."

The nervous smile returned. "Do you want a cup of coffee?"

Claire longed for a hot shower and her bed, but if she rejected her mother's invitation, Diane might never find the courage to try again.

"Decaf."

Another uncertain smile. "OK."

They moved to the kitchen—all awkward smiles and polite gestures. Like a married couple separated by war and reunited years later, they were both family and strangers, desperate for intimacy but wary of raw wounds, visible and hidden. They struggled to remember the complex dance of intimacy that others performed so naturally. Diane boiled the kettle and fixed the coffee, then joined Claire at the table.

"I went to the meeting today."

"What meeting?" Had Mom met with William's investment broker to dredge up more money?

"AA. It's Monday."

"Right."

Claire sipped her coffee to hide her surprise. She'd despaired of her mother ever returning to the support group. Now Mom had attended a meeting of her own free will.

"How did it go?"

"Better."

"That's good."

Diane shifted on her feet. "I made lasagna. Are you hungry?"

Claire blinked at her. When had Diane last cooked for her? Had she turned over a new leaf or was she trying to poison her? Claire smiled at the reflexive, cynical thought. Her mother was many things, but she was no murderer.

"Sure, I'd love some."

Diane got busy in the kitchen. The microwave hummed as she set a place for Claire at the table. Claire welcomed the plate of steaming food. The scent of tomato paste and melted cheese revived her appetite. Diane sat opposite and watched her eat.

"How is it?"

"Delicious, Mom. Thank you."

Diane smiled. She seemed relieved.

Claire put down her fork and savored the moment. "This is nice."

She didn't mean the food. For the first time in decades, she'd shared a calm, domestic moment with her mother, the kind that functional families took for granted.

Diane's cheeks trembled, and her eyes moistened. "I'm sorry."

"For what?"

"For not being there for you. Ever."

Complex emotions surged in Claire's chest. A reservoir of hurt had collected within her over the years, and now the dam walls burst. Her vision misted over, and she gasped.

A chair leg scraped on the tiles, and slippers padded on the kitchen tiles. Mom held Claire from behind, pressing her daughter's head to the soft warmth of her body and patting her hair.

Claire needed this. She'd longed for her mother's affection and despaired of ever finding it. The sudden display of mother love washed away the years, and an insecure little girl surrendered to her mommy's embrace.

A single tear splashed onto Claire's face from above. "It's OK, Claire. We'll be OK."

The pressures of the past week had crushed Claire: Two dead women demanded justice; Edward and Cynthia Hannover demanded murder; total strangers branded her a dirty cop; a psychopathic killer stalked her, day and night; and now her father's bloody legacy rose from the grave. On top of all that, Claire hurtled toward a head-on collision with forces way above her pay grade. Struggling alone beneath that impossible weight, Claire could barely draw breath.

"It's a curse."

"What is?"

"I can't escape him."

Her mother stroked Claire's head. "Your father was an evil man. But he can't hurt us anymore."

"Everybody thinks I'm like him."

The hand paused on her hair. "You're not like him, Claire. But he's your father. He will always be your father."

That was not what Claire wanted to hear. Did Diane still blame her for Tina's death? Did Claire remind her of her husband?

"I want to cut him out."

"You can't. Some things are out of our control. The first step to recovery is acceptance."

Claire stiffened. Mom meant well, but her track record disqualified her from dispensing life advice. And Claire wasn't an addict. She didn't need a twelve-step program. Her father's crimes weren't the result of her personal failings. But as his daughter, she'd carry his mark of Cain forever.

"Don't cut him out," Diane added. "That part of him inside of you helped you to beat him. Don't fight it, Claire. Use it."

Something connected in Claire's mind. Her mother's words conjured recent memories: Claire playing her "Killer Wolfe" role for Peter Knowles; Claire in the tub, pretending to belong to Johnny's murderous pack. The recollections interbred, evolving into new insights. When the primordial mist cleared, a path opened in the chaotic jungle of her thoughts. Claire was a Wolfe. To outsmart the pack, she'd have to act like one.

CHAPTER 76

Tuesday morning, Claire drove to Hannover Estate while tension pooled inside her. She'd never worked undercover before, but there was a first time for everything. That morning, she'd strapped on her new covert vest before dressing in a fresh work suit. If the Hannovers had assassinated their daughter, Claire had better prepare for the worst. She was about to confront them on their home turf.

Brightly colored flowerbeds basked in the morning sun at the foot of the Hannover Estate's tall walls and electric fencing. Claire slowed as she reached the impressive iron gates. The security guard found her name on the register and waved her inside. The Hannovers were expecting Claire, but they had no idea what she was planning.

A black hearse stood outside the pillared entrance of the mansion. Claire parked in the stony lot, joining a line of luxury cars that included two Bentleys. Her hatchback seemed painfully out of place. A young male attendant in a black suit escorted Claire around the house to a brick path that led to the family burial plot at the bottom of a manicured garden. Even in death, the Hannovers remained separate from the common people.

"I'll wait here," Claire told the attendant when they reached the low iron fence.

The ceremony had already begun. Among the stone monuments and impressive headstones in black granite, twenty impeccably dressed men and women stood around the hole in the ground and listened to the priest's recitation. Edward and Cynthia Hannover stood side by side, their designer sunglasses reflecting the polished casket that contained their daughter's mortal remains.

Two younger figures hovered nearby. Carmine's siblings, Claire assumed. They kept their distance from their parents, perhaps wary of their gravitational pull. Edward Junior hid a yawn by placing his cuff-linked hand over his short beard. His puffy jet-lagged eyelids struggled to stay open. He must have flown in for the funeral and would probably fly out immediately after. Rosalyn dabbed a tissue at the corner of her eye. She looked a lot like her sister. Were the Hannover children aware of their parents' corrupt dealings? Was that why they'd fled overseas?

Mayor Thornton stood amid the clump of friends and business associates. Claire's shoulders stiffened. What would Carmine think of her funeral, attended by the parents she despised and the mayor she'd tried to unseat? Had these conspirators ordered her assassination?

Chief Emmerso stood beside the mayor. He met Claire's gaze and inclined his head. Claire returned the silent greeting. She didn't envy him. The chief of police had to socialize with the corrupt schemers and keep his breakfast down. *Comes with the job.* Sarah Malik was wrong—Claire didn't belong in politics.

Her theory about the Hannovers and Thornton hadn't

swayed Emmerso. Was she jumping the gun? *Innocent until proven guilty.* The Hannovers deserved the same judicial process. Soon she'd determine whether Carmine's parents had ordered her death.

The priest concluded his words, the casket sank into the ground, and the funeral home attendants filled in the hole. The visitors offered the mourners words of consolation and took a brick path toward the main house where no doubt a lavish reception awaited. Edward Junior and Rosalyn split from the group and headed for the parking lot. Claire wouldn't get to speak with them today. Cynthia Hannover glanced at Claire over her sunglasses.

Claire stepped closer. "My condolences, Mr. and Mrs. Hannover."

"Thank you for joining us, Sergeant."

The husband waved toward the house. "Shall we talk inside?"

Claire followed them into the mansion. She understood what he meant. *Let's talk in private, far from curious ears.* The weight of the Glock at her waist and the bulletproof vest underneath her shirt comforted her. The Hannovers led her down a long corridor. They passed a hall of buffet tables set for a wedding feast. Claire slipped her hand into her jacket pocket and pressed a button on her recording device. Their words would be inadmissible as evidence in court. But if the Hannovers admitted involvement in their daughter's murder, a judge would grant Claire all the wiretaps she wanted.

They entered an opulent den. A large writing desk dominated the room, surrounded by oriental rugs, oil paintings, and a fireplace. Cynthia herded Claire to one of the dark leather armchairs.

Edward Hannover closed the double oak doors behind them. "Can I get you a drink?"

"No, thank you. I won't stay long."

He sat. "I trust you've made more progress since we spoke last."

"I have."

Claire studied their faces. Their involuntary responses would reveal the truth.

"You told me what to do with your daughter's murderer."

The Hannovers exchanged eager glances. Had Claire dispatched Carmine's killer already? Let them think she was dirty. Claire would leverage their assumptions to her advantage.

Edward leaned forward on the edge of his seat. "And?"

"I'll deal with him soon enough. But what about the ones who sent him?"

A look of doubt passed between husband and wife. Had their hired gun discovered their involvement, or were the Hannovers genuinely confused?

Cynthia broke the silence. "I don't understand."

"Carmine was assassinated."

"Assassinated—by hitmen?"

Claire nodded. "It seems Carmine found incriminating evidence against Mayor Thomas Thornton."

Cynthia gasped. "Tom would never do such a thing!"

Edward shot to his feet. "That ungrateful bastard!" He paced the carpet. "After everything we've done for him."

The Hannovers were not fearful. They were angry. Disbelieving. Had Claire misread the situation? Worse yet—had Sarah Malik misled her?

"Are you sure about this?" Cynthia was begging Claire to tell her this wasn't so.

"No, ma'am. It's just a suspicion. But I thought you should know. The material Carmine found concerns zoning changes the mayor expedited for a construction project."

Edward stopped pacing and stared at her, his hands on his hips. "What construction project?"

"Silicon Towers."

Glance number three read surprise. Edward ran his hands through his perfect gray hair and swore. Claire no longer needed a wiretap. The Hannovers hadn't ordered their daughter's murder. But the mention of zoning irregularities for their new high-tech center had struck a nerve. If Mayor Thornton had assassinated Carmine to cover up for Silicon Towers, then the Hannovers had unintentionally contributed to their daughter's death. She pushed her luck, hoping their guilty consciences would provide the information she needed.

"Sir, you didn't answer my question."

"What question?"

"The one who sent him—what should I do with him?"

Edward balled his hands into fists. "Nothing. Double-check your facts, Sergeant. Because if Tommy Thornton did this, I'll bloody well kill him myself."

CHAPTER 77

Captain Washington raised an eyebrow when Claire joined the team in the Newburgh PD conference room later that morning.

"Thank you for joining us, Sergeant Wolfe. Did you have a good time?"

His sarcasm surprised Claire. She had notified him that she'd arrive late at the update meeting because of the Hannover funeral. Claire searched the faces of the detectives and FBI agents for clues as to the source of Washington's foul mood but found none. Had Chief Emmerso informed him about Claire's side investigation, or was Washington jealous because the Hannovers hadn't invited him to the funeral?

She played it safe. "No, sir. Funerals aren't my thing."

Washington turned to the others. "Sergeant Wolfe attended the private ceremony at Hannover Estate."

Jealousy it is.

Gomez whistled. "I bet the buffet was great."

"I didn't stay for the reception."

Nakamura said, "I'm guessing Johnny didn't show up at the cemetery."

Claire shook her head. "No such luck. What have I missed?" The crime scene photos on the conference table lay in the same tidy groups as yesterday. Her colleagues' grim expressions meant the investigation was no closer to an arrest either. They wouldn't be happy to hear she'd been flying solo, withholding information from the team, and chasing shadows. If only she had one solid lead to show for her efforts.

Washington sighed. "What have you missed? In a word—nothing. No prints from your secret tunnel, zero hits on Johnny's identikit, and zilch on Apex at the FBI. And we're still waiting for the DNA analysis for the male decapitation victim."

Tom Brown shifted on his seat. "We'll get results any minute now. The lab has made this case a top priority."

Washington shrugged. "Don't get our hopes up. The chances of finding a match are next to zero. The only glimmer of hope comes—of all places—from Detective Gomez."

Gomez feigned insult. "Don't act so surprised." He turned to Claire. "I went through the camera footage—again. A white pickup keeps showing up near the crime scenes." He glanced at Rob. "Agent Cline says a similar Toyota Tundra followed him and Officer Long to Springfield."

This was great news. "Do we have the license plates?"

"Too grainy. Can't make them out."

Nakamura said, "It's a shame Mayor Thornton didn't install those new cameras a few weeks ago."

Mayor Thornton. The update had distracted Claire from her confession. "I have some new information."

She told the team about her meetings with Sarah Malik and Harry Wallace, as well as her suspicion that Mayor Thornton had bent the law to fix the zoning issues for Silicon Towers.

The door opened. Chief Emmerso entered the conference room and, without a word, leaned against the wall.

Nakamura summarized her revelation. "So, the Hannovers

hired Apex to kill their daughter to avoid exposure and keep their man in the mayor's office?"

"That was Malik's theory. She seems to think the Hannovers are capable of anything. At the time, I believed her. Her suspicions fit what we've learned about Apex. And when I first met the Hannovers, they told me to find their daughter's murderer —and kill him."

Jess's eyes popped in disbelief. "Geez!"

Gomez spoke to Dr. Sally Fleischer. "That would make them psychopaths. Right, Doc?"

Dr. Fleischer snorted. "You're getting the hang of this, Detective Gomez."

Captain Washington eyed Claire. "You believed Malik then, but now you don't. What changed your mind?"

It was a fair question.

"I spoke with the Hannovers after the funeral. They seemed infuriated at the mayor, not guilty. It's easy to demonize billionaires, but I don't think they killed their daughter."

"But Mayor Thornton did? And why didn't you report this right away?" The question sounded like an accusation. Captain Washington was taking her covert investigation harder than she'd expected.

Emmerso came to her rescue. "Sergeant Wolfe consulted with me on this. She did the right thing. This case is already a media sensation. One careless leak could destroy the mayor's campaign. Maybe that's why Malik shared her theory with us? I directed Sergeant Wolfe to investigate on the q.t., and in hindsight that was the right call. Sergeant, you can answer Captain Washington's question now."

Claire nodded, grateful to Emmerso for backing her up. As much as she disliked the mayor, she couldn't ignore her instincts.

"I don't think Mayor Thornton would kill to keep his office, and the Hannovers are his greatest supporters. He'd never risk turning them against him."

Washington threw his hands up. "Where does that leave us? Did somebody pay Apex to kill these women or did Johnny send us on a wild goose chase?"

Tom said, "There's another option." The older FBI agent had the room's undivided attention. "Apex crippled Malik's campaign and tried to incriminate Thornton. With the first two candidates out of the game, third place wins. Who's next in line?"

Nakamura raised his eyebrows. "You think Joe Maisel has the balls for this?"

"Who's Maisel?" Rob said. "For us out-of-towners."

Chief Emmerso obliged. "Joseph Maisel is a local doctor. He's run against Thornton for ten years straight."

"Maybe he got tired of losing?" Gomez said.

Tom's deduction animated Captain Washington. "M is for Maisel. Nakamura, interview Maisel pronto. Gomez, I want an analysis of the election polls. The last victim on the hit list might be another rival candidate. Assuming this isn't another wild goose chase."

The investigation was changing direction again and fast.

Claire raised both hands. "Wait a minute. Assuming Maisel is our man, who is his third target?"

She gazed at Dr. Fleischer, and the forensic psychiatrist thought out loud.

"The first two victims were high-status women and friends of Kitty Tucker. Both undermined Mayor Thornton in the elections. If Maisel is the Apex client, the final target might implicate Thornton more directly."

The truth hit Claire hard. "Malik. Sarah Malik is the target. She's the last living member of Kitty's group of friends."

"But Malik said she wasn't in danger," Jess said.

"She thought Thornton was behind the murders. He wouldn't strike her directly because her death could implicate him. But Maisel doesn't share that concern."

Captain Washington's eyes widened. "If we arrest Thornton for Malik's murder, Maisel wins."

Claire grabbed her phone and dialed Malik's number. She cursed her tunnel vision. The answer had stared her in the face all the time. Malik was Johnny's "cherry on the top." The homicides were not about Claire. Apex had connected with Joseph Maisel, and the murders paved his way to City Hall. *Soon this city will be ours.*

The call cut to voicemail, and Claire swore. "She's not answering." She reached for her car keys. "Detective Long, let's go. Nakamura, call a squad car to Malik's home."

"We'll meet you there," Rob said.

The officers ran for the door. Claire hoped they weren't too late.

CHAPTER 78

"Is this some kind of joke?"

Sarah Malik stared out from the back seat window of her Chevy SUV at the grassy, empty lot between two mansions in Campton Hills.

In the driver's seat, Al shrugged. "This is the address you gave me."

Sarah swore. She never swore but she was acquiring the habit. Thornton had picked off her friends and donors one by one, and now a mysterious caller had sent her across the city to an empty lot. Had Thornton invented the new donor to annoy her? Hadn't he done enough damage?

"Let's get out of here."

"Hold on. I see somebody."

Al got out of the car. A thin man with a gray suit and dark glasses approached the vehicle. He carried a briefcase. Al frisked him for weapons. More than ever, Malik was glad to have her PA. The meticulous metrosexual fulfilled her personal security needs and provided insightful campaign advice. Laying him off would be the final nail in the coffin of her political career. Her new donor's money might keep Al in her employ and breathe life into her campaign.

Al opened the back door for the visitor. Jim grinned at her with the easy confidence of a man with nothing to lose. Sarah disliked him instantly.

"I apologize for the location of our meeting. I'm in between offices."

She recognized his voice from the phone call.

Sarah turned off her phone. "I'm less interested in your office decor than in what you have to say." She kept her tone cool and collected and added a dash of suspicion to cloak her desperation—a convincing performance if she said so herself.

"Then let's get right to business." He opened the briefcase on his lap and withdrew a thick envelope. "Fifty grand should get us started."

Sarah eyed the package. She wanted to accept the donation, but the wad of cash raised red flags. Was she getting into bed with the mob or a drug cartel?

"Most people make electronic transfers."

He flashed that easy smile again. "My clients are not most people."

"Who are your clients?"

He tossed the envelope onto the seat beside her. "Concerned citizens who prefer to remain anonymous."

Sarah snickered and shook her head at her credulity. The offer had sounded too good to be true.

"Then take your money and go. I only do business with people I know and trust."

Jim's grin widened. Rejection didn't seem to bother him.

"So it seems."

He withdrew another envelope from the case, larger and thinner than the first, and handed it to her. A dark pit opened in Sarah's stomach. *Did he know? No, that was impossible.* But she had to find out.

Sarah opened the flap of the envelope and extracted a series of color photos. Her throat constricted with terror. She knew exactly when and where they'd been taken. Sarah didn't dare ask Jim—or whatever his name truly was—how he'd obtained them. Her lips trembled, and her mask of self-control crumbled.

Her eyes flitted to the window. Al stood guard outside, his back to the vehicle. He had no idea what was happening behind the tinted windows of the Chevy Suburban. He wouldn't hear her cries for help.

"Is this a threat?"

"We don't make threats, Ms. Malik." The stranger reached into his briefcase one last time. "We get right to business."

CHAPTER 79

C laire put the pedal to the metal and sped across Newburgh. Jess clung to the passenger seat but said nothing. Claire fought the urge to kick herself. Of course! Sarah Malik was the killer's next target. How had Claire not seen that! Thanks to her carelessness, the politician was probably dead already.

"There's an emergency light behind your seat," she told Jess. "Put it on the roof."

Jess contorted her body and reached for the light. She rolled down her window and placed the magnetic device on the roof. When she connected the power cord to the cigar lighter, the siren blared, and the strobe light painted the hood in red and blue.

The sights and sounds pulled Claire back in time to the Middle School Strangler case. Six months ago, she'd rushed across town to save a life but arrived seconds too late. Claire must not repeat that mistake.

Claire took a sharp corner at high speed, and Jess shifted sideways.

"I'm sure she's OK."

YOU MADE ME YOU MADE ME 371

Her words were a plea for Claire to slow down. She'd do no such thing. Claire hit the brakes to avoid ramming a van with the words Rodent Control and Removal written on the back.

"Out of the way!" Claire yelled at the van.

Jess released one hand from the seat to grab her phone. "I'll try her number again."

"Fine."

They had called Malik five times in the past three minutes. At this point in her campaign, the politician would never turn off her phone willingly. Why had Claire not taken Malik's concerns seriously? A killer had murdered her donors. Claire should have insisted on police protection. If Malik died because of her incompetence, the conspiracy theorists would claim Claire had aided the killer, and this time, Claire would agree with them.

Jess grunted with frustration. "Voicemail."

Claire jumped a yellow light. In her rearview mirror, Rob's Bureau car skidded to a stop as the light turned red. Rob was following protocol. The movies got it wrong. High-speed car chases were ancient history. Why endanger lives if a police chopper and a few strategic roadblocks cornered fleeing criminals just as well? But in this case, a few seconds made the difference between life and death.

"Call Dispatch. Ask if the squad cars are there yet and get her phone's last position from the signal towers."

Jess was still on the phone when the car halted outside Malik's mansion. Claire jumped out, drew her service weapon, and ran to the front gate. She pressed the buzzer. The house looked empty. Birds chirped in the trees of the courtyard. Johnny had the uncanny ability to gain access to his victims. Was he already inside? Was Sarah still alive? She pressed the buzzer again.

The Bureau car pulled up behind hers. Car doors opened and closed.

Rob ran to her followed by Tom. "Is she here?"

Jess joined them at the gate. "Tower data had her in Campton Hills twenty minutes ago."

"Campton Hills?" Claire repeated. "That's fifteen minutes from here. Do we have an address?"

"Only coordinates. She could be anywhere within a quarter-mile radius."

"It's a start. Johnny must have lured her there."

"Would she fall for that?" Tom asked.

"He has a talent for getting to people."

Claire turned to go when a familiar Hispanic voice spoke.

"Sergeant Wolfe."

Beyond the gate, Alexandro "Al" Menendez strode through the courtyard toward them. "We didn't expect to see you back so soon."

His gaze fell on Jess and the FBI agents. "Is everything OK?"

"We need to speak with Ms. Malik. It's urgent."

He glanced back at the house. "Ms. Malik doesn't want to be disturbed."

"It's about our conversation yesterday. There's something she needs to know."

"I'll ask her, but she was adamant."

Rob said, "Tell her it's a matter of life and death."

"And you are?"

Claire made the introductions.

The PA grinned. "You can call me Al." He was not taking the situation seriously enough. "Wait here. I'll be right back."

Something was off. After their conversation yesterday, Malik should be eager to hear what she had to say. Was Al covering for his boss? Why was Malik unwilling to show her face?

A voice called from the house. "Al, where are your manners?"

Sarah Malik, alive and well, waved at them from the front door of the house.

"Let them in."

CHAPTER 80

At the kitchen table, Diane scribbled furiously in the yellow notepad. She'd woken up that morning with a new sense of purpose. Her quality time with Claire last night had energized her. She'd started a new chapter in her life, and this time, she wouldn't waste a single page.

As much as Diane loved Tina Turner, she'd only get so far singing other people's songs. To build her career as a singer, she'd have to create new material. She needed to write her own songs.

In her early twenties, she'd made weak and haphazard attempts at songwriting. The results were corny and clichéd: Young love. Big dreams. She'd lacked life experience. She hadn't known suffering. Since then, she'd accumulated plenty of both.

"Great art comes from great pain," so they said, and they were right. Today, the words flowed, the hurt pouring out of her and onto the page in tight, simple lyrics that packed a powerful emotional punch.

The idea for her first song had taken root in her mind

during breakfast and developed as she'd dressed. Her pajama days were over, and her new routine prevented her from back-sliding to idleness and drink.

She'd sat at the kitchen table armed with a yellow notepad, ballpoint pen, and a second mug of coffee. And she hadn't budged from the spot in an hour. By the time she remembered her drink, the coffee was cold.

The thrill she'd experienced onstage returned. She was born for this. Music was her calling. And she dedicated her first song to Claire.

Last night, Diane hadn't expressed her feelings for her daughter well. Mother's love was a second language, one she hadn't spoken in years. But now the words flowed straight from her heart.

She'd started her third draft of the song when someone knocked on the front door. Claire never came home this early from work. Had she left something behind? Diane turned the notepad over. She wasn't ready to share the song with Claire yet, and she needed to work out the melody.

There was no telltale scratch of a key in the lock. No, Claire wasn't at the door. Diane had ordered a Yamaha electronic keyboard on Amazon last night. Had they delivered so soon?

Not wanting to interrupt her creative flow, she hurried to the door and pressed her eye to the peephole. A young man with dark sunglasses stood on the doorstep. He was not a delivery person. The black strap of a duffel bag pressed into the shoulder of his plain gray suit.

"Who is it?"

"Detective Johnny Norton, ma'am. I'm a colleague of your daughter. She asked me to stop by. May I come in?"

Diane's pulse accelerated. Why would Claire send a detective to the house? Was she OK? Had something happened to her? The man looked vaguely familiar. Where had she seen him before?

"Claire didn't say anybody was coming by the house."

The man grinned at her through the peephole. "It's a surprise."

CHAPTER 81

"Assassins?" Sarah Malik sat behind the enormous desk of her home office and arched an amused eyebrow at Claire. "Sergeant Wolfe, there's no need to be so dramatic."

Claire blinked at her in confusion. The politician's transformation stunned her into silence. Yesterday, Malik had begged Claire to take her concerns seriously. Today, she brushed aside the confirmation of those suspicions with patronizing indifference. Was this the same Sarah Malik?

"I know you mean well," she added. "But there's been a misunderstanding. Nobody's trying to kill me."

Claire glanced at Jess and the FBI agents. Malik's one-hundred-eighty-degree turnabout made Claire sound like a liar. Or worse—delusional.

She clenched her jaw. Claire hadn't imagined her conversation with Malik. Her days of doubting her senses were long gone. And her theory was reasonable. The killer had eliminated Malik's donors to cripple her campaign. When Malik still limped toward the finish line, attacking her was the next logical step. Her death would remove Mayor Thornton from the election race, too.

Something—or someone—had caused Malik to backpedal fast. Did her mask of invincibility hide another emotion—fear? Had Malik's survival instinct shoved her head in the sand?

Malik's eyes moved from Claire to the newcomers, sizing them up with intense interest. Did the presence of Jess and the FBI agents explain her reaction? A politician's public image was her chief asset. Malik had admitted her fears to Claire, woman-to-woman. Was she reluctant to sound hysterical in the presence of three unfamiliar law enforcement officers—or even her PA, Al? Malik needed to understand the imminent danger she faced.

"We found Carmine's and Victoria's names on the database of an assassination ring. You were right. Someone had them murdered."

Malik's composure faltered for a split second. "Then you should speak with Mayor Thornton, not me."

"We're exploring all angles. But the mayor might not be involved."

"Really?"

"The murders hurt his campaign as much as yours."

"Not if they force me to drop out. Which they won't, I assure you. Nothing will stop me from winning this election. If I lose, Carmine and Victoria will have died in vain."

"You can't win if you're dead."

That line seemed to give Malik pause. Was Claire finally getting through to her?

"Does my name appear in that database?"

"No. But we have reliable information that the assassins have one more target. To be safe, we need to put you under police protection."

"What kind of protection?"

"We'll move you to a secure location and regulate your access to the outside world."

"That's unacceptable. How am I supposed to campaign if you restrict my movement? I might not be the next target. You said so yourself."

Malik had raised a valid objection. And perhaps, an important clue? Why had the third target not appeared on the Apex site? Did the database only list successful hits, as Claire had assumed, or had Johnny misled her?

Malik seized upon Claire's silence. "Thank you for your concern, Sergeant. But I assure you, I'll be fine. Al, please show them out."

Her PA opened the door of the office, and Claire led the team outside. Two patrol officers waited on the street.

Rob turned to Claire on the sidewalk. "Is that it? We're leaving?"

Claire looked over her shoulder at the house. "Something smells wrong."

"Yeah," Jess said. "She's hiding something."

Tom emitted a world-weary sigh. "Or something spooked her yesterday, and now she's come to her senses."

"Do you think we're wasting our time?"

Tom shrugged. "We only know of a third target from Johnny, and he's not exactly a reliable source."

Claire glanced at the house again. Malik's PA strolled down a glass-walled corridor and spoke on his phone. He met her gaze in the distance and winked. Did their visit assist Malik's campaign strategy? Threats to a candidate's life created voter sympathy. How else would they spin the situation? Claire imagined the title of Bella Winters's next article. *Newburgh Mayor Prime Suspect in Murder Plot.* Claire might need a new career, after all. Had she just made a terrible mistake?

Her father's words echoed in her mind. *Soon this city will be ours.* This was William Wolfe's plan. Every detail was significant. No option was off the table, no matter how twisted. *C'mon,*

Claire, think. Claire was his daughter. She was a Wolfe. *Don't fight it, Claire. Use it.*

Claire lowered her voice. "What if M is for Malik, as we thought? The client in the Apex list *and* the appointment in Carmine's diary."

Tom chuckled. "So now Malik whacked her own donors?"

"No. She didn't look guilty. She looked afraid. Much more than yesterday. She refused to say why." And Claire understood. "They've gotten to her already."

"Who—Apex?"

"What if Apex doesn't want her dead, just to frame her for the murders?"

"To remove her from the race?" Rob said.

"Or for leverage—to guarantee her good behavior. My father said he was going to take control of the city. He had me in the police force. Now he'd have Malik in City Hall." Other connections materialized in Claire's mind. "The Apex symbol appeared on the Middle School Murder victims, but not on the buried bodies. The new homicides are an internal project aimed at extending Apex's control. Johnny led me to the Apex site, but he didn't think I'd share that with the department. The assassination list and 'M for Malik' would come to light if she didn't play ball."

"Blackmail?"

"Yes. Then Johnny fooled Carmine into meeting him at The Barnett Inn, thinking she was meeting Malik to plot against Thornton."

"How did he do that?"

Claire bit her lip. She had no answer. How had Johnny orchestrated Carmine's fake appointment with Malik that night?

"Maybe they hacked her computer?" Jess said. "Or Johnny broke into her home."

"I don't know."

Tom grunted. "Again, what's her motive for killing her friends and financiers? Framing her for their murders makes little sense."

Jess tried to rescue Claire's theory a second time. "Maybe we'd think they'd fallen out?"

Claire shook her head. "But why would falling out end in murder? Tom's right. It makes no sense."

Jess seemed crestfallen, but Claire couldn't ignore the facts.

Tom chuckled. "Look on the bright side. Malik seems to have a thing for Rob."

Rob rolled his eyes.

"She isn't into Rob," Jess said. "She had her eye on me."

They stared at her, and she blushed. Her off-the-cuff comment had thrown Claire for a loop—and opened a fresh angle on the case.

"Jess, what are you trying to tell us?"

CHAPTER 82

Shame punched Jess in the face like a scorching desert wind. She hadn't meant to expose her secret. Not here. Not now. She'd only tried to shield Rob from Tom's mocking comment. Tom had misread Malik's body language completely. But her words had tumbled out wrong. And now, on the sidewalk outside Sarah Malik's house and in the presence of two FBI agents, Jess had no choice but to come clean.

What are you trying to tell us? Jess had wanted to speak up earlier, but the personal nature of the topic made her delay the revelation. Once she came out, the two people she admired most, Claire and Rob, would never view her the same way. Then the investigation had changed direction, and Jess had convinced herself her secret no longer mattered. A serial killer had preyed on Carmine. Her love life had nothing to do with her death. Nobody needed to know Jess's secret—ever.

Her runaway tongue had decided the matter for her. After carrying the shame of her silence for a week, a part of Jess was glad to let the weight slip from her shoulders. Her insight might be the missing clue the team needed to find a killer and save an innocent life.

Jess hid her embarrassment with a nervous giggle. "Isn't it obvious? Malik isn't into guys."

Rob suppressed his smile. "How can you tell?"

"I just know. The way I knew Carmine Hannover was gay, too." There—she'd said it. She couldn't take back the words.

Claire studied her intently. "Jess, how did you know Carmine?"

Would they add her to the list of suspects? Jess had feared that, too. She had to make them understand.

"We met when I worked patrol. Dispatch called in a B&E at a jewelry store next door to her workshop. I stopped outside her display window, and we got to talking. The next day, she asked me out. Carmine was paranoid about her parents. She claimed they hired people to follow her. That's why she liked to meet at The Barnett Inn."

Memories of the hotel flooded her mind: the nauseating stench of blood and raw flesh; Carmine's naked, desecrated body on the bed. Jess couldn't breathe. Her knees threatened to buckle beneath her.

Claire touched Jess's shoulder, returning her to the present. "That's why you collapsed at the crime scene. I'm so sorry, Jess. That must have been terrible for you."

Jess choked up. She nodded and sucked in air. Rob was at her side now, too, his eyes filled with sadness. They weren't judging her. They were consoling her.

"Were you still dating when she died?"

Jess wiped her eyes and pulled herself together. "No. We broke things off after a few weeks. I knew it wouldn't last. We were from different worlds. I should have spoken up earlier, but I was in shock. And I knew it wouldn't look good. I haven't told anyone in the department. My family doesn't even know. I didn't want to mess up my new job or become a person of interest in my first case. So, I asked Captain Washington to reassign me."

Jess studied Claire's eyes, hoping she'd understand. "I'm sorry. I hadn't been in touch with Carmine for months. She'd kept her sexuality private, too. I had no idea that might help the investigation. Until now."

Jess drew a deep breath, then another. She searched Claire's eyes. Would she dismiss her from the case or get her fired from the Investigations Bureau? How were they ever going to work together again?

But Claire seemed pensive, not disappointed. "The L in Carmine's calendar was for Long. Jessica Long."

Rob reached for his phone. "I think we've found our motive."

Claire glanced back at Malik's house. "And we can guess who had planned to meet Carmine the night she died."

CHAPTER 83

Diane trembled on her bed. The killer had stepped into the house and aimed his gun at her heart. He'd moved her to her bedroom and ordered her to lie on top of the blanket. He spread her arms and legs wide and tied her to the bedposts. Now he stood over her and grinned.

"I lied. I'm not a detective. I'm...an artist."

Diane hadn't followed the news of the recent murders closely, but she'd heard enough to know what lay ahead. The killer tortured his victims before he murdered them. The deaths hadn't troubled Diane's sleep. She'd had nothing in common with the rich young women in the papers. Even when Claire had moved her to a motel to keep her safe, Diane had never thought she was in danger. Now, she knew the truth. The new chapter in her life was coming to an abrupt and violent end. The killer's lies were the least of her worries.

But he was talking to her. That gave her hope. Where had she seen his face before? If she spoke to him, maybe he'd see her as a human being? Maybe he'd spare her life?

"We've met before, haven't we?" Her voice sounded soft and shaky.

The evil grin widened. "Not exactly. But I've had my eye on you."

The killer placed his duffel bag on the dresser and rummaged around inside. He pulled on latex gloves, punctuating each movement with a rubber snap. The killer studied her with professional interest, a researcher considering how to dissect a lab rat. He placed a gloved hand on the bedpost by her foot, and she flinched.

The shock jogged her memory. "You were at The Red Keg on Sunday night. In the crowd. You heard me sing!"

His grin froze. The killer clearly hadn't wanted her to notice him. Had he discovered her there? Why was he doing this? What did he want from her?

"That was the first time you saw me, but not the first time I'd seen you. I've been watching you a long time. I've watched you sleep. Here, in your bedroom."

Shivers traveled down her spine, and her skin tingled.

"I know everything about you. We're like...family." He sneered. "I've been waiting for this moment for years. Everything I've done—all the people I've killed—has led me here, to you and this moment."

What was he talking about? He was deranged. Diane had nothing to do with those dead women—she couldn't even remember their full names.

He reached for his bag and withdrew a large knife.

Diane screamed. "Help! Claire! Somebody! Help me!"

The man emitted a chilling belly laugh. "Claire's not coming to save you, Diane. She's the reason I'm here. You've been a bad mother. I told you—I've been watching you. Kicking her out in the middle of the night? Not cool, Mom. Claire is my sister, and I'm her brother. We look out for each other."

He lifted the blade in the air. The long, sharp edge glinted in the afternoon light that beamed through the wispy inner curtains.

"You were a bad wife, too. Bill was a father to me."

Her husband's name shocked her like a bucketful of icy water on her head. Six months after she'd buried him, her murderous husband still pursued her.

"Bill is dead!" She spat the words.

All traces of humor fled the killer's face. "He lives on. In his children. In me."

He gripped her leg in his gloved hand. Diane closed her eyes. Her entire body trembled uncontrollably.

"This is for Bill."

He slipped the blade inside her trouser leg and sliced. The fabric fell away, exposing her skin to the cool air. He gripped her panties, and the pressure of the elastic band released. Tossing her damaged clothing aside, he cut away her shirt and bra.

Diane lay naked on the bed. She closed her eyes and braced for the brutal attack on her soft, exposed flesh. After an eternity that lasted probably only a few seconds, she cracked open her eyes.

The killer studied her body, and his face soured.

"An artist needs the right materials, Diane. You haven't given me much to work with."

He lowered the blade. Had he changed his mind? Was he only here to frighten her? Dear Lord, he'd succeeded!

He dug around in his bag and found a rectangular butcher knife. An evil smile curled his lips.

"I guess we'll make do with what we have." He raised the knife and flashed his eyes. "This is for Claire."

"Wait! Claire doesn't want this! We've made peace. We're good now."

The knife hovered over her body. He was listening.

"I've changed. Claire moved back in. We've started anew."

His eyes shifted as he processed her words, then the evil smile returned.

"Nothing can save you, Diane. This is what Bill wanted."

She bawled like a child, tears spilling out of the corners of her eyes. "Please, no! This is a mistake! Ask Claire! She'll tell you. Bill took care of me. He left me money!"

"Money? What money?"

Diane clung to the question for dear life. "A million dollars. He left me a million dollars. He didn't want me to suffer. Ask Claire. She'll tell you!"

This was a lie. Bill had invested the money for his retirement. He hadn't intended to die before she did. But Diane would tell a thousand lies to get away from this man and his knives.

The killer placed his knife on the dresser and picked up his phone. "Shall I call her right now?"

"Yes, please. Call her. You'll see."

Once Claire learned the killer was here, she'd send a SWAT team to rescue her. Or would she?

What if he was right? Bill had deceived her for years. Had Claire pretended to care for her, only to deliver her to this brutal murderer? No, Diane didn't believe that.

The killer snickered. Then he doubled over with laughter as though she'd floored him with a hilarious joke.

"Nice try, Diane. You didn't think I'd fall for that, did you? Bill sealed your fate a long time ago. Claire and I are working together. But she can't get her hands dirty this time. She has to stay squeaky clean. Bill's plan is perfect. It's beautiful. I wish I could tell you all about it. You'd be so proud. This is his final gift to you. But we've got a lot to do together, and I don't have all day. Let's get started."

"Please, no! I'm begging you."

He raised the butcher knife again. "This'll hurt, Diane. It'll hurt a lot."

A phone rang. The killer froze. On the fourth ring, he swore and snatched his phone from the dresser.

"Not now. I'm busy." He listened. Then he yelled. "What? Are you sure?"

He swore. He roared with frustration and ran his hand through his hair. Diane watched in horror. Something had gone wrong. Any second now, he'd vent his anger on her.

The killer inhaled a deep breath and pressed the phone to his ear. "It doesn't matter. We need to stick with the plan. I'm about to get started here." He listened again, longer this time. "OK. Fine."

He glared at Diane. "Change of plans."

Anger simmered beneath the surface. Had the caller spared her life?

He pocketed his phone and grabbed her arm. Was he going to slit her wrists and kill her fast?

Diane closed her eyes. She couldn't bear to watch. Something snapped, and the pressure on her arm relaxed. Diane opened her eyes. He'd cut the cable ties from her wrists and did the same for her ankles.

"Get dressed."

Had Claire called? Was she working with him? What were they going to do with her?

He waved the knife at her. "I said, get dressed!"

Diane clambered off the bed in a hurry.

"And look sharp, Diane. We're going to have a family reunion."

CHAPTER 84

"Back so soon?" Sarah Malik said when Claire charged into her home office with Jess, Rob, and Tom in her wake.

Al, the PA, must have stepped out. *Perfect.* Malik wouldn't throw them out easily.

Claire had chosen a risky strategy for this confrontation. Jess's confession had opened a new perspective on the evidence. Claire understood who M was and why Malik had retracted her claims about the murders. But a third life hung in the balance, and Claire had no time for lengthy interrogations to test her theory. She hoped this surprise attack squeezed the truth from Malik before Johnny completed William Wolfe's last murderous scheme.

Claire marched to the politician's desk. "You said Carmine was your friend."

Her tone was hard and accusatory, and the question seemed to knock all the fight out of Malik. A thrill ran through Claire's body. Her gambit was working.

"She *was* my friend."

"You also said you didn't meet her the night she died."

"I didn't."

"Then you've lied to us twice."

Malik shot to her feet and flushed with rage. "How dare you? Carmine meant the world to me."

"Then why'd you have her killed?"

Her eyes widened with panic. "What? Have you lost your mind?"

"Carmine met with you the night she died. You're on her calendar." That wasn't strictly true, but Malik didn't know.

"That's impossible."

"You've met her at The Barnett Inn before, haven't you? And it wasn't to discuss politics."

Malik said nothing. Her face answered the question for her. Her cheeks reddened, replacing her fury with a different emotion.

Jess stepped forward. "Carmine was your lover. She was mine, too, once. Why did you hurt her?"

"I didn't..."

Malik's lips trembled. Her need to defend her political image wrestled with her desire to respect the memory of her dead lover. The price for revealing the truth was high.

Claire helped her make the right choice. "They told you this would happen, didn't they?"

Sarah Malik shot her a quick, fearful glance. Again, Claire had hit her mark.

"If you didn't play ball, they'd expose your affair with Carmine and frame you for her murder. Victoria's, too. A love triangle that imploded with jealousy."

Malik's eyes glazed over. Her worst fears had materialized. She could no longer prevent her exposure. "Victoria wasn't... like us. She didn't know about Carmine and me." She looked Claire in the eyes, pleading. "I didn't hurt Carmine. I could never..." Her face crumpled. She sank to her chair and covered her face with her hands. "I loved her more than anything."

Claire lowered her voice. "We know."

Malik shuddered and sobbed. "He said they'd kill me if I told anybody. He had photos of us together and of what he did to her."

Claire glanced at Jess, Rob, and Tom. Malik had revealed more than they had expected. "Who said that?"

"His name is Jim."

"Jim who?"

"Just Jim. He called me up out of nowhere and gave me money. They knew I was desperate. They know everything."

Johnny had used a fake name, one of his many tools for gaining access to his victims.

Rob joined Claire at the desk. "Who sent him to threaten you, Sarah?"

"He wouldn't tell me who he represents. For all I know, he's working alone."

"What did he want you to do?"

"For now, to carry on, business as usual. To win the elections. He'll have more instructions later."

"Sarah, this murderer has one more name on his list. Did he say who he was going to kill next?"

Distress crumpled Malik's brow. "He said nothing about another murder."

Claire turned to Rob. Her frustration reflected in his eyes. They were so close. They had uncovered most of her father's plot. But without Johnny's identity or the name of his next victim, they still had no way of stopping him from completing his murderous plan.

"Sergeant, you've got to help me!"

She was right. Now she'd talked, Apex would kill her.

"We will. Officers are here already. You'll have full-time police protection."

Malik didn't seem reassured. "Victoria had a high-end alarm system, and Carmine knew karate. That didn't stop him."

Right again. Johnny always found a way to his targets. Claire had learned that first-hand.

"I'll speak with the department about moving you to a secure location sooner."

Claire's phone buzzed. Her mother was calling. She answered.

"Mom, I'll call you right back."

"Is this Diane's daughter?" The man had a Southern accent. "I'm sorry to disturb you, but I found your mother on the street. She's pretty hammered."

Claire swore under her breath. Just when she thought Diane had pieced her life together, she'd fallen right back into the bottle. *Patience, Claire.* Sobriety was a long-term struggle. At least Mom was trying.

Claire sighed in surrender. "Where is she?"

"I got her home, but somebody should keep an eye on her."

"I'll be right there. Thank you for helping her."

"You're welcome."

"What happened?" Rob asked.

"It's my mom. I need to go. I'll call Captain Washington on the way to coordinate Ms. Malik's protection. Can you give Officer Long a ride back to the station?"

"Sure. Can I help with anything?"

"No, it's nothing serious. I'll meet up with you later."

Claire left Malik's home and ran for her car. True to form, her mother had ruined her day.

CHAPTER 85

"You don't recognize me, do you?"

Johnny spoke with a Southern drawl. He savored the young woman's confused expression. She stood at the foot of the luxury apartment's four-poster bed. Her bondage lingerie was heavy on the leather and metal studs. Emily had never looked sexier.

He'd photographed her in a dozen seductive positions, then instructed his blonde female assistant to secure his model's wrists and ankles to the tall bedposts. Now, Emily seemed to regret allowing the assistant to tie her up.

She glanced at the other young woman for reassurance. "Should I know him?"

The assistant smiled mysteriously but said nothing.

Emily hadn't seen Johnny in over a year, but that didn't explain her inability to recognize her dear little brother. Besides the phony accent, he'd taken other precautions. His plan had worked like a charm.

Johnny turned to his assistant and dropped the accent. "That'll be all."

Emily gasped. He knew what she was thinking. No, it can't be him!

The assistant blew Emily a kiss and strutted out of the apartment. Her name was Rachel Morris. *Johnny's fellow pack member had lured Emily to the apartment with promises of hard cash and a career in lingerie modeling.*

Johnny stepped from behind the camera tripod and drew near. He removed the fake beard, blond wig, and sticky nose prosthetic, taking care to pocket every item. He'd leave no trace of his presence for the forensic team.

Emily's eyes bulged. "Johnny? Wow, you've...changed. It's so good to see you."

Her nervous titter betrayed her true thoughts. Win him over or he'll take revenge for what you did to him all those years. *Emily wouldn't leave this room alive, but she didn't know that yet.*

Johnny had honed his fantasy to perfection. He'd tracked Emily down and surveilled her for weeks. All that remained was to follow the script and enjoy the ride.

"I've been watching you."

She shuddered. "You have? Why didn't you say hello?"

"I wanted our reunion to be special. Memorable. I've been waiting for this moment for a long time. Don't worry." *He cast a glance at the camera behind him.* "I'll record everything."

Emily sobbed. She pulled at the cable ties, but the steel bedposts held. Pleasure surged through Johnny's body. She was at his mercy.

"I'm sorry," *she mumbled.*

"What was that?"

"I'm sorry...for what I did. I was a stupid, angry girl. I wasn't even mad at you."

Johnny unzipped his black duffel bag and withdrew the new blade he'd purchased for the occasion. He could afford to treat himself now. But his taste in knives had changed as he'd gained experience. He held the hunting knife in the air for Emily to see.

"Please don't hurt me."

He stepped closer and smiled. "Who's the boss, Emily?"

Her jaw muscles bulged with defiance. The old Emily was still in there.

"*I said, who's the boss?*"

"*You are.*"

"*Who's in control?*"

A tear slipped down her cheek. "You."

"*Good girl.*"

He licked his lips and taped her mouth shut. Then he sliced the lingerie from her body, piece by piece. He savored her every twitch and flinch as the cool blade touched her skin. Finally, she stood naked before him, and he feasted his eyes on her beauty.

"*You've taken good care of your body, Emily. Good for you.*"

This time, he didn't need to hide. Nobody could stop him. He owned her. He held her life in the palm of his hand.

"*You're beautiful. But your looks won't last forever. So, we'll create something better. Together, we'll make a timeless work of art.*"

He selected another long blade from his bag. Emily whimpered, and a final plea for mercy flickered in her eyes. He inhaled, giddy with power.

"*This is going to hurt, Emily. This'll hurt a lot.*"

Johnny took his time. He made a bloody mess. What did he care? The apartment wasn't his. When the owner returned from his ski trip, he'd have a hard time explaining the mutilated corpse in his bedroom to the cops. They probably wouldn't even notice the Apex symbol—the broken A—he'd cut into her body among the many other wounds.

Johnny washed up, packed away his equipment, and skipped down the stairs. A car waited outside. Johnny tossed his bag in the trunk and climbed into the plastic-lined passenger seat.

"*How did it feel?*" *Bill asked.*

The adrenaline rush and sense of release still circulated in Johnny's body.

"Great. Real good." He frowned. "But to be honest, I think I've developed a taste for hookers."

They laughed, and Bill pulled off. Johnny had done it—with the pack's help. Now he'd turn his attention to new horizons and challenges.

"Claire is returning to Newburgh soon," Bill said.

Claire Wolfe. Bill idolized his beloved heir and protégé. He spoke of her often, and the idea of Claire had grown to epic proportions in Johnny's mind. She was the Promised One. Displaying wisdom beyond her years, she'd inspired Bill to study forensics and police procedures. Claire was the pack's greatest asset and its future leader. And she was returning to Newburgh, the pack's base of operations.

"Seriously?"

"Yep. The Plan is finally in motion."

"That's excellent news."

The Plan with a capital P was Bill's carefully scripted design to tie up the loose ends of his first kill. The Plan also aimed to catapult Claire up the ranks of Newburgh PD. According to Bill, Claire had joined the police force and dedicated years of her life to prepare for this.

"Yes, it is. And I want you to play a key role in Phase Two."

"I'd be honored, Bill." This was a big deal. Johnny was a relative newcomer to the pack. Bill was giving him a clear vote of confidence.

"Phase Two leverages Claire's new position to give Apex control of City Hall."

"Amazing."

Bill Wolfe always dreamed big.

"It's a perfect match for your skill set."

"When do I start?"

"Later. Much later. I'm still working out the details. But you'll get to work closely with Claire."

"I'd like that."

Bill was pairing Johnny with his beloved daughter. Claire was already Johnny's soul sister. But could she be more? Would Johnny join her one day at the helm of Apex?

Bill grinned with pleasure. "I think you and Claire will get along well."

CHAPTER 86

C hief of Police Charlie Emmerso held the receiver of his desk phone at arm's length to protect his eardrums. His boss, Mayor Thornton, had chosen the wrong career path. The mayor had the lungs of an opera diva and the vocabulary of a sailor. For the past five minutes, he'd wielded both against Emmerso.

"Me?" Thornton bellowed between curses. "A murderer?"

After Claire's talk with the Hannovers that morning, Edward Hannover had confronted Mayor Tommy Thornton about his alleged involvement in Carmine's murder. The conversation hadn't gone well. When the mayor paused to breathe, Emmerso pressed the receiver to his mouth.

"Mayor, our detectives are merely following procedure. They have to eliminate all possibilities. As soon as political motives arose, all candidates became persons of interest. The investigation has not singled you out. You have nothing to worry about."

"Nothing to worry about?"

Emmerso whisked the phone from his ear again.

Thornton raged on. "Whispers of sexual harassment are

enough to kill a campaign these days. Imagine what a murder investigation will do! If the press gets hold of this—"

"They won't. We're very discreet."

"You call telling Ed Hannover *discreet*?"

Emmerso stuck his finger in his ear and worked his jaw to ease the ringing in his head.

"The FBI is behind this, aren't they? First serial killers, now a murdering mayor. I knew we shouldn't have gotten them involved. If this is what they call assisting local law enforcement, they can shove it up their asses. We brought them in to take the heat, not to burn us alive."

"Speaking of the FBI, they helped us make a breakthrough today. I can't go into the details, but we might wrap up the case soon, and I think you'll like the result."

Sergeant Wolfe had called from Malik's home. Not only was the politician alive and well, now it seemed she might have conducted a secret affair with Carmine Hannover. Sarah Malik had graduated from potential target to prime suspect. If Claire extracted a confession from the politician, his detectives might arrest the person responsible for the assassinations by the end of the day.

"You'd better pray that's true, Charlie. For both our sakes."

Emmerso launched to his feet and left his office. Thornton was right. If he didn't close this case soon, the rumor mills would do irreparable damage. But he wasn't naïve either. If the investigation didn't dot every I and cross every T, Malik's lawyers would claim the sitting mayor had abused his power to dispatch a political rival. And Thornton would feed Emmerso, his convenient scapegoat, to the DA.

Captain Washington hurried toward him. "Chief."

"Walk with me, Captain. Anything from Joe Maisel yet?"

Washington fell into step beside him. "Nakamura is with him now. His lawyers are making life difficult."

"That's to be expected."

"He's hiding something."

"Of course, he is, Captain. Most people have secrets. But did he have a hand in the homicides?"

"We've got nothing on him yet. Malik is the more likely perp for now."

"I agree, Captain. But let's pursue all options until we have our suspect in custody."

The captain's mobile phone buzzed as they reached the conference room. "It's Sergeant Wolfe."

Expecting an important update, the two officers halted in the corridor. Washington pressed the speakerphone button. Claire's voice had the distant, muffled sound of a caller using a hands-free car set. Ten seconds into her update, Captain Washington swore, and Emmerso's lunch of Fettuccine Alfredo threatened to escape through his mouth. Their promising theory about the homicides had exploded spectacularly. Mayor Thornton wouldn't be happy. And Emmerso's visit to the FBI war room had become much more urgent.

"Any news from the front lines, sir?" Detective Lucas Gomez had materialized behind them.

Captain Washington updated him.

Gomez said, "Should I keep an eye on Malik while Claire is out?"

Washington knew what he was thinking. They couldn't afford to lose Sarah Malik the way they had lost Victoria McAdams—because of inadequate police protection.

"Good idea. Liaise with Dispatch."

Gomez hurried off.

In the conference room, Dr. Sally Fleischer held her phone to her ear, her face a study of open-mouthed surprise. Emmerso and Washington glanced at the groups of crime scene photos while they waited for her to finish.

"I take it you've heard the news," Emmerso said when she put down her phone.

"That was Agent Cline. So much for Sarah Malik. This time Apex tried to snake their way into City Hall."

"So, what's their next move? Who's the third target?"

"I don't know. There's nobody left. This doesn't feel right."

Washington snorted. "Is that the technical term?"

Emmerso gave him a cautionary look. The captain had expressed his doubts about the BAU's methods before and he'd resisted her mention of serial killers. But Dr. Fleischer's intuition had proved accurate, and this was no time to needle their expert profiler.

Emmerso tried to undo the damage. "We're not asking for guarantees. But we've got a killer out there, and he's on a schedule. If you have any ideas—even vague intuitions—we'd be glad to hear them."

Dr. Fleischer considered him while she deliberated. "William Wolfe planned these homicides. He was no ordinary psychopath. What he did with the Middle School Murders was masterful. He created multiple layers of deception and misdirection. William manipulated our expectations using his knowledge of forensic psychology. We had chased a typical serial killer, but his true goals were to frame a cop for his murders and boost his daughter up the Newburgh PD chain of command. If he hadn't confessed his crimes to Claire, he would've gotten away with it."

The psychiatrist stared through Emmerso while her brain analyzed the evidence on the whiteboard of her mind.

"This time, we got lucky, too. Like his mentor, Johnny thought Claire was with the pack and unwittingly opened a window on William's thinking. Otherwise, we'd still be tracking a psychopathic stalker. There's one last target on the list. William Wolfe would make sure the final murder made sense to us. Nobody would know these killings had a political agenda." Dr. Fleischer turned to Emmerso. "We've been searching for an assassin and his client. Maybe we've been asking the wrong question?"

Emmerso's lunch churned in his stomach again. Her logic didn't bode well for a happy conclusion to their investigation. Despite their blind luck, William Wolfe's misdirection had worked. The department had chased wild geese while his minion closed in for the kill. But what question should they have asked?

Dr. Fleischer's eyes lit up. A euphoric smile parted her lips. She had figured out the answer, and she turned to the officers with an expectant glance.

"Tell me, gentlemen. What is the right question?"

She had led the officers to the threshold of a solution and dared them to take the final deductive step.

Emmerso and Washington exchanged embarrassed glances, then admitted defeat.

"We give up," Emmerso said. "What question should we be asking?"

"The question is Claire."

Emmerso waited for Dr. Fleischer to laugh at their expense, but she didn't. This wasn't a bad joke.

"I don't understand."

"Claire has nothing to do with the homicides," Washington blurted. He seemed upset at being put on the spot. "Johnny told her so."

"Correct. Johnny said William wanted to keep Claire out of this plot. Then why did Johnny carve her name on the corpses?"

"He wanted us to drop her from the investigation?"

"But why mention her at all? And if he wanted to create media hype, why not use the name Carmine or Victoria—or

Kitty? They made the gossip columns. The stalker could have obsessed over any of them. Why did William create a stalker obsessed with Claire?"

And Emmerso understood. The third victim. *The cherry on the top.*

"Because the third victim isn't connected to those three friends. She's connected to Claire."

Dr. Fleischer beamed at him. Basking in that flash of revelation, Emmerso briefly considered a career in criminal profiling.

Washington cleared his throat. "Um. Anybody want to tell me who the third victim is?"

Dr. Fleischer turned to him, all smiles. She was enjoying this, just a little. "William Wolfe wanted us to think the stalker kills to please Claire. He thought Claire killed Kitty Tucker, so he killed Kitty's friends, too. The third victim is the person Claire wanted dead the most—at least to the stalker's mind."

Captain Washington looked from the psychiatrist to Chief Emmerso, who gave him one more hint. "Somebody William Wolfe might want dead, too."

Finally, the answer flickered in Washington's eyes, and he swore.

CHAPTER 87

Claire's car barreled down the suburban roads of Newburgh. "Perfect timing, Mom."

Diane had thrown a wrench in the works during the climax of the investigation, and Claire's pursuit of the killer had ground to a halt.

She'd called Captain Washington to update him about Johnny's attempt to blackmail Sarah Malik, then focused on her mother's relapse. Diane's second drunken episode in a week disappointed Claire. Her mom had cleaned up her act. She'd resumed her AA meetings of her own accord and started singing with a band. More than that, Diane had apologized for her behavior. She'd seemed optimistic about the future. After months of stubborn refusal, Mom had stepped toward recovery and filled Claire with hope, too.

The relapse shouldn't have surprised Claire. An alcoholic never stopped being an alcoholic. Diane would battle her urge to drink every day for the rest of her life. Maybe she'd turned her life around too suddenly? Sobriety was a marathon, not a sprint. Claire needed to find new reserves of patience to support her mother's recovery. At least this time, Mom wanted to change. And, as far as Claire knew, she hadn't flashed her boobs in public again.

The killer loomed in Claire's mind. Where was Johnny? Who was he stalking? Claire had uncovered much of the plot to control Newburgh except for the identity of the third victim. Apex had murdered Kitty Tucker's friends but spared Sarah Malik, a pawn in their psychopathic chess game. Who was left to kill? Her father's ghost ruled the board. Would his next move trap Claire in a checkmate?

Claire pulled up outside Diane's home. No cars parked outside. The Good Samaritan who had taken her home must have bailed after hanging up the phone. Claire got out of the car, thumbed the remote, and walked the short path to the front door.

Details of the case floated in her mind. Johnny had led her to her father's laptop and the Apex darknet site. He believed she was with her father's murderous pack. Bill had told him about her. He'd groomed Claire for leadership. Was Johnny jealous of her? Did he resent her special treatment? Would he strike at Claire, now that Bill was dead, and claim that title for himself?

Claire fingered the house keys in her pocket. Sarah Malik surfaced in her thoughts. She was out of funds and hounded by a criminal organization. Her political career was over. But how would Apex follow through with their threat without exposing their assassination ring? The plan made no sense.

Claire unlocked the front door. She stepped inside and tossed her key chain on the telephone table. Two steps into the hall, she froze. Her mother sat on a kitchen chair, her arms behind the backrest, her face pale and tense. A silver strip of duct tape sealed her mouth shut. The man in the gray suit behind her aimed his gun loosely at Diane's head.

Johnny grinned. "Welcome home, Claire."

CHAPTER 88

"Well, that was interesting." Tom drove the Bureau car to the station, a smirk on his weathered face.

In the passenger seat, Rob stifled a grin. *Understatement of the year.* Tom always insisted on driving, and today Rob obliged the control freak. His mind was still digesting the day's revelations, and one particular revelation had thrown him for a loop.

He studied Jess's reflection in the windshield. She stared out the back-seat window. Jess had said little since coming out of the closet. The short journey to the station must be excruciating for her. She hadn't intended to disclose her sexual orientation. Now she had to endure this awkward drive with a man she'd hit on only a few days ago.

Tom glanced at the rearview mirror, the hint of a smile on his thin lips, and Rob cringed. The Master of Tact had scoffed at the pretty young detective from the start, and he couldn't resist an opportunity to rib a colleague.

"Forgive me for saying this, Officer Long, but I'd never pegged you as a..." He searched for the right word, then gave up. "That you prefer the ladies."

Jess's reflection stared at Tom and cocked her head at a confrontational angle.

"And why is that?"

Rob grinned. Jess had taken the fight to Tom, and he deserved it. He'd have to work hard not to come across as a homophobic old man. But Rob also pricked up his ears. Her recent behavior had raised questions in his mind, too.

Tom shrugged. "I don't know. You just don't look the type."

"How exactly does *the type* look?"

Rob chuckled. Tom had asked for it, and Jess had delivered. His every word sank him deeper into Politically Correct quicksand.

"I don't know." A plea entered his voice. He turned to Rob, a drowning man clutching at the nearest person. "C'mon, Rob. Help me out here."

"You're on your own, Tom."

"Thanks, pal. I knew I could count on you."

Jess stared out the window again. "For the record, I like men, mostly. But Carmine was...special."

Did she feel she owed Rob an explanation?

Tom seemed relieved to be off the hook. "Oh, I see. That's good! Double your odds when you can, that's what I always say."

Jess shook her head in exasperation but said nothing more. So, there it was—Jess was bisexual. Rob's sense for reading people wasn't completely out of sync with reality.

A phone rang on the hands-free speakers.

"Is that yours?"

"Yeah." Rob fished his phone from his pocket and glanced at the screen. "It's the lab."

"The DNA for the second decapitation?"

"Mm-hm."

Rob's heartbeat raced. If the FBI forensic lab had matched

the victim in their databases, they had discovered the killer's current identity. Finding him would be easy.

Tom said, "Twenty bucks says we got nothing."

Rob answered the call. "Ben, tell me some good news."

"Um...the Celtics beat the Lakers last night?" The Bostonian loved his basketball almost as much as biochemistry.

"Sorry, Ben, I'm a Nicks fan. You're on speakerphone. Say hello to Agent Brown and Officer Long of Newburgh PD. We were hoping you'd call about our John Doe."

"That's the other good news. We got lucky with the sample you sent us and hit an exact match on FamilyTreeDNA."

"Great!" Rob craned his neck and smiled at Jess. "Tom owes me twenty bucks."

"No, I don't. You didn't accept the bet."

Rob touched his temples to focus his psychic powers. "Let me guess. We're dealing with a male Caucasian in his mid-twenties. He has dark hair, and his name is John or Johnny. How'd I do?"

Ben laughed on the loudspeaker. "Nice try, Sherlock, but you're not even close. This guy isn't Caucasian."

Rob's excitement faded. He'd listed the characteristics of the killer Claire had described from Johnny's home visit. Rachel Morris had stolen the identity of Lisa Evans, the female decapitated victim. Johnny would've assumed the identity of someone who resembled him in broad strokes. Had they misunderstood the purpose of the decapitations?

Ben continued. "His ancestry is a mix of European, African, and Native American. That genetic profile indicates Latino ethnicity." The lab tech was right. The victim didn't match Johnny. "Which makes perfect sense once you hear his name."

"Well? Don't keep us in suspense. What's his name?"

When Ben told him, Rob's heart skipped a beat. The world shifted around him.

"Wait," Tom said. "Isn't that...?"

"Yes, it is. Turn the car around. We need to get back there, pronto." Rob swiveled on his seat. "Jess, call Dispatch. Get hold of Patrol. Let's hope that squad car is still at the house."

Jess already had her phone to her ear. "I'm on it."

"I hope this helps," Ben said.

In the excitement, Rob had forgotten the lab tech was still on the line.

"Yeah, Ben. You've been a great help. Thanks."

Rob ended the call and checked the magazine of his gun while Tom spun the car around and sped back the way they had come. The stars had smiled on them. The DNA analysis had gift-wrapped the case complete with a pretty red ribbon. But the investigation had made a colossal mistake. And this mistake might be fatal.

CHAPTER 89

"Hello, Johnny," Claire said.

She'd stumbled into a highly explosive situation but kept her voice conversational. The killer stood behind Mom, his gun to her head, his face tense. He'd secured Diane to the chair with cable ties. One wrong word or movement, and he'd blow her brains out.

Diane wasn't drunk. The mystery caller was no Good Samaritan either. Claire had run headlong into Johnny's trap. But why was he threatening her mother? Had he discovered Claire was working against him? Would he hurt Diane to punish her?

Claire's hand itched for her service weapon. Ten feet away, she had a good chance of picking Johnny off, but he'd pull his trigger before she disabled him. *Keep calm, Claire. Stay in character. He thinks you're on his side.*

"I see you've made yourself at home."

"No thanks to you. Why'd you block the tunnel?"

Rob had prepared her for that question. "I value my privacy."

Johnny scoffed. The closure of his secret entrance had angered him. Was that the reason for his visit?

Claire needed Rob now. He'd offered to help her. Had she accepted, she wouldn't be facing this gunman alone. But as usual, Claire had pushed him away. She'd done the same with Jess. When would she learn to let people in? She'd tried to protect others from her family's curse. But those fears had isolated her, becoming a self-fulfilling prophecy.

Diane whimpered. Her eyes filled with terror—and confusion. Her daughter's arrival must have given her hope. But Claire's casual banter with the gunman had dashed that hope. Claire knew the attacker. They had a history. Did Diane understand Claire was playing a role or did she think Claire had deceived her all along like William? Claire would explain her behavior later. She put aside Mom's anguish and focused on her opponent.

Johnny had a Glock 22. A standard magazine held fifteen cartridges. In terms of firepower, they were on a level playing field. Or were they? Claire's police academy training kicked in. Her instructors had drilled the Plus One Rule into her brain. Found a weapon? Look for another. Found a second? Look for a third. Was Johnny carrying more guns?

An additional problem flashed in her mind. If she won back Johnny's confidence, how would she save Diane? Her mother had seen and heard too much. Johnny would never let her live. For both she and Mom to survive, Claire had to neutralize Johnny. And to do that, she needed to get inside his head.

"I found the breadcrumb trail you left for me. Apex has a nice ring to it. So, we're framing Sarah Malik for the murders?"

Johnny sneered. "Very good, Claire."

"There's one thing I don't understand. Exposing Malik will expose Apex, too."

His derisive smile widened. *Good.* Claire's questions inflated his ego. Let him think he was two steps ahead. That false sense of superiority would buy her time and information.

"It won't come to that, Claire. We don't want to get rid of Malik. We want to control her. The death of her friends is the leverage we needed to make sure she behaves. And if she doesn't, well, Apex has abandoned that business anyway."

That business. Did Apex have others? William Wolfe had chosen to destroy his assassination ring to become a political power broker, the way a grandmaster sacrifices his queen to checkmate a king.

"Why Malik? Thornton's already in office."

"Bill considered Thornton at first. He wasn't as dirty as he seemed, and he had a well-established support base. We needed a fresh, young filly in the race. Once we broke her in, she'd yield to our will. As always, Father's plan was brilliant. First, we remove her support base, making her entirely dependent on our money. Then, we secure her loyalty with the threat of prison and a disgraceful end to her career. Meanwhile, the world would think the hits were the work of your lovestruck stalker."

Claire grunted with appreciation. "It's a good plan. And the execution has been flawless."

Johnny bowed his head. "Thank you, Claire. The media took the bait. Malik has fallen in line."

"Good job. Then I guess we're done."

Johnny scoffed. "Oh, no. We've reached the climax. Your stalker celebrates his love for you by giving you the ultimate gift." With the flourish of a magician revealing his masterstroke, he waved the gun barrel at Diane. "Behold, the cherry on the top."

Claire gaped in shock. "Diane is the third target?"

Johnny placed a hand on Diane's shoulder, and she flinched. "An end to decades of suffering. Payback for the years of psychological abuse. With the hag out of the way, you and Bill would be free to rule Newburgh and expand Apex's reach."

His words made diabolical sense. Her father had hated Diane with a passion. He'd savored her distress over Tina's death for years. But even that twisted pleasure grew old eventually. Bill turned to new projects, and his ruined wife became dead weight.

Claire forced her breathing to remain steady. "Nice."

Johnny had laid out her father's plan. He was going to execute Diane here and now unless Claire stopped him. But there was more to this gathering than William's sick plan. Claire's stalker had used knives, not guns. And the scheme didn't require Claire's presence at Diane's murder—it required her absence. Why had Johnny lured her here? The scene smelled wrong, worse even than the musky scent of men's aftershave that hung in the air. Johnny had changed the plan. Unlike Bill, he was no grandmaster. He played a different game, but he kept an ace up his sleeve, and he was waiting for the right moment to play the winning card.

"So, what's with the prank call? You could've just asked me to come over."

Johnny sneered again. He opened his mouth to answer, but a phone rang. The ringing came from Claire's jacket pocket. Was Rob calling her—or one of her team? Claire could alert them to her situation discreetly, and they'd scramble squad cars to the house. Slowly, she reached for her pocket.

Johnny pressed the gun barrel to Diane's head. "I wouldn't do that if I were you. It's rude to ignore your guests."

Claire let her hand drop to her side. The phone rang and rang for what seemed an eternity, then cut to voicemail.

Claire feigned impatience. "Why am I here, Johnny?"

"Isn't that obvious? To do the honors."

Diane's eyes widened, and her chest rose as her breathing

sped up. She glanced at Claire, pleading wordlessly for her daughter to spare her life.

"You said Bill wanted to keep me out of this project. Wasn't that the plan?"

Johnny snarled. "This'll be our little secret. Nobody has to know. You've wanted her dead since you were a kid. After the way she treated you all these years, you deserve this. Think of it as poetic justice. Here, use this. It's untraceable."

He tossed his gun to her, and Claire caught the Glock in both hands. Johnny had handed her a loaded weapon, leaving himself unarmed. Did he trust her with his life or was this a test?

Johnny stepped to the side, away from Diane. "Forensics 101. Beware of blood spatter. Bill would be proud." He chuckled. "Go on, Claire. Whenever you're ready. Just point and shoot."

Diane moaned through the tape on her lips and struggled against her restraints. Johnny grinned at Claire, daring her to turn the gun on him. Claire resisted that urge. But what was he thinking?

Claire couldn't afford to hesitate. She inhaled deeply, searching for the right emotion. Johnny was right—Diane had made her childhood a misery. Claire was a wolf on the hunt. And she'd found her prey. Claire raised the gun, aimed at her mother's head, and pulled the trigger.

CHAPTER 90

S trobe lights painted the stucco walls of Sarah Malik's house in blue and red. Rob drew his gun and sprang from the Bureau car before the vehicle came to a complete stop. Police lights meant danger and tragedy. Had he arrived too late?

Rob flashed his FBI card at the beat cop behind the gate, a mop of red hair with belly flab overhanging his belt.

"Where's Sarah Malik?"

"Inside."

The cop pressed a button on the wall to open the iron gate and let Rob, Jess, and Tom inside.

"Is there a uniform with her?"

"Yeah."

"Is Detective Gomez here?"

Gomez hadn't answered his phone when Jess had called.

"Um, I think so."

He thinks so.

Rob ran through the courtyard toward the house. With only a single officer on-site, the killer's accomplice might have dispatched Malik already.

Johnny wasn't working alone. Rob should have figured

that out earlier. The evidence had stared him in the face. If Sarah Malik lay dead in her office, Rob could only blame himself.

The front door of Malik's home stood open. Rob waited for Tom and Jess to catch up, then proceeded with caution, leading the way with his service weapon drawn. The corridors stood empty. He checked the pool for floating bodies. He reached the large double doors of Malik's office and listened. No sound came from within. He placed his free hand on the door handle and turned to the others.

"On three. One. Two. Three!"

The door was unlocked. Rob rushed inside. Malik looked up from her desk. The dark man to Rob's left reached for his gun.

"FBI!"

The wide-eyed patrol officer raised his service weapon, then exhaled heavily.

"Geez! Next time, knock before you burst in."

Detective Gomez wasn't in the room. The agents lowered their weapons.

Malik stared at Rob and Jess in confusion and rose to her feet.

"What's going on? What happened?"

"Where's your PA—Alexandro?"

Malik gawked at Rob in confusion. "Out. Why?"

"Where'd he go?"

"I don't know."

"We need his number."

Malik folded her arms over her chest. "What the hell is going on?"

"He's not who you think he is."

Malik tittered. "You have got to be kidding me."

"This is a matter of life and death. Ms. Malik—"

"If Al is in trouble, I deserve to know. He practically runs my campaign."

"Then you'll need a new campaign manager. His number?"

She reached for her phone. "I'll call him."

"No! Please. Just give us his number."

"If he needs an attorney, I'll get him one."

"Ms. Malik, if you don't comply right now, I'll arrest you for Obstruction of Justice."

Rob had to lay down the law. Denial had set in, and the seconds lost might cost lives.

"OK." She unlocked her iPhone and handed it over.

Rob read the number to Jess, who called Dispatch.

He turned back to Malik. "I'm sorry about that. I'll explain later."

Malik shrugged but avoided his eyes. While they waited for Al's current location, Rob could test his theory. Johnny hadn't lured Carmine to The Barnett Inn. His collaborator had.

"Is that a new phone?"

"Yes. Why?"

"Did you lose your other phone about a week ago?"

"How did you...?" She fell silent as the information hit home.

Rob's educated guess had proved right.

"Someone met with Carmine at The Barnett Inn the night the killer got to her. Carmine's calendar points to you. But you didn't arrange that meeting, did you? Someone contacted Carmine on your behalf—someone with access to your phone."

Sarah Malik sank onto her chair, her world collapsing. The person she'd trusted most had betrayed her.

"How did you come to hire Alexandro?"

"We met at a fundraiser for a women's shelter shortly after I registered to run for mayor."

"That meeting was no accident. The people who blackmailed you have had you in their sights from the start. And they've killed others—many others. A few minutes ago, we identified one of their victims as Alexandro Menendez. The group used his identity to get close to you. Your PA was present when Claire told you about them. They know we're onto them. They'll move fast to eliminate the last target on their list. We have to locate Alexandro—your Alexandro—before it's too late."

Malik nodded. Jess was still waiting for Dispatch to provide Alexandro's last location when Rob's phone rang.

Rob flushed with discomfort and answered. "Sally, I was about to call you." In his rush to find Malik, he'd forgotten to update the forensic psychiatrist about the DNA match. "Did you get the lab results?"

Sally ignored his question. "Is Claire with you?" She sounded uncharacteristically agitated.

"No. Why?"

"She isn't answering her phone."

"I couldn't reach her either. She left to go help her mom."

Sally swore. She never swore. *What was going on?*

"We think Claire's mother is the third target."

Dread pooled in his gut. "Diane? What's she got to do with Carmine Hannover?"

"Nothing. That's the point. Apex staged the homicides as the work of a stalker, a stalker obsessed with Claire. William Wolfe hated his wife. There's bad blood between Claire and her mom. If Wolfe wanted to get rid of Claire's mom, this is the perfect setup."

Rob swore, too. Sally was right.

Jess released her phone from her ear. "Got him! Cellular tower signals placed Alexandro in Pine Hills ten minutes ago."

"Pine Hills?" The pool of dread deepened, the rising water-line threatening to drown him. "Claire's home is in Pine Hills."

He spoke into the phone. "Sally, the accomplice is at her home."

"What accomplice? Whose home?"

Rob raced back to the Bureau car, speaking into the phone as he ran.

"Malik's PA. We found a DNA match. The decapitated man's name is Alexandro Menendez. The PA stole his identity. Dispatch traced his number to Pine Hills. Claire's walked into a trap."

CHAPTER 91

Diane stared in disbelief as Claire aimed the gun at her head. Minutes ago, when her daughter had arrived home, the fear in Diane's heart had subsided. Claire was here. She'd save her. Police officers would storm the house, arrest the killer, and free her. But the look of surprise on Claire's face destroyed Diane's hope for rescue. Her daughter hadn't expected the armed intruder. She was unprepared to defend Diane or herself. They were both going to die here.

Then her anguish turned to bewilderment. Claire addressed the intruder by name. She spoke to him as though they knew each other well. And the things her daughter said winded her. Claire cared little for Diane's survival. She jumped at the opportunity to shoot her in the head.

Diane's world narrowed to the barrel of the gun. The duct tape jammed her lips together. She couldn't even beg for her life. Why was Claire doing this? Diane had apologized for the past. They had made a fresh start. Claire had bailed her out of jail. She wouldn't kill her, would she?

And Diane understood. Claire had deceived the gunman.

She was playing a role, and the trick had worked. Any moment now, she'd turn the weapon on him and take control of the situation.

But Claire didn't take control. Her face hardened. Sparks flared from the gun barrel, and two loud blasts echoed off the walls.

Diane's head rang with the deafening sound. The acrid stench of burned gunpowder assaulted her nostrils. She blinked at her daughter. Diane had felt no pain. Had the bullets missed her? She'd heard no sounds of destruction behind her.

Claire scowled at Johnny. "Blanks? You have got to be kidding me."

Johnny trained his eyes on Claire. "How did you know?"

"How did I know what?"

He reached behind his back and pulled another gun from his belt. "Don't play stupid. You knew the gun had blanks. Otherwise, you'd never have shot her. You're not one of us."

Claire scoffed. "What are you talking about? The pack is my destiny—my father's legacy. Bill raised me for this."

Johnny shook his head. "I fell for that once. But I won't repeat that mistake. We're onto you, Claire."

"We? It's just you and me, Johnny."

"You're wrong." The voice came from the top of the staircase. A Latino with a tidy goatee and an expensive, lime-colored suit descended the stairs slowly, his gun aimed at Claire.

Diane hadn't known about the second gunman. He must have arrived while Johnny had made her dress in the bedroom.

Claire turned around. "Alexandro?"

Claire knew the second man, too, and his presence filled her with dread.

Alexandro reached the bottom step and grinned. "I told you a hundred times. Call me Al."

Johnny chuckled. "Don't you love family reunions? The last three members of the pack, all in one room. Bill would be proud. If Claire hadn't ruined it."

Claire gaped at the newcomer. "You arranged the meeting with Carmine. She thought she was going to meet Malik."

Alexandro smirked. "Very good, Sergeant Wolfe. Sarah's phone went missing. She'd never know about the messages I sent from the old device. Not that she cared. She's a sucker for new phones."

"That was risky, Al. Carmine's schedule lists the meeting."

Alexandro grimaced. "We thought Carmine would be more discreet. I only found out about her schedule today. Thanks to you."

Johnny pointed his gun at Claire like an accusatory finger. "Traitor! You told the police about the third target. You tried to ruin the plan. But you screwed up. You thought Malik was the third target, and you tried to save her."

Diane glanced from Claire to the two gunmen in confusion. She had no idea what they were talking about. But the result was clear. Claire was not working with the killers. She'd tried to stop them. Diane sobbed with relief. Claire hadn't tried to kill her. Somehow, she'd known the gun was harmless and called Johnny's bluff. But he'd been toying with her all along. He'd known Claire was his enemy and had never expected her to follow through.

Alexandro sidled closer to Claire. "Easy now. Don't move a muscle."

He reached over, slipped her gun from its holster, and stepped away. Claire stood there, unarmed and surrounded by murderers. She glanced at Diane, a sadness in her eyes.

Her lips trembled. "I'm sorry, Mom."

Claire understood how badly her act must hurt Diane. She'd never meant to place her mother in harm's way. Diane wanted to tell her it was OK. She understood now. Deep in her heart, she'd never doubted her. But the duct tape prevented her mouth from opening. Would she ever speak to her daughter again?

Diane sobbed uncontrollably. *No! We've just started over. This can't be the end.*

"Shut up!" Johnny yelled at her. "Claire, how did you know?"

Claire faced Johnny again and balled her hands into fists. Her brave gamble had failed. She was as good as dead but remained defiant and said nothing.

"Who cares?" Alexandro said. "Just get on with it."

"I care. She figured us out. What if we have a tell? For all we know, she killed Bill, too."

Al considered Claire with renewed curiosity. "Did you?"

Claire shrugged. "Maybe."

Johnny shook his head at her. "I used to envy you, Claire. Bill was a father to us. He made us who we are. We'd do anything for him. We were a family. But you were always his favorite, his one blind spot. He had high hopes for you, and you ruined everything."

Alexandro chuckled. "Not everything. We're still here. Phase Two is almost done. C'mon, Johnny. Let's get this over with. For Bill."

Johnny gritted his teeth. "Fine. For Bill."

Diane squealed with anguish. *No! Don't hurt my girl.* She willed Claire to dive out of the way and dodge the bullets. But Claire stood there, immobile, and stared Johnny square in the face.

Johnny steadied his gun in both hands and fired twice. Diane flinched at the deafening crack of the weapon so close to her ear. This time, the gun didn't fire blanks. The bullets tore into Claire's chest. The force of the impact knocked her backward. She collapsed to the floor and lay motionless while two red stains flowered on her blouse.

CHAPTER 92

R ob raced the Bureau car across suburban Newburgh and ripped through the speed limit. This time, he'd beaten Tom to the driver's seat. Claire was in mortal danger. There was no way Rob was going to waste another second getting to her.

Tom grimaced on the back seat. "Take it easy, Rob."

Jess had beaten him to the passenger door, too. The older agent had one foot still on the sidewalk when Rob had pulled off. A control freak at the best of times, Tom was the back-seat driver from Hell.

"This is probably a false alarm," Tom continued. "Remind me, why do we think Claire's in danger?"

Rob ignored his partner. "Jess, are they there yet?"

Jess had just got off the phone with Dispatch. "Not yet. Two squad cars will be there any minute."

Rob grunted with frustration. Every lost second might tip the scales from life to death. "Try her again."

"Calling her now."

Dr. Sally Fleischer hadn't been able to reach Claire on her phone either. A terrible premonition weighed on Rob's mind like a boulder. Claire had cheated death twice before. She'd taken a bullet. To hope she'd survived a third brush with the Angel of Death was asking for a miracle.

Tom yawned. "The call was probably legit. Her mother's an alcoholic. I heard she got arrested for indecent exposure last week. Lord knows what she did this time."

Tom had caught up on the department's gossip. But he wasn't factoring in more recent developments.

"Alexandro heard what we told Malik. He knows Claire shared Johnny's information with the investigation. He knows she's working against Apex. We'd assumed Johnny had used the second stolen identity, but we were wrong. Rachel Morris had a second male friend in the pack—Alexandro. He left Malik's home immediately after our visit. He must have contacted Johnny. They know we're getting close. They'll be desperate to conclude Bill's plan. And seeing that Claire stabbed them in the back, they'll want her dead, too."

In the rearview mirror, Tom shrugged. His trademark cynical confidence grated on Rob's nerves. "If they think it's game over, they'd want to save their asses. They'll hightail it out of Newburgh. I doubt they'd stick around to settle old scores. Rob, watch out!"

Rob jumped a red light to the sound of blaring horns. The near miss shut Tom up.

Rob wasn't imagining the dangers. "Don't underestimate their sense of betrayal. William Wolfe took them in as teenagers. He's their father figure. The pack is their surrogate family. Bill had intended for Claire to lead the pack one day. Turning on them was unforgivable. Killing Claire will be their new obsession."

Tom snorted, unimpressed. "If they truly cared about Bill, they'd want to complete his plan, foremost. They wouldn't invite Claire over to screw that up."

The argument made sense. But both Alexandro and Claire

had disappeared within minutes of each other. That was no coincidence.

"I hope you're right, Tom. But why isn't she answering her phone?"

"Maybe she needs some space, Rob. Sometimes I feel like screening your calls, too."

Jess snorted. Tom's cynicism had infected her. Rob eased his foot off the accelerator as he negotiated a corner. Maybe they were right, and he was overreacting. Alexandro and Johnny were probably on a flight to the Ivory Coast by now while he obsessed over Claire's mysterious unavailability.

Rob cruised down Claire's street in Pine Hills. Her white Ford Focus was the only vehicle outside the two-level home. Rob parked behind her car. The squads hadn't arrived yet. If Tom was right, they'd call off their backup.

Rob got out of the car and eased the door shut. He drew his service weapon and padded silently toward the house. The others fell in behind him. He listened for the sound of a struggle and tried to peer through the blinds.

A loud crack stopped him in his tracks. Every muscle in his body tensed. He knew that sound. A gun had fired inside Claire's home.

This was no false alarm.

CHAPTER 93

Johnny stared at the downed woman through the dissipating puff of gunpowder smoke. Claire Wolfe sprawled on the entrance hall floor, her body motionless and bloody. Johnny had done it—he'd destroyed the pack's mortal enemy. "Seeing is believing," people said. But he struggled to believe his eyes. *Claire Wolfe is dead.*

The pack's greatest asset and Bill's favorite had mutated into a formidable adversary. Did Johnny stand a chance against William Wolfe's flesh and blood? His fears had proved groundless. The makeshift plan had worked smoothly, and now his enemy lay dead at his feet. Johnny wished Bill could see him now. He'd realize that Claire wasn't his true heir after all. That title belonged to Johnny.

Alexandro knelt over Claire's body. He pried the harmless gun from her dead fingers and wiped the handle with a cloth. There was no need to check her pulse. The blood flow from her wounds had halted. Her heart had stopped beating.

A woman wailed beside Johnny, and her cries hurt his ears. He'd almost forgotten about Diane Wolfe. Still tied to the kitchen chair, the old hag bawled and babbled pathetically through the duct tape on her mouth.

"Quiet!"

She fell silent and cowered on the chair. The sight of her dead daughter had broken her. He wanted to seal her nose, too, and watch the life seep from her. But Apex had other plans for Diane Wolfe. Her death had to be perfect.

An idea entered his mind. He'd give Diane a glimpse of the pack's brilliance. She'd learn how the world would remember her, and he'd flood her final moments on this earth with anguish. Bill would have wanted that.

Johnny crouched beside her. "Your story is at an end, Diane. Claire moved back home and took over your life. You two never got along. Today, finally, you snapped. When she walked in, you plugged her twice in the heart with this gun."

He aimed the Glock at Claire's body again. "Bang! Bang! You killed her, Diane. But you screwed up. As she lay dying, she fired one last shot. You both die today. Domestic violence is so tragic, don't you agree?"

Diane sobbed softly but didn't dare look him in the eye. Alexandro pocketed the dud gun and wiped down Claire's Glock.

Johnny dangled his gun before Diane's face. "Once you're dead, I'll put this in your hand, press your finger to the trigger, and fire another round. Forensics will find your fingerprints on this gun and gunpowder residue on your skin. I'll wipe my prints first like he did for Claire's gun. Claire was a crack shot. Did you know that? She's going to shoot you between the eyes."

"Are you done?" Alexandro said. "Some of us are trying to work here."

Johnny made a sour face and stood. "I apologize for my friend's behavior. But he's right to be impatient. Our time is up." He stepped away from Diane. "Good talk. It's been fun but—"

The deafening report of gunfire startled Johnny.

He cursed Al. "Next time, warn me before you..."

Johnny didn't finish his sentence. Blood dripped from the ceiling. Alexandro slumped over Claire's body. The back of his skull was gone, and the acrid stench of vaporized flesh hung in the air. What the hell had just happened?

A female groan came from the two bodies, and Alexandro's corpse rolled onto its side. A gun barrel rested on the dead man's shoulder and pointed at Johnny's face.

No! That's impossible! Johnny had shot Claire in the chest twice. She'd oozed blood. There was no way she'd survived. But Claire's head appeared behind the gun. She snarled at him, her face plastered red with blood and gore like an undead zombie who feasted on human flesh.

"Put your hands in the air, you son of a bitch!"

CHAPTER 94

C laire aligned the front and rear sights of her Glock over her target. This was no easy task. Her chest ached, her arms trembled, and blood spatter in her eyes gave her double vision. The overlapped images of two identical gunmen gaped at her as though she'd risen from the grave. And she had. Caked in sticky human remains, Claire had passed through Hell. But her resurrection was no miracle.

Johnny's first two shots had hit her square in her chest. The impacts had pounded her ribs like hurtling baseballs, and the bruises would last for weeks. But the bullets had flattened against her covert vest. *Rob, I owe you one.*

Before she met with the Hannovers that morning, Claire had strapped the compact bulletproof material to her torso under her clothes. If the Hannovers decided to silence her, they wouldn't dispose of her easily. But stopping the first knife or bullet was only the first step. To convince the alleged psychopaths she was no longer a threat, Claire had to go the extra mile.

She'd poured a mixture of ketchup and water into two

freezer bags and taped the linings to her chest and back. Her sister, Tina, had fooled her with fake blood years ago, and the old trick would buy Claire a few seconds of grace. But the Hannovers hadn't attacked her that morning. During the day's manic flow of events, Claire had left her protective layers in place. And thank God for that. The fake blood had fooled the pack, enabling Claire to neutralize Alexandro. But one gunman remained, and Claire had run out of magic tricks.

Claire blinked hard to dislodge the blood but failed to cure her double vision. The Johnny twins raised their guns and roared a battle cry of rage and terror. Claire picked one of her attackers and pumped her trigger. The gun fired. Glass shattered on a kitchen shelf. Claire had destroyed Mom's microwave. But the twins stood their ground and returned fire.

Claire flattened her body to the floor. Bullets hammered Alexandro's corpse in the back, round after round, her human shield dancing. Claire cursed her bad luck. She'd missed her target and blown her one chance at leaving the house alive. The dead man's body wouldn't protect her much longer. She'd make an easy target when attacked from any other direction. And Johnny had leverage.

Alexandro's corpse stared at Claire with one eye, his cheek pressed against the floor. A dark, moist hole remained where her bullet had torn through his left eye and passed out the back of his skull. Blood and scorched brain matter had ruined his designer suit. "Don't judge me," the corpse seemed to say. "You're next."

And he'd be right. When Johnny recovered from the shock of her zombie resurrection, he'd destroy her. Claire had to find a way out of this death trap.

The volley of gunfire ended. Her seconds of grace ran out. Johnny had emptied ten rounds into his dead friend. Two plus ten left three cartridges in his magazine. Three were more than enough to finish this job. If he emptied his magazine, she'd improve her position while he reloaded.

Claire flexed her core muscles and hazarded another glance over Alexandro's shoulder. Diane's eyes widened, and she whimpered with relief. Her daughter was alive! Claire's double vision had cleared, but what she saw didn't reassure her. Johnny took cover behind Diane and watched Claire with murder in his eyes. He didn't take the bait and fire at her again. Instead, he laughed—the halting cackle of a hyena.

His voice filled with scorn. "You're wearing a vest." He shook his head, appalled that he'd fallen for the deception.

Claire slumped back to the floor and swore under her breath. Johnny had uncovered the sleight of hand behind her miraculous resurrection.

"What is that—ketchup?"

"And water."

There was no point in denying the facts. Johnny held all the cards. She couldn't shoot at him without risking her mother's life. Claire had to lure him into the open. But how? More than ever, she needed to get inside his head.

Claire's phone rang again. Was the department trying to reach her? Did her fellow officers know she was in trouble? Claire had to let them know.

"Answer that, and I'll shoot her in the head!"

"OK!"

"I mean it!"

"I believe you. Here."

Claire lobbed the phone over Alexandro's body. The device landed with a thump near Mom's feet, still ringing. Again, Johnny ignored the bait. Staying safely behind Diane, he waited for silence.

Claire counted each ring of the phone. Every passing

second was a lifeline. Would the department realize something was wrong and triangulate her phone's location? Had the neighbors reported the gunshots? She needed to buy more time and keep Diane alive until help arrived. What had Rob told her about hostage negotiations? *Ask questions. Understand what the other side truly wants.* Breathing hard, Claire replayed her conversation with Johnny in her mind and searched each word for a foothold.

"You were right, Johnny. What you said earlier—I knew the gun had blanks. Do you want to know how?"

Johnny said nothing. Curiosity and ego tussled with his instinct for self-preservation. Claire had been Bill's favorite, and Johnny resented that. This was his chance to prove he was better than her. Once he learned all her secrets, nobody would ever dupe him again.

"The magazine is lighter?"

Claire released a pent-up breath. This time, he'd taken the bait.

"No. The gun felt right."

"You knew I suspected you. You figured I'd never hand you a loaded gun."

"No. You hid that well, Johnny. You had me. I didn't know what to do."

"Don't lie to me! You didn't hesitate. You pulled the trigger like she meant nothing to you."

"That's because I knew you weren't working alone. But once I figured out you had a partner and he was here, in the house— then I understood you'd set a trap and the gun was a trick."

Johnny scoffed, unconvinced. "You didn't know about Alexandro."

Claire drew out her explanation, milking her small advantage to buy more precious time.

"You're right. When I walked in here, I didn't know about

Alexandro. But once I did, I knew you'd discovered the truth. And if I'd betrayed the pack, you'd want to punish me. But I wasn't the third target. Bill's plan wasn't complete yet. If you killed me, the stalker hoax would fall apart. You needed me alive until the end. Diane was the perfect bait. But baiting me was only one of her functions. Diane was the third target. She had to be. And once she was dead, you'd get rid of me, too."

Claire listened for the sound of vehicles outside. The silence wasn't a bad sign. If squad cars arrived with their sirens blaring, she and Diane were as good as dead. Alexandro had shoved his gun into the belt of his suit trousers before taking her Glock. Now Claire slipped the handgun from his belt.

"So, you changed the plan. What if the stalker didn't get to Diane? What if Diane finally cracked and shot me dead? And what if, during the struggle, I killed her, too? That'd be perfect. You'd fulfill Bill's wishes *and* get rid of me, too. With me dead, everyone would think the stalker just moved on."

Claire checked the magazine of Alexandro's gun. The cartridges had no blue paint or crimps at the tip. These babies were no blanks. A plan formed in her brain.

"So, you set me up. You positioned me in front of Diane with a gun. But you couldn't trust me with a loaded weapon. Instead, you'd have some fun. You'd tell me to shoot her, and you'd watch me squirm. And when I turned the gun on you and fired blanks, the look on my face would be priceless. Once you had a good laugh, you'd shoot me down. Two slugs to the chest would do the job. Even an inexperienced shooter like Diane could pull that off at close range. Forensics would find nothing suspicious. You'd stage two perfect murders, and I'd die knowing you were better than me—that *you* deserved Bill's love."

Claire rolled onto her side and shed her jacket. She needed

maximum freedom of movement to pounce when Johnny
screwed up and exposed himself.

"But I didn't give you that satisfaction. I fired the gun at
Diane. You should have seen the look on *your* face! I knew
you'd shoot me anyway, and I had the vest. Once I went down,
you'd kill Diane with my gun. But you're Bill's students. You'd
be thorough. You'd fire that shot from here, where I lay, and
with my hand. Otherwise, the ballistic trajectory and missing
gunpowder residue would give the game away. All I had to do
was play dead and wait until you put my gun in my hand."

Johnny snarled. "Very clever, Claire. But you still haven't
answered my question. How did you know Alexandro was
here?"

Her evasive tactics had infuriated him. *Good.*

"Don't you want to guess? It's obvious once you hear the
explanation. When a magician reveals his trick—"

"Spit it out now or I'll blow her brains out!"

"Take it easy, Johnny. I'll tell you everything. You were right.
I didn't know Alexandro was with the pack when I arrived."

"You said that already!"

"I know. I know. But the moment I came inside, I knew he
was here—in the house. And here's why. I couldn't see him. I
couldn't hear him either. But I could *smell* him. I'll never forget
that aftershave."

Claire prepared to spring from the floor. She'd delayed as
much as possible, but no officers had kicked in the door. Her
gamble had failed, and her odds for survival plummeted.

Johnny chuckled, long and hard. "Serves the bastard right. I
always knew his girly ways would get him killed. He can take
the rap for all of this. The Newburgh Slasher killed Claire and
her mother but died with them."

"That'll be a hard sell with all the lead you put in him."

His voice hardened. "I'll think of something. Get up, Claire."

"Why would I do that?"

"Stand, now, or I'll kill her."

"You'll kill her anyway."

"That's right. But I'll take my time. You don't want your dear mother to suffer, do you?"

Diane's sobs punctuated the silence. Claire *didn't* want her to suffer. But Johnny's word of honor was worthless, and Claire had no intention of dying today.

"I'm going to throw you my gun, and then I'll get up. Just don't hurt her. OK?"

"Do it."

Claire tossed her Glock over Alexandro's body. The gun landed a few feet to the side of Johnny. But he didn't leave the safety of his human shield to collect the gun. Claire had run out of options. She shoved Alexandro's weapon into her belt at the small of her back. Then, slowly, she climbed to her feet.

Johnny stared at her from behind Diane, a vicious smile on his lips. Claire tensed her muscles, ready to dive to the side and whip the gun from behind her. But the killer refused to budge from Diane. Instead, he extended his arm over Diane's shoulder and aimed his gun at Claire's head. Her muscles tensed. To pull this off, she had to time her dive to the millisecond.

"Goodbye, Claire."

Bang! Bang!

Claire flinched. The loud noises came from behind her. Someone was knocking on the front door. She kept her eyes on Johnny.

The smile dropped from his face. He put a finger to his lips and pressed the barrel of his gun to Diane's temple. The message was clear. If Claire answered the visitor's knock, Mom would die.

A familiar voice called from outside. "FBI. I'm going to open the door."

Fear gripped her laboring heart. Rob was about to enter the house. Did he have backup? Claire had failed to protect her mother and placed both their lives in mortal danger. Now the man she loved was stumbling into the kill zone, too.

CHAPTER 95

R ob turned the handle, swung the door open, and took cover behind the wall of Claire's home. His lightning glimpse of the interior told him all he needed to know—Claire was alive, for now.

Claire stood in the entrance hall with her back to the door, her hair caked with blood, her empty hands at her sides like a gunslinger. A Glock protruded from her belt at the small of her back. A man lay dead at her feet—Alexandro. Claire stared at the woman in the kitchen chair—a terrified Diane—and the gunman behind her. Johnny.

Rob had listened outside the door while Claire had spoken. While she bought time, Rob had evaluated the hostage situation. The gunman held Claire and Diane alone, but he was intent on killing them. At the last moment possible, Rob had banged his fist on the front door.

He recognized the gunman from Claire's identikit sketch. Johnny was in a fragile state of mind. He'd discovered a traitor in the pack. The traitor had killed his partner in crime. The last member of Bill Wolfe's pack had little to lose by murdering both his hostages. This was the most difficult negotiation Rob had ever faced—and the most important.

"Johnny, I'm Special Agent Robert Cline."

"I know who you are!"

Rob wasn't a faceless FBI agent. Johnny had seen him with Claire. He'd warned her Rob's investigation was getting dangerously close to the truth. But if Johnny believed he was in control of the situation, he'd be more likely to talk.

Rob gestured for Tom and Jess to go around the house. They'd arrest Johnny if he tried to escape out the back. Now, he needed to separate Johnny from the hostages.

"I understand. What do you want, Johnny?"

"I want you to see your girlfriend die."

"Nobody else has to die today, Johnny. You have better options."

"Oh, yeah? Like what?"

He was talking. *Good.* Even serial killers shared that human survival instinct. That primal drive explained why he hadn't pulled the trigger yet. Johnny knew that if he killed Diane, he'd probably die next, and deep down he wanted to live. Rob had to give him a reason to live.

"You can surrender."

Johnny cackled with disdain.

"Think about it, Johnny. How long can you run and hide? We can identify you. You have no support structure. We'll find you eventually. The sooner you put down the gun, the sooner you'll walk free. But if you kill an officer, everything changes. You'll never see daylight again. You're the last of the pack, Johnny. Would Bill want you to wipe out the pack?"

"You know nothing about Bill!"

"I know how he recruited you. He wasn't just a mentor. He was a father. Thanks to him, you learned to accept yourself.

The pack was your family and Bill's legacy. Do you want that legacy to die with you?"

Emotion thickened Johnny's voice. "Claire destroyed that legacy. She stabbed us all in the back the day she killed him."

And Rob had found his angle. "Claire didn't kill him."

"How would you know?"

"Because I was there when he died." Rob let his words sink in. "Put the gun down, and I'll tell you everything."

Rob edged toward the doorway and peered inside. Johnny stared at him. If looks could kill, Rob would collapse into a thousand bloody chunks.

Johnny's voice filled with loathing. "You killed him."

"He gave me no choice."

The sound of distant police sirens carried in the air, and Johnny's gaze shifted to the clear skies outside. The net was closing around him. Rob swore under his breath. Why had the squad units used their sirens? Johnny's sense of control was slipping away. Rob had to close the deal before the gunman self-destructed.

Johnny scoffed. "This is your plan—keep me talking until backup arrives?"

"Walk away, Johnny. Turn around and walk away. Live to fight another day. I'll stay right here."

The sirens grew louder.

Johnny steadied his arm on Diane's shoulder and aimed his gun at Claire's head. "I'm not going to prison. I'm going to finish what Bill started."

"No! Please!"

"Goodbye, Agent Cline. I'll see you all in Hell."

CHAPTER 96

Claire stared down the barrel of Johnny's gun. He rested his arm on Diane's shoulder and took cover behind her body in the kitchen chair. *You can't dodge bullets, Claire.* But she had no choice.

Adrenaline tore into her bloodstream. Time slowed to a crawl. Johnny grimaced and squeezed the trigger. Claire dived sideways and reached for the weapon behind her back. Diane pressed her feet to the kitchen tiles. Her chair rocked backward, tilting Johnny's arm upward as the muzzle flashed. The deafening crack hammered on Claire's eardrums, and her shoulder hit the floor.

Time caught up.

Johnny had missed! Diane had shoved his weapon off his mark.

"Bitch!"

He fired again, twice. But, flat against the floor, Claire made for a difficult target. She aimed Alexandro's weapon in her bloody hands. From her new position, she had a better view of Johnny, but her mother was still too close to him for comfort.

Then Diane's chair rebounded and rocked forward. She tumbled over, face-first and still attached to the chair.

Exposed now, Johnny aimed his gun at Claire and pulled the trigger. A loud metallic click echoed off the walls. Their eyes locked. Johnny had emptied his magazine. He was at her mercy.

Claire curled her finger over the trigger. Cynthia Hannover's voice hissed in her mind. *When you find the bastard, kill him!* Bloodlust flooded Claire's head. This creep had killed Carmine Hannover and Victoria McAdams. He'd carved Claire's name on their bodies. *Kill him!* He'd tried to murder Claire and Mom. *Kill him!* But Claire wasn't like him. She was not a cold-blooded killer.

"C'mon!" she yelled. "Give me an excuse."

Johnny did. He turned and ran. Claire lowered her arms, fired at his leg, and heard a satisfying yelp of pain. He crashed into the back door and staggered outside.

Claire launched to her feet and followed. Behind her, Rob called her name. She had no time to explain. *Act now, or the killer will escape.*

She raced through the kitchen and took cover behind the frame of the back door. Claire wouldn't rush headlong into an ambush.

She rounded the doorframe. Johnny lay on the ground. He writhed in pain and clutched at his wounded thigh. He was not alone. Jess stood over him, her gun drawn. It was over.

Jess took one look at Claire and paled. "Are you OK?"

Was she? Claire inspected her body for wounds, then remembered the two bloody holes in her chest and the gore on her face.

"It's not my blood. Have you got cuffs?"

Jess tossed her a pair. Claire clapped the steel restraints on

Johnny's wrists, yanking his arms behind his back and savoring his groans of discomfort.

"Claire."

Rob stood in the doorway behind her. She hazarded a smile. He could relax. They had won. With his help. And Mom's. That was right. Diane had saved Claire's life. The danger had passed. But Rob stared at her in open-mouthed shock. Something had gone wrong. Blood stained the knees of his trousers.

"Diane."

The word jolted her like a cold slap to the face. Johnny's final two rounds hadn't missed their target. He hadn't aimed at Claire.

No! Claire rushed past Rob and back into the house. Still tied to the chair, Diane lay on her side in a puddle of blood. Two small, round holes pierced the backrest.

"Mom!"

Diane didn't respond. Claire grabbed a knife from a kitchen drawer and dropped to her knees. She severed the cable ties and tossed the chair aside. The entry wounds in Diane's back oozed blood and soaked her blouse red.

"Mom!"

Her mother's eyes remained closed.

Rob joined Claire on the floor. "Paramedics are on their way."

He pressed his hands to the entry holes on Mom's back, trying to staunch the bleeding. Claire removed the silver strip from her mouth, and Diane opened her eyes.

She moved her lips. "C-Claire?"

"Don't speak, Mom. Save your strength. You're going to make it." Tears broke her voice. *Was she going to make it?* "You saved me, Mom."

Diane smiled at her. Her face glowed with an otherworldly calm.

"No, Claire. *You* saved *me*. You're my daughter, Claire. You've always..."

Claire gripped her mother's limp hands and bawled uncontrollably.

Two pale-faced patrol officers walked in through the open front door and stared at the scene.

"Call an ambulance!" Claire yelled. "She needs an ambulance!"

The officers spoke into their radio receivers. When Claire looked down again, Mom had lost consciousness.

The next few minutes passed in a blur of activity. Paramedics arrived. Hands pulled Claire away from her mother. Emergency workers transferred Diane's unresponsive body to a stretcher, lifted her into the air, and carried her outside.

Rob held Claire in his arms. She buried her face to his chest. He stroked her soiled hair and whispered in her ear.

"It'll be OK. Everything will be OK."

But nothing was OK. Nothing would ever be OK again.

CHAPTER 97

Night descended on downtown Newburgh. Claire gripped Rob's hand, and they hurried along the sidewalk. The street reeked of spilled trash and bad decisions. Her skin tingled. After three long and difficult months, closure waited around the corner. Rob had flown in that afternoon from Quantico for the occasion, and Claire was glad to have him by her side. She needed this. But was she ready for the oncoming flash flood of emotion?

Claire pointed to a neon sign down a dark alley. "It's over there."

"The Red Keg. Isn't that where Diane...got arrested?"

The scene of her mother's indecent exposure incident had not seemed like a suitable place for the tribute concert. But maybe visiting the bar would redeem those unpleasant memories?

"Frank owns the place. He organized everything."

Claire had first met Frank at the hospital's emergency ward shortly after the shootout in Diane's home. He'd seemed genuinely devastated by Mom's injuries, and Claire had bonded with him instantly. Diane had found a caring and reliable companion. Claire only hoped her mother would survive to enjoy her new relationship.

Rob held the door open for Claire, and they entered the dimly lit bar. The sounds of soft music and the scent of beer wafted through the air. A lot of people had turned out for the event, and they'd occupied most of the tables near the stage. Claire should have arrived earlier.

"Claire!"

Frank hurried over with his peaked cap and thick mustache. Claire introduced Rob, and the men shook hands.

"I saved you seats in the front. We're about to get started."

"Thank you!"

"Don't mention it."

He led them to their table, and they ordered drinks. Rob's phone rang.

He groaned. "It's Alda." Unit Chief Madelaine Alda was Rob's boss at the BAU.

"Calling so late?"

"She never leaves the office. I should take this."

"Go ahead."

He answered the phone, and Claire took in her surroundings. At a table to the side of the room, two women sipped their drinks. She knew them both. Claire hadn't told her colleagues at the department about tonight. And although she was glad to see more familiar faces, she hadn't expected to see those two together.

"That's great news," Rob said, still on the phone.

Claire raised her eyebrows, prompting him to share his secret, but he smiled mysteriously and kept the good tidings to himself. She'd have to wait.

Taking advantage of the distraction, she walked over to the other table and hit the awkward situation head-on.

"Hey, Jess."

Detective Jessica Long gave her a sheepish grin. "Hi, Sarge. You remember Sarah Malik."

"Of course."

Malik stood and shook Claire's hand. "I was glad to hear you're back at work."

"So was I."

During the first weeks when Internal Affairs investigated Claire's role in the shootout, she'd busied herself with administrative duties. She'd probed Riddle and Ember Investments, the firm that had wired Diane her million-dollar inheritance. Her research had uncovered evidence that Apex had used the front company to launder and invest its blood money. Claire had passed on the information to the FBI's Criminal Investigative Division, and thanks to her efforts, the Bureau had dismantled the financial pipeline and made several arrests. Still, Claire had been happy to return to the drudgery of her daily work routine.

"When I found out about tonight," Malik said, "I had to come. I never got to thank you for everything. I'm sure Carmine and Victoria, wherever they are, are grateful, too."

"I was sorry to hear you dropped out of the election."

The news had surprised Claire at first. Didn't Malik want to continue Carmine's and Victoria's work so they wouldn't have died in vain?

"I'm not sure I'm the right person to drain this swamp. I'm not even sure the swamp needs draining."

Claire nodded. Malik had waged a holy war against corruption only to become the pawn of psychopathic killers and an unwitting facilitator in the murder of her friends. Claire had wrestled with the same guilt after her father's death.

"I've started a new legal practice."

"I'm sure you'll do well."

Malik was making a fresh start—a life without constant reminders of her fatal mistakes. Despite their complicated interactions, Claire liked the former politician and was glad she had bounced back.

"I think Carmine and Victoria would understand, knowing what we do now." There it was again—the guilt.

"Sarah, it isn't your fault."

Malik's lips trembled. "I should have known. How couldn't I see what Al was?"

Claire had asked herself the same question about her father. "Don't beat yourself up. Psychopaths hide their true nature well."

A microphone squealed with static feedback. The event was about to begin.

"I'd better go. Speak to you later?"

Claire returned to her seat. Rob ended his call and put away his phone.

He nodded toward Jess and Malik. "Are they an item now?"

"That's the way it looks. What did Alda have to say? It sounded like good news."

"It is—"

Frank stepped onto the stage, cutting Rob short. A spotlight followed the bar's owner to a microphone stand at the center.

"Evening, ladies and gentlemen." His voice was pleasantly coarse and deep on the speakers.

The hubbub of the crowd settled.

"Many of you have heard about Diane. Some of you enjoyed her performances here at The Red Keg. What many don't know is that, three months ago, a serial killer held Diane hostage and shot her twice in the back."

A woman in the crowd gasped, and hushed voices muttered in the shadows.

Frank glanced at Claire. "Her daughter has joined us tonight. Welcome, Claire."

Hands clapped. Emotion surged in Claire's breast, and the event hadn't even started.

"But we're not here to dwell on painful memories. We're here to celebrate. Because, like her hero, Tina Turner, Diane is a survivor. So put your hands together for the one and only Diane Wolfe!"

The spotlight glided to a woman in a sequin minidress.

"At first, I was afraid," she sang. "I was petrified."

Claire gaped at the pop diva on the stage. She recognized the song immediately, but her brain failed to reconcile the confident older woman before her eyes with her mental conception of her mother. Seconds later, the band kicked into action. The crowd clapped and sang along.

Rob spoke into Claire's ear over the loud music. "I didn't know Tina Turner sang this one."

"She didn't. It's Gloria Gaynor. But who cares—she's amazing!"

Claire had urged Mom to get back on her feet and live her dreams. But formidable obstacles had blocked her progress: neglected health, alcoholism, and a violent attack that had pushed her to the edge of death. Fate had stacked the odds against her.

But Frank was right—Diane was a survivor. She had transformed her life. And witnessing the seemingly miraculous results brought tears of joy to Claire's eyes.

After "I Will Survive" Diane belted out a string of Tina Turner hits for a loving and receptive audience. Claire had never seen this side of her mother.

"Thank you!" Diane told the adoring crowd.

She took a few moments to sip bottled water and catch her breath.

"Today, I hit a personal record. Three months sober."

The audience cheered.

"The first few weeks were easy. I got all my liquids through an IV."

Chuckles circled the bar. Claire stared in disbelief. Mom had a sense of humor. Diane entertained her fans as though she was born for this and had done so for years.

"Tonight is special for another reason. My daughter, Claire, is here."

A man wolf-whistled at the back of the bar.

Diane gazed at her daughter. "Claire, without your support over the past year, I wouldn't be standing here today. You pushed me to clean up my act and reach for my dreams. You never gave up on me, even when I'd given up on myself. Thank you."

The air rang with more applause.

Diane addressed the crowd. "One of those dreams is to write and perform my own music. Should we make that dream come true tonight?"

The bar's patrons roared with approval.

"I was hoping you'd say that. This song is called, 'I Made You.' I started writing the lyrics three months ago when I almost lost everything. Now the song is done, and I dedicate it to my daughter, Claire."

Her audience applauded, then fell silent. Every soul present held its breath, sharing the sacred moment with reverence and awe. The band played a soft, slow melody—the rhythm of a heartfelt ballad—and Diane put the microphone to her lips.

"I used to say you were the problem. I used to say you only got in the way..."

She sang of a mother and her daughter—a daughter she'd never wanted. A daughter she'd resented. The story was full of false starts and wrong turns. It spoke of tragedy and loss but also love and redemption. For years, her daughter had been her biggest mistake. Now, she realized the opposite was true. Her daughter embodied the best of her. No—her daughter was better than her. The mother had learned more than she'd taught and received more than she'd given.

Claire had cried at the crime scene. She had cried beside her mother's hospital bed, too. She'd exhausted a lifetime's supply of tears. Or so she'd thought. But as Diane sang the final line of the chorus before the packed bar, fresh waves of emotion washed over her.

"I didn't make you, darling," Mom sang. "You made me."

By the time Diane finished her song and descended the steps, tears streamed down Claire's face. They hugged, and Claire savored her mother's embrace. She'd waited decades and braved mortal dangers to reach this moment and she would enjoy every second.

Diane pulled away. "I'm starving. Aren't you?"

Frank ordered food and added two chairs to their table while Diane went backstage to shower. Minutes later, they dug into their buffalo wings and steaks. This felt good. When Claire had returned to Newburgh a year ago, she'd never imagined that one day she'd share a peaceful meal out with Mom. Diane's close call with death had paved the road to full reconciliation. Maybe their family wasn't cursed, after all?

When Claire finished eating, she remembered Rob's mysterious call from Chief Alda.

"What's the good news from the BAU?"

Excitement animated him. "I bounced an idea off Chief Alda months ago, and now she wants to move forward."

Frank unwrapped a toothpick. "What's the idea?"

"A new program at the BAU. Our investigations in Newburgh got me thinking. The BAU invests a lot of resources in tracking down murderers. We studied the childhoods of serial killers to develop profiles for suspects."

Rob eyed Claire and hesitated. Had his talk of serial killers upset her?

"The same insights my father used to locate the kids he took under his wing. It's OK, Rob. I can handle it."

Her smile seemed to reassure him. "So, I got to thinking— what if we did the same thing?"

Claire understood the idea immediately. "Prevention is better than cure?"

"Exactly! What if we reached out to teens at risk and prevented them from becoming hardened criminals? The BAU could save lives instead of picking up the pieces."

Claire imagined FBI agents knocking on the doors of homes, intervening in the lives of young psychopaths, and shepherding them toward productive, law-abiding lives. The idea was breathtaking. But was such an intervention even possible?

"And Chief Alda's on board?"

"Not only her. Upper management, too. And they want me to head the new program."

"Rob, that's fantastic!"

He deserved this promotion, and his new program would make the world a better place. But a sudden realization punched a hole in her enthusiasm. Heading a new program would require Rob to return to Quantico for good. Where did that leave their relationship?

Rob grinned. "There's only one problem. To build a new program, I'll need a lot of help. I'll need to recruit people who have hands-on experience with serial killers and understand the psychopathic mindset. Such people are hard to find."

Claire smiled. He was offering her a job.

"I'll take that as a compliment."

Diane wiped her mouth on a napkin. "Where would this new program operate?"

"Country-wide, but we'll start with a test group in Quantico. Claire, I'm serious. Come work with me."

Her pulse accelerated. Claire was a capable detective. But homicide investigations had never been her calling. The past year had taken its toll on her. Her career trajectory in Newburgh forecast increasing amounts of paperwork and red tape. And relocation meant Rob would stay in her life.

Sarah Malik had made a fresh start—maybe Claire could, too? A new career—far away from her father's crimes, self-serving politicians, and creepy conspiracy theorists. Claire wouldn't be running away from her past either. She'd leverage that past to save lives.

"I can't."

"Why not?"

"Yes, Claire," Diane said. "Why not?"

"Because I have a life here."

Diane raised her eyebrows. "Me? You're turning this down because of me?" She scoffed. "I'm no reason to stay in Newburgh."

Claire's mouth fell open. "But we just reconnected. Who's going to help you around the house?"

"And what if I sell the house?"

"What are you talking about?"

Diane glared at her but said nothing. She'd become a true diva.

Frank cleared his throat. "Diane is moving in with me."

"Seriously?" Claire didn't know whether to feel happy for her mother or angry at being abandoned.

"It makes sense. She spends more time at my place anyway. And soon, she'll need to travel a lot."

"Travel? For what?"

His mustache shifted as he grinned. "You know. Singing gigs."

The talk of travel was a smokescreen. They were ganging up on her.

Diane folded her arms. "I'm just getting started, Claire. I won't let you slow me down."

Claire gave Rob an ironic glance. "They grow up so fast."

Diane had taken a bullet for her, and now she was sacrificing her personal wishes so her daughter could follow her heart. Claire had created a monster.

She sighed. Claire had tried to shield others from her family's curse by pushing them away, and where had that landed her? Now the universe was offering her a helping hand. The time had come to abandon fear, grasp that hand, and leap into the unknown.

"OK. Count me in."

Rob said, "Are you sure?"

She grinned. "If these lovebirds are so eager to get me out of their hair—then sure, why not?"

Diane and Frank beamed at her.

Rob wasn't convinced. "You'll have to retrain at the FBI academy. That'll take time."

Claire shrugged. "I like challenges, and I could do with a change of pace. Besides..." She winked. "I have a thing for the agent in charge of the new program."

EPILOGUE
NINE MONTHS LATER

"So, this is where the old grouch lives?"

Through the passenger window, Claire studied the redbrick duplex with the grassy front yard. A thirty-minute drive from Quantico toward Washington, DC, had landed them in Alexandria and outside the home of Special Agent Tom Brown.

Rob parked on the street. "Not what you were expecting?"

"I'm not sure what I was expecting. Gargoyles, probably."

Rob chuckled. "Underneath the thorny exterior, Tom's a family man. Salt of the earth."

He was right. After all, Tom had offered to host Claire's small graduation party. She should cut him some slack. And this was no time to be petty. Claire had left her family and friends behind in Newburgh, Massachusetts, and needed to build new bridges.

She eyed the line of cars on the curb. The Toyota Yaris belonged to Madelaine Alda, Rob's unit chief at the BAU and Claire's future boss. But Claire didn't recognize the other vehicles. She smelled an ambush.

"You promised me a *small* party and no speeches."

Rob grinned. "Let's go. Mary's probably wondering what happened to us."

Mary. Claire hadn't met Tom's wife yet. Soon, Claire and the senior agent would work in the same unit. She'd be wise to start off on the right foot with his wife.

Rob used the knocker on the wooden front door.

"One second," a woman called.

The sounds of hurried footsteps and hushed voices carried from behind the door. Something fishy was definitely going on in there. Claire's birthday was months away. What ambush had Rob planned for her?

The door opened, and the wafting scent of sizzling meat blew away Claire's concerns about ambushes. The ride had whetted her appetite, and her empty stomach demanded food.

A rosy-cheeked middle-aged woman smiled at them. "Welcome, Rob!"

Rob handed her a bottle of red wine and leaned in for a kiss on the cheek. "Good to see you, Mary."

Her eyes darted to Claire. "And you must be Claire."

More kisses on cheeks.

Mary beamed at her. "I've heard so much about you."

"Don't believe any of it."

The hostess's smile faltered. Dry humor wasn't her mother tongue. How had she married Tom?

Rob rescued them from the awkward moment. "Thank you for having us, Mary."

The smile returned. "Well, don't just stand there. Come on in."

They obliged, and Rob closed the door behind them.

"Where's Tom?"

"In the backyard, by the barbecue."

"I'll see if he needs help."

Out of the corner of Claire's eye, a blonde woman in a blue

dress snuck into a doorway along a corridor. A frisson of recognition jolted Claire. Had the woman slipped away to avoid Claire?

"Claire?" Rob's words snapped her back to reality.

"Um...where's the bathroom?"

Mary pointed to the corridor. "Second door on the right."

"Thanks."

Claire told Rob she'd meet him outside and headed down the corridor. Passing the bathroom, she neared the door the mysterious blonde had used to escape. Claire didn't like surprises. In her experience, they usually ended in bloodshed.

She tried the handle. The door was locked. She wrapped her knuckles on the wood.

"Hello, is anybody there?"

Nobody answered. Claire put her ear to the door but heard nothing. She reached for her Glock, then thought better of drawing her service weapon. *Take it easy, Claire. You're with friends. Nobody's stalking you. Don't ruin your FBI career before it begins by pulling a gun on your colleague's teenage daughter.* How many children did Tom and Mary have? Claire should have asked.

She stopped by the bathroom to freshen up. If Rob asked, she could honestly say she'd gone to the bathroom instead of snooping around Tom's home. In the living room, Claire found two of her fellow FBI Academy graduates nursing beer bottles as well as some BAU agents she'd met at the Critical Incident Response Group building in Quantico.

Tom stood beside a gas grill in the backyard and sported a Stars and Stripes apron. But he'd lost control of the barbecue. Chief Alda waved smoke from her face with one hand and flipped burgers with the other. True to form, their superior had taken over the situation and called the shots.

Rob sipped a Miller Lite and watched the spectacle. An

amused smile curled his lips. He was enjoying the live comedy show.

Alda ranted at Tom. "You've got to bake the wings before you grill them. Otherwise, they never cook through."

Energetic and trim, Chief Alda wore her fifty years well. Only on closer inspection did her age lines and eye bags become visible. She'd remained single, Claire deduced, thanks to her single-minded devotion to the Bureau and domineering leadership style, which spilled over into her other relationships.

Tom nodded at Claire and rolled his eyes at their boss. "Look who's arrived, Chief—the woman of the moment."

Claire stepped up. "Chief Alda, it's good to see you again."

They had met only once before at the CIRG building for Claire's formal interview.

Still gripping the barbecue fork, Alda extended her forearm for an awkward wrist-bump greeting. "Call me Madeleine—it's after hours."

"After hours?" Tom quipped. "You have after hours?"

Alda smirked. "Fair point. Congratulations, Claire. I hear you aced your exams at the Academy."

"Thank you."

Claire's dirty look scolded Rob for sharing her results, and he responded with a sheepish shrug. To be fair, Alda would receive the report soon anyway. And singing Claire's praises to her new boss couldn't hurt. According to Rob, Alda had resisted hiring his girlfriend, blaming the unit's limited budget. Claire hoped her graduation scores had justified her new boss's gamble.

Alda seemed to read Claire's thoughts. "Don't think you can rest on your laurels, Claire. I expect you to hit the ground running when you start working at the unit. Rob and Sally have a lot to prove with their new program, and the Bureau's skeptics would love to see us fail."

Claire had also doubted whether psychopathy was curable. But Dr. Sally Fleischer had collected encouraging psychological studies and prepared a promising treatment program. Everything depended on their small trial batch of criminally inclined youth. If the first group showed positive results, the agents would secure funding for larger trials and, eventually, expand their program nationwide.

Although Claire shared Alda's concerns, her stern comment reminded Claire that she was an outsider. She'd have to work extra hard to win her boss's acceptance. During her long months of training, Claire had spent her weekends with Rob. But in between those visits, she'd felt lonely and adrift. Now, those feelings returned.

She forced a smile. "I understand."

"Speak of the devil," Tom said.

Sally appeared beside Claire. "Hey, guys. What have I missed?"

Rob said, "Just a few burned chicken wings."

Alda swore and transferred the smoking wings to a tinfoil tray. Claire stifled her chuckles.

Sally nodded at Rob meaningfully, reigniting Claire's suspicions. *What is going on here?*

Rob tapped a barbecue fork to his beer bottle, and the background rumble of conversation settled. Claire stared at him with faux anger. *No speeches*, he'd promised her. He responded to her silent accusation with a guilty grin. At least he hadn't called upon her to speak.

He cleared his throat. "Thank you all for joining us today. And thank you, Tom and Mary, for hosting the party. As you know, we're celebrating Claire's completion of New Agent Training. She'll probably kill me for saying this, but Claire was one of only three trainees to graduate with honors in all three sections: academics, firearms, and physical fitness."

Her friends clapped, and Claire's cheeks warmed. Rob watched her with satisfaction.

"Traitor," she mouthed.

"What some of you don't know is that I've prepared a little surprise for Claire."

Claire knew it! The graduation party was a front. But a front for what?

Rob glanced toward the house. "Come on out, guys."

A handful of familiar figures emerged from the living room's open French doors: Diane and Frank; Chief Emmerso and Captain Washington; and Detective Jessica Long. Claire recognized her blue dress from earlier. Her former partner was the mysterious figure who had evaded her in the corridor.

Claire stepped forward to welcome her family and friends, and Rob thanked them for traveling all the way from Massachusetts. Claire's suspicions heightened. Newburgh was a five-hour ride away. Rob hadn't schlepped them here just to congratulate Claire on her graduation.

Rob handed his beer to Tom. "Now that we're all here, there's something else I want to say."

He walked up to Claire and smiled broadly. *No, he wouldn't do this here—in front of everyone—would he?*

Mary handed bouquets of red roses to Claire's friends and family. They gathered around Claire, and Sally started filming Claire and Rob on her phone.

Rob retrieved a jewelry box from his pocket and dropped to one knee. *Yes, he would.* He cracked the box open to reveal a diamond ring.

Claire should have seen this coming. She had hinted to Rob that she was ready to settle down, and they had discussed a future marriage in theory. But she hadn't expected Rob to do anything about it now.

"Claire, will you marry me?"

A rush of joy filled her, and she answered without hesitation. "Of course I will."

He slipped the ring on her finger. "This is just a placeholder. You'll get a bigger diamond when Chief Alda approves my raise."

Alda smirked. "Nice try, Agent Cline."

Rob stood, Claire kissed him, and their friends and family put their hands together.

"Sorry about the surprise," Rob said. "But I figured you'll like this one."

Claire held his face in her hands. "I do."

"Whoa. This is just the engagement. One step at a time!"

Claire laughed, but a sudden noise swallowed her cheer.

Thunder rumbled, and Claire glanced at the cloudless sky in confusion. The ground shuddered beneath her feet. Plates tinkled on a table, and Mary gasped. By the time Claire understood what was happening, the shock wave had subsided. Her friends and family stood there, frozen like mannequins, their limbs spread to keep their balance, waiting for the aftershock that didn't arrive.

Jess's nervous laugh broke the silence. "I didn't know you got earthquakes in Virginia."

They did. Claire had experienced three tremors over the past six months. But they never began with a deep rumble.

The agents traded dark looks, and Tom aired their thoughts.

"That was no earthquake."

ACKNOWLEDGMENTS

Behind every novel there is a long line of very talented and supportive people.

My team of awesome beta readers provided valuable comments and corrections. They are: Heather Bryant, Claudia Levi, Lynn Lujan, Candice Lutz, Jennifer Medina, Lara Morrison, Roger Proctor, Amy Sexton, Roxx Tarantini, Billie Wichkan, Kai Wills, and Beatrice Yeow.

My excellent editor, Emmy Ellis, made the novel shine, and her insightful tips will guide my future writings.

Teresa Collins, my trusty and talented proofreader, ensured the final manuscript is error-free and ready for publication.

I thank you all from the bottom of my heart.

~ Jamie Millen

ABOUT THE AUTHOR

Psychopaths. Stalkers. Narcissists. Killers. Jamie Millen writes about the people you hope never to meet in real life...but probably already have.

If you enjoy crime thrillers packed with nail-biting psychological suspense, unforgettable characters, and breathtaking twists, you've come to the right place.

Visit JamieMillen.com/Claire to download free stories, sneak peeks, advanced chapters, and more.

Made in the USA
Monee, IL
30 April 2024

57722611R00277